Rebel Belles

A Kate Warne, Civil War Spy Series, Book 3

Peg A. Lamphier

Writing Wench Press

Lytle Creek, CA

Rebel Belles
Kate Warne Civil War Spy Series, Book 3

Copyright © 2018 by Peg Lamphier

Writing Wench Press

Cover Art by Daniel Aley, www.flutterspace.com

Author photo by Marvelle Thompson

Writing Wench Press publishes this edition.

PO Box 113

Lytle Creek, California 92358

Visit the press online at www.peglamphier.com

ISBN: 978-1-947278-06-6

For Leo J. Burke
I'm so glad you like flannel bras.

Behind every great man
there is a woman rolling her eyes.
Jim Carey

Also by Peg A. Lamphier

Kate Chase and William Sprague:
Politics and Gender in a Civil War Marriage

❀

Spur Up Your Pegasus:
Family Letters of Salmon, Kate and Nettie Chase,
1844-73
(with James P. McClure and Erika M. Kreger)

❀

Women in American History:
A Social, Political and Cultural Encyclopedia with Document Collection
[4 volumes] (with Rosanne Welch)

❀

The Lincoln Special

Kate Warne Civil War Spy Series, Book 1

❀

The Great Show
Kate Warne Civil War Spy Series, Book 2

❀

Deadly Delights
The Perils of Petronella Crabtree, Journal 1

❀

Soldier, Diplomat, Archeologist:
The Bold Life of Louis Palma di Cesnola

Chapter 1

July 21, 1861
Washington & Centreville, Virginia

*K*ate scooped up her sturdy boots and tiptoed down the back stairs, careful to avoid the fourth step from the bottom. It creaked something awful and she didn't want to wake Louisa, who slept in the small room next to the stairs. She padded into the kitchen, sat her boots on one of the kitchen chairs and groped around for the matches. The full moon leaked light through the kitchen windows, presaging a dawn still three hours away. She scratched a match and lit the paraffin lamp they kept in the middle of the table, taking a small pleasure in its homey yellow glow.

From behind her came the scuff of a shoe and the rustle of fabric. Kate reached up her sleeve for her small pistol.

"I knew you'd try to sneak out by yo'self," a voice drawled in the dark. "I been waitin' on you."

Kate whirled, her mouth agape. Her housemaid sat on the floor, her back to the kitchen door. No longer really a girl, not yet a woman, Louisa daily showed the kind of maturity and wisdom not usually found in girls her age. Her early years as a slave in an unpleasant man's household had undoubtedly taught her things about human nature that a child should not know.

"You almost gave me a heart attack," Kate hissed. "And got yourself shot."

"Almost only counts in horseshoes Miz Kate," Louisa said in obvious disgust. She pushed herself up to her feet and pointed at the basket on the counter. "Miz Charlotte and I figured you were up to something. Especially after your meeting with Mr. Lincoln. And with Mistah Juba up in Philadelphia and Miz Hattie workin' at the hospital and Captain Hazzard at the fort there was only us to notice you acting funny. "

Kate tried not to laugh. She could disappear undercover, spying to her heart's content, but she could not keep a secret from the women in her own house. She put her hands on her hips and used her sternest teacher voice to say, "Absolutely not Louisa. You cannot come with me."

"Of course I'm coming. Miz Charlotte gave me my orders. She says if I'm with you you'll look like one of those do-gooder ladies, the kind who take their maids everywhere. We already packed food and filled a bunch of water jugs."

Kate sighed. Her housekeeper Charlotte Webster often mistook herself for Kate's mother. Kate pretended to mind, though she suspected she wasn't fooling anyone. Her own mother died over ten years ago and Charlotte's daughters both died in infancy. This fact alone made Kate loath to resist her housekeeper's maternal impulses. The two of them, the motherless daughter and the daughterless mother, needed each other.

Still, it was a bad idea to take Louisa to a battlefront. "Miz Charlotte is often right, but not about this. I cannot, I will not take you that close to the Confederate Army. If we're overrun they won't care that you're a free woman. They will enslave you and sell you south. Like they did Mr. Juba." Kate shook her head. "I can't go through that again. I won't."

Louisa picked up the basket and opened the back door. She looked over her shoulder at Kate, her lavender dress swishing as she turned. "I ain't stupid Miz Kate. And neither are you. We jess won't get caught. Now let's go. I can help you with the horses." She turned and went out the door.

There was nothing for Kate to do but follow her teenaged maid.

They walked Excelsior and Lucy down Fourth Street to Mr. Howard's Livery stable. Along the way Louisa took Excelsior's halter rope and skipped ahead of Kate, who had ahold of Lucy. Louisa adored Excelsior and he accepted her adoration. They were a funny pair, the exact opposite of each other. He was male, white, huge and elderly, while Louisa was dark, small and young.

Kate glanced over at Lucy and smiled. The horse reminded her of Hazzard. He'd delivered Lucy to Kate at the behest of General Scott and the sturdy coaching horse had come in awfully handy. Hazzard. She sighed a little. They hadn't seen each other for days and she missed him. She'd ridden down to Fort Washington last week and found him chafing under the constraints of a life teaching new recruits artillery basics. Kate also liked to think he was missing his life as a temporary operative for the Pinkerton Detective Agency. Mr. Lincoln had loaned Hazzard to the agency while they acted as a temporary military intelligence unit but these days the Army needed him more than the Pinkertons did.

It seemed to Kate that there was more street and foot traffic out than one would expect at this hour of the morning though she supposed all rules of normality were suspended when you were at war. Washington lay under the spell of a nasty heat wave, made more unpleasant because the city hadn't been cooling down at night. At least not enough. Dawn was at hours away and her light green dress already stuck to her lower back. Kate wondered if the trip out to Centreville wasn't just a self-serving way to escape the stifling heat and anxious air of the capital.

The livery stable's big double doors stood open when they arrived and the dark green freight wagon sat out in the stable's center aisle. Its lemon yellow wheels glowed in the lantern light.

Kate handed Lucy off to Louisa and stepped into the stable. "Hallooooo," she called.

Mr. Howard poked his head out of a nearby stall. "Hey there, girlie."

Excelsior bugled a loud neigh at Mr. Howard. The big horse used to live at this stable and he remembered the apples and carrots the man dispensed.

They'd just finished a round of handshaking and complaining about the weather when Kate heard a sharp, "Woof!"

She looked down to see a small, short-haired dog. He was mostly black, with a white bib, little white commas above his eyes and white feet that blended into brown then black at his knees. He cocked his head at Kate. "Woof," he repeated.

Louisa squealed with pleasure and feel to her knees to fondle the little fellow's ears.

Kate smiled at the two of them. "Who's this?"

"Oh, them rat baiting fellows left him when they cleared out. One of the Surratt boys tried him on the rats, but the poor little guy just didn't have the knack."

Kate appraised the diminutive canine before her. "He's a rat terrier?"

"Nah, he's a Feist."

Kate crooked an eyebrow at Mr. Howard.

"They're treeing dogs, squirrels and coons and such. But this one is a mite small, so Mr. Surratt thought he'd try him in the ring." Howard shook his head. "It turns out it takes more than size to make a good ratter."

Kate eyed the dog. He was about a foot tall at his shoulders, but sturdily built. She reached down and stroked his head, causing him to wriggle with pleasure. Louisa gave the dog a last pat and stood.

"He's pleasant to have around," Howard continued, "but not a durn bit of help with the rats or anything else." He paused. "We better get you hitched up and moving. Daylight's coming."

The three of them got the horses hitched to the big wagon. Louisa patted the little dog in farewell before Kate boosted her up into the wagon's high seat. Then Kate stepped on the wagon wheel hub and hoisted herself up next to Louisa. Mr. Howard handed her the reins just as the dog followed Kate's course up the wagon, from the ground to the wheel hub and from there to the wagon's floorboard and then up onto the bench seat. Louisa scooted over so he could turn around, snuggling his hindquarters between the two of them.

5

"Uh, uh," Kate admonished. "You stay here." She grabbed the dog by the scruff and dropped him over the side of the wagon, at Mr. Howard's feet. Before the stable owner could grab him, the dog sprang back up the wagon, installing himself once more upon the seat. Louisa grabbed him and looked at Kate with big puppy dog eyes. So did the dog.

Kate looked from the dog to Louisa. She turned, stared at Mr. Howard and heaved out a loud breath.

"I think he's adopting you," he said with a shrug of his shoulders.

Louisa squealed again, this time pulling the black dog into her lap.

Kate knew when she'd been defeated. "Fine."

Howard bent over and put his hands on his knees. When he straightened he was wiping tears of laughter from his face. "I've been calling him Monty, on account of he looks like Mr. Montgomery, a gent that used to keep his horse here. Diplomat fellow always wore boiled white shirts and black suits."

"Oh, Monty," Louisa sighed into the dog's head.

Kate tapped the girl's shoulder. "If he wanders away I'm not wasting time looking for him, is that clear?"

"Oh, he won't Miz Kate, you wait and see." Louisa's face lit up with complete happiness. Monty yipped his agreement.

Mr. Howard laughed again.

Pretending to be more vexed than she was, Kate clucked to the horses. They rolled out of the stable into the growing dawn of a long and terrible day.

The sun came up as they crossed the Potomac and leftthe city. Two hours later they turned off Columbia Turnpike for

Little River Turnpike. They'd stopped once so far, and then only to show the sentries at Long Bridge their pass, signed by none other than General Winfield Scott himself. As the sun climbed higher the day brightened and warmed to an unseemly degree. The countryside seemed ominously silent though Kate was unsure whether the quiet reflective of the early morning or the coming battle.

Some time not long after dawn they rolled past a deserted camp, tents in orderly rows upon a wide field bordered by a wooded, rolling countryside. The woods gave way to fields of corn and wheat. Some farms were neat and tidy, with freshly whitewashed buildings and orderly gardens, while others betrayed families living in abject poverty. Paint peeled on windowless houses, houses that seemed always accompanied by sickly looking women and children. These people would stop whatever they were doing and stare at the wagon as it rolled by, their anxiety clear by the set of the set of their shoulders.

For the past week, soldiers had streamed out of Washington City and through this Virginia countryside. There they encountered inhabitants both sympathetic and hostile to the Union Army. Kate knew the Army ordered soldiers not to pillage local farms but she also knew the space between officer's orders and real men's behavior could be as wide as the space between good and evil.

When they arrived at Fairfax Louisa helped Kate water the horses, the dog and themselves at a pump they found in the town square. Kate let Louisa and Monty run around the square for a few minutes. Kate wished for a little ball she could give the two of them, then shook her head. They weren't on a pleasure excursion. Hattie had sent them to help.

7

Three days ago her friend and sister Pinkerton came home from the Washington Infirmary looking worried. She told Kate the hospital doctors were worried there wouldn't be enough ambulances to transport wounded soldiers from the field of battle to the capital, twenty-five miles away. Hattie carried a note from Miss Barton, who headed the Infirmary's volunteers, asking Kate to broach the subject with her presidential contacts. Which was how Kate ended up with a pass signed by the General Scott himself. Kate suspected she was neither the first nor the last person bamboozled into doing something by the wily Miss Barton.

General Scott shared Miss Barton's pessimism about this first real battle of the war. He'd wanted a less confrontational approach to the war and wasn't afraid to say so. He thought they could strangle the Confederacy with a naval blockade that would crush the rebel's economy and force the seceded states back into the Union. Scott's plan had been rejected by Army command and most of the nation, who embraced the cry, "Forward to Richmond." Even President Lincoln came to disagree with his Commanding General.

Every time Kate saw the old man she was reminded of how large he was, both in height and girth. This last visit though, her primary impression of him had been one of deep exhaustion.

"There's nothing I can do Miss Warne," he'd explained. "I've ordered every available military ambulance we have to the front."

Kate bit her lip while she considered her response. "I think Miss Barton hopes you might order civilian wagons into service. As a precaution."

The old man shook his head, looking more like a tired old bull dog than the nation's best general. "I'm sorry my dear, but I won't do that. I can't order civilians to the front."

Kate leaned forward. "But if people volunteered? Accepted the risk?"

He shook his head again, his jowls wobbling with enthusiasm. "It's not that. Or not just that. Civilians create chaos. They're not trained, not battle ready, not subject to military discipline. General McDowell has enough on his plate without having to deal with helpful civilians."

They'd struck a kind of deal. He signed two dozen passes and gave them to Kate for Miss Barton to distribute to people she trusted, but he made Kate promise that no one would go closer to the battle than Centreville. So here she was, driving through the countryside, fully intending to break her promise to General Scott.

She let Louisa and Monty play for a few more minutes, then called them back to the wagon and set out again. As they left town Kate heard the first cannon's boom echo off in the distance.

They rode along, passing the remains of several more military camps on the Warrenton turnpike, each as empty as the ones they'd passed earlier. The wooden boxes strewn around the camps had CSA stamped on them, indicating they were remains of the Confederate army this time.

They reached the outskirts of Centerville by mid-morning, well ahead of the traffic Kate expected would clog the roads in a few hours. On the outskirts of town they encountered a clot of soldiers plodding back towards Washington. They walked in small groups, each man with a sizable bundle on his back, some carrying rifles, some not.

Kate felt disorientated. *Is it already over? Am I going the wrong way?* She slowed the horses and called out, "Pardon me, could anyone tell me where the front is?"

A lanky, grizzled man stopped and pointed over his shoulder. "That a way miss."

"Is it over?"

The tall fellow's companion barked a harsh laugh. "No, ma'am. We're going home to Pennsylvania." Guns rattled in the distance as he spoke. To her unasked question, he added, "We had three months of digging fortifications. Our enlistment's up and we reckon we had enough." The two of them walked on. Kate noticed they did not look back. She wondered if Mr. Lincoln had figured on the temporary nature of much of his army before he ordered them into battle. He probably had. He didn't miss much, for all he looked sleepy half the time.

Soldiers clogged the streets in Centreville though none of them seemed to be doing anything in particular. At the sight of so many men in uniform, Louisa pulled Monty into her lap and scooted closer to Kate. They stopped once more to water the horses but agreed they'd wait to have an early lunch on the other side of town.

They came to their final stop of the morning on a hill just west of Centerville. Kate pulled the horses off the road and over to an spreading oak tree that would afford them afternoon shade. A few wagons and carriages populated the hillside though they were all spread over the plateau.

Guns and cannons sounded off the left, some distance away. Figuring it would be some time before she needed the horses, Kate unharnessed Excelsior and Lucy. While she did Louisa laid out a blanket and their lunch. Kate left the horses

10

loose so they could crop at the dry grass and joined Louisa on their plaid blanket.

"Seems too pretty for a war, doesn't it Miss Kate?"

Kate took a bite of a thick ham sandwich and nodded. A line of green hills and meadows spread out before them, purpling as they marched towards the Blue Ridge Mountains in the distance. The road stretched down before them like a gray ribbon, cutting through the woods and fields towards Manassas Junction. If it had not been for the distant roar of cannon and the occasional puffs of blue smoke that rose from the trees it would have been easy to believe they were just two ladies out for a picnic. After she'd eaten, Kate dug in the basket and pulled out a battered set of brass field glasses. They were Hazzard's, but he'd insisted she take them, pointing out he'd not need them at Fort Washington. Kate felt only relief at the fact that he was missing the battle, though she took care not to say so to his face.

She turned the little screw between the two lenses until the glasses came into focus. Though the view was crisp and clear, there was nothing to see. There were too many trees in the way. Kate could see a line of baggage wagons and ambulances lined up before a narrow bridge just before the tree line that lay at the tree line.

By mid-day, carriages and horses crowded the plateau. Kate grabbed Excelsior and Lucy's reins and tied the two of them to the wagon to make room for the spectators that lined the heights. Some of them were more excited than Kate thought decent people ought to be when men were dying, unseen, among the trees. Several carriages over a lady whose dress was cut too low peered through her opera glasses and exclaimed, "This is splendid. Oh, my! Is not that first-rate? I guess we will be in Richmond this time tomorrow!"

Kate resisted the impulse to tear the woman's opera glasses from her hand and admonish the silly creature. Perhaps she could order Monty to bite the twit's ankle. She took a deep, cleansing breath. After all, the lady had expressed the unspoken hope of everyone gathered on the hill—that the battle ended with Confederate capitulation and the nation's reunion.

Sometime mid-afternoon Louisa took the blanket and crawled under the wagon for a nap. Kate was sitting by herself, peering through the field glasses when a four-wheeled carriage pulled up next her. She glanced over, surprised to find a lone woman in it. She looked away and then looked back, startled.

The young woman must have felt Kate's stare. She turned toward Kate and in a high-pitched voice said, "My goodness. You could be my sister. I mean, not my actual sister. She's still in school and doesn't look a bit like me. But you look like you could be my sister. I'm babbling, aren't I? I'm sorry. What must you think of me?"

Kate smiled. The flustered young woman's hair was almost the exact shade of auburn as her own. She also had Kate's pale skin and green eyes. Their noses were different. While Kate's nose was straight and entirely unremarkable, her twin's had a saucy little up tilt to it that made her beauty seem less arrogant and more cheeky. Kate smiled at the young woman. "It's all right. The resemblance startled me too."

Recognition dawned on the young woman's face.

"Why you're Miss Warne, aren't you? You used to teach at Miss Haines School for Girls."

Kate laughed. "Yes, I did. Before that, I was a student. You seem familiar, but I can't quite place you."

The younger woman slid over to the right side of the wagon bench, bringing her closer to Kate's wagon. "I came just as you were leaving. Allow me to introduce myself. I am Katherine Chase, but I prefer Kate."

Kate laughed. "I'm Kate too." Realization dawned on Kate. "You're Mr. Chase's daughter aren't you?"

The young woman frowned. "Now I suppose you want to chastise me for my father's abolitionist politics."

Salmon P. Chase had almost single-handedly founded the Ohio anti-slavery movement and he'd been a strong contender for the 1860 presidential nomination. Now he was Lincoln's Secretary of Treasury and either admired or defamed for his staunch anti-slavery politics.

"No, quite the opposite," Kate assured her. "I'm a great admirer. Your father took a stance against slavery long before it was fashionable to do so."

Miss Chase's face lightened. "Father is a man of principle. Sometimes too much principle—he's easy to admire, but difficult to live with."

The young women reminisced about Miss Haines School, laughing over the chemistry teacher who encouraged explosions and a French teacher who snored in class. While they talked, they kept a watch on the valley where the battle raged, the booming sometimes sounding closer and sometimes far, far away. Several times, when the booming sounded ominously close, Kate raised the field glasses to her eyes, but they continued to reveal little. She handed them over to Miss Chase, who had no more luck with them, though the visible

13

puffs of smoke suggested the had battle had shifted to the right after lunchtime.

Later in the afternoon, something finally happened. First, a horse and rider burst from the distant tree line and galloped up the road to the top of the hill. From atop his horse, the dark-suited man waved both arms like he was trying to stop traffic on Pennsylvania Avenue.

He brought his horse to a dramatic sliding stop in front of the carriages just off to their right and cried, "We've whipped them on all points. The army's taken the Rebs batteries and they're retreating as fast as they can." This pronouncement earned the rider a host of cheers from the crowd loud enough to wake Louisa from her nap. She and Monty crawled out from under the wagon, quite startling Miss Chase.

Monty leaped up next to Kate on the wagon bench. Louisa stared at the two Kate's for a moment, then excused herself. Kate made a mental note to ask the girl if she'd found a private place where a lady might relieve herself. She'd drunk a considerable amount of water in this heat and not all of it turned into sweat.

Several minutes later an older man wearing a stubby, brown and gray chin beard, approached Miss Chase's carriage. "Miss Chase, Misters Colfax and Wilson and I are going down to the bridge at Cub Run. I was wondering if you'd like to accompany us? I assure you, in light of recent news, it cannot be dangerous."

Kate almost interceded, thinking the word of one lone, non-military scout was not enough to base sureties of safety, but Miss Chase beat her to it.

"Thank you for your kind offer Congressman Ely, but Father allowed me to come only after I promised I would not

14

move past Centreville. I shouldn't want to get you gentlemen in trouble if I disobeyed."

The man made his bow to Miss Chase and left, looking chastened at Miss Chase's gentle rebuff.

Kate crooked an eyebrow at her new friend.

"Oh, it's maddening. Congressmen and senators seem to think they can curry favor with Father through me. As if he paid any real attention to me at all."

"Still," Kate said, "you had the sense to decline. I'm impressed. May I take it the Congressman referred to Senator Henry Wilson and Congressman Schuyler Colfax?"

Miss Chase nodded.

"And am I also correct in thinking you know General McDowell as well?"

"Oh, he's an old family friend. I've summered at his farm. He and his wife are the loveliest people. He'd be as mad as Father if he knew I went any closer than this."

"I'm inclined to think your father and the general are correct." Kate stared at the young woman before her, an idea forming in her mind. They watched as first one carriage and then another set off down the turnpike toward the battle. Miss Chase borrowed Kate's field glasses again and watched them go, though she said not a word.

Kate thought the young woman showed astounding intelligence and political acumen in both staying put and not disparaging men too foolish to do likewise.

"Miss Chase, I should not want to make you feel as if I valued you only for your connections, but you seem too intelligent to be treated like a paper doll. I wonder. . . ." Kate's voice trailed off. She realized she was planning for a future where today's outcome was an unhappy one. If the union ar-

Peg A. Lamphier

my really took Richmond this day, she would not need Miss
Chase. Still, it would be best to tuck this young woman into
her pocket, just in case. "Could I call upon you next week? I
assure you, I seek no political favor from your father."

It was Miss Chase's turn to arch her eyebrow at Kate.
"Why, Miss Warne, I believe you are up to something. I
should be happy to listen when you are ready to tell me." She
reached into her basket and pulled out a card case, from
which she extricated a card. With a cool smile she handed it
over to Kate.

Oh, yes. She'd do.

The afternoon grew hotter and the air stilled, which inclined most of the spectators to a soporific state. Miss Chase
announced it was 5 o'clock just when a line of ambulances
rolled into view, moving up the turnpike away from the battle.

As one wagon closed the gap between the bridge and the
hill Kate heard a man yell, "We're whipped! We're whipped!"
Behind that wagon, several uniformed men on horseback
came charging up the road and around the wagons. Then a
mass of infantry soldiers appeared out of the trees, men running and falling and otherwise engaging in a disorderly
retreat.

The two Kates exchanged horrified looks. They were
watching a rout. They turned in their seats as a line of ambulances rattled past them, each one of them empty but for their
drivers.

"Where are they going?" Miss Chase asked.

The young woman was really asking why they were running away from a battle, leaving injured men behind them.

16

"I don't know," Kate answered. "Someone will have to transport the wounded men. I'm going." She jumped down and called Louisa over. "Help me get these horses harnessed. Fast." Kate grabbed Excelsior and Lucy's halters and moved them to the front of the wagon. "Once more into the breach dear friends, once more," she told them. There was nothing for bucking up a girl's courage like Henry V's battle speech.

Louisa sprung into action, aided by Miss Chase, who dismounted her carriage and helped with the harness buckles. Once they were set Kate heaved herself into the wagon seat. The afternoon had grown loud with shouts, cannon fire, and general panic. She leaned and half yelled, "Miss Chase, I ask you now to watch Louisa for me. And the dog. I'll load up with wounded men and bring them back here. You can take them on to Centreville."

Before Miss Chase could agree Monty leaped into the seat next to Kate.

"He goin' with you Miz Kate. To keep you safe," Louisa hollered above the fray.

Miss Chase put her arms around Louisa's shoulder and waved Kate on. "Go! We shall wait as long as we dare."

Kate slapped the reins against Excelsior and Lucy's backs and they were off. Kate spared a glance at Monty. He'd jumped down from the bench and braced his white feet on the footboard. He'd be no help, but she felt better for having him along. For good measure, she hurled the final lines of King Henry's speech over the horse's backs and into the smoky air. "The game's afoot! Follow your spirit and upon this charge, Cry 'God for Harry, England and Saint George!"

She hoped the day would end as well for McDowell's army as it had for Harry at Agincourt.

17

Peg A. Lamphier

Hope would disappoint her.

Chapter 2

July 21, 1861
Between Centerville and Bull Run, Virginia

*K*ate pulled Excelsior and Lucy to a stop. Cub Run Creek was just big enough to need a bridge, but it was a narrow one. Only one wagon at a time could cross it and right now retreating ambulance wagons crowded its narrow span. She fought the urge to scream at them to hurry. She had about four miles to the stone bridge that crossed Bull Run Creek. The field hospital was there, or so she'd heard. Sweat trickled off her forehead into her eyes. She swiped at it with her forearm and looked off to her left, her eyes drawn by the not-so-distant sound of cannon and rifle fire. A gargantuan boom reverberated against her ears, and then another roaring thump, accompanied by great, stuttering flashes of light. The bridge in front of her exploded.

She yanked on the reins in surprise. No, not the bridge. A wagon had exploded. On the bridge lay a wagon in shattered bits of wood and hardware. Two horses were down, one motionless, the other thrashing and screaming. Soldiers scrambled away from the bridge like rats off a sinking ship. Tumbled off the side of the road a body lay, most of its head evaporated by the explosion. A few feet away a head and shoulders sat on the ground, not far from a set of hips and legs. An incongruous strip of green grass ran between the two chunks of body.

Monty threw himself into her lap, a quivering mass of small dog. His nose twitched in time with his quaking body. Kate watched as dark flecks of ash settled onto Excelsior's broad white back. In all the mayhem he'd horse held his ground, no stranger to mayhem and noise. Lucy shifted in her harness, leaned her shoulder against Excelsior and quieted. Kate's mind flashed to the time a bomb exploded in Mr. Howard's livery stable. Excelsior had been harnessed to the little carriage and the blast had slammed her into its back wheel. Afterwards she'd discovered her reticule tangled in the wheel's spokes. If Excelsior had bolted he'd have dragged her down the street, wounding or killing her. But then, like now, he hadn't moved an inch

Kate knew better than to leap out the wagon and rush to the downed men and horses. If there was one thing she'd learned from spending hours with a regular Army artillery officer, it was that if one cannonball or canister hit a target, others would soon follow. The Confederate artillery company hit the bridge had used fused iron cannon balls that exploded on impact. The ball's explosion not only threw molten hunks of cannonball around but caused secondary shrapnel when whatever they hit came flying apart.

The downed horse screamed again. Something dark and long protruded from its abdomen. Kate looked away. She had to listen to its death agony, but she didn't have to watch it. Somehow the big animal seemed more horrifying than the dead and dying men. Maybe because, unlike the humans, it had not chosen this war, but was an innocent victim of human violence. She thought of Hazzard, safely out of this battle— teaching men to fire artillery at Fort Washington. He'd been angry when he found out he'd not be going to battle, but she was glad for his absence.

Kate held Monty against her, watching uniformed soldiers run pell-mell, hollering and gesticulating messages she could not discern from fifty feet away. One red-faced man walked up to the screaming horse, pulled his sidearm and fired it into the horse's skull. Kate heaved a sigh at the sudden quiet.

It was short lived. Men on the far side of the bridge scrambled out of the half dozen wagons. They abandoned their wagons and horses and scrambled for cover. Three soldiers took off running across the bridge. As they passed Kate, she heard one scream at his companions, "The cavalry! They're a coming'."

Another man, this one wearing some kind of state militia insignia, shouted back, "They'll cut us to pieces." And then they were gone, sprinting up the road to join the chaos and mayhem that had once been the General McDowell's proud Army of Northeast Virginia.

Kate turned her head back to the disaster at the bridge. There was a flood of traffic behind the wrecked wagon. Once the soldiers cleared the road the turnpike would become a flood of panicked traffic back to Centreville. She would not get to the field hospital down at Stone Bridge, not today.

Kate hopped down off her wagon to check on the horses, her corset creaking at her sudden movement. Monty jumped down behind her. She patted the wagon bench. "Hop up Monty." She didn't want him lost in the chaos of an army in full retreat. Monty cocked his ears and looked at her. She

21

could see he had no intention of obeying her command. "All right then. But stay with me, you hear?" She had no idea why she talked like this to a dog she'd met just this morning, but his presence did make her feel braver.

Moving up alongside Excelsior, Kate ran her hands down over his rear legs, then his belly and front legs, before stepping to his head. She took hold of his noseband and looked him in the eye.

"You all right?"

He nickered at her and bobbed his head. Kate forced herself to focus o Excelsior as cannons boomed in the background. They'd known each other a long time and, well, it was best they have a moment together first. She kissed his nose, marveling at the silky texture, and then bumped her forehead against his. "Good horse," she whispered, and then let go of him and wiped at her eyes.

She next checked Lucy. Where Excelsior was tall and showy white, Lucy's plain brown coat and sturdy build made her appear unremarkable. In spite of the fact that they were mismatched, they made a good team, in part because she was almost as unflappable as Excelsior. After checking Lucy and applying kisses to her nose, Kate hoisted herself back up in the wagon. Monty sprung up onto the floor of the wagon before hopping up onto the seat next to her.

Kate appraised the little black and white dog. "You're quite the little trooper, aren't you?" She patted his head, surprised at how hot his dark fur felt against her hand. Uncorking a bottle of water, she took a swig and then poured some into her hand for the dog. He lapped at it. She poured him a little more, aware that the horses would have to wait until they got back to Centreville.

22

She clucked Excelsior and Lucy into motion and made a big looping turn in the road. A few hundred feet up the road she pulled over again. It was as good a place as any to wait. Since she couldn't get to the field hospital, she'd pick up men here. Behind her artillery boomed and boomed again. She twisted in the wagon seat and watched the bridge. Men were tying ropes to the dead horses to drag them out of the way. A line of soldiers held a confused mass of ambulances and rolling artillery pieces off the bridge.

She waited, wondering how it had come to this. Had the Pinkertons missed something? Had she? Surely they had. But what? What intelligence they had on the Confederates said the McDowell's army had an overwhelming numerical superiority. How did this horrifying rout happen? When she'd set out this morning, so early it was still full dark, she'd expected a difficult day, but not the utter mayhem of a full retreat.

She felt the failure in her chest, like a bullet to the heart. *Had General Beauregard known the size and location of McDowell's army? If so, how? And what part had Mrs. Greenhow played in all this? What did I miss? How many men are dead because I failed to do my job?*

Clarifying rage flooded through her. She knew Rose Greenhow's spy network had been kidnapping people of color in Washington, including her best friend in the world, and selling them south into slavery. They'd rescued Juba and his friend Columbus and a few other slaves besides and come home to Washington to end Greenhow's underground network. So far they'd failed. For weeks they'd watched her every move and found nothing, not even a lone spy caught in the act. Somehow Greenhow used the profit from her illegal slave trade to pay for the kind of spy work that could bring about this defeat. Kate was sure of it.

Shells burst overhead. Smoke hung in the air. Excelsior whinnied but held his ground. Lucy leaned into him again. Kate put her arm around Monty, pulling his warm body up against hers. They waited for wounded men, who would surely come up the road, fleeing the battle behind them.

She would expose Rose Greenhow as a traitor. Somehow. And when they hung the conniving bitch for treason Kate would stand in the front row, cheering on the hangman. She sat and watched the flood of broken men flee before her, her hate for Rose Greenhow like a flame that burned up her supply of pity.

Chapter 3

July 22, 1861
Philadelphia & Baltimore

*T*he train's sudden deceleration, combined with the squealing of brakes, woke Rose Greenhow. She blinked owlishly as she stretched her back and neck. The nice thing about sleeping on trains was that it was like time travel. One fell asleep in one place and awoke in another, all in the blink of an eye.

Around her women bustled about, collecting their bags and sundry items. Rose knew from the gossip she heard in the lady's car that the women bound for Washington were now all getting off in Philadelphia. Word had come of the Yankee defeat at Bull Run and the northern ladies were worried about the Confederate Army's advance. Rose suspected many people canceled their travel plans, having no desire to leave the relative safety of New York City for more imperiled points south. Others, like the ladies currently scurrying about the train car, decided to go as far as Philadelphia and wait there for news.

One woman, who'd been peering under her seat and the surrounding seats, stood in the aisle and burst into tears. *Oh for God's sake.* If there was one thing Rose couldn't abide, it was a whiner. It was acceptable to apply tears to get one's way, but this?

Several ladies crowded around the weeping woman, offering her handkerchiefs and patting her solicitously on the back and arm.

"I can't find the doll I bought for Baby. I've lost her present." The woman's voice climbed so high it approached a wail.

Rose mastered her facial expression. Best not to appear too disgusted.

"What if the rebels take Washington and hurt my baby?"

The cackling crowd around the crying woman that her child was almost certainly safe. Rose snorted. The child was safer in the hands of Southern gentlemen, heroes armored with the moral enthusiasm of Crusaders of old, than it was in the hands of this northern ninny.

Unable to take more histrionics Rose stood and left the carriage, taking her small carpet bag with her as a precaution against theft. One never knew what Yankees would do. Look what a coward their president was. Elected in a purely sectional contest and set on depriving the South of her sovereign rights. His arrogance provoked southerners into taking the law into their own hands. He didn't see that the South had a right to self-protection. None of them did.

So what did he do? He dressed in a Scotch cap and a ladies cloak and snuck into the capital under the cover of darkness. Why, she'd heard when he first arrived in Washington he'd surprised his Committee of Safety, who took their job so seriously they were asleep at Willard's Hotel, by bursting in the door and shouting, "Hillo! By Jingo, just look at me!"

What kind of man talked like that, let alone behaved in such a rascally manner? Presidents should speak like gentlemen. No wonder he couldn't manage against the grand Confederate Army and its glorious generals.

Rose found the ladies water closet and afterward purchased a bottle of fizzy lemon water and a sandwich at the station's tiny concession stand. Taking her meager dinner in hand, she headed back to the train. As she was about to step on board a young man stepped in front of her.

"Ma'am, the Army advises women to get off the train here. There's reports of mob violence in Baltimore and a concern that the rebel army will invade Washington."

Rose reared back her head and looked down her nose at the man. "And you are?" She didn't add 'sir," for no northerner could ever be a gentleman in her eyes.

"Lieutenant Wise, of the U. S. Army," he said, snapping to a kind of attention.

Rose continued to look down her nose at the young man, a feat that required her to lift her chin on account of him being half a foot taller than her. "I have no fears; these rebels are of my faith. My only fear is that I shall not be in time to welcome our President, Mr. Davis, and the glorious General Beauregard to Washington." Rose watched in satisfaction as the young officer recoiled in distaste.

"Ma'am, I would see those gentlemen in irons."

"You could try!" Rose barked a laugh and boarded the train. Bandying words with fools was satisfying, but not overly productive. She regained her seat and waited. Once the train commenced its journey toward Baltimore and Washington she unwrapped her sandwich, using its paper wrapping as a lap cloth. She bit into her sandwich and sighed. Dry. Why were train station sandwiches always dry?

Lord, she was tired. As much as she was loath to admit it, these days traveling wore her out as it never had before. She'd traveled all the way to California and back and never blinked an eye. But that was years ago. As her fiftieth birthday grew ominously close, every journey took more out of her. Not that she wasn't glad she'd gone to New York. She'd born eight children and all she had left were three daughters. There was nothing more important than the safety of her girls, particularly after poor Gertrude's death last spring.

Yesterday she put Leila on the best steamship she could afford for the trip to Panama. Which was why they'd ended up going up to New York. It was stupid to take a train north to catch a ship south, but tickets bought in New York were much cheaper than any of the southern ports. Poor Leila. She'd be on the ship for weeks, only to have to debark in Panama and take that awful little train across the mountains to the western coast, before boarding another ship that would take her to San Francisco. From that city, Leila would take a coach to Utah Territory, where she could wait out the war with her sister in relative safety. Not that the frontier was a safe place for a white woman of gentle breeding, but life at Fort Churchill would be less dangerous than Washington, at least until General Beauregard took the city.

She should have sent her youngest daughter away too, but she couldn't bear parting from Little Rose. Leila had to go if for no other reason than the twenty-three old was running out of marital options. Maybe the relative scarcity of women on the frontier would encourage one of the dashing Army officers to offer for her.

A woman did so like to see her girls well married. Almost as much as she liked to see Yankees whipped in battle. She was doing her part for a Confederate victory, what with her network and her own information gathering. She'd even devised a plan for getting messages out of the city and to General Beauregard. And look what he'd done with it. Sent the Yankee army packing that's what he did. She'd also used her spy network to keep out of the poor house. And returned a few nigrahs to their rightful state by selling them south. That little venture had turned out to be enormously lucrative.

There was no higher calling than outsmarting arrogant abolitionists. The Yankees were jealous that's what they were. Jealous *and* ignorant. By destroying slavery they hoped to place their own pauper population into King Cotton, thereby reaping the superior advantages of the South's system. And what would become of the slaves? How would they survive without masters?

Rose crumpled the remnants of her sandwich into the paper it had come wrapped in and shoved it into a corner of her bag. She looked out into the moonlit night, watching the gray and black countryside slide by the train as if the world was moving past her seat. She'd be home by dawn and take a bath. Then she'd lie down for a bit. In the afternoon she'd walk down to the Capitol and take a seat in the Senate gallery. She could watch the Northern senators respond to the utter failure of their "On to Richmond" campaign. That would be fun. With any luck, she'd have General Beauregard and President Davis in her drawing room before the end of summer and she could tell them all about it.

Chapter 4

July 22, 1861
Washington City

*K*ate poked her head around the tree trunk. No lights back here either. She'd already walked by the front of Mrs. Greenhow's house and it had been dark too. Hattie and she had called on Mrs. Greenhow several days ago and the lady had said she'd be absent over the weekend. She was taking her daughter to school in New York or something like that. But it was Monday night. Was Rose still gone? A small part of Kate hoped Greenhow was home. *I could wallop the wretched creature on the head, tie her up and force her to give up all her secrets at knifepoint. How satisfying would that be?* Kate's mind whirled with the possibilities, the things she could do to the traitorous Rose, and the pain she could inflict upon her. Not that it would make up for all the pain the bitch caused, but it would be a start.

Reason and reality told her it would be far better if Rose were still out of town. The regularly scheduled train from Baltimore came in at 8 and 11 in the morning and again at 9 in the evening and midnight. A check of the *New York Times* showed only one ship leaving New York for Baltimore on Saturday, but three yesterday, including one of the large Cunard steamships. Kate suspected the lady's vanity about her social position, combined with the money she made in the scheme to kidnap free people of color and sell them as slaves, would warrant tickets one of the Cunard ships. But it was all guesswork. She could have put her daughter on a ship Saturday and be home by now.

Kate stared at the back door, thinking hard. Where was Rose's slave woman? The woman always looked miserable so maybe she used her mistress's absence to leave her unhappy workplace, however temporarily. Kate checked her watch and decided to wait until midnight. If the house stayed dark, she'd make her move.

She should have done this last night, but she'd been so tired it hadn't occurred to her. Tired and frightened. The retreat became more disorderly as evening fell, compounded by sporadic explosions of Confederate artillery shells. She'd picked up four injured soldiers, drove them up the hill to Miss Chase, and then went back for more. Miss Chase took the four men and Louisa back to the city. Monty refused to go with them, much to Louisa's dismay.

On her second trip, it took Kate three times longer to traverse the distance from the Centreville heights to the bridge, fighting as she was against the fleeing traffic. She filled her wagon with injured men before she made it to the bridge. Then she'd had to turn around and fight her way back to Washington. The closer they got to the city the worse the traffic became. A long line of carriages and riders waited at Long Bridge while Army sentries examined everyone's papers. Some people failed the admittance process and were turned back, which further fouled and slowed traffic. All of which was frustrating, but not as awful as the general panic and terror that

32

rode the fleeing soldiers and civilians like a malevolent horse-man.

It was well past midnight when she delivered her load of injured men to Miss Barton's infirmary and turned toward home. Her favorite Pinkerton, Timothy Webster was sitting on the back stoop waiting for her. He took hold of the horses and sent her up to bed. She'd been up for twenty-two hours and so tired she almost cried at his kindness.

This morning as she dressed Kate thought about some-thing Hattie said last night. She'd found Hattie outside the infirmary, the street's gas lamps illuminating the chaos and dust of post-battle triage. Wagons clogged the street and the moans of injured men filled the air, making a low undertone beneath the shouts of orderlies and doctors and the thump and grind of too many wagons in too small a space. In the midst of it all, Hattie directed a pair of well-muscled black men with grim faces to unload Kate's wagon load of wounded soldiers.

Ignoring the surrounding mayhem, Hattie turned to Kate. "Bad, huh?"

Kate shook her head. "You have no idea."

"Oh, I've some idea. I've been here all day." Hattie waved at the huge three-storied hospital behind her.

Kate nodded in dumb understanding. She noticed Hattie's apron, usually a pristine white, was smeared with red gore. More shockingly, Hattie's hair had come loose from its bun and straggled about her face.

Kate gave Hattie an abridged version of her day, finishing with her worry that somehow Mrs. Greenhow's organization had played a part in the day's debacle.

"Funny, if you think about it," Hattie mused.

Kate's antennae quivered. She knew that tone. "What?"

"Mrs. Greenhow is out of town this weekend. Up to New York, or so she said. Remember?"

"Did she go? I didn't think she would. Not with a big battle brewing."

Hattie nodded. "I bet she did. She sounded serious about getting her daughter out of the city. I don't like her any more than you do, but she takes motherhood pretty seriously." Hattie paused and gave Kate a hard stare.

"And?"

Hattie shrugged her shoulders, but before she could say more someone hollered her name. "I've got to go." She shoved her hair behind her ears and hustled away to the next crisis.

Kate stood unmoving for a long minute, a small island in a sea of chaos, then crawled back into her wagon and headed for home and bed.

The next morning she couldn't believe how obtuse she'd been.

The light cast by the midnight moonlight made breaking and entering easy. Kate stepped toward the back door and peered through the small window. Nothing. No movement. No light. From previous visits, she knew the slave woman's room was just off the kitchen, to the right. Either the woman was sound asleep or she wasn't here.

Kate slid her little leather folder of lock picks out of her pocket and set to work on the back door. A few moments later it gave way with a soft snick. Kate stepped into the middle of the kitchen and listened. She tip toed over to the slave woman's bedroom door and eased it open. Empty. Next, she pushed her way past the green kitchen door, smiling as she did. The last time she'd seen this side of the kitchen door she'd been kissing Hazzard. Soundly.

She made her way down the center hall to the base of the stairs and stopped again. Should she check upstairs first? If there was no one upstairs she'd know she was alone in the house. She decided the subsequent peace of mind would be worth the stress of sneaking upstairs. She crept up the stairs, testing each riser before she put her full weight on it. The third step threatened her with a tiny squeaking groan so she stepped over it.

At the top of the stairs, she found a hall with four doors, just as she remembered. She'd been up here once while attending a party—the same party where she'd kissed Hazzard in the kitchen. One by one she eased the doors open. The two rooms on the right belonged to Little Rose, one a bedroom, one a playroom. The back bedroom had that empty feeling rooms take on when they're unoccupied. The door closest to the stairs opened to a room awash in Mrs. Greenhow's floral perfume. Kate wrinkled her nose in distaste.

Kate felt tension she hadn't known she was carrying leave her shoulders and neck. She was alone in the house. She stood in the hall thinking. Rose used the right-hand parlor downstairs for receiving and the left-hand parlor as a combination office, library and meeting room. She'd search those rooms first.

As she came down the stairs Kate noticed something she hadn't seen when she'd first come from the kitchen. A folded piece of paper lay on the floor in front of the door's mail slot. She picked it up and examined it. There wasn't much to see.

35

It had no writing on it, no stamp or postage marks, only a daub of unmarked, cream-colored sealing wax. Her heart, which had just settled down, sped up again.

Kate carried her prize into the left parlor and sat it on the large, rectangular wooden table that dominated the center of the room. She looked around the room. *There.* A small nub of candle. Spying matches on the fireplace mantel, she lit the candle and held the wax seal about four inches above the flame. After a few seconds, she checked the seal, then reapplied the paper to the flame for a few moments more. The next time she checked the seal she found it soft enough to loosen. She unfolded the paper and flattened it on the table, next to the candle. *Dammit. Code.*

Kate knew from experience that codes came with cipher keys. When the Pinkertons used a code, and they had several they used fairly often. Kate kept the cipher close by, though she never carried it with her. A spy didn't want to be captured with a cipher. She looked around the room. The room's side-wall had built-in cabinets topped by bookshelves. There was also a small writing desk in the corner. She set to work searching the room.

An hour later Kate stood in the center of the room, pushed a lock of hair away from her sweaty forehead and sighed. Nothing. She circled the room, pressing the wooden paneling and checking behind paintings. Still nothing. Not even one secret compartment. How inconsiderate of the damn woman. She stepped across the hall and did a cursory search of Rose's receiving parlor. It didn't seem likely that she would keep anything important in the room that saw the most public traffic, but Kate checked anyway. More nothing. The room had no bookshelves, no cabinets, no secret compartments, no maps, and no cipher codes.

Kate returned to the library parlor and appraised the writing desk. It had paper, ink, and pens in it. Fifteen minutes later Kate had a copy she could tuck into her pocket. She resealed the original and laid it back on the entryway floor.

At the base of the stairs, she stopped and thought. She'd been in the house for almost two hours. *Did she have time? Luck rarely favors cowards.* She scrambled back up the stairs. She'd been going about this all wrong. Men kept their most important documents and secret items in their offices, either at home or at their place of employment. Women kept their secrets in bedrooms. She'd been searching the wrong room.

The safe was about four feet tall and three feet wide, painted black with gold scrollwork. It had a door with decorative rosettes in each corner as would befit a safe of the sort that fit into a lady's closet. Across the door were the words 'Hall's Safe & Lock Company, Cincinnati.'

So far, so good. Kate pulled a tiny maroon leather notebook from her jacket pocket. She peered at a page, then another before taking a lamp from Rose's bedside table. She lit the lamp and sat it on top of the safe. The man who taught her to crack safes had copied his own notebook for her and she'd added to over the years. She'd also made copies of the notebook for both Allan Pinkerton and Timothy Webster. In fact, she'd taught both of them everything she knew about safecracking, which was about enough to open most safes, most of the time. She didn't have data on every safe ever made and safe companies were always making new ones.

She thumbed through her notebook until she came to the H section. Hall's made a bunch of safes, from massive bank safes to these smaller, one-door safes. According to her notes, small Hall's safes had three-wheeled locks. Such locks had four numbers while four-wheeled locks had five and so forth. So she had only four numbers to discover. The key to cracking a safe wasn't only in knowing the numbers, but in knowing the dialing sequence. Dialing sequences were the centerpiece of her notebook. There it was. Four left, three right, two left, one right. It made sense. It would be an easy sequence to remember because Hall intended these small safes for home use. She stuck her little red book back in her pocket, careful not to lose the pencil stub tucked in the back.

Now the numbers. George taught her two important things about safe numbers. The first was that once a cracksman had the dialing sequence he, or she, could hear the numbers with careful listening through a glass or metal tube. Second, and better, most people couldn't remember the combination, so they wrote it down and stored it somewhere near the safe. Ladies like to keep their safe combinations in one of two places: in their tabletop jewelry box or in their unmentionables drawer. Kate didn't know why people went to the trouble of locking up their good jewelry and then keep the combination to the safe in a jewelry box. She supposed most people, even the ones who bought a safe, didn't think anyone would rob them.

She swiveled and looked around the room. Thank goodness there was no bookshelf. Rifling through books was slow work. Mrs. Greenhow had a small cedar box on top of a highboy dresser. Kate checked that, being careful to note any rips in the lining under which tiny pieces of paper might hide.

Nope. Next, she opened the dresser drawers, starting with the top one and moving down. She discovered Mrs. Greenhow had a pessary hidden among her chemises in the top drawer, which startled Kate more than a little. She'd suspected the attractive widow had intimate male friends, but seeing the evidence up close was more than a little embarrassing.

Finding no papers with numbers on them, Kate turned and surveyed the room. Maybe the lady had memorized her safe combination. Doubtful. Most people didn't. Or they did but didn't trust themselves to remember it. Rose was a careful woman.

Kate stopped searching and thought. What had the cracksman said about safe combinations? *Ahhh. Right.* She grabbed the lantern and stepped over to the closet, held the lantern about eye level and looked at the walls. There. On the door frame.

67   79   115   60

Kate resisted the impulse to caper in delight. Before she started Kate checked the hall one more time. Nothing. She went back to the closet and kneeled in front of the safe. Four turns left, stop at 67, back three turns to 79, two turns to the left, stop at 115 and then back right half a turn to 60. Snick. Kate pushed down on the handle and swung the door open, again resisting the impulse to do a happy dance. There was nothing more fun than cracking a safe. If she ever had a choice between kissing Hazzard and cracking a safe she'd have to think about it for a minute. It would probably depend on the safe.

A small, dark green box sat atop a basket of papers, 'Remington' written in ornate script across the top. She pulled out the box and opened it. Inside lay a small revolver, its barrel only three inches long. It glowed like a diamond in lamp-light. She picked it up. *Oh, what a pretty thing.* Unlike her tiny Derringer's double barrel, two shot capacity, this gun had a five-shot cylinder. And it was still small enough to hide in a reticule or muff. Kate frowned. *The bitch has a better gun than me. Life really wasn't fair, was it?*

She set the pretty gun aside and pulled out the basket. Letters. And legal papers. A deed to the house. A death certificate for one John Greenhow. A hand-drawn map of something. Kate stared at it. Egad. It was the city, with all the new defensive fortification and battery positions marked by Xs and squares.

And then there it was. A single sheet of paper covered in scribbles and letters. The Cipher. Its depth in the pile suggested Rose had memorized the code and no longer needed daily contact with the key.

Kate bit her lower lip. Did she dare take it? Would the lady miss it?. She should copy it. She pulled the copy of the note she'd made downstairs out of her pocket, turned it over and laid it flat on the floor. Next, she extracted from her pocket the pencil stub in her little maroon notebook and set to work.

On the left side of the page, there were two vertical rows, one of letters and other symbols. There was another set of symbols across the top of the page for diphthongs and double vowels, from 'th' to 'ei.' Symbols for common words, including regiment, infantry, cannon, men, horses, and Lincoln, took up the rest of the page. The symbol for Lincoln, a funny little forked tree branch thingy, gave Kate the willies. She'd taken a bullet for the president not that long ago and she didn't want to do it again.

She was just putting the cipher back when she heard the bang of a downstairs door. Resisting the impulse to slam the safe shut and throw herself out the window, she closed the safe and spun the dial. She stood, taking care not to thump her boots on the floor and listened. If it was the lady of the house, she'd be upstairs soon. Kate looked around the room. The window wasn't a good option because few windows opened noiselessly.

She tip toed to the bedroom door and listened. Thumping came from somewhere below. Maybe the kitchen. The maid? Or Mrs. Greenhow? She heard steps across a hardwood floor, then the creak of that third step.

Kate dove under the bed. She didn't want to spend the night there, but the only other place to hide was the closet. If it was Rose, she'd use the closet to change into her night-clothes. Hopefully, the lady wasn't in the habit of checking under her bed for monsters. Or detectives. Kate scooted to the middle of the space, belly down should the opportunity to crawl out undetected arise. A pair of ratty carpet slippers confronted her. Thinking it would be bad if the lady in question looked under the bed for the slippers, Kate pushed them over so they just peeked out from the side of the bed.

Over the pounding of her heart Kate heard the slight swish of the bedroom door against the carpet as it opened. A set of feet shod in dark brown leather brogans came into view. A dusty dark blue calico dress hem rode above the shoes. Kate ordered her heart to slow down. It had to be Mrs. Greenhow's slave. The woman moved around the room for several minutes. Once she paused by the bed, her shoes inches from Kate's nose. After what felt like five hours and was probably only five minutes, she left the room.

41

Kate waited one long hour before crawling out from under the bed. It was longer before she found the nerve to creep down the stairs, past the sleeping slave woman's room, and out the back door.

Chapter 5

July 23, 1861
Washington City

Kate came down the back stairs into an empty kitchen, Monty hard on her heels. The coffee pot burbled on the stove, but otherwise the room was quiet. This late in the morning Charlotte and Louisa were probably doing the day's shopping. Timothy was at the hospital with Hattie. And Juba was in Chicago, at Pinkerton headquarters with Allan. They were up to something. Secret man stuff no doubt.

Last night, when she got home from Roses, Monty scratched at her door. Kate wondered if her new friend had fleas, but when she climbed into bed, he snuggled up against her leg and made a contented little doggy sound that made Kate forget about flees. Unable to wait until morning, she arranged her papers and pens around her bed and decoded the message. The words had been benign enough, but the implications worried Kate enough to keep her awake until near dawn.

She poured herself a cup of coffee and took it to the window that overlooked the walled backyard. She'd been wrong. Charlotte was hanging a load of laundry on a line strung between the house and the back wall while Louisa had Excelsior and Lucy out of their stalls. The horses were tied near the water trough to keep them from bothering Charlotte. For reasons passing understanding, the big white horse loved laundry. He'd pull it down, then try to rehang it, a process which left clothing and bedding covered in horse slobbery mud. Charlotte sent most of their laundry out to a free woman of color, but when she did wash, she did not enjoy doing it twice. Kate stepped out on the back stoop, Monty right behind her.

"Oh, there you are dear," Charlotte said over her shoulder, her words muffled by the clothespin in her mouth. She pulled it out and pinned up a kitchen towel. "Is the coffee all right? I feared it would scorch. Oh, and there's a bowl of meat scraps in the pantry for your little friend. Louisa's been to the market already this morning."

Kate crossed the yard, careful not to spill her mug, and stretched up on tippy toes to kiss her housekeeper's cheek. "Coffee's fine. I slept too long. Where is everyone?"

"Oh, here and there." Charlotte pulled a crumpled piece of telegraph paper out of her apron pocket and handed it to Kate. "This came this morning."

Philadelphia

July 23, 1861

Juba and I on morning train. Gather all for 2 PM meeting at the house. Request Charlotte and I speak before.

Mr. E. J. Allen

Kate handed the telegram back to Charlotte, who returned it to her pocket. They both knew E. J. Allen was Allan Pinkerton's favorite nom de guerre. "What's he want with you?"

"No idea dearie. Probably wants me to make his favorite cookies. He's been away from his wife's cooking for weeks now."

"But you already have, haven't you?" Kate grinned at Charlotte as she bent to pick up the now empty basket.

Charlotte surveyed her line of pinned towels with satisfaction. "Oatmeal, raisin, apple. Early this morning before it got too hot. Why don't you go say hello to your horses? And keep that old devil away from my laundry or you'll be the one rewashing it."

Kate poked her nose in the stable and promised Louisa she'd change into her scruffy trousers and come help muck out the stalls. Shoveling actual excrement was more satisfying than the metaphorical equivalent.

After stable cleaning Kate took herself upstairs to wash and change into a day dress. Monty stretched out at the foot of her bed and kept an eye on her. Kate suspected the tiny gentleman hound had adopted her. The idea pleased her more than she cared to admit.

The two of them came down stairs to find Juba in the kitchen. "You're home," she cried, throwing her arms around him.

Juba hugged Kate back, then held her out at arm's length. "You look as tired as I feel. And who's this little fellow?"

Kate introduced her best friend to her new dog, being careful not to claim him as her own in front of Louisa.

Juba crouched down and rubbed Monty's head. He kept his eyes on the dog while he said, "I hear you drove out to Bull Run."

45

"I did. I'll tell you about it later. And I was out late last night. I'll explain at the meeting."

Juba stood, nodded and pulled her back into a hug. "Sounds fine."

Though a free black man, Juba was the closest thing Kate had to a father since her parents died when she was fifteen. They'd bought their first house together, back in Chicago, six years ago and worked together as Pinkerton operatives just as long.

"You look tired too," she said. "What you been doing?"

"Ah, like you, I'll save it for the meeting. And we got hung up in the Baltimore riots. Maryland Secesh got themselves all liquored up and determined to stop northern trains going south. That town sure likes a riot."

Allan Pinkerton stepped through the kitchen door, followed by a smallish, heavyset black woman. Monty barked at the pair of them so hard his white front feet bounced off the floor, at least until Kate shushed him. She pointed at a little bed in one corner of the kitchen, put there by Louisa. He hopped in, circled and lay down, but he kept an eye on the newcomers.

Allan made a fuss over Kate, chastising her for the circles under her eyes and his belief that she'd lost weight since the last time he'd seen her. Finally, he stepped aside, making room for the woman behind him.

"Miss Odetta," Kate said, holding out both hands to greet the woman. "How wonderful to see you."

Kate wasn't just being polite. The first time she'd seen Odetta was the day after they'd removed her and several other women from a whorehouse that specialized in unusual cruelties. Odetta had been the cook, not one of the fancy ladies, but

46

even so, she'd had a hard life. They spent two weeks on a steamboat together, but when Kate debarked the boat at Memphis, Odetta still had the haunted look of a woman who'd been maltreated in creative ways. Now her eyes were bright, her skin smooth and her graying hair springing off her head in a manner that suggested robust good health.

Odetta grasped Kate's hands in her own and smiled a smile that lit up the room. "Oh, you jess being kind to an old woman. But I 'appreciate your lies." Kate was about to protest when Odetta caught sight of Louisa, who'd been peeling potatoes at the sink. "Who's this bee-yoo-tiful gal?"

Kate introduced the two of them. The two women seemed to recognize something in each other, though what it was Kate could not tell. While they made their introductions Kate turned to the stove and poured another cup of coffee. As she did Hattie and Timothy came in the back door, causing a further ruckus.

Kate made a mental note to make sure Hattie went up to bed after the meeting. Her face was grey with exhaustion and her dress dirty and sweat-stained. Kate didn't think she'd ever seen Hattie looking anything but perfectly dressed and coifed. Never. Until this war started and she went to work at the infirmary. It was as if the earth faltered on its axis a tiny bit. Kate pressed into an empty chair while Charlotte slid a cup of tea in front of her, then rooted around in the icebox. She emerged triumphant with two plums in her hand. In a trice, she had them sliced and in a bowl which also ended up in front of Hattie.

Allan asked them to take seats at the kitchen table. Not for the first time Kate wondered why the house even had a front parlor. She ought to have Juba's friend Columbus take down

Peg A. Lamphier

the wall between the kitchen and the dining room if they were going to keep spending all their time in the kitchen.

Allen took one end of the table and Kate the other after she retrieved a slim folder from the dining room table. Charlotte put a big plate of cookies on the table. The housekeeper gave both her husband Timothy and his boss Allan stern looks before she sat down, knowing as she did their fondness for sweets.

Kate looked around the table once they'd all taken their seats. Odetta sat next to Hattie, which gave Kate pause. For the first time she wondered what Odetta was doing here when she lived in Philadelphia with Hattie's mother Miz Amalie and a small host of escaped slave women.

Allan cleared his throat and began. "As you all know, last month I moved Pinkerton headquarters from Chicago to Cincinnati at General McClellan's request. He's asked me to form a secret service for the Department of the Ohio."

Kate looked up from the folder in front of her. "That's why you didn't come with us on our rescue mission to New Orleans. I wondered. It didn't' seem like you to sit out a grand adventure."

Allan nodded. "I had a telegram from the general before you all left. I didn't want to say anything at the time, not when Juba and Columbus were our first priority."

Juba grimaced a little. "I'm sorry to be so much trouble." He paused. "Though I'm mighty glad you all came. Being a slave didn't suit me at all." He shook his head and grinned a little like he was trying to make a joke, but Kate couldn't help notice how his shoulders tensed up and his eyebrows scrunched together. She still hadn't gotten the whole story on his kidnapping and captivity. She wondered if she ever would.

48

"We Pinkertons take care of our own," Allan said in a deep growling voice. He paused and looked around the table. "I'm about to tell you something that cannot leave this room. Not for a few days at least."

Allan waited for assent around the table.

"Mr. Lincoln plans to replace General McDowell."

"Well that's hardly a state secret," Timothy said. "Not after the disaster at Bull Run."

"Well, yes, but it's more than that. The President and Mr. Seward have restructured the Army. My friend George McClellan is to be commander of the Military Division of the Potomac, which will include both the Eastern theater and Washington. As a consequence, the Pinkerton Detective Agency will become the President's primary military intelligence unit until the Army can create its own."

This news caused an explosion of chatter around the table. When the excited talk died down Kate leaned forward, pushing the folder in front of her. "There's plenty to do. We've got to stop Mrs. Greenhow. She's key to all this. I know it, though can't prove it yet."

Allan held up a hand. "Kate, I know you're fair to bursting to revenge your friends, but let me finish. Please. What I've got to say will have a direct bearing on everything that happens next."

Kate fought the urge to argue. She wanted to push them all into a discussion of how best to bring down the vile Greenhow woman, but if she'd learned anything over the years, it was that when Allan Pinkerton got to plotting one could only sit back and wait.

"Our move to Cincinnati taught me one thing. The Pinkerton Detective Agency is too well known for its own good.

There were too many newspaper articles about the agency's move from Chicago to Cincinnati and its connection to the Army of the Ohio. Another move, particularly one to Washington, will cause an even greater stir."

Juba tipped his chair back and grinned. "Hard to run a secret service when everyone knows you."

Allan nodded. "Exactly. I propose we go underground."

Kate watched Allan, realization dawning as she did. "You're about to reorganize too, aren't you?"

"Right in one my dear. As of now, we are sitting in the Pinkerton Detective Agency's secret Washington headquarters. I'll keep the office open in Cincinnati and take a page out of Mr. Rice's handbook."

Juba looked over at Kate and chuckled. Their friend Mr. Rice believed in hiding in plain sight. It was an old circus trick they'd used to infiltrate New Orleans with Dan Rice's traveling circus show to rescue Juba and his friend Columbus. Mr. Rice also helped them move Mr. Lincoln across Baltimore before his inauguration by hiding him in a gaudy red and gold circus wagon.

Allan chuckled. "You take my point. I'll make a great show of focusing on railroad security from Cincinnati. I've hired some new men to do that work. Everyone knows General McClellan and I met while he was in the railroad business so they'll believe the Pinkertons are focusing on railroad protection. Plus, keeping the northern rail lines will be crucial to winning this war. So we'll have people looking over here." He waved his left hand around, then dropped it and did the same with his right. "While over here I make a show of bumbling incompetence from time to time. The president and generals will know better. The Confederates won't be so careful if they think we don't know what we're doing."

"Absolutely not," Kate said, more forcefully than she intended. "You'll go down in history as a fool."

"And?" Allan leaned back and lit the cigar he'd been playing with. "If we do this right history won't even remember most of you. Hell, Mr. Lane here's supposed to be dead."

Juba laid his hand on Kate's arm. "Katie, you know this isn't about who gets credit."

She pulled her arm away from him and glared around the table. "I know that. There's a world of distance between not being remembered and being remembered as an idiot."

Allan laid his cigar down with great deliberation. "I was with John Brown on more Underground Railroad trips than I can count and I was standing in the crowd the day they hung him. That day I vowed to do whatever it took to finish his mission. We will end slavery. By damn we will. But thousands of men will die first. If the worst that happens is that I look foolish, I'll count myself the luckiest man alive." Chin tucked like a bull ready to charge, he looked around the table. "Got it?"

They did. Even Kate, though she was loath to admit it.

After a moment he opened a folder, pulled out a sheaf of papers and handed it around the table. "Everyone take one. It's our new organizational chart. Get a good long look. At the end of this meeting, we'll destroy them."

Allan waited while they passed around papers. "As you can see, there are two columns, one for Cincinnati and one for Washington. I'll keep Mr. Bangly in Cincinnati, plus Mr. Scully. Those other names are the new men.

Kate stared at the paper and shook her head. "I can't be the head of the Washington division, not even if its secret.

Timothy's been at this far longer than I and he's older." She glanced over at Timothy as she spoke, worried he'd be angry.

He smiled at her and shook his head.

"I knew you'd buck at it," Allan said. "I already discussed it with Timothy. I'm sending him to Richmond to infiltrate the government there. It has to be you, Kate. You know the Washington underground. And you've been the head of the company's Women's Bureau for the better part of five years."

"What about Juba? Or Hattie?" Kate protested. "They could run it better than me."

Juba laughed one of his rich, rolling laughs. "Girl, you be da boss man now." He wiped at his eyes and said, "I've got my own fish to fry."

Kate saw Juba and Allan share a glance.

Hattie patted her on the shoulder. "It's all right Kate. And honestly, it's not like it means all that much."

Kate conceded Hattie's point. For the past five years, Allan handed out assignments and then let his operatives go, pretty much at their own discretion. He didn't do much bossing beyond assigning jobs. She pointed at the paper. "Fine. I'll do it. It says here Charlotte's the office manager. It doesn't seem fair to give her another job."

Charlotte slid the cookie plate over to Kate . "You may have another cookie dear."

Before Charlotte could change her mind, Kate snatched a cookie off the plate. She resisted the impulse to gobble it. Was there anything better than oatmeal, raisin, and apple cookies?

Allan pointed at Odetta, who hadn't said a word since they sat down. "That's why Miss Odetta has agreed to join us here. Juba helped me convince her."

"I didn't need much convincing, did I?" Odetta reached for the cookie plate and pushed it even closer to Kate. "I'm the new cook and I say this lady can have as many cookies as she wants."

Charlotte pulled the plate out of Kate's reach just before Kate got her fingers on a fourth cookie. "I haven't handed over my apron yet. Not before I tell you to watch that girl." She jutted her chin at Kate. "She forgets to eat. If she comes through here and even slows down, put a plate of food in front of her, real food, not cookies, and make her eat it."

Odetta adopted a chastened look, but then spoiled it by winking at Kate.

Allan cleared his throat. "The thing is we can't bring just anyone in to cook. Our secrecy needs are far too high. We can trust Odetta and she can free up Charlotte for managerial work. Right, Charlotte?"

"I'm good with numbers. I used to keep the books for my father's dry goods store."

Timothy beamed at his wife. "The boys get their brains from their mother. They'd a never got into that fancy boarding school otherwise."

Odetta stirred. "And I'd rather cook than sew." She looked over at Hattie. "Your Mama's a good woman, but she can't see how sitting and making tiny stitches is boring. I poked myself with a needle a hundred times a day. Naw, I'm a cook. Plus, I got debts to pay." She held up her hand. "Y'all don't argue. You may not a meant to save me, but you did and that kind of debt needs to be paid."

Hattie stirred in her seat. "But we sent you all to Philadelphia for a reason. We agreed it was safer for fugitive slaves than Washington. If the Confederate Army ever takes this

city, they'll round up everyone with a drop of African in them
and sell them south. You know they will."

Hattie held up her hand when Odetta opened her mouth
to talk. "I think you have a right to be here if that's what you
want Odetta, but we should agree right now: If it looks like
Washington will fall we move heaven and earth to get Juba,
Louisa, and Odetta back to my Mama in Philadelphia."

Juba shook his head. "That might be hard to do. If Washington falls the roads and rail lines are gonna be clogged with
people getting the heck out of town."

"Hattie's right," Kate said. "It's not something we can plan
for, but you three," Kate pointed around the table to Juba,
Louisa, and Odetta, "have to agree to run and leave the rest of
us if need be." She skewered Hattie with a hard look. "You
too Hattie. If you go with them you can take the horses. I
don't want Excelsior and Lucy sent south either." The thought
of sweet old Excelsior pulling an artillery piece into a battle
upset Kate almost as much as thinking of Juba and the rest
sold into slavery. She knew it shouldn't, but it did.

Odetta grabbed Louisa's hand and looked across the table
at Juba. "We'll go and we'll keep everyone safe."

Juba and Odetta locked eyes. Kate saw the two of them
make some unspoken pact.

"That I believe," Allan said, his voice as soft as kitten ears.

After a long moment of silence, Kate tapped the folder in
front of her. "What's the chain of command? I mean, outside
of this operation. We'll be in the federal government's pay,
right? Do we work for the Army? Or Mr. Lincoln and the
War Department? "

"The money comes out of War Department budget. Mr.
Lincoln would like copies of reports, but our contact will be

54

one of the under-secretaries in the War Department. I don't know who yet. I lobbied to have Captain Hazzard detailed back to us as a liaison. He's too good an intelligence asset to waste on artillery lessons for new recruits."

Hattie looked over at Kate and winked. "And far too handsome to waste on soldiers, huh Kate?"

Kate pressed her lips together and tried to look innocent. Rather than talk about Hazzard she changed the subject. "Two last details. We'll shift Charlotte's wages to the Pinkerton payroll. I'll pay Odetta and Louisa out of the household budget." Kate had a lot of problems right now but money was not one of them. Juba had a freakish talent for stock market speculation and in the last few years he'd used it to more than double her divorce settlement.

"Fine with me. But if either of you," Allan pointed at Louisa and Odetta, "do any intelligence gathering the Pinkerton's will pay you for the job. You get your orders from Kate here, but report your hours to Charlotte. She'll make sure you get paid."

Louisa nodded so enthusiastically her braids whipped to and fro, but Odetta looked dubious. Kate wondered if she was finding it hard to believe she'd be paid at all, having only recently escaped slavery, or if she intended to ignore the extra pay in favor of the debt she imagined she owed them. Seeing Odetta's face, Hattie stole a look at Kate, who nodded in response. They'd keep an eye on their new cook and make sure she didn't allow herself to be taken advantage of.

Alan stubbed out his cigar. "So it's settled then?"

Everyone agreed that it was.

He hoisted his teacup. "Then the Washington Branch of the Pinkerton Secret Service is open for business."

They all clinked tea cups and coffee mugs.

Alan looked down the table at Kate. "Kate? I know you're fair to bursting with something."

Kate took a deep breath and blew it out. "The other night at the hospital Hattie reminded me that Mrs. Greenhow was out of town."

Hattie smiled. "I thought you missed the hint."

"I almost did. I broke into her house last night." When she got to the part about hiding under the bed everyone laughed. It was funnier in the telling than it felt at the moment.

"When I got home, I used the cipher to decode the note. It's just as I suspected." She pushed the piece of paper she'd decoded over to Hattie.

Hattie read it. She finished and bit her lower lip hard enough to leave marks. "Someone delivered this the day after the battle?"

Kate nodded and pushed the letter over to Allan.

"What?" Juba shifted in his chair.

Allan shook the sheet of paper and began to read.

Our President and generals direct me to thank you for the information that led to our recent battle victory. The Confederacy owes you a great debt that it will not forget. We look forward to continued intelligence.

Capt. Jordan, Adjutant-General

"See? We missed something," Kate said. "Something big." She tried to keep her voice devoid of emotion, but some of her anger seeped in. "We need to stop this woman before she causes more damage. We'll catch her and see her hang for it. And dance on her grave. "

Hattie gasped. "That's a terrible thing to say. You shouldn't wish for a woman's death."

"And why not," Kate said, slapping her hand on the table as she spoke. "She's a traitor. She as good as murdered those men at Bull Run. She's a thief who steals human beings. There's a war on. Besides, you know if the Confederates caught one of us they'd hang us without a moment's thought. Their congress has already said so."

Hattie shook her head. "Just because they made a pronouncement doesn't mean they'll really do it. It's not right."

No one said anything. Kate waited for Allan to speak.

Allan said nothing. He didn't move. He didn't draw attention to himself in any way.

Kate looked over at her boss. He stared at the table. And then it occurred to her. She was in charge now.

Juba exploded into the quiet of the table. "This is my fault!" He stood up, kicking his chair back. "Dammit anyway. She got out in front of you all cause you took your eyes off her. To come get me. All those dead soldiers. Because you came and got me."

Everyone at the table froze and stared at Juba. Monty leaped up from his bed, hackles up and growled.

Kate patted her lap. Monty leaped into it. She smoothed her hand over the top of his silky head and took a deep breath. "And Columbus. Don't forget him. Poor Reatha was out of her mind."

"So was I," Hattie half whispered.

"You all got me out too," Odetta said, reaching out to lay a hand on Juba's arm. "I'm mighty happy to be free."

Juba shook Odetta's off and stomped toward the back door. He laid his hand on the knob, and glared over his shoulder. "You shoulda left all of us. Columbus would say the same. Thousands of men died on Sunday. Men who didn't have to die. And now those damn slave lovers have the upper hand. I'd rather be dead. We all would. So our children could be free one day." He wrenched open the door and stepped outside, slamming the door hard enough to rattle the windows in his wake.

Kate rose, but Allan motioned her back to her seat. "Sit. I'll go. I didn't rescue him." Allan grabbed his hat off the kitchen counter and left the kitchen.

"Meaning what?" Kate asked, her voice as high as a frightened child. "We rescued him so it's our fault?"

"Yeah, kind of." Timothy's voice was soft but sure. "A man doesn't like to need rescuing. Least always, not by anyone other than himself. He tried to escape, you know? And got caught."

"No, I didn't. He won't talk about it." Kate looked down at the scarred tabletop, then back up again. "At least not to me."

"He escaped in Key West, ran to a nearby military fort and got turned back over to the slavers for his trouble. They whipped him within an inch of his life for it. And now he's got to live with the fact that he let himself be taken, twice, and that he was powerless and victimized and the only reason he's free is a bunch of women came and saved him."

"It wasn't a bunch of women." Kate couldn't help it. She felt indignant and defensive. Weren't you supposed to rescue your friends and relatives? "Hazzard was with us. And Mr. Rice. And Juba didn't let himself get caught. He was just caught. It wasn't his fault. They weren't even after him. Columbus says they wanted him. On account of his size."

"Don't matter none," Timothy said, running his hand through his already messy hair. 'He feels like it's his fault. Like

58

he failed as a man. Which he's ticklish about already, being a colored and small and all the rest."

Hattie sighed. "Timothy means it's not just that he's black. Juba's not getting any younger. The slavers didn't even want him and still, they caught him. He's been taking care of you for years. That's what he does. He takes care of people. Why do you think we all live together in this house?" Hattie snorted. "He did that. He takes care of all of us. And then it turns out Mrs. Greenhow is smarter than we thought. He thinks he failed."

Kate stared at Hattie in disbelief. She wanted to say it was ridiculous. But it wasn't. She looked over at Timothy, who bit his lower lip and nodded.

Charlotte pushed herself up from her chair and looked out the window. "They're out by the clothesline talking."

Kate nodded, still processing Timothy and Hattie's words. People were too complicated for her. She was better with horses and dogs. Maybe they should just drag Rose out of her house and put a bullet in her head. They could go on with their lives like none of this ever happened.

Charlotte reached for her apron. "Kate, you make yourself scarce. He doesn't need to see you right now." She stopped, looked at the apron in her hand and with a sheepish grin handed it to Odetta.

Odetta took it with a broad smile and a nod of her head. "Mrs. Webster, I think we should send this gal up to bed." Odetta gestured toward Hattie, leaned against her chair like a wilted flower.

Hattie put up an only token protest, particularly after Charlotte assured her she'd wake her up for dinner in a few hours.

Kate peeked out the kitchen window. The two men had moved to the bench in front of the stable.

Charlotte put her arm around Kate's waist and squeezed her. "Men are funny creatures dear. They're so tender about their manhood. Best let them sort it out. Now off you go."

Kate turned and took a small step away from the window. "Do you think he'll be all right?"

"Not now. But he will be. He'll carry those scars for the rest of his life, and not just the ones we can see, but he'll learn to live with them. Like we all do. You go take a rest now and I'll send Timothy out in a few minutes. Off with you now."

Kate grabbed another cookie, called Monty and headed for the stairs. She'd talk to Juba later. And they needed a plan for dealing with the Greenhow problem or they'd end up watching the Confederate Army march up Pennsylvania Avenue. Over her dead body.

Chapter 6

July 23, 1861
Washington City

*R*ose Greenhow unlocked her front door, fumbling the key a little in the dark. It had been a wretched day. The ship docked late in Baltimore, which caused her to miss the evening train. Then she had to wait for the next train, which didn't arrive until almost midnight. She sighed as the key slipped home and the door unlocked with a satisfying snick. The damn maid should have let her in. Probably out, visiting her baby again. If the child wouldn't be valuable someday she'd have sold the brat. It wasn't like nigrah women had natural womanly feelings for their children anyway, not like she did for her daughters.

Though she'd only been gone a few days the house had that dusty, dead smell of a empty place. Rose sat her bag down with a sigh and saw a letter on the front hall floor. Grinning to herself, she bent to pick it up, her back protesting as she did. She ignored her discomfort and tore at the sheet's sealing wax. It popped right open. Rose scanned the letter, glad that months of working with the army cipher had made her fluent in the code.

She finished reading and held the paper against her chest. How very gratifying. Not only had her work resulted in a sure victory for dear Beauregard's army, but he and Mr. Davis had the good manners to recognize her importance.

Rose left her bag on the hall table and ascended the stairs with a lighter step than when she'd first approached her house. In fact, she felt like she could fly up the stairs. The letter called for a celebratory brandy.

She paused at the top of the stairs. That damned maid. She'd left her bedroom door cracked open. How many times did she have to tell her to keep the door shut? A lady needed privacy, whether she was in her room or not. The rule was doubly important if the lady in question was running a spy ring. Rose pushed her lips together in vexation, tapping her letter against the skirt of her dress. She'd have to reinforce her directives about her bedroom door with a beating. So much to do.

Rose unbuttoned her dress and stepped out of it, leaving it where it fell. She did the same for her corset cover and hoop skirt before loosening her corset strings and shrugging out of the thing with relief. A corset was an aging lady's best friend, but did they have to be so damned uncomfortable? She stripped off her chemise, noting that it smelled like she'd worn it a day too long. Naked, she approached her closet. She'd slip into her best dressing gown tonight, though she usually reserved it for gentlemen visitors. Blood red, gossamer silk clung to her body in soft folds, both concealing and revealing at the same time depending on how the fabric moved. It had cost far too much, but been worth every penny, both for the effect it had on gentlemen of a certain age and the way it felt against her naked body. She turned to admire herself in her mirror and froze.

Something was wrong. Off. What is it? Rose turned and inspected the bedroom. Everything seemed to be in its place. *No, there. The closet.* That door was open too. Rose stepped over and peered into her closet. Her heartbeat sped up. *The dial's not on 17.* She'd been born in 1817 and she always left her safe on 17. It was her lucky number. But now the dial sat at 0. When had she last used the safe?

She shook her head and bit her lip in thought. *She was never careless. The maid? No.* Ever since Rose had banished her baby the woman had been meekly obedient. *Someone else?* A fury as red as her dressing gown flooded through her. A thief had invaded her home. She looked at the door jamb. The safe's numbers were right there. *Would a sneak thief have seen them? And even if the thief had, would they have then known the dialing sequence? Probably not.* Rose knelt down and opened safe. It took two tries. That proved her theory. She had trouble getting the little safe open and she knew its combination.

She swung the door opened and peered inside. Everything appeared just as it should. Didn't it? *Did I leave my gun box on top like that?* She usually did. It made a handy paperweight. Rose sighed in relief. Someone may have tried to open the safe but they had most certainly failed.

Rose slammed the safe closed with a satisfying thunk and spun the dial, careful to stop it on 17. She hurried out of her bedroom and downstairs. She examined her parlor. It looked undisturbed, but was it? It felt wrong. Was she overreacting? Had someone been in her house? She remembered the way Jordan's letter had popped right open. Too easily. As if it had been carelessly sealed before it was sent or opened after it arrived and resealed. Which was it? Rose stamped her foot in frustration. She wanted to strangle the person who'd been in her house. She had no proof, but for a 17 turned to a 0. And her bedroom door. Still, she knew. She wasn't safe anymore.

Should she tell Jordan and Beauregard she'd been compromised? She'd lose her accolades. Her influence. She'd be just another aging widow woman scraping by in war time. *No, that wouldn't do.* Rose turned and stormed back to her bedroom, her red silk robe flying behind her like a hungry flame in the wind. She would not be reduced to a common woman. *Never.*

Chapter 7

*M*onty pushed past the door just in front of Kate. Kate would have liked to blame the manure smell on the dog, but she knew better. "We need help with the horses. We've got better things to do than this constant curry brushing and manure shoveling."

Louisa grinned at her. "I can do it, Miss Kate. I don't mind. It's just that this morning you said you'd do it."

"I did and I will. I wasn't complaining."

From the sink where she was washing dishes, Odetta harrumphed. "Lotta folks running here and there."

"See? Odetta agrees. Hey, Odetta, can I ask you a question?"

"Sho."

Kate leaned against the counter, next to the sink. "Do you think it would be acceptable to ask Samuel to come from Philadelphia and take care of our horses? And the yard? Or would it be insulting?"

Odetta stopped washing silverware and looked at Kate. "How you figger it an insult? Cause he old? Or cause he black?"

Kate bit her lower lip. She didn't know Odetta very well and didn't want to start out on the wrong foot. "He used to be a house slave, so he's used to working inside. Is outside work beneath him?" Kate shook her head. "I'm not sure what I'm asking, but I like him a lot and I don't want to insult him. Or you."

Odetta harrumphed again. "You goin' to pay him a decent wage? Is it honest work?"

Kate snorted. "Am I being stupid?"

"A bit Miz Kate, but that's all right." The older woman grinned at Kate and plunged her hands back into her soapy wash water.

"Then would you mind using some of the household money to send a telegram to Miz Amalie's house in Philadelphia? See if he'll come?"

"I can go, Miz Kate," Louisa said. "I'm off to the market." Louisa waggled her basket at Kate. "I can stop by the telegraph office on my way."

Kate looked over at Louisa. "That's a nice offer Louisa, but I wanted to talk to you this morning. I've got a plan and I need your help."

Louisa frowned. "Miz Odetta needs eggs and butter and she don't know where the market is." Louisa paused and frowned again. "And I bet she never sent no telegram either."

At the sink, Odetta stilled, then resumed washing dishes.

Kate smacked her forehead with the heel of her hand. "I forgot you're new to the city Odetta. I'm sorry. You need a tour of the city, don't you? So you know how to get around and where to find things."

Odetta looked up from the sink. "I likely do. But not today. Mrs. Webster's going to show me 'round the house today, upstairs, down in the cellar and the like. I best do that. But I need the girl to go to the market if I'm feeding eight people dinner."

Kate conceded the wisdom of the cook's point and struck a deal with Louisa. "Give me ten minutes to change my clothes and I'll go with you. We'll take the wagon and go over to the Georgetown market. We can talk on the way. And I need Monty food."

Monty's ears perked up at the mention of his name. Thinking to make it a special outing Kate added, "You can practice driving. Get Excelsior harnessed and I'll be down in a tick." Kate almost asked Odetta to write her up a list but caught herself before she did. Like most slaves, Odetta wasn't literate and she'd asked enough embarrassing questions for the day. Instead, Odetta dictated a list to Kate, who made a note to find someone to give the cook reading and writing lessons. Would Charlotte have time?

Fifteen minutes later they were rolling up Fourth Street, heading for M Street, where they'd turn west for Georgetown.

Louisa clucked Excelsior into a trot. "I used to cut across the Capitol grounds to the market, but I don't no more."

"Anymore, dear. But you're right to keep away from the Capital."

When Mr. Lincoln made his first calls for volunteers, men from all over the country poured into the city. There were regiments billeted in the Capitol building itself, and in the Patent Office, Treasury building and on the White House grounds. The Army turned the area around the unfinished monument to President Washington into a slaughterhouse while the basements of the Capital became a bakery. The whole mall, from one end to the other, teamed with men, horses, cattle and all the effluvia and chaos that came with that kind of crowding. Kate would have thought twice about cutting across the Capital these days and she was ten years older than Louisa and carried both a gun and a dagger with her everywhere. She made another mental note to get Louisa her own dagger and teach her how to use it.

Kate patted the girl's leg. "It's not fair, but girls have to be extra careful even in the best of time. Most men are good, but some are not. A few of those soldiers are surely bad men." Kate suddenly remembered the doctor that used to own Louisa. It occurred to her that Louisa needed little schooling in ways of predatory men.

Talk of the perfidy of men occupied them for the remaining blocks up to M Street. As they turned for the long run across the city to Georgetown Kate changed the subject.

"Louisa, I've been meaning to thank you for coming with me on Sunday. It was brave."

Louisa waved her hand through the air. "Oh, it weren't nuthin' Miz Kate."

"Wasn't, dear. And yes, it was. Don't discount yourself. Plenty of people will do it for you. No use giving them help. You helped me feel braver. You and Monty."

They both looked down at the little black dog. "You never once panicked and you followed directions and you were a help to Miss Chase. You were also a big help with the search for Mr. Juba last spring. I am very proud of you."

Kate paused, but Louisa said nothing. Instead, she stared straight ahead, right over Excelsior's back and head.

"Well, it occurred to me that I've been thinking of you as a girl and you're not. You're a competent young woman."

68

Still nothing. Had she offended the girl somehow? If there was anything the scene with Juba yesterday taught her it was that she wasn't great at figuring out people's feelings. Dogs were easy to understand. She looked down at Monty. He was licking his posterior with indecent enthusiasm. OK, maybe not.

Then she heard sniffling. The sniffling turned into a sob. Then another.

Rats. Kate took the reins from Louisa's limp hands and stopped Excelsior at the side of the street. She folded the crying girl in her arms. "Shhhh. It's all right. Shhhh." Excelsior looked over his shoulder, no doubt wondering what was going on. Kate had no idea. She patted and hugged Louisa while she cried, all the while wanting to kick herself. *Why do I even open my mouth? Everyone I talk to has some kind of break down.*

Eventually Louisa snuffled herself into silence. She wiped her face with Kate's handkerchief and blew her nose into it, making a wet snorting sound that made Kate smile. After that Louisa took back the reins and set Excelsior moving again. In a quiet voice, she began to talk. "I'm sorry Miz Kate. You don't know how much my life's changed since you bought me and freed me. You can't know. It's not just that I've got enough to eat and a bedroom all my own. It's the chance to do more that matters. You talk like I'm somebody."

"Oh, honey." Kate's heart broke a little. "Was there something you wanted to do. Something besides help around the house and work for the Pinkertons? Do you want me to find you a school up north? Somewhere away from the war, where you could get a real education?"

Louisa looked appalled at this last suggestion. "Oh, you wouldn't send me away, would you Miz Kate? I want to stay here and help. There's so much to do and I think I could be good. I think I could be the first black lady Pinkerton. I mean, except for Miss Lawson."

Kate laughed in relief. "My dear, you already are."

The Georgetown Market was both a building and an area. The brick building, fronted by a triple set of sixteen foot high, double doors in front and nine bays along the side, contained stalls for butchers, dairymen and produce sellers. It stood between East and West Market Streets. Stalls selling everything from roasted coffee to striped stockings lined the market. Kate and Louisa filled their baskets with cheeses, chicken and duck eggs, smoked pork belly, fresh turnip and mustard greens, three baskets of strawberries and two pints of butter. A butcher sold them a bag of beef rib bones and some yucky bits. Kate could hardly look at the bag, but Monty found it fascinating. Then they went outside to the street front stalls and bought tiny, honey-soaked pastries and several new pairs of stockings. Kate picked out a plain blue pair for herself, while Louisa chose a purple and green striped pair. They bought Hattie a pair of gaudy pink and yellow stockings, both of them knowing she'd accept them and never wear them. Still, they'd get to see her face when they gave them to her and that would be present enough. Excelsior found the apple seller and insisted they buy both tiny crab apples and large, striped pie apples. When they could hold no more they found the wagon and headed back down M Street for home.

Kate watched Louisa admire her new stockings. She'd sat down on a curb and put them on right after Kate bought them, delighted with the green and royal purple bands that circled her calves. It took the girl most of the ride home for the thrill to wear off.

Kate still hadn't discussed her plan with Louisa. She watched one of the painted omnibuses rattle by. The first time she'd seen one it had been all she could do not to stop and stare. Now she barely noticed them. "Louisa dear, let's stop at the telegraph office."

"All right. Miz Kate, did you have something else you wanted to talk about? You keep fidgeting."

"Well, there is. It makes me nervous though. I'll tell you my idea and I need you to be honest with me and tell me if you think it's a bad one or not."

"All right."

Kate smiled. The new stockings had bolstered Louisa's self-confidence.

"Here's the situation. Hattie and I have had uncounted cups of tea in Mrs. Greenhow's parlor this last month and learned almost nothing or nothing we didn't know before we left for New Orleans. Except that her contact, that Captain Jordan, is now with Beauregard and she thinks he's hung the moon."

"Who? Beauregard or Jordan?"

"Good point. Both I suppose. And you know from the meeting yesterday that Beauregard is mighty grateful to her for his victory at Bull Run."

Louisa nodded. "You said you all missed something. Something big by the sound of it."

"Whatever we're doing, it's not working. She has two circles of conspirators. An outer circle and an inner circle."

"And you and Miss Hattie be in the outer circle, right?"

71

"Right. And I'm not sure who's in the inner circle. It would be people with access to military details. Or people who know people who do. And these people could be purposefully passing her information or maybe accidentally. Flattery can pry loose a lot of information from men. Some men." Kate remembered how much Senator Wigfall revealed to her about his plan to stop Mr. Lincoln's presidency. He'd looked at her and seen a fool and a woman. Which, to him, were the same thing.

"So?" Louisa prompted Kate back to the present conversation.

Kate shook her head. She'd drifted off for a second thinking about Louis T. Wigfall. The man was dangerous even when he wasn't around.

"We need to set a watch on the house. But how do we do that? I can't station Mr. Webster across the street or in the alley. Mrs. Greenhow will notice. Adult men don't just stand around the streets these days. There are no stores or empty houses near her house to put someone in, so that's out. Then I thought of all the trees around her house. I could put men in the trees, but what's more suspicious than an adult man perched in a tree?"

"So what's the idea?" Louisa's voice made it clear she was working the puzzle along with Kate.

"Well, who does climb trees?"

"Kids. Mostly boys," Louisa answered without hesitation. "Boys climb trees. And they're small enough to not be seen."

"Ah, Louisa, you have a talent for this. I was thinking street children. They're everywhere in this city, but invisible."

"Oh, I know lots of boys like that. And they'd be glad for a job. You would pay wouldn't you?"

72

"Absolutely. Is it a good idea? Or a terrible one? Is it irresponsible to put street boys in harm's way like this?"

Louisa went quiet. She sucked in a deep breath and blew out her cheeks, then poofed out the air. "You know, I don't think it would be dangerous. Even if a policeman came, they could run and disappear in a thousand places before an adult laid hands them. They do it all the time. But I betcha no one would see them."

"That's what I thought," Kate said with relief. "But I worry I'm talking myself into it because I have no other ideas."

"No, it's good. Honestly."

Kate chuckled. "So could you round me up a gaggle of street boys?"

"Sure. When you want them?"

"Is lunchtime tomorrow too soon? We could feed them. That might buy more loyalty than the promise of wages."

"Sounds like you know boys."

"Boys, men, dogs. There's not a lot of difference. Feed them and they'll follow you anywhere." Kate glanced down at the dog sitting between them.

Monty, who'd been staring at the bag of meat bits in the back of the wagon, stopped long enough to cock his head at the two women, which made them laugh all the more.

The next day Kate dressed with extra care. She didn't want to appear intimidating or unapproachable, but she wanted to make it clear she was the boss and the job a serious one. And it was too hot for the navy wool, the one that made her look like a female army officer with its brass buttons and yellow braid. She settled on a beige and white vertical striped

gown made from lightweight cotton. It had tiny puffed sleeves
and a boat neck that ensured she'd be as cool as possible in
Washington's sticky July heat. She braided her hair into one
long tail then pinned it into a coil on the back of her head,
checked the mirror and headed downstairs.

Odetta looked up from a pile of sandwiches she was making as Kate pushed open the door from the dining room.
"Almost ready Miz Kate," she called across the room.

Kate stepped up to the counter, picked up a knife and
sliced bread for the tops of the line of sandwiches Odetta had
constructed. "It looks fabulous," Kate waved at the spread
already on the huge kitchen table. Odetta had small bowls of
watermelon and cucumber pickles set out, and larger bowls of
potato and cabbage salads.

Odetta smiled at Kate before she resumed layering thick
slices of ham on buttered pieces of bread. "I got three apple
pies hid in the pantry for later. Don't tell your horse I used up
his apples."

Ten minutes later Louisa came through the back door.
"They're here."

"Well invite them in dear," Kate said.

Louisa shook her head. "They don't believe me. You gotta
come out and tell them they can come into such a fine house."

Kate stepped into the yard to find a small band of ragged
children. Five boys, two girls, none wearing shoes, all of them
grubby dirty, stared at her. They were varying shades of
brown, but for the smallest boy, who appeared Irish. A dark-
skinned boy about four inches taller than the next largest child
stood just in front of the other six, suggesting he was, at least
for today, the leader of this motley troop. "Have you come
about the job?" she asked the leader.

74

He nodded, trying to appear older and surer than he was. "If this ain't a rum deal. You try to do us dirt and I'll see you get yours."

Kate stuck out her hand. "I promise to deal fairly with you and your friends if you are fair with me. Do we have a deal?"

He put his filthy hand in hers and they shook on it. Then they followed her inside and fell upon Odetta's feast like wolves on a mid-winter kill.

Odetta got out all the mixing bowls and filled them with warm water from the boiler on the back of the stove. She found a stack of old kitchen towels under the sink and dropped one in each bowl. When their plates were empty, she sat a bowl in front of each child. "Now every one wash up," she said in the voice that brooked no argument. "When your faces, arms, and hands are clean you may have pie. Not before."

Odetta leaned against the kitchen counter while the children splashed soapy water all over the table amidst some general complaints and protests.

Kate leaned next to her. "It's a little like closing the barn door once the cow's got out isn't it?"

"Sure is," Odetta said with a shrug, "but I didn't have the heart to slow them down before they ate. Little mites looked like they needed food more than clean hands."

Once Odetta served pie, each slice topped with a thick wedge of cheddar cheese, Kate sat down at the table, a folder and pen before her. She looked around the table, all the while endeavoring to appear pleasant and non-threatening. "All right. Now to business. Do you all understand why Louisa brought you here?"

"Ya' maid say you got a job for us," the leader said. He gestured at Louisa, who'd taken the seat next to Kate. "She also says you're a Pinkerton detective."

Realizing this deal was as much Louisa's as her own, Kate pushed a blank piece of paper and the pen and ink over in front of Louisa and gestured at her to take notes. "Louisa's not my maid. She's my assistant. We are both Pinkerton detectives."

The children looked at Louisa, eyes wide.

Kate gestured at Louisa to take charge.

Louisa smiled and turned to the largest boy. "What's your name dear?"

"You gonna turn me into the coppers?"

"No. We're about to embark upon a business deal. I'll need your names. If you don't want to give me your real names, that's fine with me, but I need something for our records."

"You can call me Jack. This here," he gestured around the table, "is Thomas, Jimmy, Patsy, Lanie, Lew and Little Red."

While Louisa wrote the names, Kate spoke again. "I need a watch on a house. You can't be seen, but there's plenty of trees on the street and in the alley to hide in. I need a record of who goes in the house, when and for how long. Can any of you write?"

Jack lifted his chin and said, "I can miss. My ma taught me afore she died."

Another girl piped up. "I can too, a little."

Kate groped for a name. "Patsy?"

"No, ma'am. Lanie."

"OK. So two of you can keep notes. The rest of you have to remember and report to the two who can write. That makes you two," Kate pointed at Jack and Lanie, "the mission

76

leaders. You're responsible for keeping a record and reporting to me or Louisa once a day. Got it?"

Lanie shifted in her seat and then spoke. "Ma'am, Patsy here can draw. Real good. Would you like her to make some pitchers? Of the people that go into this house?"

Kate smiled at the little girl. "That's a great idea, Lanie. Can you do that Patsy?"

Patsy nodded but didn't speak.

"Thank you, dear. As for the rest of you, even if you can't write or draw, watching is the most important part of this job. Watch, remember, tell. And if you see someone who looks important, make sure Patsy draws them. I'll pay you fifty cents a day.

"Jess Jack, or does he have to share?" The tiny, redheaded one asked.

"No sharing. Fifty cents each, every day."

"Naaah," the little redhead exclaimed. "Yer foolin'!"

Kate shook her head. "I'm not. This is an important job and for good work, I'll pay fair wages. It'll be a tough job. You can take turns, but it will still be lots of sitting and waiting. And Odetta can feed you lunch every day. Everyone who's not watching come here. You can take food to whoever's watching. That's when you check in. You talk to Louisa. She'll be your Pinkerton contact." Kate looked over at Louisa, who nodded in agreement, as seriously as if she'd been given control of an entire regiment of the regular army.

"Just you seven, mind you," Odetta warned. "I'll not be feeding all the city's children out my back door." The cook gave Kate and the children a stern stare. They'd argued about this point just this morning. Kate wanted to tell the new employees she'd feed anyone who came, but Odetta insisted such an offer was pure folly. Kate admitted that Odetta was right. They couldn't save all the city's street children, or at least not this week."

Jack spoke up. "So we'd be like regular Pinkertons then?"

Kate chuckled. The seven children before her were anything but regular anything. "Oh, I think you're Pinkertons all right, just not regular ones. You're more like Pinkerton Irregulars."

The gang around the table cheered and pounded on the table though probably more for their wages and free lunch than their new name. Kate looked around the table, half pleased, half anxious. They were just children. She hoped she wouldn't regret what she'd just done.

Chapter 8

July 24-25, 1861
Washington City & Shenandoah Valley

"She killed a man? How old is she?" As the question came out of Rose's mouth she wondered why she'd asked it. Were there age limits for murder?

The union army officer sitting across from Rose shifted in his seat. "Weeeell, she is just a slip of a girl. I'm sure she can tell you the story better than I can and from what I know of her she'll want to. She's a real talkative gal." He paused, then continued. "You see after we pushed the Confederate army back at Falling Waters we took control of the northern valley. The general ordered troops to go house to house in Martinsburg. Rooting out Secesh and the like. The Boyd household was flying a Confederate regimental flag. They were asked to take it down. Miss Boyd was disinclined to do so. She says one of my men threatened her mother. So she shot him dead with her daddy's revolver. I'm inclined to think the women provoked the man, but I can't prove it. Except now she's in trouble again."

"My goodness, how unfortunate," Rose murmured, attempting to appear dismayed. Her mind whirled at the possibilities. General Jackson was right about the girl. Rose had plenty of namby-pamby, gossip gathering, sit around the parlor and sip tea in outrage, ladies. Not that gossip wasn't useful. But a woman who could shoot a man? That she could use.

"And have you released her?"

"She never was in custody Ma'am, but for house arrest. President Lincoln himself sent word to treat her with kid gloves. To not inflame the locals you understand. There's a lot of Secesh sentiment in this valley, which is unfortunate seeing how close we are to Washington. Then she made friends with the guards and soon enough she was riding around camp again. She's got this big horse and she rides out at all hours." The Captain made a moue of displeasure.

Rose fought the urge not to laugh at the expression on the captain's face.

"One of my men intercepted a letter she'd written to Colonel Jackson. Damn thing had a chart of troop counts and artillery pieces. She wasn't using a code, nor did she disguise her handwriting."

The girl needed a mentor. Someone to train her up. "So if I were to take her off your hands, that would be helpful?"

"Ever so, Ma'am. She's a lightning rod and I have no idea what to do with her."

"Yes, Senator Wilson explained it all." Rose had never spoken to Henry Wilson about this girl or any other potential spy, but she didn't think it would hurt to drop an abolitionist senator's name to a Union Army officer. "I thought perhaps I'd speak to her mother and with her permission, remove the girl to a private school I know in Pennsylvania. It would get her out of the way and teach her some solid Yankee values."

80

Rose managed not to retch in disgust as she said the treacherous words.

"Sounds like a fine plan Mrs. Greenhow. I'll write you a pass."

Which was how a Union Army officer gave a rebel lady spy permission to visit with another rebel lady spy. Later, when Rose and Belle became famous, or infamous, he vowed to take the secret of his foolishness to the grave.

Rose made her way down the street toward the Boyd house. As she walked she thought about the note she'd received from dear Captain Jordan just yesterday. In it, he'd called her attention to a Miss Boyd of the Shenandoah Valley. The girl had rendered a service to Colonel Jackson, the hero of Manassas. Though the note was phrased mildly enough, Rose could feel the urgency beneath it. She hired a hack early this morning to take her up to Martinsburg, which turned out to be an unpleasant journey over a series of dusty roads. By the time she'd arrived at Captain Gwynne's office she'd begun to doubt the wisdom of leaving Washington, but her brief meeting with the captain made her feel better about her trip.

She approached the two-story, red brick house. Though she had no invitation, no mutual acquaintances and no letter of introduction, Rose Greenhow marched up the front steps and knocked on the dark wooden door.

A young woman opened the door to Rose and, as Captain Gwynn warned, almost immediately began talking. She took less than a minute to invite Rose in and offer her a glass of water before beginning her story. Rose made a note to teach the girl some much needed self-disciplined.

Miss Boyd leaned forward in her chair. "So we heard they were coming. The Yankee soldiers I mean. I sent Eliza, she's our slave, upstairs to hide the flag and Momma locked the door. And then I ran upstairs for my daddy's pistol. Then they were hammering on the door, hollering about breaking it down. Momma let them in just as I was coming down the stairs."

The girl stopped to take a breath and grinned at Rose, her cobalt blue eyes gleaming in excitement. She looked around the parlor, her gaze barely stopping on her silent mother who sat in the corner knitting something in tired gray wool.

Rose nodded to encourage the girl. Miss Boyd had told this story enough times to have it down pat and if she'd been frightened that day, she'd forgotten it in the retelling of the her tale.

"So there they were. Four of them. Are all Yankees ugly and dirty? Or just the ones in Martinsburg?" Miss Boyd meant the question rhetorically because she paused not one second in the telling of her tale. "The biggest, dirtiest one looked right at me and asked me if I was a damned rebel. I told him straight out I was a secessionist. Momma about fainted."

Rose smiled at the girl, though what she wanted to do was slap her. At sixteen or seventeen years old Miss Boyd was old enough to act like a young lady but her enthusiasm and vigor made her seem younger. Belle Boyd was an attractive thing, slim, dark-haired, with dark lashes and brows that set off the most startling pair of blue eyes Rose had ever seen. She wasn't a beauty in the traditional sense, but she had an appealing energy. That appeal would stand her in good stead when prying secrets out of military men.

Belle rushed on with her narrative. "Then they told Momma they intended to use our flag pole for a Union flag. And they weren't nice about it neither. Momma was very brave. She said we'd all die before we let them do such a thing. Then the big one grabbed Momma by the neck and pulled her up against him. Then he tried to kiss her."

Belle shuddered at the memory though to Rose's practiced eyes it looked rehearsed and theatrical. Rose glanced over at the mother, but she seemed to not be hearing their conversation at all. The ugly thing she was knitting had grown larger.

"Everyone knows what animals the Yankees are. I was sure my mother was about to be ravaged by all four of them. Right in front of me.

Rose thought to test the waters. "Were you not worried for yourself dear?"

"I was not. I had Daddy's pistol. I pulled it right out of my pocket and pointed it at the dirty Dutchman. And guess what I said? I said, let go of my mother. And what did he do? Well, he did not let go of my mother like I told him to. That Yankee grabbed her bosom. So I shot him. Right in the heart. He fell right there," Belle gestured toward the front hallway, "and bled all over the floor. Eliza had a time scrubbing up the mess he made."

It didn't take a trained spy to notice that the young lady took no responsibility for her actions. She shot a man and blamed him for the mess. And made her slave clean it up. Belle Boyd was a cold piece of baggage and thank goodness for it.

"I dared the others to shoot me, but they were not so fallen as to shoot a woman. Instead, they locked me in my room."

"What happened then?" Rose asked just to see what the minx would say.

"Why General Patterson himself came to the house the next day. Right handsome he was too," Belle paused and added, "for a Yankee. He brought some other fellows with him, one to take notes and one to ask questions. Well didn't I just tell them how awful his men had been? How they'd been coarse in their language and behavior. I could tell he wanted me to be all weepy and sorry for what I'd done, but I wasn't. Not a bit. But he wanted me to, so I cried and said how afraid we'd all been. Then he said he'd protect us by putting Yankee guards around the house. Like he thought I was too stupid to know he was putting me under house arrest. Can you imagine? For protecting my mother's honor and the honor of southern women everywhere?"

The more Rose heard the happier she was. This girl had courage aplenty and she wasn't a fool. Just rash and untutored.

"That's quite a tale, Miss Boyd. And how did you come to be passing letters to Colonel Jackson?

The second half of Miss Boyd's story had the intrepid rebel girl flirting with her guards until they let her leave the house. Before long she was riding her horse around the union army camps talking to any soldier who would talk to her. Which was quite a lot of men. She counted tents, cannons, and horses, memorized the numbers and wrote it all down every evening. Then she'd write letters to Colonel Jackson and get the neighbor girl to deliver them to the Confederate camp in nearby Winchester. Or sometimes she'd go herself.

"My dear daddy is in the Jackson Brigade, though he didn't have to enlist at all. Not at his age. They fought at Ma-

84

nassas. That's where all Jackson and Johnston's soldiers are now. Daddy's brave, almost as brave as Colonel Jackson and we're very proud of him. I think he's proud of me too. He calls me his 'Little Rebel Belle.'"

When Belle stopped for a breath, Rose fixed her with her sternest look. "My dear, that is quite a thrilling tale. You quite literally got away with murder."

Belle opened her mouth to talk some more, but Rose shook her head. "No. Just listen. Let me tell you what you did wrong. First, you brought yourself to their attention with the murder. A good spy, an effective spy, lives in the shadows. Second, in talking to so many soldiers you have opened yourself to accusations of impropriety."

Belle opened her mouth again, this time presumably to object, but Rose quelled her again. "Don't argue with me, my dear. The truth is a fast girl may get information out of men, but she'll never get information out of gentlemen. And the gentlemen will be the ones with information worth having. Third, you did not try to disguise your communiqué, using neither code nor altered handwriting. In doing so you laid a trail right back to your door, which once again violated rule number one. Your enemy caught you and thereby you called attention to yourself."

"But I showed those nasty Yankees we secessionists are not to be played with."

Rose glanced over at the mother. Still nothing. Rose didn't understand women like Mrs. Boyd, women who had nothing to say, no ideas, no reason to live beyond keeping a clean house and serving her family. The lady would play no further part in her daughter's future if Rose had anything to say about

Peg A. Lamphier

it. The girl had too much potential to be left with this gray woman and her gray knitting.

Rose shifted her gaze back to Miss Boyd. "My dear, you have a decision to make. Do you want to play at rebellion or would you like to do real work for the cause? If it is the first, then I will wish you well and take my leave of you. But if it is the latter, then you will listen and follow my orders. I can teach you to be an effective agent for the Confederacy."

"You?" Belle looked Rose Greenhow up and down. "What do you know of such things? Have you killed a man?"

It was all Rose could do not to slap the little baggage for her impudence. Instead, she gathered her dignity about her like a shawl and said, "My dear. I have killed hundreds of men. Do you know how many men the Union Army lost at Manassas? No, you do not. Almost 3000 northern soldiers died in one day. Twice as many as our boys. And do you know why? No, you do not. Because no one knows, but for two men, one of them General Beauregard."

Belle gaped at Rose.

Rose guessed few people in Miss Boyd's life had bested her. Certainly her mother had never taken her in hand.

"You foolish girl. Did you ever wonder why General Johnston up and pulled out of the Shenandoah just two days before the battle of Manassas? Because I sent dear Beauregard intelligence about the size and makeup of the Union Army. It turns out McDowell's force was much larger than anyone thought. If Johnston hadn't reinforced Beauregard at the last minute, our brave boys would have been beaten by McDowell's numerically superior force."

"I don't believe you," Belle said, her lower lip stuck out like a petulant child. "I've never heard of you."

86

"Of course you haven't, you simpleton," Rose snapped. "That's my entire point."

Rose stood to go. "I'll be at the Inn until tomorrow noon, registered as Mrs. Jordan. Think hard about what I've told you, Miss Boyd. If you'd like to make a real difference come see me. And if not, I wish you well in your efforts to annoy men who know exactly what you are."

Rose swept from the room, using the same imperious posture and walk she'd learned from Dolley Madison twenty years before. As she shut the front door, she could only congratulate herself on how well it had gone. It was child's play for a woman of her experience to manipulate a chit like Miss Belle Boyd.

As Rose expected, a subdued Belle Boyd called at the Martinsburg Inn the next morning and asked to speak to a Mrs. Jordan. The two women met in the inn's parlor. After almost two hours the inn's porter, a young, spotty faced fellow, asked the two ladies if they'd be needing lunch. Rose sent him away with an imperious wave.

"Well?" The fat innkeeper looked up from an account book, where he was tallying the past month's receipts.

The porter shook his head. "They don't want any drink or food."

"Ladies," the innkeeper spat out. "They have nothing to do but sit around yakking their heads off. Neither one of 'em looks like they've ever done an honest day's work and never plan to."

It turned out he was right.

Chapter 9

July 28, 1861
Washington City

*K*ate heaved another fork of clean straw into Excelsior's stall, wishing all the while that Samuel would hurry and get here so she didn't have to do this anymore. He'd sent a telegram Friday saying he'd take the job, but he hadn't said when he'd arrive. Until then she and Louisa continued to share stable duties.

She forked up some more straw and turned to pitch it forward when someone grabbed her from behind. Without thinking, Kate reached behind her and grabbed a handful of shirt, pushed her bottom into the assailant's hips and squatted. She lifted with her legs and yanked with her arms forward, slightly rounding her back as she did. The maneuver rolled her attacker up and around her right hip, flipping him into the pile of straw in front of her. She grabbed for her dagger, glad she'd left several of her shirt buttons undone in the heat. She crouched into fighting position, her dagger hand coming out of her corset just as her attacker rolled over.

"Brava!" Hazzard's hands came up into a slow clap. "Just like I taught you."

Monty came running in from the yard, where he'd been sniffing at things unseen, barking like a dog possessed. He launched himself at Hazzard, becoming a black and white flying blur. Hazzard snatched the little dog out of the air and held him above his head. Monty wriggled and yipped at this interruption of his attack.

Hazzard. She'd just pitched Hazzard across the stable. *Well, it serves him right.* She pushed her dagger back into her corset front and appraised the man she loved. *Oh, he was a pretty man, wasn't he?* She walked over and plucked Monty from Hazzard's grip. She reassured the little dog she was fine and set him down in the straw. Then she looked at Hazzard, sprawled in the straw. He seemed fine too.

Kate threw herself down on the straw and rolled atop Hazzard before he realized what was happening. His arms came up around her, pressing her chest against his. She kissed him harder, twining her tongue with his. He moved his mouth down along her jaw, working his way to that sensitive spot behind her ear. She loved the way his mustache felt against her neck and ears. It always made her wonder how it would feel other places. She intended to find out one day.

When she thought he'd been kissed enough she sat up, her legs straddling his abdomen. "Happy to see me, aren't you?" She could feel his emphatic pleasure at the moment.

He circled her waist with his hands and squeezed. "Of course. After our trip to New Orleans, I got used having you around."

With Mr. Lincoln and General Scott's approval, Captain George Washington Hazzard accompanied a small cadre of Pinkertons and Mr. Rice's circus on the mission that rescued Juba last spring. He also taught Kate how to fight with and without dagger, one he'd given her. And when she killed a woman who'd been trying to kill her first, he'd been proud of her. Kate thought that's when she really knew he was the man for her. Most men would have been horrified to find themselves courting a killer, let alone a lady detective and spy.

Kate leaned down close to his face, her chest brushing his. "Louisa and I got up early and drove to Bull Run. We were up on the hill above the battle. If you'd been in the fight I don't' know if I could have stood it. It was terrible."

He pulled her closer and kissed her again. When he finished, he held her eyes with his own. "Now you know how I feel when you throw yourself into danger. It scares the hell out of me. I'm a soldier and there's a war. You better understand that if this," he squeezed her waist, "is going anywhere."

Kate looked into his eyes. They looked black from a distance, but up close she could see tiny yellow flecks in the dark parts. "I know you're a soldier. I still don't want to see any battle you're in." She paused and then in her softest voice she admitted, "I'd want to be with you. Helping."

He blew out a breath. "Oh, my dear, fierce tiger." He wrapped his arms around her and rolled her over.

His body, hard and supple above her woke things in Kate she'd long forgotten. And things she'd never known. In a rush of tenderness and passion, she decided. She wanted this man for her own. Not to marry, but to love. Really love.

"Ahem."

Hazzard half rolled, so they both ended up on their side. Above them, in the doorway of Excelsior's stall, stood a white-haired black man, grinning so wide his teeth showed.

"Is this the stable or the bedroom? I need to know if I'm reporting for my new job."

Kate unwrapped her arms from Hazzard's and struggled to her feet. Samuel had arrived. *Dammit.*

Kate ahd Hazzard took Sameul to the house, where Charlotte took charge of their new stable man. Odetta insisted Kate go upstairs and change, on the premise that gentlemen callers did not prefer their women in manure-scented trousers. Kate considered telling Odetta that her recent experience said otherwise, she didn't want to scandalize her new cook. Odetta might have worked in a whorehouse, but she had an inflexible sense of correct behavior.

When she came back downstairs a crowed had gathered around the kitchen table. Everyone but Hattie, who was working at the hospital, was there. Hazzard, Juba, and Timothy, stood against the wall, while Charlotte, Louisa and five of the seven Irregulars sat at the table. The children all had a fried pie in their hands. Kate took the last empty chair hoping for her own fried pie. Odetta handed her one as she hustled between the stove, pantry, and table, setting out lunch.

Hazzard cooked his eyebrow at Kate. "You running an orphanage now?"

Before Kate could answer Timothy did, his tone a tiny bit defensive. "She's got a good idea if you ask me, using the kiddies to keep an eye on Mrs. Greenhow."

Kate swallowed her bit of pastry as she appraised Timothy. He didn't know Hazzard very well. "It's all right Timothy. Rose is out of town so we haven't learned much." Kate looked around the table at the children. "Or she was. She's back now isn't she?"

They agreed she was.

"And I was asking around town," Juba said. "The disappearances or kidnappings or whatever you want to call them, they seem to have stopped." He paused and rubbed at his face. "Which makes sense if the New Orleans slave markets don't re-open until fall. So we're not going to catch her at slave stealing this summer."

Kate glanced at Juba. It occurred to her that there wasn't much he could contribute to this case, a fact that could not be helping him recover from his kidnapping. She turned over an idea she'd been keeping in the back of her mind.

"Besides," Little Red piped, "We ain't orphans. We're Irregger Pinkertons."

Kate smiled at the small red-headed boy. "Irregular, dear. And yes, you certainly are." Three days ago she and Hattie visited Lansburgh's department store and bought a new dress for each of the girls, new trousers for the boys and stockings and shoes for all the children. And because Lanie and Jack could write and Patsy could sketch, they stocked up on pencils and half-sized notebooks. It had been fun to buy all the stuff and even more fun to see the children's faces when she distributed the clothes.

Louisa piped up, pulling Kate back to the present problem. "So this lot was about to report. Like they do every day." She caught Kate's look and corrected herself. "Like they do every day."

Lanie scrabbled around in her dress pocket.

"Patsy's been busy. She draws everybody. Then we saw them toffs and we got to thinkin' they might be 'portant. So we played some stickball in front of the house and along came this gent and Little Red ran into 'em and fell down like and cried and cried. And Patsy, she jess run right up like to check

93

on Red and she got a close look. So she drew the feller real good like. Then only a mo' later along comes another toff, so we run the same gaff and now we got pitchers of both. Patsy's really good." She finished her story beaming with pride, which she shared by grabbing Patsy's hand.

Lanie pushed several sheets of paper over to Kate, who took them up and studied them, surprised at their quality. Some were no more than quick pencil sketches, but she'd captured the essence of each personality. One sheet held two detailed portraits that looked skilled enough to frame and hang on a wall. "Patsy, these are really good."

Patsy bit her lower lip and stared at the table, kicking her feet at her chair rungs.

Seeing her struggle, Lanie came to her rescue. "I allas tell her she could be one of them artists for the newspapers. Maybe even the National Era. I seen it on newsstands. Patsy's good enough right now. Oh, and we got days and times these gents and others were at the house. Here." She pulled out another sheet of paper, this one with columns of words and numbers.

Kate looked at the sketches again. They'd labeled one sketch 'Mouse,' while another sketch read 'Snooty.' "Well, it seems I was wrong earlier. The Irregulars have found plenty."

Kate put her finger on 'Mouse.' "That's Eugenia Phillips. Hattie and I met her at one of Mrs. Greenhow's card parties. Her father has a pile of money and her husband used to be a congressman. So she has excellent connections, but if she's up to something we haven't been able to catch her." Kate shifted her finger to another face, this one labeled 'Flower." "And this is Lily Mackall. She's at Mrs. G's house every time I'm there. She's young and gushes over Rose so it's hard to take her seriously. "

94

"Which might be why she's in Greenhow's coterie," Hazzard cautioned.

Kate nodded. Last winter, before he joined the Pinkerton's efforts, Hazzard infiltrated a group of Illinois secessionists. As a result, he had more espionage experience than the average artillery officer.

Juba nodded in agreement. "How many times have you used the 'helpless woman' act?"

"It's a fair point. But it doesn't feel like Miss Mackall is acting. If you met her you'd know what I mean." Kate tapped the sketch of the snooty fellow. "That's Edward Van Camp. He's a doctor or a dentist depending on what story he's telling that day. He's either wealthy or pretending he is. Mostly he's smarmy and impressed with himself. And this one is Rose's lawyer. Pringle. I can't remember his first name. I've only met him once. Hattie and I are sure they're both guilty of something, we just don't know what."

Lanie pushed the paper with columns of numbers in front of Kate. "That one doesn't come too often, but see?" She put her forefinger on the list. "The others are there most days."

Kate looked around the table at her Irregulars. "This is really good work gang. Anything else to report?"

"Nah," Lanie said.

"All right, everybody grab another cookie and off you go. Oh, don't' forget lunch for Jack and Lew."

"We still on the job?" Lanie asked.

"Sure you are. Where would I get a better crew? Keep checking in with Louisa every day."

The bunch of them milled around the kitchen for a couple of minutes while Odetta and Charlotte stuffed their pockets with food.

As they were filing out Kate called out, "Patsy?"

The small brown girl turned, her cookies clutched to her chest.

"You're sketches are wonderful. Keep up the good work."

The little girl appraised Kate with big owl eyes. Then she nodded and was gone.

Odetta watched the children out the window, then turned back to the table. "Don't it jess break your heart." She said it in a statement, not a question.

Hazzard sat in one of the now empty chairs. "Are they all street children, or just poor children with parents and homes?"

Odetta shook her head, then chucked a tea towel up over her shoulder. "Don't rightly know."

Charlotte added, "They don't talk about it and I hate to ask."

Kate made another mental note and then thought better of it. She couldn't do everything herself. "Charlotte, I wonder if you and Odetta could figure out where those children sleep. Also, we need a bigger kitchen."

Charlotte smiled. "I was wondering when you would notice. You want to take that wall down." She pointed at the wall between the dining room and kitchen.

"Yep. And the sooner the better. We can get rid of that fancy dining room table out there. Find us something like this," Kate tapped the scarred table, "but bigger."

Charlotte bustled off to her makeshift office, dragging her husband along with her so they could talk construction plans. Juba pushed himself off the wall and announced he was going downstairs to take a nap. Kate watched him leave the kitchen. He rarely took naps. She remembered back after her parents died. She'd found refuge in sleep. Maybe that's what he was doing.

Hazzard patted her hand. "It going to take time, but he'll be fine." He slid the remaining sketches in front of Kate. "Recognize these other gentlemen?"

She held the papers up to the light and frowned. "I don't know. You?"

Hazzard paged through the papers. He stopped at one. "This is Major Keyes. No. I think he's a colonel now. He used to be Third Artillery, but I heard he's one of General Scott's military secretaries now."

"Then take that one," Kate said. "Can you find out what he's doing at Rose's? "

"Absolutely. The military takes care of its own. In all the ways possible." Hazzard folded the sketch of Colonel Keys into a small packet and slipped it in his jacket pocket.

Kate pulled out the two larger, more detailed sketches from the pile. "Both of these look familiar, but I can't place either one. I know someone who might know." She looked up at Hazzard. "I've got to go change into something a little nicer, then I'm going calling. If you've got time I think you'd enjoy coming with me."

"I take it you're not calling on Mrs. Greenhow?"

"No. A new acquaintance. You have to see her to believe her." When Hazzard agreed to accompany her it was all Kate could do to keep hid her grin of delight. This was going to be fun.

An hour later Kate and Hazzard stood in front of the Secretary of Treasury's house. They'd walked over, having only to cross the hospital grounds just to the west of Kate's house, to E Street. A short one-block walk south to 6th Street brought them to a square brick house that seemed to impose on its corner lot like a grumpy bulldog. Sweat trickled down Kate's back as she looked up at it. For its size and supposed grandeur, it was one of the ugliest houses she'd ever seen.

As they walked up the steps Kate pulled the card Miss Chase had given her out of her reticule. "Brace yourself," she said from the side of her mouth just after Hazzard used the front door's brass knocker. A tall, lean, light-skinned black man opened the door.

Kate held out the card. The man took it with a white gloved hand, examined it and let them in the house. The interior was dim and cool, the foyer paneled with dark wood and holding an expensive looking hall table. The pocket doors to the rooms on both side of the hall were pulled closed.

"Wait here please," the man said. He walked away, his step deliberate and dignified.

Hazzard crooked an eyebrow at Kate.

"Just wait." Kate fidgeted with her blue gloves. Were they too bright? She should have worn the plain white ones. But a visit to a cabinet member's house seemed to require more than simple white cotton gloves. Plus, the blue ones matched her day dress of blue dots on a cream background. The blue underdress and the ribbon trim were the same color as the gloves. So why was she so nervous? Miss Chase seemed like a nice young woman for all she was Salmon Chase's daughter and the second only to Mrs. Lincoln in the lady's political hierarchy.

The parlor pocket door slid open and a butler stepped through. "Miss Chase will see you now," he said, disapproval stamped on every word and gesture.

"Let them come in Marshall," came a clear voice from inside the room. "And ask Cassie for tea, please?"

Marshall stepped back and Miss Chase stepped into the doorway, her dove gray dress almost entirely obscured by a voluminous white apron. "Oh, how wonderful," she said, her face lighting up with quiet pleasure. "I'm so glad you came." She stepped forward and grasped Kate's hand, pulling her forward into a gentle kiss on the cheek. "Come see what I've been up to." She stepped back into the room. Kate glanced over at Hazzard. His mouth gaped open. He tried to speak but failed. Kate grabbed his hand and pulled him after Miss Chase.

They stepped into the front parlor, or what had been the front parlor before being converted into a makeshift hospital ward. A man lay tucked into the sofa, and two more on cots along the wall. An older gentleman in a priest's collar sat on a low stool between the two cots reading the Bible aloud. He stood as Kate and Hazzard entered the room, closing the book with one of his fingers in it to hold his place.

Miss Chase gestured to him. "Allow me to introduce Bishop Charles McIlvaine. He is an old family friend and an invaluable nursing assistant."

McIlvaine nodded, expressing his pleasure at meeting them. Kate watched spellbound as his fine white hair waved in the air around him. Between his hair and his beatific expression, he looked like a corporeal angel. No wonder the man was a bishop.

Before Kate could speak the man on the sofa grabbed McIlvaine's wrist and groaned, "God damn it."

The bishop rounded on the man and with a fierceness that belied his angelic looks said, "There are ladies present sir. Your profane language is uncalled for."

The soldier grunted an apology to the two Kates.

McIlvaine laid a hand on the man's forehead, his face softening. "God can help you much more than the devil can, my son."

Miss Chase reached over and squeezed the bishop's hand. "I'll leave you to it then. If you need anything, ring the bell." She led them from the parlor, down the hall to the kitchen. There she took a tea tray from her protesting housekeeper and led them into the dining room. Hazzard still hadn't strung together more than a few polite words.

Once they settled in the dining room Miss Chase eyed her male guest. "Jarring, isn't it?"

He looked from one Kate to the other. "Not jarring exactly. Certainly odd. All this beauty in one space confuses a man."

"Oh, I see how it is," Miss Chase said. She looked over at Kate. "This one is trouble, isn't he?"

"You have no idea."

Hazzard watched as the ladies shared a look beyond his powers of interpretation.

Miss Chase poured them both tea as she spoke. "As you see, I have turned my father's household into a temporary infirmary. I had two more men but they've recovered and returned to their regiments."

"I thought you were delivering the men to the hospital."

"I was. I didn't want Father to worry, so I stopped here first. Just to run in and tell him I was safe. He saw the injured men and insisted we take care of them ourselves. With Marshall and Cassie's help."

Hazzard put down his teacup. "I have heard your father is a man of deep principle. I'm glad to hear it is true."

Miss Chase smiled. "Oh, I'm sure you've heard plenty, not all of it nice. He can be rigid and rub people the wrong way. Saints are easier to admire from afar than they are to live with. He's a good man, for all his prickliness. He's not here or I would introduce you. He spends ever so much time at his office at the Treasury. But where are my manners? You didn't come here to talk about Father. Or my makeshift little hospital."

Kate pulled the two sets of folded papers from her reticule. She looked at both sheets and put one back. She unfolded one paper and pushed across the table. "Can you identify either of these men?

Miss Chase raised her eyebrows at Kate's tone, but took up the papers and examined them. A moment passed. She raised her head. "What are you up to?"

Stalling for time, Kate answered, "I'm a Pinkerton operative."

"That's not what I meant and you know it."

Kate could only stare at the younger Kate. She hadn't thought to concoct a story for why she needed these sketches identified. She glanced over at Hazzard.

He shrugged his shoulders.

Miss Chase refilled her teacup, took a sip, then sat the cup back on the saucer. "Would it help if I tell you what I suspect?" She paused, then continued. "I think it would. In a conversation where Father told me Mr. Lincoln had taken a shine to me, thus raising Mrs. Lincoln's ire, Father also told me Mr. Lincoln admires intelligent women. To demonstrate his point, Father told me a story of a young woman who prevented Mr. Lincoln's assassination through both intellectual endeavor and feats of physical daring. I admit I discounted the story as too far-fetched to be true. Mr. Lincoln does like a tall tale and Father is too earnest to know he's being teased."

Kate heard Hazzard gulp his tea.

"I think you are that woman." Miss Chase held up a finger that commanded their silence and attention. "You were brave enough to go down to the battle. You had military grade field glasses, which are hard to find these days. You had a pass signed by General Scott. I know because I examined it when you took a necessary break. I asked myself what kind of woman could command General Scott's attention just days before a battle. I know the old fellow you see. Then you show up here in the company of an artillery officer. I happen to know General Scott assigned an artillery Captain to Mr. Lincoln on his trip from Illinois. It was in all the papers. And Father was interested, thus I was interested. Lastly, and a point you should appreciate, Miss Henrietta Haines insisted upon sharp thinking in all her students." She stopped and smiled at the two of them. "How'd I do?"

Kate wasn't sure what to say. "You searched my wagon?"

Miss Chase smiled an arch little smile. "Just so. Because I am a cabinet member's daughter and Father's hostess, many people attempt to win my favor. I protect myself from such people though it makes me few friends."

Kate relented. "I bow to your keen perspicacity and offer my own assessment. Contrary to gossip, you are no mere society belle, interested only in the latest fashions and balls. You are loyal to Mr. Lincoln, though he defeated your father for the party's nomination, because you, like your father, are committed to ending slavery. Also, if Miss Haines educated you then you know the value of both honesty and discretion. Thus, when I tell you I am a spy, working under the aegis of the War Department, I know that you will guard that secret with your life."

Miss Chase reached her hand across the table. "Ladies do not shake hands, but I suspect neither of us is, in our hearts, a lady."

As the ladies shook hands Hazzard threw back his head and snorted a laugh.

Miss Chase's mouth curved into a catlike smile and returned to the sketches. "How did you come to have these? It's important that I know."

Kate turned to Hazzard, eyebrow crooked in question.

He leaned back in his chair. "You said you can trust her. Now trust yourself."

She took a deep breath and dove in. "I have operatives watching the home of one Mrs. Rose Greenhow." At Miss Chase's blank look Kate added, "She's old guard Washington so you wouldn't know her. Been around forever. She knew Dolley Madison, or so she's fond of saying again and again. She is also a Confederate spy. In fact, we think she is the head of the Washington underground. The Pinkertons do not wish to make a move against her until we better understand that underground's command structure and information pipelines. We also have proof she played a role in the Confederate's recent military victory, but we do not yet have the details of what information she collected or how she communicated that information."

Miss Chase stared at Kate, her mouth open, eyes wide. "You're kidding? All those dead men? That was her?"

Hazzard said, "Not all her. There's plenty of blame to go around. The military high command was not ready to take this war seriously. They are now."

"I should hope so," Miss Chase said. "But Mrs. Greenhow?"

Kate shook her head. "We don't know. Which is why we're watching her house." Kate tapped the sketches. "These two men, among others, were seen entering Mrs. Greenhow's house on more than one occasion, though not together."

Miss Chase picked up the sheets of paper. "These two men?"

Kate nodded.

"And you say there were others? May I see them? The ones you put away?"

Kate shrugged. "My source made several sketches but made it clear that only three of them looked like important men, the sort of men you would know. Which is why we're here."

Hazzard spoke up. "I've already identified the third man."

"Still, the grouping might tell me something."

Kate shrugged and dug the reserved sketches out of her reticule. She held the sheaf of sketches to Miss Chase. She opened them, leafed through them and handed all but one back to Kate. "You were right. I know none of those people. Kate lined up the reserved sketch with the other two. She tapped the new addition and looked at Hazzard. "And you say you know this man?"

104

He didn't answer.

Kate nudged him. "You can trust her."

He sighed. "It upsets me to say. That is Colonel Erasmus Keyes."

"Ah, that explains it. He's connected to this man." Miss Chase tapped the sketch in the middle. "And you're sure this Rose woman is a spy?"

Kate nodded again.

Miss Chase made a fist and held it up to her mouth. "This is terrible," she muttered, half to herself. She blew out a breath, sat back and then sat forward again.

She tapped the middle sheet of paper. "I am sorry to tell you that this is Mr. Henry Wilson. He's a second term senator from Massachusetts and an ardent abolitionist. Father admires him a great deal. He is also chairman of the Senate Committee on Military Affairs."

Both Kate and Hazzard froze. The information Wilson could betray boggled the mind.

"I'm afraid it gets worse," Miss Chase said. She tapped the last sketch. "I'm surprised you don't recognize this man. Perhaps because one sees his name more often than he is himself seen. Clearly, you don't go to the same parties I do. This is Mr. William Seward."

Hazzard spat out a profanity, then shocked at his own breach of propriety, immediately apologized.

Miss Chase shook her head. "No need Captain. I suspect we ladies feel the same.

William Henry Seward was a giant in antislavery politics and the front-runner for the presidential nomination before Mr. Lincoln rose to prominence. And, as the Secretary of

State, he was the second most politically powerful man in Washington, behind only the president.

And he was on intimate terms with a known Confederate spy.

Chapter 10

July 29-August 1, 1861
Washington City

"I don't know." Juba rubbed his jaw and looked bemused. "It's just crazy enough to work."

Kate stopped pacing and looked at Juba, hands on her hips. "You think?"

"It's your idea, girl. Don't you think it'll work?" He gestured at the nearest chair.

Kate sat down with a sigh. "I wasn't sure. For the past two days, I've been vacillating between thinking it's a brilliant idea and thinking it was the dumbest thing I've ever considered." She knew Juba would go along with the plan even if it was harebrained and dangerous.

Kate eased back in the chair. Juba's taste far exceeded her own, as did his ability to feather his nest for maximum ease and elegance. His basement apartment had dark blue satin upholstered furniture, walls in a lighter blue, down pillows and velvet curtains. Posters and handbills from minstrel shows lined the walls, many of which had featured either Master Juba or Boz's Juba in large print toward the top. Once he'd been famous, perhaps the most famous dancer in all of North America. He'd also been the first black man to headline a minstrel show, at least until the demands of fame almost killed him. So he retired. Or he tried to. Years ago, when Kate was still in school, he had to fake his own death to get away from minstrel shows. He killed Master Juba and left Juba Lane in his place, Juba being as common a name as John amongst free blacks.

Kate sipped her tea and considered Juba. "I thought it could work, but I wanted to check with you. If we get caught we could still get away with it, if you know what I mean. I can pull off a convincing crazy woman act if someone figures out I'm a woman pretending to be a man. But I worry about you. We'll be in slave territory."

"Which is why I'll be fine. They'll not suspect me of anything more nefarious than having a loony mistress. In fact, they so want to believe in slave loyalty they might like the idea that the crazy woman's slave is trying to help her."

Kate fiddled with the fringe on her armchair. "So there's relatively little risk, right?"

Juba snorted in disbelief. "There's a ton of risk. Someone finds us out, you likely to get shot. And there's always jail. And what happens to people in jail. And don't forget, governments hang spies."

"True, but I don't think they'll hang a woman. Not with all their talk about the holy sanctity of white womanhood."

"I thought you wanted Mrs. Greenhow hung? She's a spy and a woman."

"I didn't say we shouldn't hang women, only that I don't think southerners would. They're too invested in ideas that don't allow it. All that Southern womanhood business."

Juba sat forward, straining towards Kate. "Here's what I think. I think it's dangerous, but it needs doing if we're going

108

to plug the information drain between this city and Richmond."

Kate agreed. "It's not like we can expose either Senator Wilson or Secretary Seward, not with so little proof of wrongdoing. I'm not inclined to even tell Allan about them until we know more."

Juba cocked his head at Kate. "You sure?"

"No, not at all. From what I've heard of Seward he's both powerful and prideful. Heads will roll if the Pinkertons accuse him of treason with no proof. And the first head will be Allan's. I know less about Senator Wilson but I can't imagine he would be any more amenable to weakly supported accusations of treason."

"So we keep Allan in the dark? About Seward and Wilson?"

"Yeah, that. But we have to tell him about our plan. We might need his help." Kate retrieved a satchel she'd left on Juba's table. "OK. We'll do it. I've made lists." She retrieved her bag and moved to the table, pulling a slim set of papers as she did.

Juba joined her, pulling the top sheet of paper towards himself. "What have you got here?"

"An identity. A genealogy, really. I visited the Congressional Library yesterday after we left Miss Chase's house ."

"Hazzard go with you?" Juba had a hard time imagining the buccaneering Captain Hazzard in a library.

"No. He has his own assignment. He's chasing down a Colonel that might be in Mrs. Greenhow's pocket. Like a senator and secretary of state weren't enough." Kate looked over at Juba's mantel clock. "He'll be by for dinner. Anyway, the library. They have a copy of Burke's Peerage. If they hadn't I'd have gone to the British Embassy."

"And you found something? Someone?"

Kate smiled across the table. "I did." She pushed another set of notes over to him. "In 1835 the 8th Lord Tracy of Toddington died, leaving no male heirs. The Tracy line is officially extinct. But, the last Lord had a daughter, Henrietta, who married a cousin. When the Henrietta's father died the Queen made her husband Lord Hanbury-Tracy. And the new Lord and Lady Hanbury-Tracy have no children." Kate beamed at Juba. "Brilliant, isn't it?"

"It is? It's convoluted. And confusing."

"I know," Kate said with evident delight. "The existence of Lord Hanbury-Tracy disguises the fact that the Tracy line is extinct. If anyone in Richmond knows that I can claim to be the new lord, from a side branch of the family. We'll be in and out before anyone finds out otherwise."

Juba grabbed at his brandy bottle and frowned as he poured himself a considerable drink.

"You just don't like all the Lording business." She pushed yet another sheet of paper over at him. "Here's a list of what I think we need. What am I missing?"

Over the next two days, they collected Lord Tracy's effects. Samuel and Juba visited Mr. Howard and hired a black barouche and a pair of matched chestnut horses. Charlotte contacted a man in New York who handled all the Pinkerton forgeries. Her husband Timothy had once been a New York City policeman and he'd arrested the fellow back in the early

1850s. They'd gone easy on him in exchange for use of his services.

Juba loaned Kate his well-used, but high quality traveling trunk. 'Buy a new trunk' had been fourth on her list, but he'd pointed out that Lord Tracy would be a seasoned traveler. New trunks would give her away as surely as a bad English accent. Which they also worked on. Long ago, Juba had performed in London and England's other major cities. The English went crazy for American minstrelsy, erroneously believing it an accurate representation of American life and slave customs. He'd once even performed for Queen Victoria. As a minstrel performer, he met London workers, Welsh miners, street urchins and members of the peerage and he could mimic them all.

Kate picked up the upper-crust accent in a matter of days. The key was to pretend she had a mild form of lockjaw and a stick up her hindquarters.

Pretending to be shopping for Kate's brother, they bought two new suits, one in formal black and one with a hunter green coat and green and gray checked trousers. She also bought a velvet-collared smoking jacket and a set of riding clothes. Juba served as their tailoring dummy when the proprietor insisted he needed one day to make alterations. The tailor also sold them several embroidered waistcoats of the sort that suggested frivolity. Another tailor had a supply of London-made shirts, along with a tooled leather cigar case embossed with the British lion. They bought Juba a plain black suit and a ridiculously high top hat. Juba bought her a fresh supply of manly toiletries, including shaving soap, which Kate thought was stupid until Juba pointed out that the scent of shaving soap would provide masculine verisimilitude. Af-

111

terwards they visited the British embassy and converted a hundred dollars into gold sovereigns. Juba also bought a boot shine kit from a street vendor to complete his disguise as a professional manservant.

Then they spent one entire afternoon trying to perfect a fake mustache. It did not go well.

"I'll have to just go clean shaven," Kate teased as she stripped off their fourth mustache attempt. "With the carriage and the waistcoats, no one will mistake me for anything but a effete dandy, anyway."

They got it right when they tried a bushy, tailing mustache. They'd been working with small, neat mustaches on the principle that an English Lord's facial furnishings would be restrained, but all of them looked like just what they were, fake mustaches, good enough for the stage, but not realistic enough for close up work. The bushy mustache covered more of Kate's face, and thus more of the glued area.

Kate looked at herself in the mirror. "It looks like I've got a dead muskrat on my face," she pointed out with a laugh. But it looked real. Horrifying, but real.

"You'll look like you're overcompensating for being a little fellow. And people expect the titled classes to be ridiculous," Juba noted. Once they quit laughing they agreed on the muskrat mustache.

Friday afternoon they dressed downstairs in Juba's apartment, he in his bedroom, she in his dressing closet. Kate pulled on a gentleman's small clothes, noting as she always did that they were fewer, lighter and less constraining than lady's undergarments. She strapped on her breast binding and pulled on a muslin undershirt, then a linen shirt and buttoned on a starched collar. She stepped into the loose trousers, attached the suspenders and pulled them over her shoulder, before buttoning up an embroidered lavender silk waistcoat.

Several years ago she'd made a faux male appendage from some rolled up handkerchiefs, which she pinned into her drawers, but she'd found the prosthesis so distracting she'd gotten rid of it. The trick was to walk as if you had the appendage, whether you did or not.

Her forays into male disguise had taught her that most of it was about attitude and posture. Men were sure of themselves. They walked into rooms like they owned them and they rarely expressed doubt or asked questions. It helped that social convention that said men wore pants and women wore skirts. People saw pants and thought man, even if the 'man' they saw had smooth skin a high pitched voice. In fact, Kate had heard there were women passing as men in the army and she believed it. People saw what they wanted to see.

She slung a royal purple cravat around her neck but left it untied, that skill being beyond her. Lord Tracy's manservant would do that sort of thing, anyway. She pulled on silk socks and a pair of shiny calf-skin half boots. Her boots had a two-inch heel, plus an inch of lift hidden inside, increasing her height a crucial 3 inches.

Last, she shrugged into a black frock coat made from superfine wool broadcloth, into which they'd added padding to give her some much-needed bulk. Kate tucked a pair of white calfskin gloves in her pocket, gloves being a good way to hide her small hands and settled a black silk top hat on her head. She stepped in front of Juba's mirror and frowned at her reflection. Pretty good, but for the one glaring problem.

She knocked on the dressing room door and called out to Juba. "You ready for me to come out?"

113

"Bring on Lord Tracy," Juba boomed.

Kate stepped out of the dressing room, paused and with a sweep of her hat, bowed to Juba. She waved the hat around her head. "You see the problem?" She kept her voice at the bottom of her range when she spoke.

He sighed. "I was hoping we wouldn't have to. You have such beautiful hair. And you won't be Lord Tracy forever."

"True, but Lord Tracy is a vain bugger. While most English gentlemen are wearing their hair at their earlobes, I think my lord could have shoulder length hair, pulled back into a little club, like the military men used to do. It'll give me enough to make a bun with when I return to ladyhood, 'specially if I use a rat."

"A rat? In your hair?"

She smiled at him. "Not the four-legged kind. More like a cushion for hair. Women with thin hair use them."

Juba shrugged his shoulders. "Lady stuff is ever mysterious." He dug a pair of scissors out of a side table drawer.

They returned to the mirror. She unpinned her braid from its bun at the back of her head. "You ready?" Juba asked.

"Yes," she said. She wasn't, but she didn't have much choice. Not if she was going to shut down Rose's underground.

Juba took hold of her braid, pulling it gently away from her neck. Kate heard the scissors cut through her hair. She tried not to cry. *It was just hair. Wasn't it?*

Juba cut and snipped for a few more minutes, then rebound her hair into a short tail. Kate moved her head to and fro. It felt so light. So free. Maybe it was just hair. She straightened her shoulders and looked at him in the mirror. "Juba?"

114

"Hmmm," he murmured.

She paused, unsure what she meant to say next.

"What girl?"

"Do we need to talk?" She gulped and went on. "About what happened to you."

"Maybe," he said. "Why do you ask?"

"Well, what I'm wondering is if this plan of mine is a terrible idea. Part of me wants you to go with me just because. And another part thinks it might be good for you. But I'm worried too. Worried this might be a terrible idea. Maybe even selfish."

"'How you figure that?" His tone was mild, but Kate could see his shoulders tense as they spoke.

"I'm asking you to play slave servant to Lord Tracy. I get to act all high and mighty and you have to spend a couple of weeks acting like a slave. In the south." Unspoken was the fact that he'd just returned from the south and was, at least as far as the slave dealers who bought him were concerned, an escaped slave."

"But you want me with you, anyway?"

"Yes." She blushed with shame. "You're my partner. And all the family I have. And now that Samuel's here, well he can help you with whatever you're doing with Columbus. You're up to something, you two, but it's none of my business until you make it my business."

"I should have known better than to keep a secret from you. I'll talk to you about it, but not right now. I'm coming with you, come hell or high-water." He sat down his scissors and put both his hands on her shoulders to turn her. "I got two things to say to you. One long overdue. The first is there's a world of difference between playing a slave and being a

115

slave. The space between those two things is filled with choice. I didn't choose to be captured and sold. But as a free man and a Pinkerton, I can choose to play a slave, knowing I'll be working to eradicate slavery while I do. See?"

She nodded, more relieved than she had words to say.

His hands tightened on her shoulders. "And we are family. I should have told you a long time ago but the longer I kept my secret, the harder it was to tell. I told the story in the belly of that slave ship one day and once I said it out loud the secret seemed less important."

"I know we're family," Kate said. She knitted her eyebrows together, his worried face making her uneasy. "You're my uncle Juba. Not my real uncle, of course, but Momma and Poppa always said you were family. And you took care of me after they died. You still do."

He shook his head. "You don't understand." His hands tightened on her shoulders. "Your father was my brother. My half-brother really."

Kate's eyes went wide. She leaned forward. "Huh?"

"When my Daddy met my mother, she was a widow with a little boy. That was your dad. My Daddy married her though he was as dark as any African and she was Irish. They lived in New York, in a slum called Five Points and they had me. Then my mother died trying to have another baby. Not long after that, a gang of Irishmen killed my daddy for living with a white woman. They hung him from a lamp post. I was only six years old and your father, well he was fifteen and he took care of me after that. Eventually, we ran away to the circus."

"Why didn't you ever tell anyone," she asked. What she meant was 'why didn't you ever tell me?'

116

Juba shook his head. "It felt dangerous to admit to being brothers, what with Phin so pale skinned Irish and me so dark. They lynched Daddy for race mixing didn't they? We got in the habit of not talking about it. The only person we ever told was your mother before Phin married her. Not that she minded. She wasn't that sort of woman." Juba stuttered to a stop and squinted his eyes at her. "You're not too mad are you?"

Kate bit her lower lip. She could see why he'd told no one this story. And her parents *had* told her to call him Uncle Juba. Did blood change anything? She shook her head. "No, I'm not mad." She reached out and touched his temple where his hair was turning gray. "You've always been family. Blood might be thicker than water, but it's not so thick as love."

"You are my sweet girl." He wrapped her up in one of his best Juba hugs.

She inhaled his particular scent, a mix of spicy hair tonic and sunflower soap, happier than she'd been in a long time. She wasn't an orphan after all. Not really.

He let her go and tapped her on the nose. "Now turn around. I need to finish this haircut."

She kept her Lord Tracy garb on through dinner, much to Louisa's delight. She hovered around Lord Tracy, peppering him with questions about England and the queen. Kate made up a story about a country estate full of unicorns and dwarves that had the girl speechless with laughter. Lord Tracy also practiced stories of trout fishing and pheasant hunting with Hazzard and made lascivious passes at Charlotte, who blushed so furiously Kate felt compelled to apologize for his lordship's temerity. Odetta disapproved of Lord Tracy's flirta-

117

tious behavior or at least she pretended to. A wink at Kate as the cook passed the beans gave her away.

Samuel, who'd seen more than his fair share of toffs in his years working for upscale New Orleans brothels, watched Kate throughout dinner before awarding her with a solemn nod of approval. Monty remained unfazed by the whole performance, affirming Kate's suspicion that her dog was smarter than most people.

After dinner, Hazzard asked Kate to go for a walk.

"You want me to change?"

"Never." He smiled his piratical smile as he swung his hat upon his head. "Let's take Lord Tracy out and see if he passes muster.

As they headed for the front door he caught up a little tapestry bag and slung it over his shoulder. They walked down the street and circled the hospital grounds, passing the Chase house about halfway around. It lay cloaked in darkness. Kate wondered if the sick men were asleep or gone.

Hazzard waved his hand at the house. "There's a reception at the White House for Lord Lyon, the British ambassador. It was in the newspaper." He slowed and stopped on a bench that sat under a massive, spreading oak tree.

Kate followed him, glad for the opportunity to sit down. Her new boots chafed her heels. "Thank goodness we're too lowly for an invitation."

"Oh, I don't know. Lord Tracy might be a hit with the ladies."

Kate smiled into the dark. "And some of the gentlemen, no doubt."

Hazzard threw back his head and laughed. "I suppose I should feign shock and dismay that a lady of my acquaintance

118

should know of such things. Particularly a lady I think of as my own."

Kate punched his arm to turn his declaration into a joke. She worried about this very thing—the male tendency to treat women as property. "I'm not your lady. I'm no one's lady but my own."

He turned toward her, bringing his mouth up to her ear. His mustache tickled her ear as he said, "Oh, you are mine, but no more than I am yours. And only yours."

Before her heart could leap out of her chest Kate turned, grabbed Hazzard's cravat and pulled his mouth to hers. After a few deeply satisfying moments she pushed away from him. She breathed out. "Hazzard."

"Kate?" he whispered.

"I don't want to." She stopped.

"I told you, my dear. I can wait as long as you need."

She shook her head. "No, not that."

He issued a low chuckle. "Then what?"

"I know you haven't asked, and I know ladies aren't supposed to bring it up, but I don't want to marry. Not anyone. I was married and I don't care to repeat the experiment."

"My dear, marriage is for producing children. I should think a lady spy and an Army officer would not want children at the start of a war. Am I correct?"

"It's just that," Kate felt herself blush. "Damn. This is hard. I'm saying I think would like to enjoy the pleasanter parts of marriage, but without becoming Mrs. Hazzard. Not tonight, but eventually."

His laughter rolled across the hospital grounds. "Oh, my dear Tiger. You are the most surprising, unconventional, delightful woman I have ever met. And I love you for it." He paused and dug around in his bag.

Kate bit her lip. Here's where she was supposed to say she loved him too.

Before she could speak he drew a mid-sized box from his bag and held it out to her. "This is for you."

She opened it to find a Colt pocket revolver, like Mrs. Greenhow's, but better. Kate grinned in delight. This one had a pearled handle. The bitch no longer had a better gun. She held it up to the light coming from the street lamps. "So pretty."

Hazzard laughed again. "I shall never have to buy you jewelry. Only deadly weapons."

"How did you know?"

"Juba. You tell him everything and sometimes he passes the information along. I'll come by first thing tomorrow morning for a shooting lesson."

"I know how to shoot a gun," Kate replied absently. She was too busy examining her new revolver to bring much fervor to her argument. Besides, the dagger lessons she'd had with Hazzard had been delightful. Shooting lessons would be at least as pleasant.

"You know how to point a derringer in the general direction of your target and pull the trigger. Which is all one needs to know with derringers. This, my dear, is a real gun. It's smaller than a standard revolver, but don't let it fool you, it's a deadly weapon. Never aim it at someone unless you intend to shoot them and never shoot unless you aim to kill. You get one lesson before you go and you must promise that Lord Tracy will practice."

120

Kate nodded and put her new gun back in its box. It seemed less pretty now.

He reached into his waistcoat pocket. "One more thing." He drew out an engraved brass pocket watch and held it in the palm of his hand. "My father's father gave this to him when he left for Harvard. My father gave it to me when I left for West Point. I'd like you to have it."

Kate looked at the shining thing and shook her head. "I can't take your watch."

He leaned in close and slipped it into her waistcoat pocket. "Lord Tracy needs a good pocket watch. And that watch will remind you I am ever with you."

Kate thrust her hands into her jacket pocket. "It's a family heirloom."

"You're my family now."

Her heart almost exploded. Almost.

They were locked in an enthusiastic embrace when Kate heard someone say, "Disgusting. This used to be a decent neighborhood."

Kate drew back from Hazzard, confused. He looked her up and down, forcing her to remember she was wearing Lord Tracy's clothes. Hazzard threw back his head and laughed. She joined him.

It would be a long time before she laughed so hard again.

Charlotte handed Kate a telegram the next morning. "It came hours ago, at dawn. Looks like the boss is up to something."

Bleary-eyed from her late night, Kate poured herself a cup of coffee with one hand and studied the telegram in the other hand. She sat down at the table just as Odetta slid a bowl of oatmeal in front of her.

Aug. 1

Cincinnati, Ohio

Request Mrs. Barley and friend change course. Same plan, but come to Cincinnati first. Ship everything by rail. Will meet you at the depot.

E. J. Allen

Kate frowned at Charlotte. "Darn it. We're all set to pick up the barouche from Mr. Howard this morning and head for Richmond. And how'd Allan know what we're doing in the first place?"

Charlotte frowned right back at Kate. "You didn't think I was going to let you go into enemy territory without telling him, did you?"

Kate beat back a sigh. She'd never won an argument with Charlotte and she wasn't likely to now. Juba's footsteps thumped on the stair behind her. Kate waited for the door to squeak open and held the telegram up above her head. She felt him pluck it from her hand.

"Huh," he grunted. "Boss like to make his own plans. I 'spect his General McClellan is up against something out west. I better tell Mr. Howard to put the horses and carriage on the train."

Odetta laughed a grim little laugh and handed Juba a bowl of oatmeal. "Newspaper says General McClellan's got troops harassing the Confederates from the north and west. They gonna wish they'd taken this city when they had a chance."

Charlotte plucked her glasses out of her apron pocket and perched them on the end of her nose. She picked up the telegram from the table and examined it again. "Hold on." She left the room and returned with a trains schedule. "There's a 3

PM train to Baltimore. You can take the B & O from there to Cincinnati."

She looked over her glasses at Kate. "Your captain sent a note this morning. You're to meet him at 9 down at the Navy Yard for target practice. Juba can get everything packed and to the depot while you do that."

Juba swallowed a big bite of oatmeal. "But who's going to Cincinnati? Kate and me? Or Lord Tracy and his slave?"

Kate bit her lower lip as she thought. "I can't see any reason Lord Tracy has to go to Cincinnati. We don't need to sneak into a Northern city held by the U.S. Army." She sighed again. "Damn it. I thought Allan understood how important it is to stop Rose and her network."

"Oh, he understands all right," Juba said, leaning back in his chair. "I bet it turns out fine."

Kate shook her head, mostly to herself. Juba and Alan hadn't seen the debacle of Bull Run. They hadn't seen the dead men and horses, hadn't smelled the gunpowder and fear, hadn't heard the booming of the guns. She knew Rose Greenhow had something to do with that mess. In the darkest part of the night, she would lie awake and try to convince herself none of the dead could be laid at the Pinkerton's door. But she didn't believe it. It had been their job, no, her job, to stop Greenhow and she'd failed. And now, when she had a plan to address her failure, Allan wanted her to do something else. She didn't like it. Not one bit.

Chapter 11

August 3-4, 1861
Cincinnati, Ohio to Guyandotte

*K*ate shook the black cinders off her skirt as she stepped out of the train, trying to hold on to both her carpet bag and Monty's leash. Summer train travel meant the rail car's windows were open, causing co al cinders to blow in and get on everything and everyone. Also, if she were honest, she'd spent the last hours on the train feeling cross about the cavalier way that Allan changed her plans.

"Woof."

She looked down at the little dog. Her little dog. He strained at the leash, watching someone off to the left. Taking her cue from Monty, she looked up and over. Allan Pinkerton strode across the cavernous depot, a serious look on his face. He stepped up to her, took her carpetbag from her hand and said, "You've got less than an hour to get changed and get down to the docks. I've booked passage for Lord Tracy and his servant on the *Cricket*, steaming west on the Ohio River."

Kate glanced around. No one was around, so there wasn't much chance anyone overheard. The Cincinnati train depot was built so trains pulled right into it through one end and left through the other end. At over 400 feet long and a hundred feet high, the building echoed with the tumult of the train engine and people.

"Well, hello to you too. And thank you for asking. Our trip was fine," Kate snapped at her boss. She looked up and down the track until she found Juba in the distance. The Baltimore station master had refused to let him ride in first class with Kate. She wanted to make a fuss about it, but Juba pointed out they wouldn't appear to be together when they arrived in Cincinnati, which might be for the best. Particularly since they had no idea what Allan was up to.

Allan leaned in and kissed her cheek. "I'm sorry my dear. I really am, but time is short. The station master has agreed to let you use his office—you'll change there." Alan grabbed her arm and tugged her along. "This way."

Kate looked down the track at Juba and gave her head a minute shake. He nodded back at her. She saw him take a seat on one of the outside benches just before Alan whisked her inside.

"But I don't have my things," she protested. "Lord Tracy's trunk is back in the baggage car."

Allan smiled in triumph. "I had a man waiting. He pulled your trunk from baggage the moment the train stopped." Allan took Monty's leash and herded her towards an office door at far end of the building.

Twenty minutes later Lord Charles Tracy emerged from the depot master's office and strode over to Allan and Juba, silver-headed walking stick hitting the marble floor with marvelous, self-centered, echoing thumps. He stopped before the two men and bowed with a flourish of his perfumed handkerchief. Monty barked his approval.

126

Juba jumped to his feet. "My Lord," he said with a deep bow. "Your baggage is ready for transfer." He stepped up to Kate and straightened her cravat.

The four of them made their way to a hansom cab waiting outside the depot's large, arched doorways.

Once they were settled inside the cab and the driver directed to the wharf, Allan pulled an envelope from his pocket and handed it to Juba. "Two tickets for the *Cricket*. Your itinerary is also in there. And a note from the president. Read once you're aboard and destroy it."

Juba tucked the envelope inside his jacket.

Kate settled Monty on her lap and looked at the two men, fighting the urge to smack both of them upside their heads. "I don't suppose either of you would care to share any information with me, would you?" She shook her head and thunked her silver duck headed walking stick upon the floor of the carriage. "If you're scuttling my plans I at least deserve to know what I'll be doing instead."

Allan sighed. "I owe you an apology, Kate. This Greenhow thing is important, but Mr. Lincoln thought you might help General McClellan on your way to Richmond. He also has an errand for you once you get to Richmond. They've got a congressman held as a prisoner of war there—a fellow they captured at Bull Run— and the president wants you to check on him."

Kate's heart sunk. She'd just gone from having one job to having three. Still, she was going to get to Richmond.

Allan watched Kate's face. "There's a benefit to this change of plans too. Your Lord Tracy might be less suspicious if he came to Richmond from the west. It'll take longer, but it increases your chances of success. None of which I could ex-

127

plain in a telegram and dared not commit to a letter, even in cipher."

She'd read enough of the newspapers to know McClellan's army was poised to strike at Richmond, through western Virginia. A series of hasty calculations brought her to a conclusion.

"Your general doesn't know how big the western Confederate Army is, does he? He needs a report on troop locations and numbers before he attacks. Not knowing Johnston left the Shenandoah Valley for Manassas Junction proved disastrous for the Union Army."

Allan nodded. "If we'd known he'd gone south to reinforce Beauregard the Union Army would not have attempted that disastrous flanking movement."

Juba shifted in his seat. "I'm sorry, but I still don't understand why we're here. You could send anyone across the river to spy on the Confederates. You don't need us. We could be in Richmond right now if you'd let Kate do it her way."

Kate nudged Juba with her shoulder, glad of his support.

"The Confederates are being mighty cagey," Allan explained. "There's only one road of any importance between the Ohio River and Richmond, the Kanawha Turnpike. The Confederate Army has the turnpike blocked at Charleston and we haven't been able to get a man past that block to the other side. And believe me, we've tried."

"Charleston? You want me to go through Charleston on my way from Cincinnati to Richmond? I need to be in Richmond before Christmas." Kate heard her voice spiral up in anxiety. She wasn't a geography expert, but she was sure South Carolina wasn't wedged between Ohio and Virginia.

Monty kept his eyes on Allan, ready to spring to Kate's defense if the moment required. Monty didn't particularly care for men and right now Kate agreed with her dog.

Juba laughed at her impatience and patted her knee. "He means the Charleston in Virginia. It's a little town about two day's ride from here. We performed there back when I was with Pelham's Serenaders."

"Right," Allan said. "You two can pretend you've just come up the Mississippi from New Orleans, touring the country. Since you've just come from New Orleans you'll be able to fake the details should anyone ask you what you've seen. You'll take the *Cricket* up the Ohio River, get off tomorrow and take your carriage to Charleston. I'm hoping Lord Tracy will get past the Confederate pickets. If you do you'll be in Richmond within the week."

Kate nodded, feeling some of her anxiety drain away. This might work.

Allan looked out the carriage window and then pulled his watch from his waistcoat pocket. "We're running out of time. The Cricket leaves in less than half an hour. You'll find more information in the envelope with the tickets. His lordship's carriage is on its way to the steamship as we speak, the loading of which should help you with your lordly personae. Your cover story is just as you concocted, but Lord Tracy is heading for White Sulfur Springs. It's a well-known resort just past Charleston where the idle rich take the water. Once there, you'll announce your intention to visit Richmond."

"I presume you mean these springs are behind enemy lines?" Kate smiled at Allan, feeling less cranky with him by the minute.

"They are. A day's ride past Charleston. Along the way, you'll write letters to Mr. Vallandigham, an Ohio Democrat well known for his sympathy to the Confederate cause. I shall cause those letters to be intercepted and sent to me. Juba has a bottle of ferrous sulfate disguised as hairdressing oil for use as invisible ink should you think it necessary."

"Cross write it, or just use the back?" Rich folk might use a whole piece of paper to write a letter that left some of the paper blank, but poorer people never did, preferring smaller pieces of paper with words covering both front and back of the paper, sometimes written over twice, once on the vertical and other on the horizontal.

Allan nodded. "Use the back. I think it's safe to assume that an English lord would be a careless user of paper." The carriage slowed and stopped as he spoke. Allan looked out the window. "I'll stay out of sight. It's show time."

Allan and Lord Tracy shook hands while Juba jumped out of the carriage and with much pomp, propped open the door and pulled down the carriage step. Kate watched Monty jump out of the cab before she leaned forward. She whispered in Allan's ear, "You really are the most infuriating man." Then, just before she exited the carriage, she kissed him on the cheek. She stepped out of the carriage, her silver walking stick and brass jacket buttons glinting in the bright western sun. Juba kowtowed and bustled about collecting Lord Tracy's traveling trunk and several cases of champagne that traveled with him, so that he created a small tornado of chaos in the Lord's wake.

In Lord Tracy's wake, Allan's laugh echoed from the carriage.

130

The Cincinnati docks teamed with men, both white and black, loading barges and steamboats with barrels of whiskey, flour, cornmeal, salted meat and more. Steamboats lined the docks, creating a forest of smokestacks, flag poles, and guy lines. Passengers scurried to and fro, some followed by carts laden with fine leather trunks, others carrying their belongings in sacks and baskets. Lord Tracy moved through it all as if he were above the dirt and noise of the quay, assisted in his forward progress by his manservant who allowed no one to impede his Lordship's parade of one.

Kate's heart leaped at the site of the *Cricket*. English lords traveled in high style. The double-deck ship sported a fresh coat of whitewash with bright red trim, shiny twin black smokestacks and both stern and bow boxed paddle wheels. As they stepped aboard the ship whistle sounded, high and clear. Juba took out their tickets and handed them to the man standing at the top of the ramp who directed them to their private cabin on the ship's upper deck.

Though they had the best suite on the ship, their quarters were cramped and hot. Even Monty objected by placing his feet on the open cabin window and staring out at the shoreline. Juba shut the door and turned. "I think ole Lord Tracy would take an interest in the ship's departure. Why don't you find a deck chair and look grand? I'll unpack and make friends with the help."

Kate looked in dismay at the massive traveling trunk that contained the accouterments of her manly performance. Juba caught her gaze and pushed her toward the door. "Don't you worry none. We both got a part to play. Go."

Kate spent the afternoon lolling about, speaking loudly and authoritatively on a variety of topics, many of which Lord

131

Tracy had no knowledge. As always, it was intensely liberating. And no one ever suspected her, at least not as far as she could tell. The nice thing about living in a world where the rules for men and women were both rigid and completely different was that the roles, behaviors, and mannerisms of manhood, once observed, created an ironclad false identity.

Kate and Monty spent the first afternoon aboard ship on the main deck, making occasional forays into the ship's grand salon for rejuvenating beverages. She feared that by the end of the day the fish in their wake would be tipsy from all the brandy she spilled overboard.

The ship seemed populated in equal numbers by Union soldiers and Virginia gentlemen. The two groups of men stayed separate from each other though Lord Tracy talked to men in both groups.

Two civilian gentlemen approached Lord Tracy after dinner with a bottle of Kentucky whiskey and asked him if he'd like to join them. Kate stood and shook their hands.

The older of the two gave Lord Tracy an astonished look. "Are all English gentlemen little bits, or just you sir?"

"Daddy!" the younger man exclaimed, reddening in embarrassment. He held out his hand. "I apologize for my father." He introduced himself and his father as Virginia landowners on their way back home from Chicago where they'd sold the past year's cotton crop at higher prices than they would have gotten at home.

Lord Tracy assured both the men he had taken no offense. "My mother, the dowager Lady Tracy, is a tiny woman. It's no wonder her children are modestly sized, to my father's everlasting mortification. Though what he thought would happen when he married Mother I'll never understand. I once

132

had to call out a man who insulted my size. Rapiers at dawn. I scooped out his eye and left him squealing on the dueling grounds. It took the scoundrel weeks to die from the infection, but no one over suggested I was less than a man again." The two men looked chastened and there was no more discussion of Lord Tracy's size.

Lord Tracy and his new friends lit their cigars, cupped their snifters of brandy and looked out over the river. The sky turned red and purple as the sun set, its reflection lighting up the river with a soft glow. Frogs sang their songs loud enough to be heard over the steam engines, creating a soothing background song. Monty, who'd had a large dinner of meat scraps, flopped down on the deck and closed his eyes with a little, doggy sigh.

The older man seemed perplexed about his Lordship's destination. "You didn't notice there's a war on?"

Kate, who'd earned top marks in her history classes at Miss Haines' school, put her education to use. "War?" she scoffed. "You call this a war? One battle, with the ruffians routed back to their federal stronghold? That's not war. My father was in the Crimean War. Now that was a war." She sipped her brandy for emphasis and, when prompted, shared details from that war, some real and some made up, being sure to favorably compare the Confederacy to the British empire.

Because his Lordship declared his southern sympathies, the two Virginia men made several sweeping assertions of southern superiority and the ease with which the Confederacy would win the war. To Kate's dismay, no matter how she prompted the men they would not speak of anything more than generalities. Instead, they took an interest in Monty, which sparked an enthusiastic discussion of the best dogs for hunting squirrels, coons, possums and even deer. She took care to note the peculiarities of southern gentlemanly behavior, including their casual approach to the King's English.

When a brace of Union officers joined them, the talk turned to the attractions of the area. Lord Tracy asked about the fabled White Sulfur Springs and was assured the waters would be good for a sickly fellow like himself. One of the Virginians even called him 'consumptive,' an adjective that pleased Kate to no end. Better they think his Lordship sickly than suspiciously unmanly. She made a note to cough delicately into one of Lord Tracy's monographed handkerchiefs for the duration of the trip.

Kate woke the next morning with a sore head and a sick stomach. She'd dumped most her booze over the side, but she'd still drunk far more than she intended. Juba brought her a pot of coffee and a damp cloth for her forehead and ordered her to stay in bed. She used the morning to examine Allan's carefully prepared itinerary and notes and then wrote a letter to Mr. Vallandigham.

She emerged from her cabin in the late afternoon when the sun no longer threatened to make her head explode. Most of the other men aboard ship seemed no more inclined to repeat the previous day's bacchanal than Lord Tracy, so she spent a quiet afternoon in a deck chair, Monty nestled in beside her, reading Dickens and sipping weak tea.

The ship steamed into Guyandotte, Virginia just before sunset. They disembarked the *Cricket* with much noise and fuss. Kate wanted to make sure people noticed Lord Tracy's traveling trunks, cases of champagne and loud insistence on the town's best hotel. When his Lordship's servant dropped his trunk Lord Tracy excoriated the cringing black man, much to

134

the satisfaction of one Virginian gentleman who admired the Englishman's command of his servant. At one point in their burlesque performance of master and slave, Kate caught Juba's eye and almost burst into laughter. It was less funny when she remembered that they were now in Confederate territory

An hour later they checked into a rough little hotel not far from the river. They ate a paltry dinner of thin stew made with unidentifiable meat, checked on the horses and went to bed, his Lordship in a hotel room and Juba in the stable. She lay in her lumpy and not entirely vermin free bed that night trying not to worry. So far, so good. She'd pulled off the Lord Tracy charade for a day and a half, some of it in close proximity to men. At least she assumed they were men. How many women dressed as men might be around? If the reports about women in the army were correct she wasn't the only one. Still, all it would take was one slip to reveal her. One moment where she forgot to walk like a man, forgot to keep her voice low or moved her hands wrong and she'd be found out. If that happened she'd never get the information against Rose Greenhow that would put her in jail.

Long ago, before her parents died in a circus tent blow down, the famous Blondin gave her lessons in the art of walking the high wire. He said the key to wire-walking was both to forget one was on a wire and to never forget you were on a wire. A wire walker needed both bravery and perfect balance, and both required a kind of selective awareness. The next few days she'd be wire walking and if she fell off the results would be disastrous.

The birds sang in the pre-dawn light before sleep found Kate.

135

Chapter 12

August 4, 1861
Washington City

*R*ose Greenhow held the piece of paper up to the light and shook her head. "This will not do Miss Boyd. Not one whit." She set the paper down and pointed at the writing. "Right here. You wrote '200 mip.' It should read '2000 men.' If you can't get your ciphered messages right, there's no reason to send them. You must commit the cipher to memory and your memory must be flawless."

They were in Rose's library parlor, sitting at the large table that took up the center of the room. The closed curtains made the room dark and stuffy.

Belle pushed her chair back so abruptly that it fell over. "I hate this," she shrieked. She looked down at the fallen chair, kicked its padded seat and threw her pen across the room. It hit the floor with a ping and slid up against the rug in front of the empty fireplace.

"My dear Miss Boyd," Rose said as she crossed the room, "You say you are the daughter of a gentleman, but you behave like an ill-mannered hoyden." Rose bent and picked up the pen. "See here? You've bent my best steel nib. You lack self-control."

Hands on hips, Belle stamped her foot. "I didn't come here for school. Why can't I keep the code on a piece of paper? I could hide it in my corset or my bonnet. Or anywhere."

Rose leveled her sternest gaze at Belle. "Because it might be discovered, you ninny. A great number of us use that cipher."

"Bosh."

"You forget yourself, Miss Boyd. A true woman is self-controlled, patient and modest. She does not stamp her feet, throw pens or get caught by the Union Army passing ill-disguised dispatches. And she does not endanger an entire spy network by riding around with the cipher code in her corset." Rose crossed her arms and stared at her recalcitrant pupil. "Pick up your chair and sit down."

Belle stuck her tongue out at Rose.

"Pick. Up. The chair. And sit. Down." Rose heard her voice get louder with each word. This girl really did try her patience. "Now. Or I send you back home."

Belle picked up the chair with a thump and sat, her lips so tightly pressed together they all but disappeared..

"Miss Boyd, we've had this talk and we'll have it one more time. But this is the last time. Do you want to make a difference? A real difference? Or do you want to ride your horse around the countryside attracting attention?"

Belle laughed a tinkling little laugh. "Both!"

Rose steeled herself against defeat. Belle would be a magnificent courier if she could just bring the girl to heel. "Because what we do here is serious Miss Boyd. The fate of the nation may well hang upon the endeavors of southern women. Failure will destroy everything we hold dear."

"I know that," Belle said. She started to rise but sunk back to her seat under the narrow eyed scrutiny of her mentor. Before Belle could continue the argument a knock came at the door.

Rose pointed at the door. "Good. This is someone I want you to meet."

The pocket door between the parlor and the hall slid open. "Miss Duvall for you, Mrs. Greenhow," Rose's slave woman announced.

A slight, dark-haired, dark-eyed young woman stepped into the parlor. She held out both hands to Rose. "My dear Mrs. Greenhow, I am once again at your disposal," she said and kissed Rose on the cheek.

Rose returned her compliments before turning to Belle. "Miss Boyd, it pleases me to introduce to you Miss Betty Duvall."

Belle stood and made a small curtsy in Miss Duvall's direction. The two young women eyed each other like two junkyard dogs facing off over a meaty bone.

Rose saw the unspoken competition and smiled to herself. Pretty girls were the same everywhere, blind to everything but their own teacup sized circle of popularity. "Miss Boyd, you see that Miss Duvall is young and pleasant to look upon and she is my best courier. She carried my messages regarding the union army's strength to General Beauregard, alerting him that McDowell had a much larger army than we had thought. It was she that got a message through to General Johnston in the Shenandoah telling him to turn south and reinforce Beauregard. I and others gathered the intelligence, but Miss Duval delivered it to the generals. She has never been caught. She does not call attention to herself. She does not flirt with

139

officers. She does not seek fame or adulation. She does only her duty as a loyal southern woman. In short, she is everything I want you to be."

This speech did not endear Miss Duvall to Miss Boyd. Belle scowled at her rival.

Seeing her mistake, Rose took another tack. "Miss Boyd, you show tremendous promise, both as a courier and as an intelligence gathering resource. Where Miss Duval is cautious, you are fearless. Miss Duval has not the nerve to gather information and pass it on. She is a courier only." Rose's voice trailed off. She looked over at Betty Duvall, spread her hands and shrugged her shoulders.

Betty took her cue. She stepped up to the table and rested a hand on Belle's shoulder. "Let's you and I study the cipher together. I learn things better when I have a friend helping me. And as soon as you learn it, really learn it, I'll show you how I get across Union lines to the Confederate Army. I can take you right to General Beauregard and introduce you. And maybe you can teach me to be braver."

Belle's eyes brightened. "I'd rather see Colonel Jackson. I know him from home and my father's in his brigade."

"I can take you straight to General Jackson. Once Mrs. Greenhow says you're ready." Betty smiled and took a seat next to Belle.

"General! Oh, I hadn't heard. He was a colonel when I saw him last." Belle's voice went up several octaves in her excitement.

Rose moved over to her desk to find a new pen nib. Behind her, the two young women chattered about their favorite generals like debutantes discussing their favorite beaus. Rose vowed she would carve this wild young woman into an exem-

140

plary spy, one discrete enough to slip behind enemy lines unnoticed, bold enough to discover the enemy's secrets and courageous enough to get critical information to the men who needed it most. She was perfect. Or she would be. If she'd just stop kicking chairs and throwing pens.

Rose delivered a new pen to Belle. "Betty, you have two days to impress our cipher upon Miss Boyd's brain. On the third day, I'm sending you both across enemy lines."

The women gathered around the table and returned to work. Outside the birds sang in the trees, oblivious to the darkness in Rose Greenhow's parlor.

Chapter 13

Aug. 5-6, 1861
Guyandotte Ohio & Charleston Virginia

Kate sat in the back of the barouche feeling as grand as a sultan on tour. The carriage was glossy black with gold trim on its body and wheels befitting the grandness of an English lord. The main body of the carriage had room for four people on its two seats. Lacking companions Lord Tracy rode in solitary splendor with the collapsible half hood up to provide his lordship much-needed shade. Juba sat on the barouche's high front seat, handling the reins for a pair of matched black horses, both as glossy as the carriage. He maintained a soft conversation with the horses as they rolled along. Monty alternated between sitting in the back with Kate and perching on the front seat with Juba.

So far the day had gone well. She'd crawled from her bed at dawn and, after dressing in his lordship's casual suit, walked along the river for about a quarter mile, found a fallen log and used it for target practice. After a half hour she could hit what she aimed at some, if not all, of the time. Most importantly, she could reload the revolver without fumbling.

Kate yawned and yawned again on her walk back to the hotel. She nearly always had trouble sleeping while on a mission, but last night their innkeeper kept them up past midnight, regaling his Lordship with stories of Guyandotte's brief history. Five years previous an abolitionist established a mixed-race colony just west of the town, upsetting the pro-slavery Virginians already in the area. The two political poles split the town into warring factions. Then Virginia seceded, making Guyandotte part of the Confederacy until the Union Army arrived only weeks before and wrenched the town from Confederate control.

The Union Army still had control of this part of Virginia. A soft-spoken colonel warned his lordship that Union held territory ended just south of town, making travel in that direction unsafe. Lord Tracy blithely brushed off the colonel's warnings, assuring the man that his British citizenship would protect him from harm. Kate didn't mind that the colonel thought Lord Tracy was a fool. She agreed with the colonel.

They drove south after a meager breakfast on a road made of compacted rocks and gravel. The macadam surface made for a considerably less dusty drive than the day before. They left early enough that the air had been cool and fragrant with growing things. Even as the sun climbed higher in the sky, the day stayed pleasant, helped along by the fact that the road followed the tree-lined Guyandotte River all morning.

For lunch, they stopped at a farmhouse where a young woman sold them a half dozen ham biscuits and a small basket of last season's apples. They ate lunch in the woman's front yard, under the shade of a waxy leafed magnolia tree. The farm woman had been delighted to meet an English lord, at least until Monty chased her chickens. He didn't catch anything, but the ruckus caused their hostess considerable dismay. After the Great Chicken Caper the young woman frowned at his Lordship several times when she thought he wasn't looking.

Once they got back on the road Juba told Kate that the farmer's wife had taken him aside and offered him asylum. "I had to act like I didn't understand her meaning or she'd have freed me against my will." Juba chuckled at his story, but Kate could tell the abolitionist lady's efforts had gone a long way to making his slave act more tolerable.

That afternoon the road left the river and turned east, towards Charleston. The roadside woods grew denser as they rode into the Virginia foothills. With the afternoon sun at their back, the carriage's soft top provided Kate consistent shade. The warm air and gentle rocking of the carriage, and the white noise of the wheels on the gravel road, combined with a full stomach, lulled both Kate and Monty to sleep. She awoke when she felt the carriage slow. The length of the tree shadows told her it was late afternoon.

"We coming up on a sentry in the road," Juba said in a low voice. "Best wipe the drool off your chin and get your papers ready."

Kate looked down at her shirt front. *Good lord, I have drooled all over myself.* For a moment she was glad Hazzard wasn't here to see her, then changed her mind. He wasn't the sort of man to be put off by a little nap drool. She groped her upper lip, making sure her mustache was affixed and tugged on her gloves to hide her hands. Then she pulled out her little packet of papers and peered out the carriage door. She kept one hand on Monty's collar as they slowed. A wagon, guarded by a lone soldier, blocked the road. As Juba pulled the carriage to a stop a contingent of horsed soldiers, two in gray uniforms, two in blue, appeared from the trees at the side of the road.

145

One man in gray detached from the group and rode up to the barouche's door.

Kate kept a tight hold on Monty so he wouldn't jump out and frighten the horses. "May I help you, Sergeant," Kate asked, taking care to keep her voice low and relaxed. Monty wasn't so careful. His hackles came up as he issued a low growl. Kate gave his collar a little tug to shut him up.

"Present your pass. Please." The man had not taken care to keep his voice low and relaxed.

Kate pretended not to notice the Sergeant's crankiness. "I am unsure what you require sir. I do not carry a pass." She paused, pulled out her pocket watch, mostly so he could see it, and looked back at the soldier. "I'm traveling from New Orleans and am presently on my way to White Sulfur Springs to take the waters. We hoped to spend the night in Charleston."

"That's nice sir," the man said. "But you need a pass to enter the city."

"My good man," Lord Tracy pronounced, in his most officious voice. "I heard the States were a civilized place to visit. I was not aware that a Lord of the British Empire needed a pass to travel the public roads. Perhaps you could enlighten me? Was I misinformed?"

The sergeant shifted in his saddle and looked perplexed. "What?"

Juba spoke for the first time. "Sir, you are addressing Lord Tracy of Toddington. The *ninth* lord."

The sergeant paled and shifted on his horse again.

Lord Tracy doffed his hat at the poor soldier. "And allow me to introduce my valet and driver Lane, late of New Orleans." Kate figured her meaning was not lost on the sergeant. Lord Tracy wasn't just English aristocracy, he was a pro-

146

slavery aristocrat traveling the southern states with a slave he bought in New Orleans. Kate watched the poor man think, his gears grinding slowly but surely. *Just let us pass.* She sent her thoughts out to him, hoping just this once she could control a man with mind power.

The sergeant heaved a sigh. "I should take you to see the colonel. He can decide."

Kate pursed her lips in faux disapproval, hoping to disguise her delight. Lord Tracy would have more success with an officer.

"Lead on Macduff," she said with a grand wave of her gloved hand.

"Right this way yer Lordship," he said and turned his horse. Then he paused and over his shoulder said, "Only you got me confused with somebody else. I ain't Macduff. I'm O'Reilly. Sergeant O'Reilly."

He rode ahead of them. Kate watched Juba's shoulders shake with quiet laughter.

The sergeant escorted their carriage down the road a piece before asking Lord Tracy to disembark and follow him across a beaten down meadow filled with off-white military tents. At the meadow's far end stood a white, two-story farmhouse. O'Reilly told his Lordship to wait on the house's broad veranda while he checked on his colonel's availability. Kate took it all in, from the field artillery to the number of tents. She knew from Hazzard's artillery lessons she was looking at a row of twenty-year-old twelve-pounders. Despite their age, armies considered them an artillery workhorse. Fort Washington had a bunch of twelve-pounders on its lower walls, though the ones before her rode on sturdy wheels so a horse or mule could pull them.

Lord Tracy soon found himself seated in front of Colonel George Patton. The man had a high forehead, wavy brown hair, a matching beard and brown eyes. Though he looked no more than twenty-five years old, he wore an immaculate gray frock coat with gold stars at his collar.

The young colonel introduced himself and welcomed Lord Tracy to the First Kanawha Infantry Regiment.

Kate told Colonel Patton her story, emphasizing Lord Tracy's desire to spend time among the natural aristocrats of the South and enjoy Virginia's famous hot springs.

"My good sir, no Virginia gentleman would detain even the lowliest subject of England, let alone one of its lords." Patton paused, blushed a faint pink and asked, "But I should see your papers."

Kate passed her traveling credentials across Patton's desk, sure they would pass muster. The Pinkerton's New York forger was the best in the business.

Patton examined Lord Tracy's papers and declared them satisfactory. "I'll write you pass to Charleston, but once there you must see General Wise. He'll be the one to approve a pass on to White Sulfur Springs.

Kate tried not to appear as if she'd not almost peed her trousers. General Wise was ex-Virginia governor Henry Wise and the man who'd ordered abolitionist John Brown's execution. His reputation suggested he was not a nice man and would be less susceptible to an English Lord's travel needs than young Patton.

Patton then invited Lord Tracy to take dinner with him that evening. His lordship reciprocated with an offer to share some of the wine he'd brought from New Orleans.

Patton agreed to the plan and Lord Tracy ordered his slave to bring 3 bottles in from the carriage and stow them in the cellar. He also ordered his servant spend the evening in the kitchens with the slaves that cooked for the regiment's officers. Kate made Monty go with Juba, but only after the colonel admired the little black dog, tried to pet him and was nearly bitten for his efforts. Though she admired Monty's dislike of Confederate army officers, Kate didn't need the little beast foiling her plan to coax secrets out of the young colonel.

When Lord Tracy's servant and the dog left the room Kate turned to Patton. "Now sir, while the wine cools, perhaps you could take me on a tour?"

As they walked, Patton talked. A lot. He proudly explained that he'd designed his regiment's uniforms himself and from there launched into a detailed description of the regiment's defense of the turnpike and James River. They also toured the fortifications his troops had thrown up north of the camp and explained that he and his 900 men could defend against 10,000 Union soldiers. Kate scrambled to remember everything the young man said.

Over dinner, Patton grew even more voluble, particularly after Lord Tracy favorably compared the Confederate fortifications with English fortifications in the Crimea. Of course, multiple bottles of champagne didn't hurt either. After dinner, a bevy of majors and captains joined them, each with their own flask. Before midnight the well-lubricated officers acted out regimental drills, all with explanations about how the drills prepared the enlisted men for particular battle strategies. Kate was hard pressed to believe her luck

The next morning Lord Tracy thanked his host for his remarkable hospitality and handed him a letter. "I wonder if you would mind posting this. As you see, it's addressed to my good friend, Congressman Vallandigham." The two men agreed the Confederacy had no greater friend in the North than Vallandigham.

"I'll have my aid put your letter in the morning post." Patton held out his hand. "Perhaps we might meet again someday my Lord."

Lord Tracy made a small bow. "God willing, Colonel. I thank you for the most remarkable evening I've had in a long time." Kate had never said anything truer. She hoped General Wise would prove half so amenable.

It turned out he was not.

It began harmlessly enough. The road was smooth, the weather pleasant, the scenery lush and green. Charleston, which turned out to be a little town of brick and white clapboard buildings. They crossed a sturdy stone bridge, past a pretty Episcopalian church and down the town's main street. Soldiers crowded the streets, most of them rougher looking than the soldiers they'd seen mustering in Washington.

A group of rough fellows stopped and stared as Lord Tracy's equipage rolled past. One bearded man made a display of spitting a large wad of chaw onto the sidewalk at Lord Tracy's passing. Determined to appear unimpressed, Kate asked Juba to stop the carriage. The conversation between the spitter and

Lord Tracy was not a congenial talk, but his Lordship did pry the local hotel's whereabouts from the man.

Two uniformed officers stood in front of the Kanawha House Hotel when Juba stopped the carriage. Both wore gray though only one carried a shotgun crooked over his arm. Juba glanced over his shoulder at Kate, crooking his eyebrow in a question. She nodded and he dismounted to open the carriage door. Kate mustered her Lord Tracy, tipped his silk hat at the men and glided past the both sentinels and into the hotel. Kate paused in the doorway as her eyes adjusted to the dim light of the hotel's front desk foyer. She identified the front desk and clerk and asked for a room.

"I'm sorry sir," the round-faced man said with evident relish, "but my hotel is booked by General Wise's staff." He looked over Kate's shoulder as he spoke. She turned and saw the shotgun-wielding officer standing in the doorway behind her. He appeared to be doing his best impression of a dangerous man.

In her loudest, most English lord voice Kate announced, "That is most unfortunate. Colonel Patton directed me here, knowing how anxious General Wise would be to make the acquaintance of the Ninth Lord Tracy of Toddington. I should hate to return to London with reports of how the Confederacy made me unwelcome."

The shotgun wielder turned, glanced at the gleaming black and gold barouche, with its top-hatted driver, then back at Lord Tracy. The innkeeper saw the glossy carriage too. It turned out the inn had an empty room after all.

An hour later a dark-skinned porter delivered Lord Tracy's trunk to his room. Juba unpacked while his Lordship had a talk with the shotgun-wielding officer, whose attitude had become less hostile and more toady. Lord Tracy learned he would meet General Wise at dinner that evening. His lordship also learned that while the hotel had a room for an English Lord, it did not have room for black servants. The porter directed Juba to the stable out back. Juba tipped Kate a wink before he left and promised to be back in time to help his lordship dress for dinner.

Kate used the interim hours to stroll around Charleston. The town was smaller than she'd expected and chock full of Confederate military personnel. An hour or two spent in a bar down the street, nursing a whiskey garnered her a host of informational tidbits from well-lubricated soldiers. She learned General Wise had alienated the town when he usurped the local government with a high-handed zeal. He compounded his unpopularity when he tried to take a widow woman's home as his headquarters. The lady refused to vacate the house and he'd threatened to burn her out. The doughty lady held her ground, protecting her house with an old shotgun. Wise had to locate his headquarters at the hotel, much to the delight of the locals.

Lord Tracy also discovered Wise had a regiment of 1600 men just to the north and another 1000 men stationed to the southeast where they controlled the road to White Sulfur Springs and Richmond, effectively blocking the only southerly route out of town.

As she walked back to the hotel Kate couldn't shake the uncomfortable feeling she and Juba had driven into a trap.

Chapter 14

August 6-8, 1861
Charleston, Virginia

esplendent in Lord Tracy's black superfine coat and red calfskin boots, Kate stepped into the hotel dining room, determined to beard the lion in his den. The innkeeper directed his lordship to a table across the room from the General's table. From the shrimp bisque to bread pudding, Wise ignored the English lord dining on the other side of the room. When a pair of white-gloved, black-skinned waiters cleared desert Lord Tracy rose and approached the General.

Kate planted herself in front of the general and made a formal bow. In response, Wise leaned back in his chair and, cigar in hand, and spoke to the other men at his table. He waved his huge black cigar about, leaving trails of pungent smoke like a purgatory escapee, all the while ignoring the man standing before his table. After a long minute Wise turned his gaze to the English lord. When he did Kate had to fight the impulse to step back. The general had deep-set, black eyes as cruel as any bird of prey. A large beaky nose presided over a steel gray chin beard that failed to hide thin, pinched lips.

This was no toothless lion, but a hardened old beast capable of wily misdirection and casual cruelties.

"General Wise, I presume. Allow me to introduce myself. I am Lord Tracy of Toddington." Kate laid one of his Lordship's calling cards on Wise's table.

Wise nodded his head like a potentate considering whether to lop off a clumsy servant's head. Kate stood her ground. They scrutinized each other like a cobra and a mongoose.

Wise ground out his cigar and heaved himself to his feet. He held out his hand. "Brigadier General Henry Wise, at your service. What brings you to Charleston in the middle of a war?"

He didn't add "you damn fool," but the sentiment was clear in the general's intonation and facial expression. *So much for the pleasantries.* Kate coughed delicately into the handkerchief she had grasped in her hand. "There was no war when I made my travel plans. My health is not what I would wish and was told that White Sulfur Springs offered revivifying effects rivaling those of the great resorts at Bath."

"English are you?"

Kate tried not to laugh. The general had mastered the art of being unimpressed. She tipped her head. "Just so. As I said, I am Lord Tracy. I thought a man of your standing would help me reach my destination." Kate noted that Lord Tracy was an accomplished flatterer.

"Well, I might." Wise walked away from his dining companions without a word or look back. Kate followed and moments later found herself in a small downstairs hotel room that had been converted to an office.

Wise waved Lord Tracy toward a chair and took his own seat behind a paper-laden desk. He took a cigar from a box on his desk and lit it. He did not offer one to his guest. "I assume you want a pass?"

"Yes, sir." Kate dug into her jacket pocket and withdrew the pass she'd used to get into Charleston. "Colonel Patton issued me a pass for Charleston and directed me to you for further guidance." Kate held the paper out to General Wise.

He waved it away, squinting at his lordship as he did. "Are you unaware that there's a war on sir?"

"I understand your confusion General. As I said, my travel plans were made well over a year ago. I sailed from Liverpool six months ago. At the time there was no war. And now I am loath to return without a full exploration of your new nation."

Wise snorted. "That's exactly what I'm worried about Sir."

Lord Tracy reared back his head and squinted at the general. "Do you call my honor into question sir?" Affront filled every word. Lord Tracy pushed back his chair and stood. Kate twitched her upper lip, causing her mustache to bristle. Or at least she hoped that was what it was doing.

Wise sat up as if he'd just realized he'd insulted a member of the English aristocracy. He stubbed out his cigar and waved Lord Tracy back to his seat. "I am not accusing you of anything, your Lordship. But these western counties are full of Copperhead traitors. They'll invite the enemy in, feed him, shelter him, arm him. There is a spy at every farm and in every home from Charleston to Richmond. I cannot be too careful."

"General, you have my word as a gentleman I am not a traitor to your cause." Kate felt comfortable in her vow, seeing how she wasn't a man, let alone a gentleman.

"I understand, but I must use every precaution or fail this new nation," Wise said. He pressed his lips together so tightly they nearly disappeared.

"I see General. Even a man such as myself may fall under suspicion." Lord Tracy stood back up, pulled down his waistcoat and turned to go. There was no point in alienating the old snake before she got what she wanted. "Perhaps I should apply to the British embassy in Richmond for a travel permit?" Kate realized her mistake the second the words were out of her mouth.

Wise harrumphed, then stood. "Perhaps you should." He knocked his fist on the top of his desk and bowed. Lord Tracy had been dismissed.

Kate walked nonchalantly up the stairs and down the hall to her room, taking care not to hurry. Her heart galloped in her chest, threatening to over-take her reason. Did he know? Had he seen through her disguise? Why else would he be so rude? Or was he always so nasty?

She stepped into her room. Juba lounged in the corner chair, a book in his hands, Monty tucked in between his leg and the chair arm.

Monty jumped down to greet her with a soft woof. Kate sat on the bed and patted it. The little dog leapt onto the bed, circled once and settled in next to Kate.

"Innkeeper ain't gonna like a dog on one of his beds," Juba said in a lazy drawl. He closed his book and put it on the side table.

"I thought you were banished to the stable."

"Us nigrah valets are allowed in da' big house 'till Massa done got hisself upstairs. Cain't expect you fancy white fellers to undress yourselves, now can we?"

"A fair point, but there's no way you're going to undress me."

Juba dropped his slave patois. "I should hope not. Too bad I can't send Captain Hazzard up for that task."

"Juba!" Kate pretended ladylike outrage, but her heart sped up again. Why did even talking about Hazzard threaten her composure? Damn the man.

"I take it you had trouble with General Wise?"

"Aargh," Kate groaned. She told him about how the general ignored Lord Tracy during dinner and all but insulted him in their interview afterward. She finished her story with her fear he was on to her.

"And I can't apply to the British consul for help. They'll know there's no such person as Lord Tracy of Toddington. I don't know why I said it."

Juba shook his head. "I been talking to the servants. Wise is a right bastard. I'd be willing to bet he's giving you a hard time just because he can."

Kate stood up and peeled off her evening coat. "Either way, he's not inclined to let Lord Tracy go traipsing about the Virginia countryside."

Juba helped her pull off her boots. She groaned as they came off her feet. The lifts in them made her feet hurt like the dickens.

"The good news," Juba said as he opened his boot polish kit, "is that I might have found a way around the old devil. Word is he's in a power struggle with General Floyd.

"Floyd? Not John Floyd?" Kate's eyebrows stretched up in astonishment.

"The same."

Peg A. Lamphier

Kate and Juba looked at each other over Lord Tracy's boots. Last December they'd discovered a plot to kidnap then-president Buchanan. At about the same time Buchanan discovered Floyd had been raiding the war department, diverting federal money and military equipment to pro-slavery states. He'd also been implicated in the theft of bonds worth thousands from the Department of the Interior, money intended for Indian schools in the west. Buchanan forced Floyd's resignation and let the presumptive kidnappers think he believed Floyd was the problem. Buchanan had known the truth, but blaming Floyd and getting rid of him solved a host of problems and rid the federal government of a man so crooked he had to screw his pants on each morning. Though they'd played a central role in Floyd's disgrace, neither Kate nor Juba had ever met the man.

Juba flipped is boot brush in his hand and brushed a boot. "Wise and Floyd hate each other. Floyd was governor of Virginia before Wise, about ten years ago. The feud goes back at least that far. Anyway, the Confederate war department assigned both men to this county. To make matters worse, they're both brigadier generals, so there's wrangling about who's senior and in charge. And Wise hurt his case when he allowed General McClellan to push him south about two weeks ago. That's how he ended up here in Charleston."

Kate sat cross-legged on the bed, rubbing her tired feet, but looked up to catch the gleam in Juba's eye. "So where's Floyd now?"

Juba grinned. "About a half day's ride. just outside of Fayetteville. We could be there and back tomorrow and no one the wiser. Especially if we left that big carriage here."

"Horses?"

158

"Got 'em. These mountain fellers are horseflesh rich and cash poor. A couple of men came to a cash understanding with his Lordships' valet."

Kate smiled. "And if someone does notice we're gone they won't question it. People expect the aristocracy to waste time riding around for no reason." She jumped up and kissed him soundly on the cheek. "You're a wonder Juba."

"That I am," he agreed. He set Lord Tracy's gleaming boots on the floor, rose and kissed the top of Kate's head, wished her goodnight and left. She could hear him whistling all the way out to the barn.

Juba knocked on her door just after dawn. Kate checked her reflection in the small dressing mirror. The muskrat mustache took some effort to re-affix each morning and she didn't always get it on straight the first try. Juba wordlessly handed her a mug of coffee and a ham biscuit, both of which she made short work of as they made their way to the stables.

They took a small road out of Charleston that meandered through a wood of oak and poplar. The trees grew so large they created a verdant archway above the road. Lush green grasses and shrubberies took up the space between tree trunks. A small river glimpsed through the trees, burbled off to their left. At mid-morning Confederate sentries stopped them, but Patton's' pass and a story of how an English Lord wanted to meet a former Buchanan cabinet secretary, opened the way.

They'd tried to leave Monty back at the inn, but he declined to cooperate. Instead, he demonstrated his skill at horseback riding, leaping up to Kate's booted foot and from there launching himself up to the saddle. He settled in be-

159

tween her legs, rear end on the saddle, front paws on her right thigh. As they rode along, he would periodically leap down and run alongside the horses, treeing errant squirrels with great fits of high pitched barking.

They reached Floyd's encampment well before the lunch hour. Another meadow full of pole and canvas tents spread out before them. Lord Tracy once again presented his pass, this time to a pimple-faced private and asked to speak to General Floyd. Flustered by the sudden appearance of someone as grand as Lord Tracy in the backwoods of western Virginia, the young man took them straight away to a set of larger white tents marked "Regimental Headquarters."

Kate heaved herself off her horse, resisting the temptation to rub her behind. There was nothing she loathed more than riding side saddle but riding astride presented its own agonies. They waited while the private stepped into the center tent. After a moment he stepped out and motioned Kate inside.

Lord Tracy handed his reins to his servant, commanding him to water and rub down the horses while he waited. A faint "Yassuh, Massa," came from him as Milord stepped into the general's headquarters. From the corner of her eye, Kate saw Juba grab Monty so he didn't follow her.

Floyd sat at a small wooden field desk, two folding chairs arrayed before him. He had a Turkish carpet on the ground and a narrow rope bed off to the side. Lord Tracy swept off his hat as he approached Floyd, who pushed himself to his feet, moving like an aged dog awoken from his nap. His resemblance to an elderly hound extended to his face where his eyes and cheeks drooped in the manner of a man not unacquainted with dissipation.

160

Once again Kate introduced the ninth Lord Tracy of Toddington.

Floyd eyed his visitor and said, "Well, ain't you a little small for such a big name?"

Kate sighed. She was developing a healthy appreciation for the difficulties faced by smaller than average men. She took a chance with her answer. "It's never hurt me much with the ladies. They prefer a tall title to a tall man." Lord Tracy winked at the general as he spoke.

General Floyd guffawed in surprise and gestured for her to take a seat. "Well, at least you aren't a namby-pamby fellow. What brings you here, sir?"

Kate told her story again, finishing with the rather rude treatment Lord Tracy met at the hands of General Wise.

Floyd shook his head. "Wise is misnamed. He's a fool who sees spies everywhere. He's jailed dozens of men in this county alone and alienated just about everyone, even his own men."

They were in the midst of a congenial talk about Wise's shortcomings when Monty burst into the tent and launched himself onto Lord Tracy's lap. Kate grabbed the little black dog by his scruff to prevent him sailing off the other side.

"What's this!" Floyd's eyes sparkled with delight. "This your little feller?"

Lord Tracy petted Monty's head and admitted it was his dog.

"Where did you get him?"

Kate's mind scrambled for a story. "I won him in a steamboat poker game between New Orleans and Memphis. I was going to dump him overboard, but he's grown on me."

"I should say so," Floyd said. He stood, walked around his desk and approached Monty. "May I?" He held out his hands.

161

Kate nodded, patted Monty's head and handed him over to the general.

Floyd ran his hands over the little dog, then rubbed Monty behind his ears. Monty relaxed under Floyd's hand.

"You've got a way with dogs Sir," Lord Tracy said.

"Oh, he's a fine little fellow. A classic Mountain Feist and a southern dog through and through. You're lucky to have him. Game little buggers. Tell me, does he chase varmints up trees pretty good?"

Lord Tracy grinned. "How did you know?"

"I had me one of these when I was a boy. Scout. He was little like your feller and the other boys like to make fun of me and him, but when he got to squirrel and coon hunting, no dog could beat him. Good old Scout." Floyd got a little misty and hugged Monty close. The little dog wriggled in the General's arms, clearly finding this hugging thing beneath his canine dignity.

Kate gave Monty a stern look. This was no time to be a bad dog. Monty looked whole-heartedly innocent, as only a dog can do. Kate took it to mean he agreed to a nice.

Floyd handed Monty back to Kate and returned to his desk. "Tell you what. I will write you that pass for Richmond, for two reasons. First, I like your dog. Second, it'll tweak ole Wise if I do." He picked up his pen, rifled through the papers on his desk and found what he was looking for. "But I warn you," he said as he wrote, "The old bastard is as likely to tear this here pass up as he is to honor it, so use it wisely." Floyd realized what he said and guffawed again.

Kate left Floyd's tent under a pall of befuddlement. She knew the man was a pro-slavery fanatic and a political conniver, thief and embezzler, but she liked him. And so did Monty.

They made it back to Charleston in time for dinner. Lord Tracy passed General Wise in the hotel lobby, but the General ostentatiously took no notice of his lordship, which was fine with Kate. On the way back to town they'd discussed their strategy.

"I'd like to just make a run for it, but it's a bad idea," Kate said. "Wise is likely to detain us, particularly if we're carrying a pass signed by Floyd."

Juba agreed. "What we need is a distraction. The pass will only work if his men don't get a direct order from the general himself and that means he needs to not notice our going."

Kate thought a moment. "If our letter got through to Allan, it might encourage the Union army to make a move south. That would distract Wise."

"You think we can get another letter through?"

They agreed to try. When they got back to the hotel Lord Tracy took dinner in his rooms and caught up on his correspondence while Juba returned the hired horses and found his own dinner.

Several hours later Juba knocked on his lordship's hotel door and entered. "I came up to get milord ready for bed, but I've changed my mind."

Kate crooked an eyebrow at Juba.

"Weeeell," he drawled. "I passed the hotel bar on my way up the stairs. "The place is full of Confederate officers. They're well in their cups."

Kate smiled. "Methinks Lord Tracy is thirsty." She rose, slipped on her coat, checked her mustache and straightened her cravat. "You wait here. I'll be back in an hour." After his success with Floyd, Monty went with her.

Lord Tracy's second visit to a drinking establishment proved as rewarding as his first. He joined a bevy of officers at the hotel bar, most of them young men engaged in a hearty round of complaining about their General, though they did interrupt themselves to admire Monty. Once Kate answered all the dog-related questions flung at her the officers returned to their previous conversations. They thought their general over-cautious, over-suspicious and under-prepared to lead an army. Lord Tracy shared his own sad story and everyone agreed that the small English Lord's own story of woe was unfortunate and uncalled for. United by whiskey, the men agreed that an English lord was a natural companion for southern gentlemen. The men also thought English guns might soon help turn the tide of the war. It was an idea his Lordship might have given them.

The men also told a story about how Wise summoned Colonel Patton to the hotel earlier that day. According to Wise's aide-de-camp, a plumply pink young man in a too-tight officer's tunic, Patton backed up Lord Tracy's story of their meeting. Rather than reassuring the General, Patton's information made Wise cranky.

The young men ended the evening by issuing an invitation for Lord Tracy to visit their camp tomorrow. Major Wright promised to call for Lord Tracy in the afternoon and treat him to a tour of nearby fortifications, a dress parade and a round of artillery practice.

Lord Tracy retired to his rooms exhausted and tipsy. Kate flung herself on the bed and watched the room spin, pleased enough with Lord Tracy's evening to attempt a song. She could hear it fine in her head but had trouble getting it out. Meanwhile, Juba pried her boots off and rolled her out of her jacket and waistcoat before pulling a blanket over her and leaving her in darkness.

Before she fell into a drunken sleep, she made a note to find Monty a meaty bone as a reward. It was clear to Kate that Virginia gentlemen liked dogs more than they liked foreign aristocrats.

Just as promised, Major Wright rode up to the Kanawha House Hotel at the dot of 2 PM with an extra horse in tow. Kate stood up from her seat on the hotel's front porch, squinting into the sun at Lord Tracy's escort. Though the major was only two or three years younger than Kate's twenty-six years, he vaulted from his saddle as if unaffected by the gallons of whiskey and beer he'd consumed last night. Kate hadn't been able to do much more than hide her head under her pillow and moan into the sheets all morning. About noon Juba brought her two pieces of dry toast and a small pot of coffee. Then he washed her hair in a basin of cool water. It felt heavenly and by the time she dressed and took herself downstairs she felt almost human.

Her hangover proved worth every throb and stomach twinge when Major Wright treated Lord Tracy like a long-lost friend. They took a two-mile ride to the major's encampment, where his Lordship enjoyed a tour that outdid the one he'd taken with Colonel Patton. When they arrived the enlisted

165

men were lining up for dress parade, though their ragged appearance belied both 'dress' and 'parade.' Almost all the men were unshaven and none of them wore uniforms. They looked like the farmers and laborers they were, wearing an assortment of homespun, handmade clothing and sporting hats that looked to have seen quite a lot of outdoor activity. Wright's colonel explained his regiment's rationing system, including a verbal treatise of the yeoman farmer's nutritional needs. After a series of poorly, but enthusiastically executed drills the colonel dismissed the men. Major Wright took Lord Tracy on a tour of earthwork fortifications. Some of the earthworks had tangles of felled trees and shrubberies about 50 yards in front of them. Kate couldn't help but be impressed with the hard labor that had gone into the whole arrangement of ditches and dirt walls and she tried not to think about the men who would die should these structures come to use.

Though the entire afternoon turned out to be an intelligence bonanza, though Kate had trouble concentrating. All she could think about was getting out of town. They'd been in Charleston for three days and still had no escape plan. A mental clock ticked relentlessly in Kate's head, every minute another opportunity for Rose Greenhow to undermine the Union army with her intelligence network. Tick, tick, tick.

That evening Lord Tracy wrote yet another letter to Mr. Vallandigham. Anxiety pecked away at her as she wrote. Juba must have noticed because he left Monty with her for the evening. Tucked into bed with her dog, Kate decided. They'd try to get out of Charleston tomorrow, General Wise be damned.

166

Chapter 15

August 9-11, 1861
Western Virginia

he echo of thumping boot steps woke Kate with a start. She rolled over and looked out the window. The weak light of almost dawn limped through the glass. Crowd sounds came from the street in front of the hotel. She pushed herself out of bed and looked out the open window. Uniformed officers, some horsed, some not, milled in front of the hotel, clogging the street in the predawn light.

Hmmm.

A knock came at her door. She opened it to find Juba. "What's going on?"

He grinned at her. "Cox's army is on the move. He's coming this way."

"Cox?"

"He's in charge of the Kanawha Brigade under McClellan."

"Oh, right," Kate said, feeling stupid. She really ought to memorize the army's command structure.

"Wise is taking his army out to meet him." Juba paused and grinned. "Moving northwest."

"So we should head southeast." Kate looked around the room. "Give me ten minutes to get dressed and pack up."

"Slow down missy. Wise is downstairs. Stay in your room, out of sight." He gestured at the room's window. "The minute he leaves town I'll harness the horses and we'll high-tail it out of here." Juba left Kate alone in her room. The minutes ticked by with excruciating slowness.

Not long after dawn General Wise took his army and marched out of town. Juba and Kate had no trouble clearing the sentries on the eastern road, not after they flashed Floyd's pass.

Kate spent the morning expecting Wise's soldiers to catch up with them and turn them back to town, but Floyd's pass worked its magic at every roadblock. After dark, covered in dust, they arrived in White Sulfur Springs. A sign on the outskirt of town read "Welcome to the Queen City of Watering Places." Eager to get to Richmond, Kate wanted to avoid the town's famous resort and push on. Juba pointed out they'd need to describe the resort with some accuracy if asked about their reason for traveling in Virginia. Plus Richmond was still two days drive away.

They approached the resort's hotel along an oak-lined winding lane that gave way to a formal English garden. The scent of flowers filled the evening air as they rolled up to the hotel. A row of elegant white cottages lay off to the right, their small size emphasizing the main building's grandiosity.

"Wow," Kate said in a low voice intended only for Juba.

He turned and looked back at her from his perch on the driver's seat. "Wow is right."

She knew from Allan's briefing letter that a consortium of wealthy Virginians had recently refurbished the main building. It loomed up against the darkening sky, a huge, many-columned, multiple storied architectural mongrel somewhere between Greek Revival and Ostentatious Wealth. Kate could see how rich plantation owners and their families would flock to such a place.

With the war just down the road, the hotel had plenty of vacancies. Lord Tracy took a suite on the second floor large enough to include a small room for his valet and dog. The suite's sitting room had a thick blue and cream carpet, blue velvet drapes and shining mahogany wainscoting. It looked like heaven and Kate couldn't wait to leave it. Once they'd taken delivery of his lordship's trunk Kate shut the door and leaned against it.

"How long do we have to stay?"

Juba scrubbed at his face. "I'd rather be in Richmond too."

"I have an idea," Kate said with a wicked grin.

He smiled back at her. "When do you not, my dear?"

The next day Lord Tracy rose to a leisurely breakfast and then he took himself off to the hot springs fed baths. There he engaged a small room where he might soak in privacy. Meanwhile, his valet Lane and dog drove into town to buy boot polish and hair tonic. At least that's what Juba told the hotel porter.

Three hours later he returned, waving a telegram envelope in the air. He approached the desk and inquired after his lordship's whereabouts, all but wringing his hands in a parody of anxiety. A somber clerk located Lord Tracy at his lunch on the west verandah.

169

"Thank goodness I've found you, your lordship," Juba said in a voice loud enough for the ladies at the next table to overhear him. "There was a telegram waiting for you in town."

Lord Tracy sighed a bored sigh and held out his hand for the envelope. He tore it opened, glanced at it and swore. "This is damnable news. I've only just arrived." He sighed and tucked the envelope into his coat pocket. "King and country must come first."

Once in the suite, Kate turned to Juba. "So it's all right?"

"Easy peasy," Juba said with a smile. "I had this whole elaborate story concocted, but there were four people in the telegram office when I walked in. And a pile of blank telegram forms and envelopes right there on the table, ripe for the taking."

Kate drew the envelope out of her pocket and handed it back to Juba. "You better burn this so a maid doesn't find it and wonder why his lordship left a blank telegram laying around."

Lord Tracy's valet informed the chief desk clerk that the British consul in Richmond required Lord Tracy's presence. Within the hour their carriage was out front with the trunk strapped to the back.

That night they stayed at a small coaching inn outside a tiny town called Clifton Forge. The next day they made it to Charlottesville. Kate knew they were pushing the horses too hard but she couldn't bring herself to slow their trip. They could rest in Richmond.

For the last leg of their journey to Richmond, they took the oddly named Three Chopt Road. On their way out of Charlottesville, they passed Monticello, which sat on the south side of the road, on a small rise.

"Pretty isn't it," Kate said from her seat at the rear of the barouche. Monty put his white toes on the carriage door and stared at the house. Kate suspected he smelled something he wished he could chase.

Juba snorted. "If you like houses paid for with slave labor."

Kate stared at the grand brick and white columned house on the hill. She'd read somewhere that president Jefferson kept a slave woman as his concubine and had a handful of children with her. Monticello, like the fancy resort in White Sulfur Springs and every other grand building and house they'd passed, was built from the profits of slavery. They were pretty things hiding an ugly reality. For all the pro-slavery people's protestations of the benign nature of their peculiar institution, there was nothing noble about denying an entire group of people's freedom. Nor was there anything commendable about a system where men owned women. Any man could be corrupted by power.

And all the talk about the supposed inferiority of black people was, at least in her estimation, complete nonsense. No one she'd ever met was smarter, kinder or more dedicated to doing right than the man driving Lord Tracy's carriage. No one.

And even if the slavery people were right, that blacks weren't as intellectually capable as white folks, it still wasn't fair. She remembered a speech she'd read in the newspaper a few years ago, one given by a black woman at a woman's rights convention in Ohio. The woman, who called herself Sojourner Truth, pointed out that no one treated black women like they were delicate flowers or ornaments of the home. She could work as hard as any man and had. She'd mocked notions of female delicacy by her very presence.

171

Truth was right. Men were always saying women weren't smart enough or strong enough for equality. Same with black folk. But if they were right, shouldn't a just nation help those less capable, instead of enslaving and oppressing them? Didn't democracy demand tolerance and kindness? And why didn't democracy create tolerance and kindness? Was it that hateful thinking was easier? Were people better at hate than love? Hate seemed to come easier to a lot of folks. And didn't hate and the love of power kill democracy? The very democracy these people said they were trying to protect?

Maybe that's why she did what she did. Because she wanted her country to be fairer and kinder. Or maybe she just didn't want to be someone's wife, bored to death, trapped in a house, washing diapers and cooking dinners for a man who, according to the law, owned her body, her work, her children, her life. And weren't the two reasons really the same?

Chapter 16

August 12, 1861
Richmond, Virginia

*K*ate stared over the carriage door. She'd expected yet another quiet southern town, but from what she'd seen the new capital of the Confederacy was as vital as wartime Washington. Maybe even more so. Juba brought them into town on Brook Run Road, which turned into Brook Street, an angled throughway that cut diagonally across streets set out on a square grid, not unlike the big avenues in Washington. Along the way, they'd passed two foundries, three tobacco factories, and a nail smithy. The buildings holding these concerns were open to the street, offering passers-by a glimpse of the multitudes of dark-skinned men that toiled inside.

"I'd forgotten how black this city is," Juba commented over his shoulder. About half the people they saw were black or mulatto though whether they were slaves or free blacks was impossible to know.

Kate, who was tired of riding in the back of the little carriage, dug around in her carpetbag. As she pulled out a tattered envelope she asked, "You've been here before?"

"Yep. Southern folk love a minstrel show. The Pelham Serenaders played this city a dozen times, back in the early fifties. You've been here too. You were just a little mite, not much higher than Monty." Juba patted the little dog's head. Monty struggled with the carriage ride, torn between riding in the back, snuggled against Kate's leg and riding up front with Juba, where he could put his feet on the splashboard and keep an eye on everything around him. He'd been jumping between the two positions since they'd rolled into Richmond.

"Was that one of Mr. Rice's shows?" Before they died Kate's parents worked for a handful of circus owners, but Dan Rice remained her favorite for a lot of reasons. And he'd helped rescue Juba this past spring.

Juba shook his head. "I got to tell you, I can't remember. It was that summer when you gave your first performance up in Washington. We moved south after that, performing in all the decent sized towns."

Kate smiled at Juba's back. She only vaguely remembered her first ventures into the circus ring, standing on the back of a horse as it cantered around the ring, but she did remember the look on Momma and Poppa's faces as she rode circles around them. She sighed, opened the envelope and extracted a sheaf of papers, thumbing through them for Allan's instructions.

"Do you know the Spotswood Hotel? Allan says Lord Tracy would stay there."

Juba shook his head. "Nope. I expect it's new. I'll ask someone."

Brook Street ended at Broad Street, which was as broad as its name suggested and full of wagons, carriages, and people.

Juba called over to a dark-skinned man dressed in the ragged clothes of a working man and asked him for directions.

The man peered into the back of the carriage at Lord Tracy, who ignored him. "The Spotswood jess the sort of place for your Massa. Jess go on down the street here and turn toward the river at the street just past the theater where the train stops. It'll be down there, past the capitol. You'll know it when you see it. It be a carriage trade sorta place."

Juba thanked the man and clucked the horses back into a walk. They passed a variety of shops, businesses, and small factories as they make their way down Broad. Wagons crowded the streets and people filled the city sidewalks. Only the churches they passed seemed quiet and she suspected that was only because it was Monday.

Seven blocks down they came to the train depot. Like the depot in Cincinnati, this depot was open on both ends. Trains pulled in, turned on a large half circle loop, before going out the way they'd come in. Kate often wondered why railroad companies didn't cooperate in building central depots, instead of this plethora of depots, one for each rail line, with the terminuses blocks and even miles apart. If this war went on like Hattie thought it would people would come to regret this willy-nilly railroad arrangement. The Union army lost the battle of Bull Run for a lot of reasons, but she knew chief among them was that Confederate General Johnston had put his Shenandoah Valley Army on a train and moved them to Manassas far faster than any army could have marched. But moving troops and supplies that way would be hard in cities where the depots weren't connected or even close together.

"We're here, Milord," Juba announced.

Kate jerked her head up. While she'd been musing on railroad logistics they'd arrived at the Spotswood Hotel. Once again, Richmond astonished her. The hotel was almost as big as Washington's massive Willard Hotel and considerably newer. The window glass sparkled in the sun and the exterior woodwork had that fresh, just painted look.

White-gloved bellmen ran up to the carriage as Juba pulled it to a stop in front of the hotel. Juba stepped down from the carriage and once again the two of them enacted their Lord and slave performance as they entered the hotel. The desk clerk informed Juba that rooms were $3 a night and suites $5.

"A room sir?" Juba drew back his head in pretend shock. "For Lord Tracy? His lordship will need your best suite."

Kate nodded in the clerk's direction and returned to looking bored.

While Juba took care of the pesky realities of money, luggage delivery and stable needs for the horses, Kate wandered over to the doorway of the dining room. Darn. They'd just missed breakfast and dinner service didn't start until 3. The menu had oyster soup, lamb, veal, turkey, ham, potatoes baked and boiled, rice, beets, pound cake with custard sauce and more on it. Her stomach rumbled. The dry biscuit she'd eaten at the coaching inn this morning was long gone. Then Kate remembered room service and felt immeasurably better.

An hour later, with the trunk unpacked and a platter of sandwiches laid to waste, Kate once again drew out her sheaf of notes from Allan and handed a page to Juba.

"The Richmond directives," she said.

He studied the pertinent page, then looked up. "You don't suppose he's kidding do you?"

176

Kate shook her head. She should have told him sooner but the last few days they'd moved from one crisis to another. Now she wished she'd already discussed it.

He shook the paper at her. "It's madness. If we're caught, they'll most likely hang us."

"True. But Mr. Lincoln asked us to try. So we will. We'll walk right into Libby Prison and find Congressman Ely. And gather enough intelligence so that someone can come back later and break him out."

Juba shook his head.

Kate laughed a dry, humorless laugh. "It gets worse. I met Congressman Ely the day he got himself captured."

Juba's eyes widened. "What if he recognizes you?"

Kate shrugged. What if, indeed?

Libby Prison hunched on its corner like a sleeping beast. It looked like what it was, a former warehouse, made grimmer by its three stories of barred windows and guards at every exterior door.

From the hotel, they'd walked down Carey Street, past a row of tobacco warehouses, a machine shop full of smoke and the sounds of hammering, and a tired-looking tenement building that proclaimed itself the Richmond Poor House.

"You know how up north the rich folk visit asylums and prisons just to see the poor unfortunates?"

Kate saw where Juba was going. "That's genius. I can be one of those despicable people who tour other people's misery for entertainment."

Juba grinned. "The poorhouse gave me the idea."

Lord Tracy and his valet presented himself to the soldiers stationed outside Libby's wide front doors and requested an audience with the prison's commanding officer. A private showed them into a makeshift waiting room. A clerk in lieutenant's bars sat at a small desk before a door. He commanded them to wait and then ignored them, returning his attention to an account book on the desk before him.

Lord Tracy's valet dusted off a section of the wooden bench with a lawn handkerchief before his lordship would sit. A young woman with soft brown skin sat on another bench, head down, two covered baskets at her feet. After a few moments, a door at the far end of the room opened. A lady stepped out, followed by a man in uniform, his hand hovering at her waist as if he wanted to push her out the door but dared not touch her.

The lady was small, Kate noted, even shorter than her own five foot, four inches. She wore a plain dark brown dress, but it fitted her slim form in a manner that hinted at expensive tailoring. Her dark blond hair was pulled back into a soft bun, from which curls escaped, softening her facial features, which were elfin sharp. Her chin jutted like a lady accustomed to getting her way.

Lord Tracy popped to his feet as the lady entered the room. The woman glanced over at him and dismissed him, turning her attention back to the man behind her.

"Thank you general," she said in a voice both soft and unyielding, like an iron hand in a satin glove. "Mother and I believe Christian charity should extend to all God's creatures, even poor benighted Yankees. I am grateful that you are sufficiently a gentleman to agree with us." She glanced over at the young woman, who rose and carried the two baskets over to her.

Kate watched the general kiss the lady's hand. His face was a magnificent wreck of sagging skin, drooping eyes and an unformed bread dough nose, topped by a nest of white hair unacquainted with comb or brush. He also wore the stars of a brigadier general's on his uniform collar and had the assured air of a career officer. He directed the enlisted man at a second interior door to open it and the lady, accompanied by her basket-laden servant, walked through.

The clerk rose and had a whispered conversation with the General. "Fine, fine," the General said and turned to Lord Tracy and his valet. "General John Winder at your service," he said, holding out his hand. Lord Tracy bowed and introduced himself. Both the men ignored Juba, who hadn't moved from his seat on the bench. General Winder motioned for Lord Tracy to follow him into his office.

Kate took a seat before Winder's desk, which was no bigger than the clerk's desk outside the general's door, but covered with papers. The whole office looked like it had been thrown together by someone who didn't care how things looked.

Lord Tracy rested his hands on the head of his walking stick. "General, let me be frank. I am not just another rich idler seeking to entertain himself by gawking at those less fortunate than myself. Rather, I have heard good reports about the Confederate government's treatment of prisoners and wish to observe for myself." Neither Kate nor Lord Tracy had heard any such thing, but a good spy never let truth impede a solid cover story. "I am sympathetic to your nation's cause, having some understanding of the realities of a natural aristoc-

racy and the burdens imposed upon men such as ourselves."
Here Lord Tracy waved his gloved hand at both the general
and himself. "I have been touring the south, from New Orleans to Memphis to here and I am impressed with the officers
and gentlemen that have received me. I hope to take favorable
reports of your new nation home to my friends who sit in the
House of Lords."

Winder swelled at the flattery and offered his lordship a cigar. They puffed away for a while, chatting about the
similarities between people of African and Irish descent and
other topics designed to make the speaker feel like a god
among mortals. At last, the General stubbed out his cigar and
offered Lord Tracy free reign of prison. He scribbled out a
note and handed it over, waving at the messy pile of papers on
his desk. "I'd accompany you, milord, but I've got the devil's
own pile of paperwork here."

Lord Tracy stepped back into the anteroom just as the lady
in the brown dress did.

A guard in a gray Confederate uniform was just behind
her.

"Damn Yankee sympathizers," he spat out in a voice low
enough that General Winder wouldn't hear him through the
door. "You ask me, you're no better than them soldiers who
killed my brother."

The lady hunched her shoulders under his tirade, but the
look on her face told Kate that his harangue was neither new
nor just begun. Her maid followed her, her face screwed tight
with controlled anger.

As they stepped further into the room, the guard spat on
the floor and then put his hand on the lady's lower back and
shoved her. She stumbled.

180

Kate acted without thinking. Lord Tracy stepped up and put his hand on the guard's shoulder. "I say, sir, this is a lady. I insist you apologize."

The guard was an older, grizzled looking man not much taller than Lord Tracy, though his gut swelled out before him like the prow of a ship. He pushed the lady once more, then turned his gaze and glared at his lordship.

Betting the guard acted more on instinct than on reason, Kate held out Lord Tracy's gloved hand. The guard grasped it. Kate squeezed the hand as hard as she could and pumped it up and down. "Nice to meet you, sir," she said in her deepest voice.

The guard's eyes widened. He turned away, but Kate held on to his hand. She pivoted to her left and swung his arm around his back. Using both hands, she shoved his arm up and in. The guard bent over to escape the agony of this new position and screamed in surprise and hurt.

His left arm flailed behind his back, whacking Kate on her left hip, then her shoulder. A finger caught his Lordship's cravat and tore at it. She shoved his arm another inch higher and growled into his ear, "Stop it. Right now. Or I break your arm."

The man's flailing arm stilled. So did the room, quiet but for the shuffling of feet and the guard's panicked huffing.

Kate's attention returned to her surroundings. Behind her the general's door open. The lady and her maid stood frozen to Kate's left.

When she heard General Winder laugh Kate let go of the guard's arm. He stumbled away, toward his commanding officer, cupping his elbow in his left hand. The general pushed the man into his office and shut the door.

As he did the Lady made a small coughing sound and looked pointedly at his lordship's neck. Kate pulled her cravat together into a lumpy knot and straightened her jacket. Juba came up beside her and laid a hand on her shoulder. His wordless reassurance did little to slow her galloping heart.

What had she just done?

Nothing terrible resulted from Lord Tracy's scuffle in Libby Prison's anteroom. Miss Van Lew assured Winder that Lord Tracy had only been protecting her honor. The lady then sketched an outline of the soldier's behavior and Winder apologized for the affront. After everyone assured each other of their mutual admiration and respect, Winder retired to his office to deal with the guard. Kate watched as Miss Van Lew took her leave, sweeping her dark-skinned maid along in her wake.

Afterwards, Winder's lieutenant clerk gave Lord Tracy a tour of the prison, while his lordship's valet waited in the receiving room. They began in a long, low room on the prison's first floor. The lieutenant explained that they kept officers and civilians in this room. Prisoners were fed two meals a day and allowed visitors like Miss Van Lew, who often brought them books, food, and other luxuries. They kept enlisted men on the second floor. The clerk did not encourage his lordship to visit those rooms.

Kate looked around the large room. Despite the clerk's attempts to paint the prison in the brightest light possible she noted that the room was hot, stuffy and smelled just like what it was, a holding pen for too many men with too little access to basic sanitation. More than one rat ran across the floor as she made a circuit of the room, each of them as sleek and well fed as pampered pets. The men had made beds of piles of straw and ragged blankets, some of them cordoning off small private areas with rope strung with articles of clothing.

She understood the charitable impulse of ladies bent on doing good deeds, but room's appearance left Kate shocked that General Winder considered it a suitable place for ladies to visit. Either he took a laxer view of female propriety than did many gentlemen or Miss Van Lew had more steel in her than her gentile appearance suggested. Kate suspected the latter

At the far end of the cavernous room, several men gathered around a disreputable looking table playing cards, a large piece of paper tacked to the wall above them. She stepped towards the men. The top of the page read "Richmond Prison Association." Below these words were a circle made of small, many-legged bugs, lice she presumed, in the center of which someone had printed, "Bite or Be Damned."

The clerk saw her interest and waved at the group. "Congressman Ely started the Association to entertain the men. Sometimes they sing or put on plays from memory. They're harmless so the General lets them carry on." The clerk pointed. "That's the congressman there. Shuffling the cards."

His lordship looked at the army clerk, his eyebrows high with disbelief. "You've got a United States Congressman in this prison?"

"Sure do," the clerk said with more than a little delight. "Some South Carolina boys caught him during the big battle."

Kate eyed the congressional prisoner, surprised she hadn't recognized him. He was much changed from when he'd approached Miss Chase and asked her if she wanted to go

183

downhill, closer to the battlefield. He looked gaunt and tired, like a man who wasn't getting enough food or sleep. Kate stayed back from the group. She didn't think Ely would recognize her, given he'd only met her once and then in women's clothes and mustache-less, but she didn't want to take any chances.

As they left the room Kate fought the urge to sigh. It was one thing for Mr. Lincoln to want to break a congressman out of an enemy prison, but another thing entirely to do it without getting caught. She hoped she didn't get sent back to do the job. If she got her wish and saw Rose at the end of the rope, what would that spell for northern spies caught by the Confederates? Would the much-touted southern chivalry extend far enough to allow clemency for lady spies? Kate suspected it would not.

Kate was explaining the prison layout to Juba over a magnificent repast of roast turkey, baked sweet potatoes, and pickled beets when a knock came at the door. A look from Juba sent Kate hustling into the suite's tiny dressing room. She'd been eating dinner in their suite in Lord Tracy's smoking jacket and soft trousers, but she'd removed her mustache and loosened her hair. She left the dressing room door cracked open an inch and peered through it.

A bellman stood at the door, his silver hair a sharp contrast against his ebony skin. He held a sealed piece of paper in his hands. "A letter for your man," the fellow said to Juba. "Delivered to the front desk not five minutes ago." Juba gave the man a coin for his trouble, shut the door and leaned against it.

Kate stepped out of the dressing room. "A letter?"

Juba frowned and nodded.

"But who knows we're here? It's not like Lord Tracy has any friends in Richmond. Open it." Kate's voice cracked with anxiety.

Juba broke the thick wax seal, read the note and frowned some more. Then he held the note out to Kate.

Aug. 12th

Lord Tracy (or whoever you are):

I know your secret. I look forward to our discussion of its implications. My mother and I request the pleasure of your company at dinner tomorrow evening, 7 PM. Please bring your valet with you.

Most cordially,

Miss Elizabeth Van Lew

2300 East Grace Street

Richmond

Kate looked up at Juba. A sour taste flooded her mouth as her stomach rolled over, threatening to disgorge her lovely dinner. The note fluttered to the floor, settling on the flowered carpet like a fallen butterfly.

Chapter 17

August 16, 1861
Washington City

Belle tugged Zephyr to a halt and patted his neck to quiet him. This was it. She needed to get through the federal pickets without being searched. She reached up and patted her hair at the back, reassuring herself the small packet of papers was still tightly encased in her bun and thought about her dilemma. She couldn't sneak past them through the woods as she'd planned. The trees and under-growth were too thick in this part of Virginia, even for a horse as grand as Zephyr. Then she remembered what Mrs. Green-how said.

"Act like a trollop and you'll be treated like a trollop. Act like a lady and you'll be treated like a lady." Mrs. G seemed to think Belle could be rash and unladylike, but Mama said she was just high spirited. Men liked a high spirited girl, didn't they? Still . . . Think of the glory that would be hers when she delivered these messages to General Beauregard. She tight-ened her grip on Zephyr's reins and dug her heels into his flanks. Unused to such cavalier treatment, he squealed with indignation and leaped forward. Belle whacked him again and again with her heels, then commenced a high pitched hollering. "No! Stop! Help!"

Zephyr charged out of the brush and onto the road, just beyond the union soldiers' barricade. She forced him to run right at the soldiers, sawing his reins back and forth so he'd look erratic. Confused and angry as he was, her horse gave every appearance of being a panicked runaway. She knew what the soldiers saw. A coal black, out-of-control stallion and a frightened damsel in need of rescue.

One of the blue-clad soldiers leaped in front of Zephyr and waved his arms, causing Zephyr to veer off to the left. Belle kept up her high pitched screaming until one man grabbed the stallion's bridle and pulled him to a stop. She slumped in faux relief, then kicked her leg over her sidesaddle and slipped off her horse, sobbing and wailing to beat the band. She threw herself into the arms of the nearest soldier and soaked on his scratchy wool uniform with tears. Behind her, Zephyr snorted in disgust, but the soldier patted her hair and murmured tender words of safety into her ear. She quieted her sobbing, wiped her cheek against his damp tunic and looked up at him, batted her eyelashes and gasped, "You saved me!" He smiled at her, briefly tightened his grip on her, then remembered his manners and released her. She collapsed onto the dusty road in a faint. It was, if she had to say so herself, a magnificent performance.

After a moment she let her eyelashes flutter. She threw in a soft moan and brought her hand to her forehead.

"Are you all right Miss?" Belle opened her eyes and stretched out her hand. A Union soldier, not much older than she, pulled her into a sitting position. He had a pinkish freckled face and wide, honest blue eyes. Soft orange curls peeked from under his cap, making him look like an Irish angel.

The face of an older man appeared over the angel's shoulder. "Can you stand Miss?"

She nodded.

"Help her up son," the older man said. He looked less wide-eyed than the boy, but no less concerned for her.

When she was on her feet, she thanked the two men for helping her. "My horse ran away with me, you see. Papa said he was too much horse for me, but I wouldn't listen and he took off and I couldn't stop him. It was so terribly frightening." Belle pushed out her lower lip and quivered it a little, all the while trying not to laugh. She'd had perfect control of Zephyr since she was ten years old. These fools had no idea that southern girls learned to ride right after they learned to walk. "And now I'm behind enemy lines and I am your captive." She shivered her body, being careful to push out her bosom as she did.

"You poor thing," the angel said, unable to take his eyes from her chest.

The older man ignored her breasts and examined her face. "You're from south of here? Confederate territory?"

Belle nodded, letting her lip quiver a little more. She blinked three times in succession.

"But you came from that way." The older man pointed behind them, up the road to the north.

Belle clutched at the younger soldier's arm and wailed. "I don't know! The brute was running and running through the trees. I was too busy trying to stay on and I was ducking branches and I couldn't see which direction we were going."

The angel straightened his shoulders and puffed out his chest. "Can't you see Sergeant? Her horse got all turned around and now she's lost. She's lucky she didn't break her pretty neck."

Belle gasped and swayed on her feet. "It was ever so terrible. I shall never ride that horse again. I beg you to permit me to return to my family's farm."

Before either man could answer a tall man in a captain's coat and insignia walked up to the little group. "What's going on here?"

Belle stared at the captain's fluffy side whiskers and collar length hair. The man looked a good deal like her Daddy.

"A beautiful captive, Sir," the angel said, his voice so high with excitement he squeaked.

"Well," the captain huffed. "We can scarcely think of detaining a little scrap of a girl. Where do you live Miss?"

"In town, sir. Manassas. Just down the road."

The angel looked at his sergeant and captain.

"It looks as if the private here would like the honor of escorting you at least part-way home. We can't take you all the way home, mind you, not with the Confederate army in camp there." The captain looked over at the angel.

"Oh yes sir," the young man replied, his eyes shining with expected pleasure.

"But sir," the sergeant said, "what if she's a spy? She came from that way," he pointed north again, "not from Manassas direction."

The captain frowned. "Sergeant, don't be a tartar. She's just a girl. We must claim the honor of restoring her to the custody of her family."

190

"And if they take the private prisoner? What then? Is she worth the trade?" The sergeant gave Belle the gimlet eye.

The captain snorted. "I have no fear those wretched Rebs will take a Union soldier so close to our lines.

Belle spoke up, trying to hide her indignation at their conversation. She'd show them. "Captain, I would be glad to take a pass and leave your man here, safe and sound. I'm sure Zephyr has tired himself out and won't be any trouble on the way home."

"Absolutely not. The private will walk you down the road a piece. You tell your Mama you're far too young to be out alone on a horse that large and ill-trained. I know there's a war on, but that's all the more reason for young ladies to take care."

Belle seethed with indignation at his words. Zephyr ill-trained? Her Mama remiss? The arrogant Yankee needed a good horsewhipping. Instead, she smiled and in a flash, she'd swung onto her horse. The private took Zephyr's reins and led them off down the road. She turned in her saddle and blew a kiss at the skeptical sergeant and his presumptuous captain. Fools!

The sweet-faced private took hold of Zephyr's reins and walked down the road. They talked as they walked, he of his home in western Massachusetts, where his parents and six brothers and sisters lived, she of an entirely fictional family. She didn't dare talk about her real parents. She'd give too much away. Mrs. Greenhow would be proud of her, what with her being so careful and all.

After ten minutes or so he stopped in the middle of the road and returned the reins to her. "That's as far as I go,

Miss." He laid his hand upon her booted foot. "You take care now, you hear?"

She beamed at him, using her most brilliant smile, then she leaned down and placed a kiss squarely on his forehead. "Thank you," she whispered to him before straitening and clucking Zephyr into a motion.

As they trotted down the road he yelled after her. "Wait! You never told me your name."

She turned and looked over her shoulder.

He stood like a lost waif in the middle of the road.

"Belle Boyd, Rebel Girl, at your service!" Then she kicked her horse into a gallop and took off down the road, leaving her angelic squire with nothing but dust to remember her by.

She made it to the Confederate Army's camp before dinner, her hair and spirits entirely intact.

Chapter 18

August 12-15, 1861
Richmond, Virginia

hat secret did Miss Van Lew know? That his lordship is a fake? And what could she do about it? And why ask them to dinner? Would she bribe them? Kate tried not to worry. She'd find the answers to her questions tomorrow, one way or another. Still, sleep eluded her while questions whirled and skittered in her head.

Somewhere near dawn, she fell into a fitful doze only to be harried by dreams of being chased by an invisible monster.

She awoke bleary-eyed and unprepared to meet the day. Monty caught her mood and whined nervously while Kate dressed. Juba ordered up breakfast, but in the end neither one of them ate a bit. They tried to make plans for an investigation of Beauregard's headquarters but made little headway on that either. It was impossible to concentrate with the specter of the hangman's noose suspended above them.

Kate suggested they leave the room for lunch, but a stern look from Juba persuaded her to stay put. If the Confederate authorities suspected anything at all their best course of action was to keep a low profile. They took lunch in the hotel room, though neither of them ate much. Afterwards Juba took

Monty for a hasty walk around the block. While they waited for evening they agreed that if dinner went poorly, they'd try to escape the hotel that very evening, under cover of darkness. On foot if necessary.

Come six o'clock Juba helped Lord Tracy in his jacket of black superfine and white tie. They re-stuck the mustache onto Kate's face and checked the mirror. She looked like Lord Tracy. Kate checked Hazzard's pocket watch, partly for the time and partly for reassurance. It was time. The two of them headed for a hansom cab, leaving Monty in the hotel room with orders to behave himself.

An earlier discussion with a bellman persuaded them to ride to the Van Lew house. "That's a Church Hill address," the man said, "Where the quality folk lives. It's a good fifteen blocks away."

I spite of the distance Kate thought the walk might be good for her anxiety, but Juba pointed out that a toff like Lord Tracy wouldn't walk anywhere in evening clothes. "Best keep up appearances as long as we can."

The cabman took them south, around the Capitol complex, where the provisional Confederate Congress sat in special session. Kate briefly wondered about her old friend Senator Wigfall and then remembered he'd been made a brigadier general and put in charge of a Texas brigade. She should inquire about that brigade's location. She wouldn't want to run into her old paramour while rambling about Virginia. Louis T. Wigfall might see through the mustache and men's clothing. He wasn't quite as big a fool as most people thought he was.

The cab took them up the gentle incline of Grace Street and stopped in front of a house that must have been the jewel of the neighborhood. The three-story white house occupied an entire city block, surrounded by an ornate iron fence painted to match the house. Clipped privet hedges and glossy leaved magnolia trees ran down the side of the house, shielding it from prying eyes, while a floral scent hung in the air, suggesting a profusion of unseen flower beds. Kate and Juba exited the cab and approached the front door, both of them careful to appear nonchalant. Doric columns and twin curving staircases announced the front door.

Kate turned to Juba, careful to keep her voice low. "Are we in the right place? The lady we met yesterday didn't seem grand enough for this house."

Juba snorted. "The note said 2300 East Grace Street."

Juba knocked and they waited. Kate's anxiety rose to such an extent that she startled when a man opened the door and invited them in with an air of distant politeness. He led them through the marble-clad entryway and into a large, high ceilinged, book-lined room. Kate tried not to goggle at her surroundings. Lord Tracy would have seen English manors grander than this house and libraries with many more books. Kate Warne, on the other hand, only rarely saw houses this palatial.

Two ladies sat, their skirts spread about them, at the far end of the room before an empty fireplace. The younger of the two, whom Kate recognized as Miss Van Lew, rose to meet them. She held a small white hand out to Lord Tracy, who kissed it. Then, in a move that couldn't have surprised Kate more, she held out her hand to Juba.

"Allow me to introduce my mother, Mrs. Eliza Van Lew," Miss Van Lew said with a faint bow of her head.

Lord Tracy approached the older lady, intent on offering her a bow. Instead, he gaped at her. "My lady, your daughter is the very image of you. Why you could be sisters." The two ladies did look alike. They had the same slight build, the same elfin features, and the same astute gray eyes.

Mrs. Van Lew smiled and blushed a faint pink. "You are too kind. I had my dear daughter when I was sixteen."

When they'd all taken their seats, Juba included, Miss Van Lew rang a silver bell next to her chair. The butler appeared with a bottle of claret and a tray of glasses. Miss Van Lew directed the man to pour everyone a drink. When he poured a small glass for Juba and handed it to him without comment Kate wondered what was going on. The quality didn't invite servants to sit in their parlors, let alone offer them libations. When the butler finished handing out drinks Miss Van Lew looked up at him. "William, I wonder if you could find Mary and ask her to join us. And tell Caroline and Elizabeth that we shall begin dinner in one-half hour."

They sipped their wine and waited in silence. Kate thought her head would explode if the Van Lew ladies didn't start talking soon.

A slim, dark-skinned black woman appeared in the library's double doorway. She was young, or at least no older than Kate herself, dressed in a white dress sprigged with lavender flowers. Kate recognized her as the same young woman who'd been with Miss Van Lew at Libby Prison.

Miss Van Lew motioned the young woman over. "This is our protégé Miss Mary Ann Richards. Mary Ann, this is . . ." Miss Van Lew paused before going on, "Lord Tracy and his companion Mr. Lane." Mary Ann nodded her way around the room, stopping in front of the double sofa where Juba sat. She smiled at him as she took a seat next to him.

Once again, Kate tried not to goggle at her hostess. Her protégé? And why introduce Juba that way? What were these two southern ladies up to?

Miss Van Lew clapped her hands together twice. "Now we're all together, I rather feel as if we might put you out of your misery Lord Tracy." She said his name with a clear note of disbelief. "I know you are not Lord Tracy. I would wager this house that no such person exists. I know you are a woman." A small smile curled at Miss Van Lew's thin lips.

Kate fought the urge to rise and flee. This was the worst possible thing. She looked over at Juba. He shrugged his shoulders, hands palms up in a gesture of helplessness.

Mrs. Van Lew leaned forward. "Lizzie, you are scaring them. We assure you there is no danger here. In fact, I owe you a debt of gratitude for your defense of my daughter yesterday."

Kate looked at the older Van Lew woman. She wore a kind, patient expression on her face. Kate heaved a great sigh. "Then what do you want. And how did you know?"

"Your throat," Miss Van Lew explained. "In the scuffle with that disgusting man at the prison your cravat came loose."

Kate reached up and touched her silk cravat, wondering why it mattered.

"Ahhh. The missing Adam's apple," Juba said. "Men have them. Women do not."

Kate gaped at Miss Van Lew. "And you noticed that? Just after you'd been accosted?"

"In my business, my dear, I notice a good number of things that go unseen by most people."

"Your business?" Kate felt as if they were having two conversations, neither of them seated in reality.

"Well it's the same as yours, isn't it? I'm a spy. We all are." She gestured around the room at her mother, Miss Richards, and William, who'd been leaning in the doorway watching the conversation. She smiled at Kate and Juba, her eyes bright with amusement. "I'll admit I've seen more than one woman passing as a man. Mary here's done it a time or two."

The young woman smiled. "It's easy really. No one expects women to dress as men so they don't see us when we do. People see trousers and stop looking."

Kate nodded in agreement. "The walk's important too. And the attitude."

The two women smiled at each other in common understanding.

Mrs. Van Lew spoke up. "We also know of at least one passing woman in the Confederate Army. I'm sure there's more."

Kate wanted to ask for details but stopped herself. The woman soldier might be a Confederate but she was entitled to her secret. "I suppose both armies have women in them."

Juba nodded. "Kate here can't be the only Northern woman looking to help her country and unwilling to do it by rolling bandages and holding knitting sales."

"Not that there's anything wrong with such pursuits," Mrs. Van Lew said with a gentle smile.

Miss Van Lew chuckled. "No Mama, there is not. But we can do so much more." She gestured at Kate and Juba. "It occurs to me that we have not yet been introduced."

And thus Kate Warne and Juba Lane met Eliza and Elizabeth Van Lew, two women who had put their entire household of ex-slaves to work developing a pro-Union Richmond resistance movement.

Kate had to laugh when they ate dinner in the kitchen. Did all spies congregate in kitchens? Mrs. and Miss Van Lew led them through a magnificent, high ceilinged dining room with a grand, dark wood table large enough to seat thirty dinner guests, though it was currently empty and dark. They went down the servant's stairs and into a ground floor kitchen. The table was as large as the one in the dining room, though not nearly so grand, particularly as it was covered in plain white plates and wooden cups.

Mrs. Van Lew introduced a raw-boned, copper-colored woman named Caroline as the cook and a smaller, younger and darker woman as the cook's assistant. The latter informed Kate her name was also Elizabeth, but to avoid confusion she went by Betty.

"I'm sorry if we offend you by eating in the kitchen," Mrs. Van Lew said, "but both Caroline and William refuse to sit at the dining room table.

"Ma'am," William said in a voice that suggested they'd had this very argument many times before, "if someone saw us there'd be trouble and you know it. It's just too dangerous."

Betty piped up, "And just who will be looking in the dining room windows of the grand Van Lew mansion, anyway?"

Caroline wiped her hands on her apron and shook her head. "You never know. Not these days. Them fanatics are on the lookout for spies everywhere. And you know Miz Eliza doesn't fit into society, her being from Philadelphia and all."

Kate looked at Mrs. Van Lew, who was busy gesturing people to their places at the table. "Really? You're not a Virginian?"

"No dear. My dear father was the mayor of Philadelphia back before the turn of the century. We've lived here for fifty years, but as far as Virginians are concerned, we're Yankees. Or at least I am. My daughter is only slightly less suspect."

"Virginians take their bloodlines seriously, whether in dogs, horses or humans," Miss Van Lew explained as she took her seat.

An hour later they'd eaten their way through most of a Virginia ham, a pot of rice and about a half-dozen dishes of pickled vegetables and mountains of talk.

Kate and Juba explained that they were Pinkerton detectives hunting evidence of a Washington resistance movement funneling information south to Richmond.

Miss Van Lew, who insisted they call her Elizabeth, talked about how she and her mother disapproved of secession and slavery. She explained how they'd been buying and freeing slaves ever since Mr. Van Lew died eighteen years before. According to them William, Mary, Caroline, and Betty were all free and had the paperwork to prove it. They continued to work for the Van Lews and pretend to be slaves because otherwise they'd have to leave Virginia. They all had family in Richmond and didn't want to move north until everyone was free.

"Besides," Mary said, "if we stay, we can work to destroy slavery from within."

200

"Everyone here can read," Elizabeth said with some pride, "and write too. Mary's as well educated as I. And she's right. We can do more against slavery in Richmond than in any northern city."

Mary nodded. "The Van Lews sent me to Philadelphia for school, after which I spent a few years teaching in Liberia."

Juba reared back his head. "Liberia? In Africa? You've been there?"

"Oh, I have. It was wonderful and awful," Mary said with a frown. "It's a tale for another day, but one thing I learned is that I'm not an African. I am an American. That's why I came back."

Mrs. Van Lew smiled and patted Mary on the shoulder. "We were happy to have you back. You are so very dear to us."

Kate could scarcely believe her eyes and ears. They had mixed race dinners at their house in Washington, but this was another order of magnitude in its defiance of the accepted social order. Just eating dinner together was a gargantuan act of courage.

Eventually, talk turned to the Confederate prisons and the union prisoners they held.

"As I'm sure you know," Elizabeth explained, "thousands of Union soldiers were captured in the aftermath of Bull Run. The Confederate Army converted several tobacco and cotton warehouses into prisons, including the one in which we met yesterday. And the hospitals are full of wounded southern men."

"Not Union soldiers?" Kate asked.

"Some," Elizabeth conceded, "but our army dumps most of the wounded Union soldiers in warehouse prisons. They are left to fend for themselves as best they can. Southern ladies have been most eager to volunteer goods and services to bene-fit southern soldiers, but not Union ones. Mother and I have tried to fill that gap."

"It's difficult," Mrs. Van Lew said. "We are already sus-pected of being Yankee sympathizers, though I admit that so far our great wealth has shielded us from the worst criticism. Still, it is dangerous."

"I expect it is," Kate agreed.

William agreed. "I have told them and told them to stay home, but no, they won't."

"William, what kind of women do you take us for. If we were the type to cower in our houses, only doing what was expected of us, where would you all be right now?" Mrs. Van Lew pressed her lips together and squinted at William.

Kate glanced over at Juba. Mrs. Van Lew looked like a sweet old woman, but she had steel in her spine.

The older woman sighed. "I'm sorry William, but I'm too old for cowardice. Still, we must be careful."

Elizabeth shifted in her seat. "Which is why Mother and I have devised a two-fold plan that will allow us to continue to help those poor union soldiers. We're planning to volunteer to nurse Confederate soldiers too so Richmond sees we attend to all sufferers, not just the Yankees. Also, I thought we might appeal to President Davis for a letter of permission. With his approval, no one would dare criticize us. Dear Mr. Davis is above reproach amongst even the most fanatical pro-slavery men and women."

Kate gave Elizabeth a sharp look. "You know the Presi-dent?"

Before Elizabeth could answer her mother spoke up. "Of course, we do dear. We are very rich and we live in the biggest house on Church Hill. We may be Yankee upstarts, but we're still important members of Richmond society. Mr. Davis has only been in Richmond a few weeks, but he's been out in society, though without his wife. She's not arrived in Richmond yet and so the President has had no parties. Indeed, when we visit him we're hoping to offer him the use of some of our people as servants so he might begin with his social obligations."

"Clever," Kate said with a suppressed laugh. Kate looked over at Juba again.

He saw what she was thinking and nodded his head.

"Do you think Mr. Davis would like to meet an English Lord?"

The two Van Lew women shared an amused glance. "Oh, I think it can be arranged," Elizabeth said. "We have an appointment to see him tomorrow. Your Lordship could come with us. But only if you do us a favor in return."

"Anything," Kate said. She couldn't believe their luck. An audience with the Confederate president presented a huge opportunity, so long as long she didn't get caught. Mrs. Van Lew had seen through her disguise and the president might too. She'd have to take particular care with his lordship's cravat.

The Van Lews called for Lord Tracy at ten the next morning.

"Mr. President's been unwell, my friend Mrs. Carrington tells me," Elizabeth explained the night before, "so he's been working from the house instead of his office at the Capital."

Eliza and Elizabeth rode in a glossy red and black coach, pulled by a set of matched chestnut coaching horses. William sat in the driver's seat attired in a black coat and top hat. His lordship stepped into the carriage after making a show of being unimpressed with the equipage. As they rolled away Kate saw Juba and Monty heading out for a walk. She wished she was with them and not on her way to see the president of the Confederate States of America. Last night it had seemed like a good idea, but this morning it felt like utter folly.

They rode around the Capitol grounds and up Thirteenth to Clay Street where they turned. They came to a stop in front of a house nearly as grand as the Van Lews. Two story, double columns flanked the front steps of a white neoclassical mansion set with a wide front porch and three French doors, each placed between the four columns. The whole effect was one of pleasing symmetry and opulent excess.

Lord Tracy stepped out of the carriage before handing out the Van Lews. Kate fussed with her neck cloth as she followed the ladies up the walk. She'd worn Lord Tracy's finest clothes and hat, had reviewed her walk and accent with Juba this morning before leaving the hotel and made sure she was carrying her forged identity papers, but no amount of preparation could shake the icky feeling in the pit of her stomach. It was hard to imagine how they would treat a woman caught dressed as a man, spying on the Confederacy in the President's office, but she was pretty sure it would be bad.

A butler as finely dressed as William but older, let them into a square entry hall with wallpaper so red it hurt Kate's eyes.

Mrs. Van Lew laid her calling card on a silver tray and announced, "Mr. Davis is expecting us." The butler took the ladies shawls and his lordship's hat before leading them past first floor rooms empty of anything but carpets and up the stairs, where he knocked on the first door. The silent butler waited a moment and let them into the room.

Kate followed the Van Lew ladies into a nearly dark room. She swallowed hard. Now would be a bad time to vomit.

The room was large but details were hard to see. Heavy maroon velvet curtains covered the windows and the room's one light came from a tabletop lamp in the room's back corner. The room was stifling hot and still. The aroma of lamp oil competed with a faint scent of putrefaction.

"Please forgive me, ladies," a man said. "My eye is suffering another bout of inflammation and can tolerate no light."

Kate strained to see the speaker. He was medium height and lean, but with the posture of a man much older than he appeared. He'd risen from behind the desk and turned towards Eliza and Elizabeth Van Lew, exposing the left side of his face. Kate had to stifle a gasp at the sight of the man's eye, which was swollen and damp with leaking fluid.

Eliza Van Lew sketched a shallow curtsy. "I appreciate you seeing us in spite of your health Mr. President."

He bowed at the ladies and stepped toward them. "You also see the half-dressed state of the house. My wife and children are scheduled to arrive in two week's time. I depend on Mrs. Davis to put the house in order. I should hire servants before she gets here, but until then I have only Jefferson. I've had him since college so we rub along together well and he knows how to treat my eye."

205

Elizabeth stepped forward. "Perhaps Mama and I could help you with servants Sir. We have several slaves with not enough to do, what with our social life constrained as it is and our time spent nursing wounded soldiers. We could loan you one or two."

Davis smiled, then winced and reached for his eye. "How generous of you, Madame. I'm sure my wife would appreciate it if the house were in a semblance of order when she arrives. Thank you."

"Any help we can provide the President of our new nation is thanks enough. I shall send Mary and Caroline to you. My two best girls." Elizabeth turned and beamed at her mother, who smiled back. Kate thought the ladies looked ready to break into a jig, but Mr. Davis either didn't notice their glee or chalked it up to their delight at doing him a favor.

Davis smiled again and peered around the Van Lew ladies to Lord Tracy.

Eliza swept her hand out toward his lordship. "I take great pleasure in introducing you to Lord Tracy of Toddington. He is the eighth lord of that name."

"Ninth, milady," his lordship corrected with a faint smile. Kate stepped forward and held out her hand to Mr. Davis, hoping he didn't hear her heart pounding. "Not that it matters one whit Mr. President, but my father, the eighth lord was particular in these matters and I believe in honoring my father." There, Kate thought, let's hope that's the right mix of self-deprecation, grandiosity and filial piety. Would a gentleman ask about the eye? Would a gentleman ignore the eye? What should she do? Dammit, she would expose herself if she kept thinking like a ninny.

Jefferson Davis confronted the issue for her. "Lord Tracy, I am sorry to meet you in such circumstances. My doctor says I must keep the room as dark as possible to minimize the inflammation. I know in this dark I appear like a sneak thief, but my doctor says he does not understand why my eye has not already burst. I'd very much like to avoid that occasion and so we meet like this." He gestured for them to sit, dug a handkerchief out of his jacket pocket and wiped his face before sitting himself.

Though she'd been prepared to despise the Confederate president, Kate couldn't help but admire the man before her, who worked through the clutches of what was obviously an extremely painful affliction. He questioned Lord Tracy on his travels and plans for the future. At one point he asked for his lordship's papers, which he carried over to the room's only lamp and examined closely. Kate's heart stuck in her throat while he did so, but he handed the papers back to her with no comment.

Davis returned to his desk, wiped his face again and finally spoke. "And how may I help you, Sir?"

"Mr. President, I would like to tour your nearby military encampment so that I might accurately report back to my countrymen about your new nation's martial needs. I hope to sway my friends in the House of Lords to my way of thinking."

"Which is?" Davis's tone suggested he was entirely uninterested in the answer, though the tension in his body said otherwise.

"Sir, no country on earth is better suited to understand this nation and its stance on slavery than England. We can only admire the way slavery has transformed brute savages into

207

docile laborers for the superior race. We only wish we could accomplish as much with our Irish problem."

"You quote me?" Davis tilted his head at Lord Tracy.

Kate was glad she'd done her homework. "Your address to the Confederate Congress in April, Sir. I hope you don't mind. I thought it was a grand speech. I'm honored to sit in the same room with the man who gave it." Had she pushed the flattery too far?

Davis didn't seem to think so. He puffed out his chest and nodded. "And Yankee abolitionists? What do you think of them?"

"Zealots sir and the worst type at that, liberal zealots. And like all liberals, they are unrealistic and uninformed. They imagine Liberty for all, which is ridiculous. We might as well lay down with dogs and dine with swine. We English understand the natural order of all things."

Davis's face, what little of it Kate could see, brightened. "May I presume that you would like to meet with General Beauregard?"

Kate wanted to caper about the room but retrained Lord Tracy to a polite bow. "Very much, Mr. President."

"Then it shall be done." Davis reached for his pen, dipped it into a small pot of ink and scribbled out a short note. He set it aside and looked over at Eliza and Elizabeth. "And how can I help you, ladies?"

Kate stifled a laugh. In allowing two Van Lew 'slaves' in his household Davis had done quite enough. The Van Lews assured the president they had visited to offer him their help and wanted nothing in return.

That night Kate wrote her final letter to Mr. Valandigham. She wrote on both sides though if anyone were to examine the letter it would appear that she'd only used one side.

Chapter 19

August 16-18, 1861
Manassas, Virginia

They left Richmond late the next morning, after calling at the Van Lew mansion, this time with Monty along for the ride. After admiring the little dog, Elizabeth and Eliza got down to business. Elizabeth handed Kate a small packet of papers they wanted his lordship to get through the lines and to Washington.

"We want to establish an information pipeline from Richmond to Washington," Elizabeth explained. "We'll work on establishing a network of couriers here in Richmond. What we need from you is an endpoint. Someone who will take delivery on our intelligence dispatches. Someone who will take our work seriously."

Elizabeth, Eliza, Kate and Juba were standing on the back portico of her house. A deep porch and shade trees created a cool space against Richmond's summer heat. The Van Lews had the backyard landscaped so it framed an unimpeded view of the James River, several blocks distant. Heedless of the view Monty scampered around the back garden, lifting his leg on every other plant.

Kate could scarcely believe women raised in this level of elegance and privilege would risk it all to end slavery. They stood to lose their home, their positions, their entire world. History books never recorded that kind of bravery, the quiet and yet obdurate resistance of people who were not soldiers or generals and never would be. People who fought against ignorance and hate because it was the right thing to do could do a great deal of human good, but books rarely remembered them. And history rarely recorded any women at all. Books made it seem as if only men mattered, and then only powerful and rich men.

Juba smiled. "Miz Van Lew, we are not exaggerating when we say we can take your information to President Lincoln himself. This one here," he nudged Kate with his elbow, "took a bullet for him back in March. He owes her his life and he knows it. He'll see the value of your work and honor it."

Eliza blinked rapidly. "Even if we are just women? Virginia women?"

Juba nodded. "Mr. Lincoln trusts Kate. She'll tell him to trust you and he will. And he can tell his generals if need be. One of them is likely to need a Richmond spy."

Kate nudged Juba back. "He trusts you too." She turned and faced Eliza and Elizabeth. "I'm trying to prove that one of the most dangerous Confederate spies in Washington is a woman. I plan to expose her so she's hung for treason. I'm afraid once I expose a lady spy it will be more difficult for other ladies. I suggest you make haste in putting together your network because the period when women are above suspicion or below notice is rapidly coming to the end."

"A good news, bad news proposition to be sure," Elizabeth murmured. "We're using slaves too, or people that look like

212

slaves to those who believe in that sort of thing. I'm hoping we all stay invisible."

The ladies shared a look. Each understood full well that her work succeeded in great part because most men didn't view women as rational human beings. That fact was irritating but helpful in the espionage business.

Elizabeth laid a hand on Kate's arm. "And about that other matter, your congressman. I can visit him or get a message to him. There might be something I can do. I know for sure there are men in Libby planning an escape. Maybe we can get Mr. Ely in with that group."

Kate nodded in relief. With Rose Greenhow running amok she didn't need another job. "Then I'll tell Mr. Lincoln you're working on it."

Kate called Monty and they made their way to the front of the house where the barouche waited.

Before they left the Van Lew house Elizabeth touched Kate's elbow again and smiled. "Did I tell you we sent Mary Ann to Mr. Davis this morning?"

Kate almost laughed. "Can I assume he thinks she's an ignorant and illiterate slave?"

"Why of course," Elizabeth said. "Is there any other kind?"

The two women shared a smile. Kate wished Miss Van Lew lived in Washington. It never hurt to have another friend.

Juba went down to the barouche which he'd left on the street, and opened the door for Lord Tracy and Monty. The two Van Lew ladies waved an enthusiastic goodbye to them all and they drove away. Juba looked over his shoulder at Kate as they made their way down Broad Street toward the road north, out of town. "I hope they're careful. All of them. I'd hate for something to happen to that household."

213

Kate nodded her agreement, not sure she could trust her voice. It was funny how some people could feel like family after only a few hours.

They spent a hot dusty day on the road. Soldiers stopped them twice on their way, but both times Lord Tracy presented his pass signed by President Jefferson Davis himself and both times they were waved along their way. Monty continued to growl at everyone and the soldiers continued to not take offense. Late in the day, they came upon a tiny town. Juba slowed the barouche and turned around. "I was hoping to make it to Fredericksburg but," he waved at the failing daylight.

Kate peered around the carriage door. "Maybe there's an inn ahead. Even if it's tiny and grubby let's stop. I don't want to be on the road after dark."

Juba chucked the horses into a trot. Not long after they came to a small town called Spotsylvania, and found the Spotswood Inn, which was decidedly un-tiny and un-grubby. Kate stared at the building in wonder. The Inn featured the South's favorite architectural embellishment, a set of two-story white Doric columns holding up a wide front porch. The large square building behind the columns appeared freshly white-washed. While she was admiring the building slaves hurried out to take their horses and bags, reminding Kate that behind all this lovely southern architecture lay the rotten heart of human bondage. Kate turned on her Lord Tracy act, which seemed to delight the rotund innkeeper to no end. He let them a double room so that Lord Tracy could keep his valet close.

They slept in soft feather beds, a cool breeze wafting over them from the room's open windows. After a breakfast of pecan waffles and smoked bacon, Lord Tracy and his valet driver continued their journey. They drove along for a couple of hours, then watered and rested the horses in Fredericksburg before pushing on to Manassas Junction, heading northeast until well after lunch. At Dumfries, they turned left, crossed a large stone bridge over an almost dry creek and headed northwest for the last leg of their journey to the Confederate Army's largest encampment.

From her seat in the back, Kate called out to Juba. "Does this feel too easy?"

He nodded. "Kinda makes a body nervous doesn't it?"

Then it all went sideways.

The road from Dumfries to Manassas was narrow and looked to have been considerably churned up by the passing of Beauregard's Army of the Potomac the month before. The trees leaned in over the road in places, making it seem as if they were traveling down a long, leafy tunnel. As they came over a small rise Juba pulled the horses to a stop. "Got your revolver handy?" he called over his shoulder.

Kate jerked out of her doze. Her revolver? She groped for her jacket, which she'd removed and laid on the seat. The revolver. Where was it? There.

"Got it," she said in a low voice. She pushed her pretty gun up her jacket sleeve and crooked her elbow just enough to hold it there. Then she checked her mustache, pressing it onto her lip with anxious fingers. "What's going on?"

"Four men at the bottom of this hill. Just standing there like highwaymen."

"Should we turn back?"

Juba turned and looked back at her, eyes narrowed. "You want to?"

Kate shook her head. "You have your gun?" They'd argued about him carrying a gun. She'd given him her old pepper pot derringer, but he hadn't wanted it, arguing that a black man with a firearm was asking for trouble. "Then you better not get caught," Kate told him. "Also, we can pretend your lordship insisted on it."

He patted his vest pocket. "Right here."

"Well . . . If we must die, let us encounter darkness as a bride and hug it in our arms."

Juba heaved a sigh. "Really? Shakespeare? Now?" He clucked the horses into a walk. She grabbed Monty's collar and pulled him close.

Minutes later they were in the middle of a robbery. The four men were Confederate soldiers out scavenging. Having run into a richly appointed carriage packed with baggage and crates they were disinclined to let Lord Tracy pass. All four of them had rifles and two of them had handguns tucked into their belts.

"And do you think," Lord Tracy asked in his most supercilious tone, "that your commanding officer would approve of you robbing an Englishman? Particularly one with the king's ear? And the ear of your president?"

All four men laughed at this.

A scrawny man wearing sergeant's stripes stepped forward one step. "Colonel Shanks ain't gonna care. He hates you rich fellers jess as much as us all."

216

Juba looked over at Kate. Even they had heard of 'Shanks Evans,' a man notorious for his abrasive personality and battlefield brilliance. The story most often told about him was so outlandish it was hard to believe. Apparently at the battle of Bull Run the colonel had a man follow him from skirmish to skirmish with a small barrel of whiskey lashed to his back. When the day was done Shanks Evans had emptied the cask and was not only alive, but appeared no worse for wear.

Lord Tracy heaved a sigh. Men fighting for Shank would not be amenable to reason.

One of the other men, this one rusty-haired and fat, stepped up to the carriage. "Why look at that. Fancy pants got himself a nice little Mountain Feist. I alas wanted one myself."

The man in sergeant's stripes waved his rifle at Monty. "They are powerful good at treeing squirrels and the like. We could sell him. Hand him over, sir."

Kate sighed, grateful that her Lord Tracy disguise was holding. Men like this did terrible things to women. On the other hand, they were generally kind to dogs.

She scooted over to the edge of the carriage and handed Monty out over the edge to the ginger-haired man. A stench of body odor rode the air around the man as he reached out to take Kate's dog. He grinned at her, his teeth black with rot.

The little black dog squirmed in the man's arms.

Much to Kate's surprise, the wretched man thwacked Monty on the head. Monty yelped and looked at Kate with rolling eyes. Kate decided these men would suffer. It was one thing to be a fat and disgusting rebel, but a man who would hit a dog was no better than a child beater. Maybe worse, considering some of the children she'd met.

"Quinn, step back," the Sergeant barked. The fat man backed. "Now you all git out of that fancy wagon and git yourself on down the road."

Juba looked back at Kate. She shrugged. They didn't have much choice. Not right now. She stepped out of the barouche. Behind her she heard Juba climbed down from the driver's seat. She shot Monty a reassuring look. This would end badly for someone, but not the dog. Men like this would not best her.

"Empty your pockets," the sergeant ordered.

Kate turned out her pockets, handing over Lord Tracy's over-sized billfold, which contained not only numerous bank notes but Lord Tracy's forged identity papers and the hand-written pass from President Davis. The smallest man stepped up to take the packet of papers. He also reeked of body order and unbrushed teeth. Kate felt her gorge rise, along with her temper.

"And now the carriage," the sergeant barked. "You nigger, step away from them horses afore I shoot you in the head." Kate looked over at Juba. He'd been edging towards the front of the carriage. If Kate had to guess he'd been planning to spook the horses to cause a diversion.

Kate looked at the men. Three of them clustered around Lord Tracy's billfold, chortling over the bank notes it held. The redheaded one had Monty squeezed under his arm.

Off to the side, Kate saw the sergeant pull his revolver from his belt, cock it and step towards the front of the carriage. He raised his arm and pointed the gun right at Juba.

Kate was half glad they'd given her no choice. She straightened her elbow and let her revolver slide down her arm and into her hand. She sighted down the revolver. If it

218

were done, best it were done quickly. Kate's gun fired .31 cal-
iber soft lead bullets and, at short range, it was deadly
accurate, particularly when fired by someone who'd been target practicing. And she had. She gave her head a tiny shake
and pulled the trigger.

The back of the sergeant's head slammed forward like he'd
been hit with a bat. He stumbled and fell, dead by the time his
face smacked into the dusty road.

Fourteen things happened at once. Or so it seemed. Monty
made a savage sound, something like what you'd think a wolf
sounded like when it was killing something. She wheeled and
pointed her gun at the men behind her, but the smallest one
had already turned tail and bolted down the road. The fat
redhead, the one called Quinn was trying to pull Monty off his
neck. He grabbed at Monty's little body, but the dog's legs
were kicking and clawing in a frenzy of black and white fur,
his teeth locked on to the man's throat. Quinn screeched and
hit the dog. Then Monty was flying. He hit a bit of brush and
half yelped, half shrieked. Quinn turned and ran.

The last remaining man turned toward the man Kate had
shot, tripped, scrambled to his feet. He grabbed the dead
man's arm, and pulled, flipping the body onto its back. Realizing his friend was dead he let go and scrambled into the brush.
At her back, Juba made a grab for the carriage horses and
missed. The spooked horses took off down the road, the barouche bouncing and clattering behind them. A rear wheel
ran over the dead sergeant's head, causing it to crunch open
like a dropped watermelon. Juba turned and fired the Derringer after the fleeing men. There wasn't much chance of hitting
them at that distance, but the shooting sounds seemed to encourage them along their way. Seconds later the three men

burst out of the underbrush, each of them mounted on a scrubby mountain pony, and took off up the road. They were gone from sight in the blink of an eye.

Kate stepped toward where Monty landed, just as the little dog limped out of the brush. He stood in the middle of the road, his hackles up, growling. Kate called his name. He ran at her, favoring his right front leg as he did and leaped into her arms. "My hero," she said in his ear and hugged his quivering body. He smeared blood on her shirt but she didn't care, not right then.

Before she could check and see if the blood was his or the man he'd attacked, Juba tapped her on the shoulder. He jerked his chin at Monty. "Did I see that right?"

She nodded. "That man would have shot you, so I decided to shoot him first. When he turned his back on me I knew I could. But I figured I had about a fifty percent chance of one of those other men shooting me before I turned around. Monty kept that from happening."

Juba leaned over and kissed the top of Monty's dusty head.

She looked at Juba. "You all right?"

"Yep. You?"

She looked at the corpse in the road and shook her head. "I keep killing people." Kate ignored the sinking feeling in her gut. Or she tried to.

He nodded once, then glanced around. "That's a conversation for later. You drag that fellow out of the road and hide him in the brush before someone comes along. And then stay hidden. I'll fetch the horses. No telling how far they ran, but I'll get them turned around and come back for you." He turned to go. "Want me to take the little guy?"

Kate hugged Monty closer to her, then loosened her grip on him and set him down. "He's the hero of the day, so he gets to do whatever he wants."

Juba grinned, then turned and set off up the road in a loping run. Monty didn't follow him.

"I guess you're with me," she said. She gestured at the dead man. "I'll grab his arms if you grab his feet." She paused and smiled. Monty was taking a moment to lick blood off his front paws. "Fine. I'll do it myself."

She looked down at the dead man. Only moments before he'd been a living human being. Not a very nice one, at least not this afternoon, but someone, somewhere loved him. And here he lay in the road, gray brain goop leaking out of his skull like cheese curds gone bad.

She grabbed his cooling hands and dragged him across the road. He was heavier than she'd expected and his cracked head kept snagging on the bumps and ruts in the road. And he stank of voided bowels and old sweat. Kate averted her eyes from her burden and pulled harder. The birds, which had quieted after the gunshots, sang again.

It took awhile to get the dead sergeant off the road. She'd have liked to pull him deeper into the woods, but the tangled underbrush wouldn't allow it. Monty trotted along with her, finding the whole operation intensely interesting. Kate bent some branches over the body and left it. She crept to the side of the road and crouched down behind a thick bush. Monty crawled into her lap. The birds sang. The wind blew through the trees.

Kate hugged Monty and tried not to cry. She remembered his limp. She ran her hands over his body, probing and patting for injuries. He didn't want her to touch his front leg, but

221

it didn't seem broken or cut. Kate guessed one man had used the leg to pull Monty off the man's throat. She turned his head towards hers and looked at his doggy face. He had blood on his muzzle, up where his tongue couldn't reach it. She pulled her shirt tail out of her pants, spit on it and wiped her dog's head. He returned the favor by licking her hand. She found his warm tongue comforting and spent a few minutes weeping into Monty's fur.

They waited. Birds sang, squirrels capered and the world moved on as if she hadn't killed someone. Monty pricked his ears. A jangling sound came down the road, then the clopping of hooves. She realized she hadn't brushed the blood or drag marks out of the road. What if it wasn't Juba? She ducked her head and prayed.

"Kate," Juba called in a soft voice.

She loosened her grip on Monty and the two of them scrambled out onto the road. Kate kicked dirt over the mess the dead man's head left on the road and moments later they were gone, following their would-be-robbers up the road. Behind them and before them, the birds still sang.

"Dammit boy, fill up this damn decanter." Colonel Nathan Evans held out a rough glass whiskey decanter to his fourteen-year-old body servant and slave. The youth scuttled over, snatched the bottle and took it over to a small table in the corner of the tent. On it stood a tapped cask. The smell of aged Kentucky whiskey filled the tent as the amber liquid trickled into the bottle.

While his bottle filled, Evans appraised the three privates who stood before him. The red-headed one had a bloody scrap of fabric wrapped around his neck. "And you left Sergeant Stone behind?" God's teeth, but enlisted men could be dumb as rocks.

"Yes sir," snapped the oldest looking man "That fancy feller started shooting and we thought it best to skedaddle."

Evans turned toward the ginger-haired, fat man. "What's your name and what happened to you Private?"

"Private Quinn sir. The man's dog attacked me. Sprung right at my throat."

The older fellow snickered.

Evans glared at him, then turned to the older man. "What?"

"It was a little bit of a thing, sir. The dog I mean. No bigger than a possum. Quinn here nearly let the little feller git the best of him."

Evans sighed and returned his gaze to Private Quinn. "You let a dog beat you? A small one? God's teeth man. How can I win a war with men too stupid to outwit a dog?"

Quinn stared at his colonel, mouth gaping in an effort to formulate an answer.

Evans ignored him. "And these papers?" He looked down at the over-sized leather case in his lap. From it, he'd pulled a set of papers that testified to the carrier's identity. There was also a travel pass signed by Jefferson Davis. "It didn't occur to any of you wooly heads that robbing an English aristocrat was a bad idea?"

The three men shook their heads in unison.

"Especially one who knows President Davis?" He roared these last words. Then he had a blinding thought, followed by a moment of hope. "Did you tell them who you are?"

"No sir," one man barked.

223

Quinn shuffled his feet.

Evans pinned the shuffler with his eyes.

"I might a mentioned your name, sir. And Sergeant Stone called me by name."

"You damn fools," he roared. "I told you to rob the gentry, but I didn't ask you to cause an international incident. Get out of my sight before I have you all shot for stupidity. And no more scavenging. You're too damn dumb to leave camp. Wait. Was anyone with this fellow?"

"He had a nigger driver, Sir. With a gun."

Evans snorted. By God people were stupid. You didn't give guns to niggers. "Are you numbskulls still here?" he yelled at the men.

The men scrambled out of the tent, bumping into each other as they went. Evans grimaced at the papers in his lap. If Beauregard found out his men had harassed this English fellow he'd be cashiered out of the army. He needed to put a lid on this whole damn thing and quick like.

A black arm intruded upon his musings, holding his whiskey decanter before him. Evans took it and gazed fondly at the boy before him. "Will, you should be in bed," he said softly. "Wait. Pull off these here boots first." The child, who was no more than ten years old, knelt before him and pried off first one boot, then another, exposing threadbare socks redolent with the smell of unwashed feet. Evans ruffled the child's black hair and then pushed him toward the door. "Keep out of trouble, you hear."

"Yassah," the boy said in a high cracked voice before he backed out of the tent.

Evans gulped whiskey straight from the decanter, then hooked a straight back wooden chair with his sock-clad foot

224

and pulled it in front of him. He plunked his feet on the chair bottom, took another gulp of whiskey and stared at his legs. They were pale, scrawny and knock-kneed. At West Point, he'd earned the nickname "Shanks" because of them. It was a nickname that had always enraged him. Now that war had come he had a chance to make a new name for himself. No more "Shanks." While other men quailed and shit themselves in the hot press of battle, his heart took flight. It always did. Fear, which dogged him most days, flew away in battle, leaving him exhilarated and energized when bullets flew and cannon boomed. No more being stalled at Colonel—he'd be a general or he'd be damned. But his chance would disappear in a cloud of ignominy if this damned English Lord showed up demanding redress. He'd be Shanks forever.

Maybe nothing would come of it. He took another pull from the bottle. Best to be realistic. Either the English bastard was heading here or he'd high tail it back to Richmond, where he'd surely go running to President Davis. Unless he could intercept the fellow and make him disappear. And sell the Englishman's slave in Richmond. That would net him a tidy sum. He could buy better whiskey.

His boy poked his head through the tent flaps, his eyes wide with fear and worry. "Sorry sir, but Captain Lewis says he needs to see you right away."

Evans heaved a great sigh. The shit was about to fly.

Chapter 20

August 19-20, 1861
Manassas, Virginia

They reached the main Confederate camp at Manassas Junction just as the sun slid past the horizon. Juba slowed for the sentries who blocked the road and Lord Tracy reached for his papers. Then Kate remembered. In her mind, she saw the three men. They'd been digging through h Lord Tracy's packet of money and papers when everything slewed sideways.

"Juba," she hissed, "My papers. They're gone."

He looked over his shoulder and in a calm voice said, "Confederate deserters robbed Lord Tracy." He paused. "Right?"

Kate shrugged, then straightened her shoulders. This would take some serious acting.

"Halt!" A man stepped out and approached their carriage.

Monty barked.

Kate grabbed her dog and mustered all the indignant entitlement she could imagine. "I am Lord Tracy of Toddington and I would like to report a robbery. I had a pass allowing me to inspect this camp signed by president Davis himself, but four villains in the uniform of this army attacked me. I demand to speak to your commanding officer about these miscreants and recouping my losses."

"Huh?" The man, who wore sergeant's stripes, had expected nothing like Lord Tracy to appear on his road.

Kate repeated herself, this time using shorter words.

"Well, we'll see about that," the sergeant drawled. "My captain will not be happy to have his supper disturbed." He turned and barked at the knot of men behind him, "Private Wills, go fetch the captain." He turned back to Kate and Juba. "Meanwhile we'll wait." One of the men stepped forward and took the reins from Juba.

They waited almost an hour. The graying light turned the sky deep blue, then purple. An evening star appeared in the gathering gloom before the private returned. He snapped a salute and said, "Sorry Sergeant. Captain Lewis went to check with Colonels Evan's. I had to wait. The Colonel wants to see them first."

Dammit. Kate looked over at Juba. Colonel Evans? Shanks Evans? Had they ridden right into men under the same command as their robbers? *What were the chances Evans was just now hearing of his men's trouble on the road?* Kate thought the chances were pretty good.

Juba twisted in his seat and shared a look of astonishment with Kate.

Under her breath, she muttered, "Out of the frying pan and into the fire." It wasn't Shakespeare, but it would do.

Colonel Evans was a singularly unimpressive looking man. He wasn't much taller than Kate, but he had a barrel-shaped torso that made him seem bigger than he was. His body balanced on a pair of stick-like legs so crooked they touched at the knees. All that, together with a high, broad forehead and pale eyes and the colonel bore an unfortunate resemblance to a large toad. Unfortunately, the toad was looking at Lord Tracy as if he were a juicy fly.

"And why should I believe this story of yours," the Colonel asked, spitting his words as if they were to acid.

Kate looked over at the packet of papers lying on the man's desk. "Because sir," she said in her snottiest Lord Tracy voice, "you have my papers right there." She pointed at the Toad's desk.

Evans walked over and picked up Lord Tracy's billfold. "These could belong to anyone."

Kate wished Juba was here to see the Colonel's performance. "That's not true, Sir. The papers belong to a man both English and aristocrat. How many men like that do you suppose are in northern Virginia right now?"

"That there's my problem," the Toad said. "I don't know. I'll have to put you in the brig while I sort this out." He jerked his chin at his men. They grabbed Kate and shoved her out of the colonel's tent into the cool night air. Juba stood outside, flanked by two privates.

Kate realized the cold truth of their situation as the men marched the two of them into the dark. The colonel had no intention of letting his men's activities become a matter of military record, which meant Lord Tracy and his servant had to disappear, probably into a discrete hole in the ground.

The soldiers marched them down a row of tall, framed wall tents, to a log cabin so small they both had to duck their heads as the men shoved the two of them through the door. Kate stumbled, then regained her footing when Juba grabbed her arm. They heard the jangle of keys, the snap of a padlock and the sound of men marching away.

She and Juba were alone. Locked into a windowless, one room cabin.

"That went pretty well."

Kate turned toward the sound of Juba's cheerful voice. "You're kidding right?"

"Nope. The door doesn't fit the door frame and I didn't see them search you. They didn't, did they?"

Kate thought for a moment and chuckled. Dear, dear Juba. "No. Colonel Toad didn't touch me. Thank God."

Juba snickered. "He is a toad, isn't he? Got your lock-picks?"

Kate pulled the small leather encased tool set from her inside jacket pocket. The picks made a small clanking sound as she did.

"Wait," he said. "I've got a packet of Lucifer's somewhere."

Kate heard the rustle of clothes, then the strike of a match. She held her lockpick set up to the tiny flame and pulled out her smallest twist wrench and the hook pick.

Juba shook the match out before it burned his fingers. The stink of sulfur hung in the dark. "Hold on. It didn't sound like they left a guard, but we best check."

The door hinges creaked, then the lock rattled. A sliver of dim light appeared in the space between the door and the frame. Kate's eyes adjusted to the improved lighting. Juba stepped back. "No pressure, but I suspect they'll be back as soon as they've dug a hole big enough for you."

"And you," she amended.

He shook his head. "Nah. Just you. I'm valuable. You're the one that's a problem. Cause you're white."

"Rats," Kate muttered. "Here I thought we might spend eternity in the same grave, Uncle of mine."

"No such luck, your lordship. Now quit chattering and pop that lock open."

The grin in Juba's voice made their situation more tolerable. Thankful she had small hands, Kate reached through the crack in the door and grabbed the big padlock. It keyhole was on the side of the big lock, which helped the work. She pushed the short end of the L shaped wrench into the lock and pressed down. With her other hand, she went fishing for pins with the hook.

She worked the lock for a long minute, then withdrew the hook pick and turned the wrench. The padlock snapped open with a satisfying, if too loud, click.

Minutes later they were in the trees behind Colonel Toad's tent, where they waited for someone to notice they'd escaped. After nearly an hour voices came from the Toad's tent. Then a yell.

"What do you mean they're escaped? How? Dammit, all!" More hushed voices followed, then a thud hurried footsteps.

Kate peeked from behind a tree. The Toad and two men were walking up the tent row toward the tiny jail. She stepped back toward the Toad's tent and drew out her dagger. She kissed its hilt for luck and cut a slit in the tent's rear wall.

Before she could step in, Juba pushed her aside. "Let me," he whispered. "He won't kill me."

She wanted to argue, but he had a good point. "Table to the left." Remembering they were facing the opposite direction from earlier in the evening, she corrected herself. "No. Your right."

Kate stood watch while Juba searched the tent. About three seconds before she had a heart attack an arm holding Lord Tracy's papers popped through the back tent wall. Juba followed. They crept back into the trees.

"Now what do we do?" Kate tucked Lord Tracy's identity papers and traveling pass back into her jacket. "We're fugitives in the middle of the largest Confederate Army encampment in Virginia." It seemed worse when she said it out loud.

Juba didn't even hesitate. "We finish the job."

Kate bit her lower lip and thought for a moment. "So we find Beauregard, where ever he is, and tell him about the Toad?"

Juba nodded. "Discretely. Lord Tracy can't be pushing the General into a corner over one of his best fighting men."

"And if we handle it right Beauregard will be indebted to his lordship."

"Let's hope so. With your papers in hand, he has to treat you fairly, even if he doesn't want to." Juba turned in a circle. "Now how do we find Beauregard?"

It turned out that finding General Beauregard was the easiest thing they had done all day, even though they had to lurk through the shadows like sneak thieves to do it. Using the alleys behind the rows of tents they made their way toward the center of the camp and looked for the largest, busiest set of tents. One of the wall tents was bigger than the others. It also had a wood-framed door built into it and an awning out front large enough to accommodate several long tables. Lord Tracy showed his pass from Jefferson Davis to the soldier standing outside the general's door and demanded to see the general. Once again, Juba waited outside.

Beauregard resembled the Toad only insofar as neither one of them was over tall. In all other details, the man seated before Kate was the Toad's exact opposite. He had a trim build, a face like a fox and a uniform so perfectly sponged and pressed it appeared brand new. His tent contained a neatly made up camp bed, two straight back chairs, a small, unlit stove and a desk behind which he sat.

He leaned back in his chair as Lord Tracy began his story, but the more his lordship spoke, the more Beauregard leaned forward. She told the story of the robbery pretty much as it happened, leaving out the man she'd killed and didn't discuss their confinement at all. As Lord Tracy's tale came to the close of her tale Beauregard had his elbows on his desk, hands clasped before him.

"That is a fascinating story. You're asking me to believe Colonel Evans assisted you after his men robbed you. Furthermore, you say he sent you to me after returning your papers, which he retrieved from his men." Beauregard spoke English with a soft French accent that Kate suspected made him deadly with the ladies.

Lord Tracy clasped his hands behind his back and clicked his heels together with a little bow. "Let us say that is precisely the tale I am prepared to tell. If you so wish."

Beauregard crooked an eyebrow at Lord Tracy. "And if I don't wish?"

"Then I have another version. One less complimentary to the Colonel and the Confederate Army. It is not a tale I wish to tell. I would not deprive you of a capable field officer for no more reason than wounded pride. If you require the strict

233

truth from me I shall give it to you, much to the detriment of your Colonel." Lord Tracy paused, rocking upon his heels. "May I assume you would prefer to avoid unpleasantness?"

The little general regarded Lord Tracy for a moment and then inclined his head and smiled. "Would you take a brandy with me, sir? Or would you prefer to retire for the evening? I'm sure we can find an empty tent for you and your man."

Lord Tracy settled himself into a camp chair. "A brandy would be delightful. If you would do me a favor sir."

Beauregard poured a glass of amber liquid and held it out to his guest. "I am at your disposal, Your Lordship."

Kate agreed, but didn't say so. "Could you send a man to fetch my dog? I would hate to think he is still held hostage now that I am free."

Beauregard blanched as he took in the implication of his lordship's words.

Kate took a sip of excellent brandy and eyed the general over the rim of her glass. Politeness was all well and nice, but she needed him to understand the depth of Colonel Evans' depravity and the immensity of the debt he owed Lord Tracy. Beauregard sent a man to fetch Monty. Their reunion was most satisfying.

The next morning, after all too short slumber, Juba waited on his lordship at breakfast and returned to their tent, leaving Lord Tracy with Beauregard's staff. Lord Tracy was drinking his third mug of coffee when Beauregard joined him.

Beauregard admired Monty, who sat at Kate's feet under the table. After a thorough ear rubbing the general offered Lord Tracy a tour of the camp. "Or would you prefer to go about on your own?" Beauregard hastened to add, "Either way is fine with me, but you might enjoy the knowledge a guide could offer."

Lord Tracy agreed that a tour would be most delightful. By mid-morning, they'd seen about half the camp, led by a lieutenant so eager and amenable that Kate wanted to take him home and feed him cookies. The young man provided horses for the three of them, assuring Lord Tracy that his carriage horses were being cared for by men in the Thirtieth Cavalry. Monty trotted alongside them, signaling his happiness by peeing on as many Confederate tents and wagons as he could manage. Kate had never been prouder of her dog.

The young man introduced himself as Lieutenant Floyd of the Twenty-Fourth Virginia Infantry, a regiment in Colonel Early's Sixth Brigade, over which General Beauregard had command as the top general of the Army of the Potomac. Kate's brain reeled at the names, numbers and military hierarchy, though a glance at Juba suggested he understood the Lieutenant just fine. She again made a note to have Hazzard explain military structure to her one more time.

His lordship asked young Floyd if he was related to the Confederate General John Floyd. The young man's answer led to a convoluted Floyd genealogy that suggested five or six degrees of separation between the two Floyds. Still, the young man seemed proud of his relative, though more because he'd become a brigadier general than for his service to the federal government.

They rode through the army camp, zigzagging their way through regiments from Louisiana, Mississippi, South Carolina, Arkansas and Virginia. Each regiment grouped their tents around a regimental headquarters, notable for the relative

comfort of framed wall tents for officers and rough log buildings not unlike the one Evan's men had imprisoned them in
the night before. Rows of tents for enlisted men surrounded
each headquarters, divided by dusty throughways wide
enough to drive a wagon through. The enlisted men's canvas
and pole tents were staked so close to each other they looked
like a herd of pointy sheep. Most of the tents were only open-
ended canvas staked into a triangle, though some regiments
used the larger, conical Sibley tents. The combined scents of
cooking and coffee rode the air, along with wood smoke from
the hundreds of fires that dotted the camp. Men, both white
and black tended the fires and a fair number of women.

In fact, there were more women in camp than Kate expected. Most of them bustled around smoking fires, which
they seemed to use primarily to cook large pots of stew,
though some appeared to be heating water for laundry. A few
gaudily clothed women lounged here and there, clearly in
camp to engage in the world's oldest female profession. The
Lieutenant pretended not to see any of the ladies, an oversight
Kate found unsurprising and disappointing.

After they'd toured Colonel Hampton's Legion and were
making their way back to Beauregard's headquarters for lunch
Kate spied a young woman galloping through the camp her
black horse glossy with sweat. She took several small jumps
over logs the men had lying about for benches, her black hair
flying behind her like a flag. She rode with confidence, a feat
made more impressive because she rode sidesaddle and held
the reins with one hand, using the other to wave at men as she
called out greetings.

Kate thought the girl looked familiar and broke the silence
about women to ask about her.

Lieutenant Floyd whipped off his hat. "That is Miss Belle Boyd. A lovelier, braver girl there never was." He waved his hat at Miss Boyd but either she did not see him, or pretended not to see him. She was out of sight moments later after which a downhearted Floyd jammed his hat back on his head. Then he brightened. "If we hurry she'll still be at the General's tent." He turned his horse to go, not looking back to see if his lordship, valet, and dog were following.

Juba watched the Lieutenant ride away. "Wonder what that's all about?"

Kate shook her head. "Pretty girl. Young, romantic army officer. You do the math. Did she look familiar to you?"

"Maybe," Juba drawled. "She was moving pretty fast."

"I'm thinking she was one of little Patsy's sketches."

"Hmmm. Could be."

When they arrived back at General Beauregard's head-quarters young Floyd discovered Miss Boyd had already come and gone. His face fell so precipitously that Kate feared he would burst into tears.

"Why didn't she stay?" the crestfallen Lieutenant asked his general.

Beauregard smiled like a man who remembered youthful infatuation. "She's having lunch with Colonel Jackson. And Jackson's got her father with him. You go join them. You can tell the Colonel I'd like to see him after lunch."

Juba led the horses away, but not before casting Kate a meaningful look. Monty gave her his own meaningful look, though his was more about water and food than spycraft.

"I'm afraid it's just stew for lunch," Beauregard said. They took a seat at the same table they'd used for breakfast. A bowl of bread and another bowl that smelled like lamb stew sat in the middle of the table next to a pile of smaller tin bowls and a mug full of spoons. "The cook makes great bunches of it which we eat over and over again. The most you can say is it's honest food." The general half filled one bowl and set it on the ground for Monty. The little black dog ate his lunch with unseemly haste.

"And your wife, sir? May I ask if there is such a person?" Lord Tracy asked in between spoons of stew, which was more delicious than it had a right to be.

"There is. I remarried last year, a widow. The new Mrs. Beauregard is a lovely woman, but I find I still miss my first wife. I suppose it is impossible to become attached to someone and stop when they pass beyond this vale of tears. Are you married your lordship?"

Lord Tracy smiled in what Kate hoped was a self deprecating manner. "Sadly no, though many an ambitious Mama's has pinned their hopes on me, or more accurately, on my title and fortune. I find myself unready for the matrimonial institution." Kate took another bite of her stew and tried to look modest. "Though this camp seems to have a lady or two that might tempt a gentleman. We saw an interesting girl on a big horse as we were coming back."

"Oh, you mean Miss Boyd," Beauregard said, reaching for the bread. He buttered a piece of bread and bit into it. "She is too forward and obvious for my taste and yours as well, as you would see if you met her. She's good enough for the boys I suppose. Damned useful girl though."

Kate's heart quickened. "How is that?"

Beauregard eyed Lord Tracy. "What I tell you here is in confidence, understand? I speak of this because I trust you."

The business of Lord Tracy's arrest and near murder lay unsaid between them.

Kate nodded. "Sir, I come to the end of my American sojourn impressed with your nation's ideals. As I told dear President Davis, I hope to return to England and convince my high placed friends to support the Confederacy." Kate thanked the gods in the heavens that the Confederacy needed the English, both as military allies and as trading partners. Without that underlying desperation, none of this would have worked.

"Then tell your friends our cause is so just that it inspires southern women to brave feats of patriotic duty. Miss Boyd showed up here two days ago with messages from one of our nation's best-placed spies, who is also a woman." The general paused and took a bite of his lunch. "The girl acts as courier for a resistance network in Washington headed by this woman. Having delivered her messages," Beauregard gestured to the small camp desk inside the tent, piled high with papers, "Miss Boyd continues to act as courier around the camp, carrying messages from one regimental commander to the next."

Kate's heart leaped again. Were those messages from Rose Greenhow sitting on the desk right behind the general? She reached for a piece of bread and buttered it, trying to appear calm and unruffled as she did. "So you admire her? For her bravery?"

"She has courage to spare, though I think she flirts too much. We southern men know our women are our greatest strength and one the Yankees, in their arrogance, underestimate."

"English gentlemen believe much the same about our women." Sensing an opportunity, Lord Tracy swept his nap-

239

kin off his lap and learned towards the general. "Would it interest you to know General, that I set out on my journey with three cases of French champagne and have an entire case of the stuff left? Perhaps this evening you and some of your men could join me at my tent and toast the bravery of southern women?"

Beauregard thought Lord Tracy had a splendid idea.

Chapter 21

August 20-21, 1861

Manassas & Centreville, Virginia

Juba shook his head. "It's too dangerous. And he's bound to have his own man for that kind of thing."

They were standing inside their borrowed tent arguing about the coming evening.

"He might," Kate argued, "but if he agrees it would give you a legitimate reason to be in his tent."

"And I'd be the first person he'd suspect if he figures out someone's been through his papers. And by extension, he'll suspect Lord Tracy."

Her plan was simple. Lord Tracy would offer her valet's services as a bootblack when Beauregard arrived for their evening champagne. Once he agreed she could send Juba to Beauregard's tent to retrieve the boots. While there Juba could look for papers sent to the general from Rose Greenhow, if he found them, use the general's boots to remove such papers. He could then take then return to their tent, copy anything worthwhile before returning the papers inside the shined footwear.

"It could work," she insisted.

He shook his head again. "No, it could not. And you need to quit trying to keep me safe." He put his hands on his hips and gave her a hard stare. "Don't think I've forgotten about yesterday either. You killed a man you thought would hurt me."

"He would have," Kate said, her voice rising higher than it should, given she was pretending to be a man. She bristled her muskrat mustache at him to compensate for her girlie voice. "He'd cocked his revolver and was pointing it at you."

"Oh, honey," Juba said to his niece, his voice soft and sad. "You can't keep me safe for the rest of your life. And you can't live in fear of letting me down. You didn't let me down. You came and got me. And I helped you rescue the others. I'll always help you."

He watched Kate decide whether to argue with him. Part of her believed it was her fault he'd been kidnapped and sold into slavery and another part of her knew better. Both parts worried Juba because when she wasn't blaming herself she blamed Mrs. Greenhow. And the thing with Greenhow was personal, no matter how much Kate tried to dress it up as loyalty to the Union. Kate didn't want to see the woman hanged for being a spy, she wanted revenge for his kidnapping. That kind of thinking shriveled a person's soul.

"So I suppose you have a better plan?"

"I don't know about better, but at least one that doesn't automatically implicate you." He told her his idea.

"You'll have to be fast," Kate said. "The cigars ought to keep them in place for a while. I smoked one with Colonel Patton back in Charleston and it took nearly an hour." Kate shuddered. "I'll stall on lighting them as long as I can, but after I do they'll be like a ticking clock."

Before he could reply Kate let loose an enormous, jaw-cracking yawn. She picked up Hazzard's watch from the little desk inside the tent and peered at it. "We've got a few hours before dinner. Time for a nap."

Kate fell asleep about three seconds after she laid down. Juba took longer and when he did fall asleep a nightmare about being caught in Beauregard's tent and sold into slavery woke him up. He gave up on sleep after that.

The evening jogged along pretty well as planned. Until it didn't.

General Beauregard arrived just before the light failed. He brought his staff with him, including an artillery colonel, a captain from the quartermaster's office and Lieutenant Floyd. Young Floyd hauled two more chairs. Lord Tracy, dressed in his hunter green coat, received the men as if they were in the parlor of a ducal castle and not sitting in the dust in front of a tent. His lordship had his dog tied to his chair, on the excuse that the little fellow had taken to wandering off at night. Juba poured out the first three bottles of champagne into an assortment of camp mugs, making sure each man had a full glass and that Lord Tracy an extra bottle. Then he retired to his Lordship's tent.

Juba lifted the tent's back wall and crawled under. Their line of tents backed up against the rear walls of another line of tents, creating a narrow alley of a sort. From the smell, Juba guessed soldiers used the alley as a latrine. Juba smiled in satisfaction. The tomcat piss odor would keep men from using the alley as a thoroughfare. He counted tents until he came to Beauregard's.

The back wall of Beauregard's tent contained a button flap that could be opened in hot weather to allow a breeze to flow right through the tent. Juba hadn't ever been inside, but Kate's description included the fact that the buttons were inside the tent. Beauregard also had a wood floor in his tent, though the tent canvas was not tucked under it, probably to allow the sides to roll up in hot weather.

Juba squatted down and leaned in close to the tent. He listened. Nothing. He slid his hand through a gap in the buttons and undid one, then another and another. Quiet as any sneak thief he slipped inside. He stood still for a moment, letting his eyes adjust to the interior gloom. He patted his jacket pocket, checking for Kate's lockpicks. She'd insisted he borrow them, though he didn't think he'd need them. Military men lived peripatetic lives among shared goods. Juba doubted the desk in this tent was Beauregard's personal furniture. Rather it was the desk that came with the tent. Men used to that arrangement would keep keys with the desks.

He groped around the desk's exterior with no success. He knelt and examined the desk's kneehole. *Still nothing. Where could the damn thing be?* Just as he was about to resort to the lockpicks he glanced at the desk's deepest drawer. *Oh, for goodness sakes.* Juba resisted knocking his head against the desk for his own stupidity. A key jutted from the lock.

As he pulled open the drawer, he heard a shuffling noise at the front of the tent. *Shit.* He looked back at the tent flap. He'd left it unbuttoned. *No time.* He crawled into the desk's kneehole, held his breath and prayed.

He heard the wood-framed door open, then boot heels on the wood floor. They paused.

A bead of sweat ran down's Juba's forehead and into his eye. He blinked. The boots moved again.

"There," he heard a male voice mutter.

Juba heard the clink of glassware, the same noise he'd heard the night before when Beauregard and Lord Tracy shared a brandy while he waited outside. Juba's heart pounded so loudly he felt sure the interloper would hear him.

Footsteps again. A boot stepped around the desk, then another. Juba stared at the man's legs. His heart stopped. One boot lifted and nudged the drawer closed. Then the boots walked away. Juba heard the flimsy tent door open and close. Silence returned.

It took a few moments for Juba's heart to start up again. When it did it galloped around his chest as he crawled out from the desk. The damn nightmare had almost come true. He pulled the drawer open again and tiptoed his fingers through Beauregard's files until he found one labeled 'Washington.' He pulled it out and opened it. A sheaf of telegrams, scraps of paper and small notes lie inside. Several documents were written in a familiar cipher. He snapped the file closed and tucked it inside his shirt before he closed the desk drawer, careful to leave the key where he found it. Juba crept out of the tent, all the while wondering how he'd find the courage to return the file less than an hour from now.

Back at Lord Tracy's tent, he laid the file on the desk, before peeking out the front of the tent. He'd been gone less than fifteen minutes, but his lordship's guests had already drunk their way through four bottles of champagne. He fetched four more from the creek. Kate crooked her finger at him. He lowered his head to hers and she murmured, "Cigars just lit." Louder she said, "How many bottles left after these Lane?"

"Four, more sir," he said with a little bow of his head.

His lordship nodded and waved his servant away.

Juba spent the next forty minutes copying everything in the file in a barely legible scribble. Some of it he didn't understand, but the documents not in code left him breathless with rage. How had Mrs. Greenhow gathered so much information? He remembered Mr. Wilson and Mr. Seward with dismay. Heads would roll when Mr. Lincoln and his generals saw this stuff. And maybe Kate would realize her fondest wish, Mrs. Greenhow kicking at the end of a rope. The thought made Juba uneasy.

Kate's head throbbed like a base drum the next morning. She sat at the edge of her cot, head in her hands, trying not to moan. Monty jumped up on the camp bed, jiggling it when he landed. Kate winced, then squinted at her dog. Eyes clear, ears forward, his small body coiled for action, he was an advertisement for temperance. "These southern men do two things really well: drink and talk."

Juba handed her a cup of coffee he'd begged from the baker's tent, one laced with a shot of brandy. She sipped it and gagged and held it out to him. He pushed the cup back toward her. "Trust me. A little hair of the dog that bit you will help."

She sipped her coffee. "Did we talk last night? I can't remember."

"No, we didn't talk. You staggered in mumbling about God only knows what and passed out three minutes later."

Kate sniffed at herself. She was wearing Lord Tracy's outfit from the night before and it badly needed a wash. So did
she. "How'd you do?"

He grinned at her. "Got it. Everything we need to sink
Mrs. Greenhow's operation. I've wrapped the copies in oil-
cloth and tucked the whole mess in the champagne crate,
under the empty bottles."

Kate emptied her mug. Juba was right. She felt better. Not
well enough to drink champagne anytime soon, but at least
her head didn't hurt so much she yearned for death. "I'd love
to take a look, but you're right to hide the stuff and leave it.
Oh, last night Lord Tracy expressed an interest in meeting
General Johnston. His lordship's good friend Gustave said to
come by this morning for a pass to Centreville."

"Gustave? Centreville?"

Kate smiled. "Lord Tracy and General Beauregard have
agreed to use their Christian names with each other. His first
name is Pierre, but he prefers Gustave. And Johnston is up at
Centreville."

Juba held out his hand for Kate's mug and refilled it from
a larger one he'd borrowed from the bakers. He left the brandy out this go round. "I thought the Union held Centreville."

"I was just outside Centreville the day of the battle, and the
Union had control of it then. That's where the crowd gathered to watch the battle, such as it was. But after their defeat
the Union army pulled back to Washington, leaving the town
undefended. Johnston moved his army in to fill the void."

"And how far is Centreville from Washington?"

"Half a day's ride," Kate replied with a grin. "Shall we go?"
Sensing a shift in the action, Monty jumped off the bed and

trotted outside, presumably to perform some last minute urination chores.

Lieutenant Floyd brought the barouche around to their tent along with a note from Beauregard introducing them to General Johnston. He also brought Beauregard's regrets. The general had a staff meeting this morning and couldn't see them off. Floyd hopped down from the carriage and after admiring its shining black paint and gold painted trim, handed the reins to Juba and shook Lord Tracy's hand. "Wait till I write my mother and tell her I met a real lord. And you were nice as peas." Young Floyd shook his head in wonder. "Who knew war could be such an adventure?"

Kate looked over at the young man. He wasn't really that young. A year or two younger than she. Old enough to know better. She leaned forward from her carriage seat and asked, "Did you see much action in the late battle?"

Floyd fairly bounced on his toes. "I was with the General at his headquarters. I ran messages."

Lord Tracy nodded, shook the young man's hand and wished him well. She hoped he never got closer to war than message running. The world needed more wide-eyed romantics and fewer cynics hardened by violence.

On their way out of camp, they rolled past Colonel Evan's tent. The Toad sat out front eating his breakfast. Lord Tracy's driver tipped his hat at the man as they drove by.

"General Beauregard sends his regards," Lord Tracy called out to the Toad.

The Colonel gaped at them, his fork frozen halfway to his mouth as they rode out of sight.

248

Kate endeavored to keep a straight face. She failed.

Hundreds of cattle being driven down the road to Centreville, on their way to becoming supper for thousands of soldiers, slowed their progress. After following the cattle herd for twenty minutes Juba gave up and pulled the horses over to the side of the road. While the dust settled, they planned their return trip home.

"The way I see it," Juba said, "our problem isn't getting out of Johnston's camp, it's getting through the Union pickets between here and Washington."

Kate lolled back in the seat, her eyes half closed, her hand on Monty, who was dozing next to her. The bumping and bouncing on the road wasn't doing her head any favors. "Don't worry. I've got that covered. But we need to get rid of Lord Tracy before we leave town."

She explained what she was thinking. This time Juba thought her plan was pretty good.

Once again Lord Tracy presented his papers to Confederate pickets set up at the edge of town. The soldiers manning the barrier were more impressed with the note from General Beauregard than they were the one from President Davis. As they made their way into town, they passed gangs of men cutting down pine trees. No doubt Johnston's Army of the Shenandoah was larger than the town could accommodate. Kate didn't envy the men who would inhabit the rough little cabins the military liked to build. They also passed several fortification construction sites. She suspected there was more fortification work on the north side of town, facing Washington and the Union Army.

Soldiers at the barricade directed them to Johnston's headquarters in town. They rode down a main street crowded with

249

wagons and soldiers in a profusion of noise and color and dust. Everyone seemed busily on their way to some important event or another. No one paid any attention to them. Kate supposed she looked like any other rich slave owner, come to town on errands.

When they found the Centreville Hotel, they discovered it had been transformed into a hospital. Juba jumped down from the driver's seat and looped the carriage reins around the hotel's hitching post. He took a moment to examine the horses, then stepped back to confer with his lordship. "I don't think anyone's paying any attention to us at all."

Kate agreed. "Interesting, isn't it?"

"New plan?"

"I should think so."

Juba grinned and climbed back into his seat. "Shall we find the most disreputable livery stable in town?"

"What a delightful idea." Kate tried not to laugh. It was lovely to be heading home finally.

Juba drove Lord Tracy up and down Centreville's few streets looking for livery stables. The first one was too well maintained. Even its sign looked new. Juba looked over his shoulder at Kate. She shook her head. They kept looking. On the northern outskirts of town, they found it. The small barn, sheathed in gray unpainted boards, tilted to the west as if it were tired of standing upright. The words 'Conway's Livry' were painted on the building, apparently by someone who couldn't spell.

Juba pulled the barouche up to the leaning building. The carriage looked like a society lady in a waterfront tavern.

"Kin I help you?" The voice came from the barn's dark interior. A gangly, pale-skinned man stepped out into the light, blinking like he hadn't been outside all day. He wore a shirt and trousers of butternut homespun, over which he'd hung a grease-spotted leather apron. Kate watched him as he realized who had pulled in front of his stable. He straightened his scrawny shoulders, wiped his hands on a dirty apron and stepped toward the barouche.

Juba jumped down from his perch atop the barouche's driver's seat and opened the carriage door with a flourish. Lord Tracy swung his top hat onto his head, grabbed his silver-headed walking stick and stepped down from his carriage. Monty jumped out behind Kate and went looking for something to pee on.

"My good man," his lordship declared, "I require your services." Lord Tracy did not offer his hand to the man. Kate didn't dare look at Juba for fear she'd break into laughter. "I need a place to store my carriage and trunks for several days."

The man spit a wad of brown tobacco goo on the ground before he spoke. "And your horses?" The greedy glint in the stable owner's eye was unmistakable.

Kate had no doubt that if she left the carriage horses here, he'd sell them to the Confederate Army within the hour and report them stolen.

Lord Tracy looked down his nose at the man. "I think not. I require storage, not stabling, for two days. My man and I shall use the horses to tour the camp. We'll return the morning after tomorrow."

"Jeb Conway at your service, sir." Kate watched the man lick his thin lips, his tongue like a furtive pink worm testing the air.

His lordship turned to his valet. "Lane, this will do, don't you think?"

251

Juba grinned back at her. "It's perfect, sir."

While Juba and Mr. Conway unharnessed the horses Kate removed items from the carriage. First, she retrieved the oil-skin-wrapped package from the crate of empty champagne bottles. Next, she crawled into the carriage's back seat and bumped a panel under her seat with her fist. It popped open, revealing a hidden storage space. Monty stuck his nose into the space. "Hold on boy," she said and pushed him aside. She removed the second packet of papers from the compartment, closed it back up stepped out of the barouche for the last time. The Pinkertons would owe Mr. Howard a fair bit of money for its loss but it would be worth it. She glanced over at Juba and Conway. They'd freed the horses from the carriage. Juba saw her looking and walked Conway over to his back room, talking loudly about his lordship's saddle needs.

Juba negotiated the sale of two saddles and bridles from Mr. Conway. While he did Kate tucked her packet of papers into the small of her back, where they'd be covered by his lordship's frock coat. Then she found two empty bottles and filled them at the well. She also made sure Monty had a drink before they left.

Twenty minutes later they were horseback, heading back toward town at a sedate walk, Monty scampering alongside. Juba spotted a break in the trees at the side of the road and rode into it. Kate and Monty followed him. They stopped in a clearing about twenty feet off the road.

Kate looked back at the road. "I'm trying to feel bad about stealing that man's saddles and bridles." She patted her saddle, inviting Monty to jump up with her. In a whirl of dark fur and scrabbling feet, he joined her atop the horse.

Juba shrugged. "When we're not back by Thursday, he'll rifle through the trunks looking for valuables and find a buyer for the carriage. It'll be gone before the weekend's out or I miss my guess. He'll get a good deal more for it than these ragged saddles are worth."

"And if he's asked he won't admit to ever seeing his lordship. If anyone comes looking for him." Kate smiled at the thought of Lord Tracy's demise. The constant performance of masculinity had worn on her. She'd been walking and talking like a man so long it had become second nature, but she missed the gentle swing of a skirt and the sisterhood of other women. Most of all she missed not having to be on guard every minute of the day. "If we pull this off his Lordship's disappearance will make people nervous. They'll either think poor Lord Tracy met his end in an illicit robbery and is buried in the Virginia woods, or they'll suspect the truth. In which case neither General Beauregard nor President Davis will want to admit they were taken in by an imposter."

Juba looked around the woods that surrounded them. "And you think we can get through Confederate territory?"

Kate nodded. "We're still Lord Tracy and his valet. If we're caught, we'll say we got lost. But I don't think we will be caught. We just stick to the woods and hop back on the road when we're past Confederate lines."

"Hop?"

"Well, you know." Kate grinned at her uncle and set her heels to her horse.

Their escape turned out to be more arduous than Kate predicted. The Confederates held the road all the way to Fairfax, which meant they traversed the seven miles zigzagging through the underbrush, fording streams and tramping through briars and over fallen trees. The heat didn't make their day more pleasant, nor did the flies. After several hours of winding through the woods, they had a brief discussion about the wisdom of returning to the road but decided not to.

The Confederates had another camp that spread out to the west of Fairfax, so they turned east, past a series of fortified entrenchments. The day dragged on and the temptation to return to the road mounted each hour. Just before dark, they saw a huge pile of fallen trees and a knot of Confederate soldiers blocking the road. The men were on the west side of the barricade, with two-wheeled cannons pointed east.

"You think?" Kate asked Juba in a whisper. Monty growled, reminding Kate of his presence. "Monty," she hissed. She patted her saddle again and he jumped up with a whine. She wrapped her hand around his muzzle and shushed him.

Juba motioned for her to stay. He slipped off his horse and crept closer to the barricade. Kate could barely see him through the trees and the gathering dusk. After an interminable time, he crawled back to Kate and Monty. "I think this is the last Confederate outpost. They're way more alert than the sentries we've passed. And better armed."

Kate shook her head. "We should have asked someone when we had the chance so we weren't reduced to guessing. Amateur mistake."

"True," Juba said. "Next time we get ourselves disguised, infiltrate the enemy's army and copy their intelligence reports we'll try not to be so dumb about it." Juba paused and rolled his eyes.

It was Kate's turn to snort. She let go of Monty with one hand and patted the packet of papers at the small of her back. "I never did look at these."

254

"Then let's get home and spread them all over the kitchen table. I 'spect little Louisa will be a dab hand at deciphering the code. And Odetta will have something cooking."

Kate nearly cried at the thought of a meal eaten in her own kitchen. She wiped at her eyes with the back of her hand and kicked her horse into motion. It was time to go home.

They crept through the woods for another mile or so. Dark fell as they rode. They had a decision to make. Hunker down in the trees till dawn, or take to the road and ride home in the dark.It was an easy decision. They rode home by starlight and crossed Long Bridge into Washington not long after the moon rose.

Chapter 22

They gave their stolen papers to Allan as soon as they arrived home, who insisted they go through the pile that very minute. Kate cast a longing glance at the stairs, thinking of her bed, but instead she and Juba joined Allan at the kitchen table. Seeing it all from the safety of their kitchen been revelatory to Kate, who hadn't seen the most damning items collected by Juba the night before their flight north.

They found Rose's July 9 note to Beauregard detailing the Union Army's preparations for attack in Northern Virginia. Another group of messages detailed McDowell's military strength, including lists of regiments and numbers of men in each. Other papers contained regiments locations and destinations. There was also a hand-drawn map marking the sites of Washington's new defensive fortifications, though Juba admitted he'd copied it so hastily it might bear little resemblance to the original. Kate made a note to have Hazzard to check it anyhow. He'd been dividing his time between artillery training at Fort Washington and fortification inspections for General Scott so he'd know if the map was important.

Most alarming, for its content and its timing, was a message dated the same day as Bull Run that read: *Wilson to join McClellan's staff. Shall have greater access very soon.*

Kate held that one out to Allan. "Miss Chase identified Senator Henry Wilson as one of Mrs. Greenhow's visitors. Is this him?"

Allan heaved a sigh. "I suspect so. There's some reorganization going on. General McClellan's getting ready to take command of the Union army. Poor McDowell is on the way out. Miss Chase's father championed McDowell's command appointment, but no one could save his job in the wake of the Bull Run debacle. Though these papers," Alan waved his arm over the table, "make it clear the defeat was not entirely McDowell's fault. The Rebs knew everything."

"And Wilson?" Juba asked, redirecting the conversation. "I thought he was a senator and the chair of that military committee."

Allan shook his head. "He is. But he's been organizing a volunteer infantry regiment and has promised it to McClellan. Looks like McClellan might have rewarded him for it."

Kate tapped the paper. "Well, we don't know how Rose is connected to Wilson or what she's getting out of him. She could be exaggerating the Wilson thing." Kate thought about the sketches she had, the ones Miss Chase identified as Senator Wilson and Secretary Seward. And even if Wilson visited Rose, there was no evidence he was doing anything more dangerous than calling on an attractive widow.

Allan nodded. "He's a senator so we must go carefully." He stood. "Let's take this to Mr. Lincoln without delay."

Kate thought about her bed with renewed longing, but agreed to go with Allan. Juba agreed to go too, but not before

258

casting his own longing looks towards the door that led to his downstairs apartment.

John Nicolay, one of the President's two private secretaries, ushered Kate, Juba, and Allan into Lincoln's cluttered office. Each time she saw Nicolay she was struck by the contrast between his appearance and his job. He looked like a romantic poet, all soft hair and soft eyes, but he essentially ran the man who ran the nation and he did so with an iron hand. No one saw Lincoln unless Nicolay let them in.

Mr. Lincoln sat at the large table that dominated the center of his office. He stood, waved them over and took his seat again. "Miss Warne, Mr. Lane, and Mr. Pinkerton, come in. I'm afraid I've got a busy day and can only spare you a few moments."

Kate took a seat at the table, pushing a pile of books out of the way so she could see her president. He looked good today. His suit seemed to be relatively new, his cuffs had only a few ink stains on them and he'd brushed his hair recently. New maps had appeared on the office walls since she'd last been here, hiding much of the forest green wallpaper.

After greeting Mr. Lincoln, Allan looked over at Kate and nodded. She pushed a file folder over in front of Lincoln. "Mr. Lane and I collected these documents, which are copies, from General Beauregard's desk only three days ago. I'd like you to take a few moments to peruse them."

Lincoln's eyes wrinkled at the corners. "As you wish Madame," he teased. But he opened the file. Ten minutes later he'd run his big hand through his hair enough time that his hair stood on end. He raised his head and spoke. "This is terrible. You say you got them from the General's desk?"

Juba spoke up. "I did, while Kate here kept Beauregard busy."

Kate grinned at Juba, who winked back at her.

Lincoln noticed the exchange. "That's a story I'd like to hear someday. Can I assume you have more evidence besides this?" He waved his hand at their papers.

"You can sir," Allan interjected. "The Pinkertons have been watching Mrs. Greenhow for months now. We know many if not all of her co-conspirators and sources. Miss Warne has been in Greenhow's house and in her safe, where she found several other damning documents, including a copy of the cipher code she uses."

Mr. Lincoln shoved back his chair, stood and walked to the window. Kate wanted to talk, to say anything, but she'd learned he'd make up his own mind in his own time. He couldn't be pushed, that much was for sure.

He paused there, framed by the gold velvet curtains, hands behind his back, looking out. "So many men," he said to the window. He shook his head and turned. "And am I correct in recollecting she funded her activities through the illegal sale of free persons of color, including our friend Mr. Lane?"

Juba nodded but didn't say anything.

Kate swallowed, momentarily unable to trust her voice. All the tension of living undercover, the near constant fear of discovery, the danger, the man she killed, all of it welled up in her all at once. "Yes, sir," was all she could say. She scrupulously avoided looking at Juba.

Lincoln's eyes grew sad. "I understand the country owes both of you a great debt for your services this past month. Mr.

Pinkerton tells me that in addition to your mission to find evidence against Mrs. Greenhow you toured several Confederate encampments and sent him several detailed letters."

She took a gulp of air and pulled herself together. "Yes, sir. And I've got more to report." She glanced at Juba. "We do. Once we arrived in Richmond, it seemed ill-advised to send any more letters."

Lincoln glanced at Allan and chuckled. "Serves the copperhead right."

Allan smiled at the president. "I thought you'd appreciate the irony in using an anti-Lincoln, anti-war Democrat's name for our little undertaking."

Juba sighed. "Sirs, may I ask what you intend to do about Mrs. Greenhow? And her spies? She's got so many we ran into one while we were in Beauregard's camp. Pretty gal riding a huge horse, galloping around like she belonged there. Apparently she crosses the lines with impunity."

Kate shot her uncle a grateful look. Thoughts of the rebel girl had been troubling her some now that she had time to think about it.

Lincoln sat at the table again and steepled his hands before him. In his deep, lugubrious voice he said, "It seems we have no choice. The lady must be arrested and jailed. It's the only way to stop her network. Cut off the head and the body will die. We've got some Confederate prisoners of war in the Old Capitol Prison so she should feel right at home. Maybe we can trade her for Congressman Ely."

Kate resisted the urge to leap up and do a happy dance on the room's green carpet. Having the lady arrested was the first step to the gallows. Instead of capering around like a mad woman she stood and smoothed down her skirt. She'd work

261

on getting the rest of them arrested once Rose was safely behind bars.

The president raised his hand. "Now hold your horses there missy. You and Mr. Lane will spend the rest of this afternoon reporting on what you've learned about the Confederate army. Mr. Stanton's been assisting Mr. Cameron of late so you can talk to him. Mr. Nicolay will escort you to the War Department and remain to take notes."

"But the arrest . . ." Kate stuttered. She didn't want to sit around talking when she could be escorting Mrs. Greenhow to jail.

"The arrest can wait until tomorrow," Lincoln said with a gentle smile. "In the meantime, Mr. Stanton awaits." He stood and walked to his desk. They'd been dismissed.

Kate felt like a woman on the edge of greatness. Yesterday she met with Mr. Stanton, who agreed it was time to take action against the Greenhow network. Then she'd had the rest of the day to herself. She took a three-hour nap, crawled out of bed and took Excelsior for a leisurely ride through Rock Creek Park. Then last night she slept in her own bed for twelve glorious hours. Best of all, Rose Greenhow would end her day in jail. And she had a note from Hazzard saying he'd be by tomorrow.

She sighed in happiness as she entered the kitchen. As always, it smelled like warm bread, coffee, and home, but now there was twice as much of it. While she and Juba traveled south Charlotte paid Columbus to take the wall down and repaint. She'd also found another table and placed it end to end with their old one, making one long, mismatched table.

Juba, Samuel, Allan, Timothy, and Charlotte sat at the one end of the table, mugs of coffee before them, while Odetta pulled a pan of sweet rolls from the oven. Louisa was at the sink, elbow deep in soapsuds, talking to Monty, who was keeping his eye on the sweet rolls. Only Hattie was missing.

After a round of good mornings and cheek kissing Kate asked about Hattie.

"She was up afore me," Odetta said, looking up from a bowl of powdered sugar she was whisking into a glaze, "like she been for weeks now."

"She spends pretty much every day at the hospital," Charlotte added. "Other days she goes over to Miss Chase's house. They've got a man over there who took a turn for the worse so Miss Chase needed nursing help. Hattie says the fellow has gangrene and the doctors keep chopping parts off him."

Kate shuddered. "Gross." It was one thing to shoot a man in the head and drag his stinking, brains-leaking body across the road and into the brush, it was a whole other thing to nurse sick men. "Still, I should pay a call on Miss Chase and offer my help. Maybe after we arrest Madame Greenhow." Kate grinned. Today that awful woman would begin her punishment for what she did to Juba and Columbus. And what she'd done to the Union. "Louisa, before I forget—anything to report from our Irregulars?"

Louisa turned from the sink. "I got some more notes from the kids. And some sketches, but it didn't look like anyone new."

"They're still coming by every day?"

Odetta laughed a deep belly laugh. "Those ragamuffins like to eat you out of house and home Miz Kate."

Kate frowned. "Is it too much trouble Odetta?"

"Oh, no. Nothin' like that. Children brighten up a day, don't you think? If you don't mind, I don't mind."

"Then let's continue the experiment. Louisa, would you put the papers you've collected on the desk in my room. I'll look at them as soon as I have a minute."

Just then the doorbell rang. Kate turned, but Charlotte rose from the table. "I'll get it dear. I'm expecting a telegram from Timothy Junior. He's coming here for a few weeks before school starts again." Charlotte bustled from the room, her cheeks rosy with happiness.

A few minutes later Charlotte returned to the kitchen looking disappointed. "It's from Mr. Lincoln," she said, holding the envelope out to Allan and looked apologetically to Kate. "It's addressed to Mr. P."

Allan opened and read the telegram, then looked at Kate. He shook his head. "You're not going to like it." He held the slip of paper out to Kate.

August 23, 1861

Have rethought our plan. Seward concurs. This morning place G under house arrest only. While doing so send Mrs. Barley to me. I will be in my office.

A. Lincoln

"Dammit Allan. I wanted to haul that awful woman into jail today. And arrest the rest of them tomorrow." Kate thought of that rebel girl riding through Beauregard's camp and resisted the impulse to crumple the telegram into a ball and hurl it across the kitchen.

Instead, she handed it to Juba, who read it aloud. "Of course Seward concurs. He's terrified of what she'll reveal once she's in jail. I mean, he's married and he's the Secretary of State for God's sake."

264

Odetta poured Kate another cup of coffee. "Who's Mrs. Barley?"

Juba spoke up. "When Mr. Lincoln met Kate, she was using her Mrs. Barley personae. He thinks it's funny to call her that still."

Odetta nodded and slipped a plate of glazed sweet rolls onto the table before she patted Kate's shoulder. "Mr. Lincoln got a plan, you count on that dear."

Kate wanted no more plans. She wanted to arrest the bitch responsible for Juba's enslavement. She wanted to hear the doors of Greenhow's cell clang shut. She wanted the wretched creature punished for her crimes. What she didn't want was for the woman to stay in her nice house, surrounded by all her nice things, as if she hadn't betrayed her country and left a swath of suffering in her wake.

"Fine." Kate stood to go. "I'll dress and go see Mr. Lincoln. Juba, would you come with me?"

He shook his head. "He asked for you, not me and that man never makes mistakes with words. Besides, Columbus expects me this morning ."

Samuel pushed back from the table. "Miz Kate, you want me to harness Excelsior to the shay? Or Lucy?"

Kate ignored Samuel and opened her mouth to argue with Juba, but stopped. She'd gotten used to having him with her, but he was right. Mr. Lincoln hadn't asked for him, which meant Mr. Lincoln wanted to see her alone. The thought kicked up a nest of butterflies in her stomach.

She turned to Samuel. "Saddle Excelsior. The sooner I'm done with Mr. Lincoln the sooner I get over to Mrs. Greenhow's house. And Samuel? Thanks for your help."

The old man's face crinkled with pleasure. He glanced at Juba and the two of them went out to the yard. Kate walked over to the back door and watched them walk across the backyard, Juba talking, Samuel listening. Whatever they were up to, it wasn't her business and they'd tell her about it when they were ready.

She looked over at Allan. "Will you hold off on the arrest?"

He shook his head. "Sorry Kate, but we need to move on this now. You know what kind of connections she has. The longer we hold off the more likely it is she finds out. And it's house arrest so you won't miss anything. Come to Mrs. Greenhow's as soon as you're done with the president."

"Fine," she repeated, thinking quite the opposite.

As she made for the stairs Allan called out to her. "It will take days to undertake a thorough search. You're not going to miss anything."

She looked at her boss and sighed. "Fine."

Twenty minutes later she and Excelsior were headed for the President's house. Louisa produced a bone that convinced Monty to stay home though Kate thought that Mr. Lincoln would enjoy meeting her dog. Not today though. She wanted to be mad at the president for chickening out. What was it with men and pretty women, anyway? After all the evidence did he still doubt Greenhow's guilt? And if the Secretary of State and a senator had been indiscreet, wasn't that their fault?

Excelsior nickered as he trotted down F Street. She patted him on the neck and assured him he was the prettiest horse in the world. It took less than ten minutes to ride to the stables, on the west side of the President's House. Kate kissed Excelsi-or's nose and handed his reins to the gray-haired groom. Like most visitors, she used the west entrance, both for its proximi-ty to the stable and because it wasn't so grand as the formal north entrance. Retracing her steps from the day before, she made her way upstairs to Mr. Lincoln's office. Just as she topped the stairs Mr. Lincoln emerged from his office.

"Good, you're here." He strode toward her, seeming to need fewer strides than other men to cover the same distance. He was smiling. "You're angry with me and you have a right to be. Walk with me."

Befuddled, Kate let him sweep her back down the stairs.

They strode down the first-floor hall, heading for the west entrance again. "I got to thinking last night. About how we'll need you and others to cross Confederate lines again." He paused at the door and looked down at her. "Eventually someone will get caught. You know they will. How we treat Mrs. Greenhow and her friends may very well determine how the Confederates treat our people one day." He looked down at her with a crinkly smile. "How *you* might be treated one day."

He pushed open the door and strode out on to the lawn, waving his arm. Kate stared after him. What the hell was he up to?

Two boys appeared on the lawn, running pell-mell from a low, swampy area on the far side of the grounds. "Papa," one of them shrieked. Mr. Lincoln stopped and watched them, his face beaming with pleasure. They ran straight to their father and stopped, both of them gasping and talking at the same time. "We let them turtles go, just like you asked Papa," the larger one said with a gap-toothed grin.

267

The smaller one laughed. "Alice will never catch them and cook them now."

"That's fine news." Lincoln rested his large hand first on one boy's head, and then the other. He turned to Kate. "Boys, may I introduce to you Miss Katherine Warne. Miss Warne, my sons Willie and Tad."

Kate held out her hand, first to Willie, the taller of the two and then to Tad. "It is very nice to meet you. Why have you been freeing turtles?"

The boys looked at their father, their faces glowing with pride. "It's a secret," they said in near unison.

The president bellowed out a laugh. "That it is my boys. We're running veritable terrapin underground railroad. Now run along." Mr. Lincoln waved the boys away. He watched them run across the lawn, thumbs tucked in his suspenders like a man at a county fair. After awhile he turned to Kate and said, "The British ambassador, upon hearing I enjoyed turtle soup, made me a gift of live soft-shelled turtles. The boys saw them in the kitchen after which I didn't have the heart to condemn them to the soup pot. But I don't want the ambassador to know we scorned his gift, so I swore the boys to secrecy."

Kate tried not to laugh and failed. "You are training your sons in spycraft."

"I suppose I am." He gestured her down the path so they could continue their walk. "I'm sorry if I was abrupt earlier. All this military business has me running in circles. I'm heading for the Winder Building for a meeting with the generals. Walk over with me."

Kate agreed. Not that she had much choice in the matter.

Lincoln spoke as they walked. "I am not insensible to the outrage you feel regarding Mrs. Greenhow, but the president's job is to protect the nation and its citizens. I wouldn't be doing that if I threw a woman who'd once entertained presidents and senators into jail like a common trollop. Particularly one working for the Confederacy. Southerners are sensitive about the treatment of white ladies."

Kate snorted.

"You disagree?"

Kate sighed and said nothing. She wondered if he'd heard about the connections between Rose and his secretary of state. And one of his most staunch senatorial supporters.

Lincoln shot her a hard look. "By God Miss Warne, so few people speak frankly with me. I wish you would."

"Well, we've got evidence that Mr. Seward visits Mrs. Greenhow. And Mr. Wilson."

"I remember. Mr. Seward has many enemies, but I need him these next four years. A public scandal would force his resignation and I would like to avoid that. I don't mean to be indelicate Miss Warne, it is widely known that Mrs. Seward has been an invalid for years and does not leave Auburn."

Kate snorted again. "That fact hurts his case. Trust me, sir, men like to brag to women with whom they are intimate."

Lincoln stopped walking and turned to face Kate. "I suspect you're right, but whatever Mr. Seward's indiscretions, the damage is done and the country needs him. And I assure you, my changing orders from prison to house arrest are not to protect Mr. Seward, but to protect you and all the Union spies. I prefer prisoner exchanges to executions. And if we keep Mrs. Greenhow under house arrest, we have a powerful bargaining chip. Also, you must admit that keeping her on a loose leash allows her to reveal more of her methods and sources."

Kate ground her teeth in vexation. "But if we jail and try her, her sources and methods become meaningless."

"Perhaps. And perhaps not. You must admit we don't know the extent of this network."

They walked along in silence for a few moments. The white brick Winder building lay just before them when Kate spoke again. "Sir, you know I will abide by your decisions, even if I disagree. But you should not forget that, though she is a woman, Mrs. Greenhow is dangerous." Kate paused and before Lincoln could reply she took a deep breath and continued. "You said earlier that my work did not differ from hers. You are wrong sir. I am a loyal citizen working to stop people who want destroy democracy with tyranny and slavery. In seceding they have engaged in a massive act of treason. She is a traitor who profits from the sale of human beings and as such she is an enemy to the Union government."

Lincoln stopped on the sidewalk before the Winder. "Has it occurred to you Miss Warne, that loyalty is a subjective idea. You believe you are loyal when you lie and steal from Confederates to uphold your vision of this nation. They believe they are loyal for the same reason. Like you, they believe they are right and they are willing to die for their ideas. You and I do not have to agree with them to recognize that fact. But we should at least acknowledge that they too see themselves as honorable and patriotic."

"But they're wrong, Sir."

He held out his hand to her.

She offered her own.

He enveloped her hand in his own, squeezed it and let it go. "I would not see you hanged in retribution for Mrs.

Greenhow." With that he turned and walked into the Winder building, leaving Kate to stare after him.

He was wrong, wasn't he? She'd seen first hand the havoc that woman created, the suffering that resulted from her work.

Kate turned for the short walk back to the White House stables. Mr. Lincoln wouldn't be the last man to treat Madame Rose with kid gloves. Allan had a tender spot for ladies too. She should know. She'd used it to get him to hire his first female operative. Kate glanced at her watch and picked up her step. Rose's house was less than three blocks away.

As she walked Kate made a vow to herself. She would bide her time and if Mr. Lincoln and the authorities wouldn't do it, she would. She'd kill Rose Greenhow herself.

Chapter 23

August 23, 1861
Washington City

*R*ose pulled her bonnet down against the sun's glare. A lady of her age could not be too careful and her olive tinted skin tended to darken if exposed to sunlight. She'd learned that lesson the hard way when she lived in Mexico, back when she was a new bride. A trickle of sweat ran between her shoulder blades, reminding her to hurry home before the heat overwhelmed the day. She should have sent her cook to the market, but the woman couldn't seem to pick the best peaches, the ones just coming on ripe. Little Rose did so love peaches and after Gertrude's death this spring Rose to liked to indulge her baby girl. Besides, Little Rose was such a good girl, so loyal to her Mama and so delicate about Mama's private time with gentlemen.

She swung her net bag of peaches by her side and quickened her step towards home. Not a block away from her destination she heard someone call her name. Rose looked up. Mrs. Mills stood at her front fence across the street, a chunk of her apron gripped in her hands. Her neighbor waved her over. Rose noticed Mrs. Mill's eyes darting toward Rose's house. Rose crossed the street, using the opportunity to glance over at her house. Two dark-suited men stood in front of her stoop, their arms clasped behind their backs.

Rose felt almost relieved. She'd been expecting something like this since the night she discovered someone had violated the sanctity of her home. And lately every time she left the house she felt watched. More than once she thought she'd been followed. She thought she'd feel frightened when the moment came but found she was not. Instead, she looked forward to jousting with the Yankees. She stiffened her spine. They were no match for Rose Greenhow, of that she was sure.

Mrs. Mills met Rose on the sidewalk. "Those men have been there for over an hour."

Rose nodded that she'd heard and then in a loud, carrying voice asked Mrs. Mills about her children.

"They're feeling much better," Mrs. Mills replied in a voice as loud as Rose's. Rose and Mrs. Mills chatted for a few minutes about the children's recent bout with fever, trying to appear as normal as possible. As she prepared to go home Rose leaned into Mrs. Mills again. "Stay here. If I raise my handkerchief, all is not well. Be on guard. If it goes bad once I'm inside I'll send out an alarm."

Mrs. Mills face turned white. In a squeaking voice, she asked, "What if they arrest you?"

Rose laid her hand on Mrs. Mills arm. "Just be ready." She turned and walked the final few houses down the street to her house, chin up, shoulders back, her spine ramrod straight.

She approached her house. The two men blocked her way. She tried to step past them.

The smaller of the two made a throat clearing noise and then said, "You are Mrs. Greenhow, are you not?"

274

Rose turned and glared at the little man. He had the barreled shaped body of a peasant and the thick unpleasant beard of a ruffian. Scotch, no doubt. Or worse, Irish. She raised her chin and looked down her nose at her questioner. "I am. What do you want?"

"I am Detective E. J. Allen of the Washington Metropolitan Police and you are under arrest."

Rose's heart galloped. "By whose authority?"

He took one step closer to her. "By sufficient authority to get the job done."

The taller and younger man stepped forward but said nothing.

"Humph." Rose held out her hand. "Then let me see your warrant."

"You are a spy Madame and I have no need of a written order. You must have heard that Mr. Lincoln suspended habeas corpus. You will comply with your arrest or I shall take you by force. It makes no difference to me. Either way, my people will search your home and detained you." He squinted his eyes and stared at her, daring her to defy him.

"My goodness, have I no power here?" Rose wailed. She pulled her handkerchief from her pocket and dabbed at her eyes, making sure Mrs. Mills could see the scrap of white cotton.

Signal sent, she tucked her handkerchief away. She stepped up one more stair so she was higher than the mean little man. "I have no power to resist your arrest, but if I'd been inside my house when you came I would not have let you in and if you had gained entrance, I would have killed you before I submitted to this illegal detainment."

The taller man leaned back his head and barked out a laugh. "You coulda tried Madam. And you'd be worse off than you are now. If that's possible."

The smaller man only looked disappointed. He removed his slouch hat and held it to his chest. "Ma'am, we both have families who would miss us if you were to indulge in a fit of murder."

Rose fought the urge to scream in vexation. These ruffians understand nothing of loyalty. She gathered her resolve and let the two policemen into her home.

Twenty minutes later two more men joined the original pair. They forced Rose to sit in a corner chair of her library parlor, her bag of peaches at her feet, while they searched the room's cabinets and bookshelves. Before they began, they drew the curtains. Rose smiled in grim satisfaction. They wanted no one to see what they were doing. Was there any greater proof of their moral profligacy?

Rose reviewed her options. She could resist but suspected it would net her little advantage. She must gather her courage for her next great battle. Before her was the fruit of abolitionist rule, proof that while men like Seward, Chase and Lincoln were in charge of the nation no respectable woman was safe.

She gathered her resolve once again and asked, "What are you doing here?"

Mr. Allen turned toward her, the book he'd been rifling in his hand. "Why Madame, I would have thought it was obvious. We are searching your home for evidence of treason."

Rose leaped from her chair and strode over to a large vase that stood on a pedestal stand in the corner. "Then let me help you." She tipped the vase and reached inside, pulled a folded piece of paper from within and held it out to the detective. "There," she said, unable to keep the triumph from her voice.

He took the paper and unfolded it.

Rose straightened her already straight back and smiled. Weeks ago she'd made a copy of the letter Jordan sent her on behalf of President Davis and General Beauregard, transcribing it from cipher to plain English. Now she wanted to rub this nasty little man's nose in her triumph.

He glanced at the note, refolded it and slid it into his pocket. "I've seen this already Ma'am, but it was nice of you to be helpful."

Damn the man. She'd meant to puncture his ego, but her arrow had gone astray. *What was it Mama used to say?* The devil is no match for a clever woman. She folded hands in her lap and considered her options. It was time to call in reinforcements.

"Gentlemen, could you bring my daughter to me ? I ask because she is just a little girl and may be afraid, what with recent events and all." She gestured around her library at the men searching her books and papers.

The detective glanced at the taller man, who nodded and left the room. Moments later he returned with a small girl in tow. The moment Little Rose entered the room she ran to her mother. "Oh, Mama! Those men wouldn't let me see you. I was scared!"

Little Rose cried prettily on her mother's shoulder while Rose petted her and made little murmuring sounds. After losing Gertrude this past spring and sending Leila west, she treasured her Little Rose more than ever.

After less than a minute the child had ceased her weeping. Rose held her daughter at arm's length and looked her in the eye. She tried not to smile, but it wasn't easy. Little Rose had the prettiest blue eyes. "Are you hungry darling?"

Little Rose remembered her cue. "Yes, Mama," she said in her most babyish voice. "And ever so thirsty, too."

Rose turned her daughter around and gave her a gentle push. "Go see Cook. She'll make you some lunch. And take these with you." Rose handed the bag of peaches to her daughter.

"Oh Mama, peaches are my favorite," the little girl cried in delight. She kissed her mother on the cheek and skipped from the room, swinging the peaches just as her mother had done not long before. The men took no notice of the girl's departure.

Little Rose stopped skipping the moment she was out of sight. Her Mama needed her and she would not let her down. She pushed the green door to the kitchen open and stepped inside. Their slave woman hunched in a kitchen chair, lips pressed together as she peeled potatoes.

Swinging her peaches up onto the table, Little Rose stared down her nose at the cook. It was an expression she'd seen her mother use to great effect and she'd been practicing it in her mirror. Someday she'd be as great a lady as Mama. "Mama says you are to make me lunch. I shall be back in ten minutes."

Rose walked out the kitchen door to the backyard. A large oak tree stood at the edge of the yard, its branches spreading over the board fence that enclosed the backyard. Rose

278

grabbed an old chair she kept back here for just this purpose and hauled it over to the tree. Balancing on the chair, she reached up and grabbed the tree's lowest branch. Her feet scrabbled against the rough bark of the tree trunk. She hooked the branch with her leg and swung herself astride a thick. jutting branch. Her heart pounded with excitement. *Mama needs me.*

Little Rose inched out along the branch, the scratchy bark rubbing against her legs through her cotton pantaloons. When she'd crossed the fence Little Rose leaned over until she could see the street, careful to keep her legs clamped on the branch. She saw them. It was just as Mama said it would be. Mrs. Mills and Mrs. Crumpler stood together, in front of Mrs. Mills' house.

Little Rose let loose with her loudest yell. "Mama is arrested! Mama is arrested!" Little Rose watched as the two neighbor ladies spun towards her and then, hearing her warning, scurried away. They'd pass the word and before long Mama would have help.

The back door slammed. Little Rose looked back over her shoulder. The icky old bearded man from Mama's parlor glared at her from the back steps. He put his hands on his hips and yelled at her. "Get down right now. Before I give you a good paddling."

Little Rose smiled as she climbed down. The man was angry so she'd done the right thing. Mama would be proud.

The man grabbed her by the arm and dragged her into the house without another word. He hauled her into the parlor and handed her over to the tall man.

"Take them both upstairs and lock them in their rooms." Little Rose frowned at the men. They didn't have to be so mean. She snuck a peek at Mama, who rewarded her with a wink. Mama stood and walked towards the stair. Rose followed her, emulating Mama's ladylike silence. The mean man locked her into the spare room, two doors down from Mama's bedroom. Little Rose threw herself on the bed and reviewed her moment of triumph. She'd done just as Mama had told her.

Her stomach gurgled and rumpled her happiness. She should have eaten lunch before saving Mama.

Rose frowned at the sound of her bedroom door locking. She surveyed her room. *What to do first?* She looked at her bookshelf, then at her closet. The portfolio or the safe? The safe was secure for now, wasn't it? Or was it? She bit her lip, concentrated and decided.

Grabbing up a little footstool, she hurried over to her corner bookshelf. The library downstairs held her dead husband's books and things he'd collected on his travels. The variety of languages and topics impressed everyone who saw them, but they weren't hers. Her books were here, in her room. Rose pulled back one of her velvet curtains and found the pocket sewn into the bottom. Slipping a thin portfolio out of the pocket, she carried it over to her dressing table. *Would they search her?* Surely even Yankee traitors wouldn't be stoop so low as to force a lady to undress. *Dare I take the time?* And yet, what choice did she have?

Rose unbuttoned her dress, slipped it off her shoulders and reached around to the small of her back to loosen her corset strings. She wriggled her torso until the whalebone lined panels loosened. Folded papers disappeared into her corset. Once

280

the portfolio was empty, she re-tightened her corset strings, pulling them harder than usual, an action resulting in an enhanced décolletage. She slipped her dress back on and buttoned it once again. The fabric strained around the buttonholes, but not enough that most men would notice. Men noticed a lady's bosoms, not her tailoring.

Next, she took a seat on her maroon velvet footstool, reached for her button hook and unbuttoned her walking boots. Thank goodness she'd had them made a little large. A mature lady's feet did tend to swell in the afternoon. In her stockings, she walked over to her closet and knelt before her safe. A few seconds later she had the safe open, pulled out another sheaf of papers and carried them back to the footstool. Rose leafed through the papers, selected four of them and set the others aside. She slipped two each into her boots, then pulled her boots back on and buttoned them up. Something crashed downstairs. She heard raised voices, then footsteps on the stairs. Rose smiled. It was one of her friends, come to help in her hour of travail.

A knock came at the door. Rose glanced in her mirror, smoothed her hair and called, "Yes?"

"Rose dear, I'm here. To comfort you."

Rose's heart soared. It was dear Lily Mackall, her most loyal co-conspirator. The key scratched in the lock and the door opened. The bearded detective stood at the door, Lily behind him.

"Madame," the detective said, "I'm going to allow your friend to visit you. You should remember this kindness the next time you think of threatening myself or my men." When she didn't respond he stepped aside for Lilly.

Rose let Lily into the room and slammed the door in the detective's face. The stupid fellow understood nothing. She'd once been a power in this city and she would be again, and when that fine day happened she would see to it he lost his job.

"Rose!" Lilly cried and threw herself into Rose's arms.

Rose pushed her back, harder than she meant to. "No time," she hissed.

Lily's hurt expression transformed to one of doe-eyed hope. "What do you need?"

Before Rose could answer she heard the front door again. Rose's heart swelled with gratitude. Her friends were rushing to her defense. Rose pressed her ear to the door again. She heard voices, then arguing. One of the voices was female. She really did have the most loyal friends.

"You've got to be kidding me!" The woman's outraged screech echoed up the stairwell. The voice sounded familiar, but Rose couldn't place it.

Someone ran up the stairs, their feet thumping on each riser. "The key, dammit!" The woman's voice rose to an unladylike bellow. "Hurry!"

Rose grabbed Lily and pulled her away from the door just as it flew open. She gaped at the woman who stood in the doorway. She was tiny, but her body vibrated with an energy that suggested she was no parlor princess accustomed to gentle conversations about tatting and tea parties. Her auburn hair straggled from its bun as if she'd been in some kind of scuffle, while her green eyes spoke of barely contained murderous rage. It was General Scott's niece. Rose couldn't believe her eyes. Why would Miss Scott be here? And why was she so angry? Then the pieces fell into place .

Chapter 24

August 23, 1861
Washington City

*K*ate leaped off Excelsior and threw his reins to a young man in military blue posted at Rose's front door. Before he could question her she was bounding up the steps and through the front door. "Allan!" She stood in the hall, just inside the door and hollered for her boss.

Allan poked his head around the pocket door. "Yes, dear?" His voice was as mild as hers was agitated.

Kate took a deep breath.

"How was Mr. Lincoln?" He stepped toward her, a book in his hand.

"Fine," she said, trying to keep her voice calm.

"You have been using that word an awful lot today." He squinted at her. "Is everything all right?"

"Yes, it's . . . ." She caught herself before she said 'fine' again. "The president plans to use Mrs. Greenhow's treatment as a model, should the Confederates capture one of us. And while doing so, use her as bait."

Allan nodded. "It's a good plan."

Kate interrupted him. "Where's the lady of the hour?"

Allan looked up the stairs. "Well, we had a little contretemps, so I sent her and her daughter to their rooms. I thought a little time alone might settle her down though I just allowed one of her lady friends up there. I'm hoping it will settle her down."

"You've got to be kidding me! Allan!" She turned and ran towards the stairs.

Allan's head reared back. Kate rarely yelled at him. He watched her bound up the stairs. He followed her.

She rattled the doorknob to Rose's room and turned on Allan. "The key, dammit." He looked at her like she'd lost her mind.

Allan dug in his waistcoat pocket and pulled out a small black key. Kate grabbed it from his hand, thrust it into the lock and turned. She burst into the room. Rose had her arms around her friend's waist. Miss Mackall looked terrified. Rose looked like a woman getting away with something. Kate wanted to pull her revolver and shoot the bitch in the head just to wipe that smirk off her face.

Kate rounded on Allan. "I cannot believe you left her upstairs alone. And then sent a friend up to help her with whatever unholy thing she's up to in her bedroom. She's completely unsupervised."

Allan looked down at his feet and shuffled them.

His chastened look made Kate flush with shame. "I'm sorry. But you are too trusting when it comes to women. I should have been here all along." Kate paused, resisting the impulse to plant a kiss on his cheek as a way of further apology. Instead, she pushed him toward the bedroom door. "You go back downstairs. We ladies need a little privacy."

284

Rose raised her chin and looked down her nose at Kate. "You are not General Scott's niece. I never trusted you. What sort of woman would pretend to be gently born, partake of my hospitality under false pretenses, and now act so unladylike a manner?"

"I'll have none of that Lady of the Manor nonsense from you." Kate spat her words at Rose. "You may call me Mrs. Barley. And I will call you Rose."

Through all this Lily Mackall had uttered not one word. Kate examined the woman who was Rose Greenhow's most loyal companion. With her pink cheeks and soft, brown hair and storm gray eyes she looked barely twenty years old. Kate, in her guise as a young woman eager to betray her country, had met Miss Mackall several times, though she recalled little about her. She was one of those women who faded into the background, being neither so beautiful nor so brilliant as to call attention to herself. Should she get rid of the girl? Or make her stay? Would Rose be more difficult to handle with or without an audience? And what damage could Miss Mackall do outside this room? Kate decided.

"Miss Mackall. Sit over there." Kate pointed at the deep red footstool near the bed. "Not one word from you."

Lily sat, put her face in her hands and wept.

The moment Kate looked away Rose had sidled over to her dresser. She pulled open the top drawer and, before Kate could stop her, pulled out her revolver. She pointed it at Kate. "Get out or I'll shoot. And I will kill you. My nerves are so steady I could balance a glass of water on this gun."

Kate stared at the woman and her weapon. Then she strode across the room and wrenched the gun from Rose's

285

hand. Lily screeched. Rose screeched. Kate resisted the impulse to screech too, in the spirit of the moment.

Instead, she spun the gun barrel. "You stupid cow," Kate said as she turned. "It isn't loaded. If you own a gun, you ought to be trained to use it." She shook her head in disgust. Rose Greenhow hadn't been to the George Hazzard School of Dangerous Weapon Handling.

Rose's mouth opened and shut like a fish pulled from the water.

"And you left your safe open. You're not great at this stuff, are you?" Kate backed toward the closet and reached into the safe. She pulled out revolver case and loaded the gun from the short row of bullets inside. Behind her Rose mumbled insults, her voice too low for Kate to catch the exact words. She did understand the general idea though.

"Yes, yes," Kate said. "I get it. I don't like you much either. But I've got the loaded gun. And I know how to use it." She pulled a chair away from the wall and sat down. She waved the little Colt at Rose with a lazy twist of her wrist. "I need you to take your clothes off. Slowly."

Rose adopted a tone of haughty condescension. "Is this how women of your sort entertain themselves? I suppose you are one of those pseudo-women who enjoys this sort of thing? Or a prostitute?" Rose's eyes glowed with fervor at this idea. "Certainly! You are a prostitute. A woman so coarse she would ask a lady to disrobe. What a whore you are!"

Lily looked up from her footstool, aghast at her friend's language. Rose shut up. Kate looked at Rose, then at Lily, then back to Rose. She waved the gun at Rose.

Rose ignored her.

Kate fired a shot into the wall only two feet from where Rose stood. Plaster dust flew. Lilly screeched, but Rose didn't even flinch. On the other hand, she did begin unbuttoning her dress.

Kate couldn't remember the last time she'd had this much fun.

As expected, Rose's clothing yielded a wealth of information. She'd first pushed off her dark blue dress and stepped out of it, leaving it puddled on the floor.

"I'm not your maid," Kate said with a wave of the revolver. "Pick it up and hand it to me."

The lady huffed in disgust but did as Kate commanded. Kate felt the dress, listening for the telltale sound of crinkling paper, but found nothing. She dropped the dress on a chair and pointed the gun at Rose. "Next."

"Is this necessary," Lily squeaked from her stool.

Kate glared at the girl who shrunk back into herself. Kate almost felt bad. It was too much like hitting an already cowering dog.

Rose loosened the strings that held hoop skirt at her waist and slid it down over her plain, muslin petticoat. The hoops collapsed into each other, one after another as they hit the floor. Rose looked down her nose at Kate yet again.

Kate tipped her head made a bored little circle with the revolver's muzzle. "You know what to do." Rose huffed and puffed, but delivered the hoops to Kate. Still nothing.

They repeated the process with the lady's petticoats and corset cover. Once down to her corset, chemise and drawers

Rose refused to continue. "It's not proper," she said in a voice as tight as her clenched fists.

Kate snorted. "If you ask me, betraying your country isn't proper either. Stealing free men and selling them into slavery isn't proper. Getting arrested for espionage isn't proper. Lady, taking your clothes off is the least of your problems right now."

Rose raised her chin and straightened her spine. "You know nothing of loyalty. I have revolutionary blood in my veins and was tutored in government by the greatest American who ever lived, Mr. John Calhoun. Unlike you and your uncouth cohorts, I understand freedom. Freedom of speech. Freedom of thought." Her voice rang with righteous indignation.

Ah, a speech. I'm must be getting close. Kate twirled the revolver's muzzle again. "How about the freedom to not be shot in your undergarments?"

Rose stared at Kate.

Kate stared back. "You know what interests me?"

"Gin houses and sailors?"

Kate tried not to laugh. One had to admire the lady's spirit. "No. What interests me is that you haven't asked what this arrest is about."

The lady arched her eyebrows and widened her eyes in a parody of innocence. "Why should I care about the petty concerns of tyrants and prostitutes?"

Kate shook her head. "Wrong again. You haven't asked because you know why we're here. And you're acting like a complete bitch because you're badly frightened." Kate paused and thought. "I take that back. You're a bitch even when you're not frightened."

288

Rose glared at Kate. "Do you think I care one whit for the opinion of such an ill-bred, ill-dressed creature as yourself?"

Kate looked down at her outfit. She was wearing her Garibaldi shirt and navy blue skirt. "This is my favorite outfit, I'll have you know."

Rose snorted in derision. "Exactly my point."

"Madame, you are not in the position to give fashion advice," Kate said, waving her free hand at Rose's state of undress. "Take. Off. Your. Corset." This time Kate used her gun hand to emphasize her sentence.

The lady relented and reached behind her back to loosen her corset strings. "And you wonder why I have no respect for Yankees."

Kate rolled her eyes. Rose pushed her corset down over her hips. Sheaves of papers fell to the floor. Kate stood and stepped toward Rose. "Step back, into the corner. Right there. If you move, I'll shoot you. And keep in mind I hope you'll give me an excuse."

Lily watched in abject horror as Rose backed into the corner. Kate bent and picked up the papers, trying to both collect them and not take her eye off her captives. It occurred to her this would have been easier if Hattie was here. The next time she planned on holding a woman at gunpoint she'd remember to remember lady friends.

Kate collected the papers and laid thm on the bed. She looked at Rose and considered her options.

"Lily, I'm going to search your friend and to do it I will have to turn my back to you. I'll be holding the gun. If I hear so much as a rustle from you I'll turn and shoot, no questions, no warning. Do you understand?"

Lily nodded, her eyes as large as teacups.

289

Kate stepped up to Rose and patted her down. The lady wore only her chemise and drawers, so there wasn't much between Kate's hands and the lady's skin. Her breasts felt slack and her belly pooched out. Kate suspected the great bulk of Rose's seductions took place in the dark. She stepped back, satisfied the lady had no more papers on her body.

A minuscule smile of triumph snuck onto Rose's face.

What had she missed? Kate examined her captive from head to toe. *Oh, for goodness' sake.* "Your boots, if you will. Lily, you can help."

Kate's realization wiped the smile from Rose's face, a fact Kate enjoyed almost as much as finding the stash of papers inside the lady's boots.

Kate collapsed onto one of Rose's velvet-covered parlor chairs, waking Allan who'd been dozing on the chair's matching settee. He jerked awake and popped upright like a Jack-in-the-box. Startled at his own swift movement looked about wide-eyed, came to his senses and scrubbed at his face. Kate tried not to laugh and failed. Hattie appeared in the parlor doorway, took in the scene with a soft smile. She approached the other chair, swept her skirts under her and perch on the chair's edge.

Kate frowned at Hattie. "How do you do that?"

"What?" Hattie widened her eyes and batted her eyelashes at Kate, a parody of innocence.

"That." Kate waved her hand in Hattie's direction. "You worked at the hospital most of the day and you've been here for coming on six hours and you've got not a hair out of place, not a wrinkle on your dress." Kate didn't need a mirror to know her hair had sprung from its bun and her skirt was covered in dust smudges.

"My dear," Hattie said, looking down her nose at her friend, "Unlike you, I am not a trollop."

"Oh, no, not you too," Kate groaned. "I've had all I can take. I almost shot her just to shut her up."

It had been a long afternoon. After she forced Rose to undress she'd considered doing the same to Lily but decided not to. After all, the girl been alone with Rose only a few minutes before Kate's arrival. Kate did pat Lily down and found what she expected. Nothing. Then she'd faced a dilemma. She could put the ladies in another bedroom, but without searching the room first she couldn't be sure Rose wouldn't destroy documents there too. But she couldn't search Rose's bedroom room while the rebel ladies watched.

To solve the problem Kate called Allan upstairs and had him to escort the ladies to Little Rose's bedroom. She reasoned the child's room was most likely the room least likely to contain hidden papers. Also, though Kate hated to admit it even to herself, she felt a little sorry for Rose's daughter and thought her mother's company might make the girl's day less frightening. Rose heaped insults upon insults on Kate as they moved the two women down the hall and continued to excoriate her every time she checked on them, in spite of her daughter's presence. The verbal barrage had driven Kate to the edge of sanity.

Allan watched Kate and Hattie giggle at each other and then interrupted. "Are you ladies done?"

"With what? Abuse from Madame la' Rose or the urge to murder her?" Kate asked.

Hattie giggled again. Kate joined her.

Allan stood up and pulled down his waistcoat with all the dignity he could muster. "You're both exhausted and none too coherent. Go home, sleep and we'll come back tomorrow. I've got soldiers on all the doors. Timothy went home hours ago. He'll be back to head the night watch." A stern look from him set the two women to giggling again. He sighed, pulled his pocket watch out and snapped it open. "It's almost midnight. He'll be here any minute. Maybe tomorrow we should get Odetta to join us as chief cook."

It occurred to Kate that she hadn't seen Rose's slave all day. She sat up straight and wiped at her eyes. "What happened to Rose's cook?"

Allan heaved a sigh. "Don't spread this around. Mr. Lincoln would have kittens if he thought I was liberating slaves in contravention of the law, but that's what I did. Juba took her to Columbus and Reatha."

"Oh Allan," Kate sighed. Allan Pinkerton didn't just disapprove of slavery in a general or theoretical way, he'd spent the last ten years working for the Underground Railroad. She pushed herself upright, walked over to her boss and kissed his cheek.

His face turned pink with pleasure.

After a moment of silence, Kate spoke. "How's it going down here?"

Allan rocked back on his heels. "Not bad. We've searched both parlors and Charlotte's made a start on organizing the papers. It's a huge job. Half of it needs decoding, all of it needs reading. I'd like you two to help with that tomorrow. No doubt Mrs. Greenhow's entire network now knows she's being detained and her house searched. The rats will scatter, so we have no time to waste. Hattie, can you take a day off from the hospital?"

Hattie nodded and stood. "Let's all go home." She linked elbows with Kate and Allan and moved them toward the front door.

Allan stopped at the door. "I sent Excelsior home with Juba hours ago and had him bring back Lucy and the shay. Go home. I'll wait for Timothy." He pushed them out the door and shut it behind them.

Hattie stopped on the front stoop and looked back at the house. "He's not leaving is he?"

Kate shook her head. "Probably not." She nodded goodnight to the soldier standing at the foot of Mrs. Greenhow's stairs and looked up into the night sky. The moon rode low on the horizon, three-quarters full. She thought about the reams of paper that needed examination. They'd need help or the job would take forever. Someone they could trust, someone smart. Kate smiled. She knew the perfect woman for the job.

Chapter 25

August 24, 1861
Washington City

*K*ate took a cup of coffee from Charlotte and blew on it. "Where is everyone?" It was only a few minutes after seven, but the house had none of its usual early morning liveliness.

"Juba and Samuel left for Columbus's place about ten minutes ago. They took Monty with them, to help with a squirrel problem at the feed store. Allan and Timothy didn't come home. No surprise there." Charlotte yawned and refilled her own mug. "Where was I? Oh, right. Samuel hooked Lucy to the shay for Hattie. She'll check into the hospital and then meet you over at the Greenhow place. Oh, and Samuel said to tell you he saddled Excelsior for you. And Odetta's says she'll bring food over today so you all don't starve. She and Louisa left for the market already." Charlotte shook her head. "I tried to talk her out of it. We could call Willard's and have food delivered, but Odetta's of the mind that catered food is akin to abuse. She insists on bringing lunch."

Kate shrugged. "She wants to help. If she could read, I'd put her to sorting papers. Louisa too, but she doesn't read well enough for the work I'll have today." Kate gulped down her coffee and set the mug in the sink. "Hazzard said he'd be by this morning, but I don't know if that means 7:30 or just before noon. I don't want to hang around all morning waiting for him. You'll be here, right?"

Charlotte nodded. "Someone's got to hold the fort. I'll feed your irregulars if they come by, but what do I tell them?"

Kate pursed her lips. "Hmmm. Tell them they're still on the job, but I want them to take today off. The Army's guarding the house and I want no one hurt by an overzealous soldier. Tell them to check in here every day, lunch time," Kate shot Charlotte a grin, "and when I've got time, we'll have another meeting." Kate paused. "Charlotte? "I know you're busy, but would you go to the telegraph office this morning? First thing? I want to get back to Rose's house. Oh, and maybe I should leave a note for Hazzard. In case you're not here."

Charlotte dug into her pocket and pulled out a small notebook and a stubby pencil. "Write it all down, dear. And then off you go."

Hazzard stepped into Rose's kitchen, closed the door and leaned against it. He stared at Kate for a moment before speaking. "We've got a problem."

Kate felt her heart plummet. "We do?" He was in uniform and he was beautiful. And he was about to leave her. Probably for a more conventional woman.

He nodded, his face expressionless.

Crap. She'd been gone too long. Her job wasn't ladylike. There was a war on. There was someone else. Someone who didn't shoot people. Kate swallowed hard and stiffened her spine.

Before she could speak, he did. "I think about you all the time. When I'm teaching men to load cannons, I think about you. When I'm inspecting fortifications, I think about you. When I'm in bed, I think about you. And then I can't sleep." He spread his hands. "What do I do?"

"Oh," she squeaked. She pushed back her chair and threw herself into his arms.

His lips met hers as he backed into the kitchen door. He kissed slowly as if he had days to waste in kissing. Her ex-husband had always rushed, like kissing was something he had to get through to get what he really wanted. Hazzard never, ever rushed. She pushed into him, her breasts tight against his wool jacket. She could feel its double row of brass buttons against her chest. Her clothes felt tight. She reached up and pulled his head tighter to her, shuddering as his lips left her mouth and explored her jawline and then her ear. He growled a little, a small animal sound she'd heard before. A sense of peace flooded through her, longing transformed into belonging. The world narrowed down to the two of them, their arms, their mouths creating a tiny, perfect universe where she was safe and unafraid.

He tugged at her flimsy bun, knocking it loose so he could run his fingers through her hair. "I like this hair," he whispered. "It feels like quick silver."

Kate was about to tell him how much she enjoyed his mustache when the door bumped the two of them forward.

"This feels familiar doesn't it?" He backed them more tightly against the door, holding it shut.

Dazed, Kate pulled back from Hazzard. They'd kissed against this very kitchen door before, months ago and been interrupted then too.

297

She pulled his head back down to her mouth. "We have a talent for picking the wrong place," she whispered into his hear. The door bumped again.

"Kate?"

Kate sighed. It was Hattie. She nipped at Hazzard's ear lobe and let him go.

He growled once more before stepping back.

Hattie's voice came at the door. "Should I go away?"

Hazzard crooked an eyebrow at Kate.

She looked back at the piles of papers on the table, torn between duty and desire.

He shook his head. "Your work comes first." He opened the kitchen door and allowed Hattie into the room.

She stared at the two of them, first Kate, then Hazzard, then back to Kate. "You two should go away for a few days. Someplace far away from all this," she gestured at the table. "It would be easier for the rest of us."

"Hattie!" Kate felt herself blush.

Hazzard threw back his head and laughed.

Hattie turned to him. "Oh, you can laugh all you want lover boy, but it's exhausting for anyone in the same room with you two. One gets the feeling that any minute one or both of you will snap and do something horrifying and embarrassing to the rest of us." Hattie rolled her eyes. "Something more mortifying than the longing looks and near-constant grappling with each other."

"Near constant grappling?" Hazzard stepped toward Hattie, his eyes twinkling, and dropped a kiss on her forehead. "You exaggerate my dear."

She pushed him away, toward the door. "I don't," she said, trying to keep her mouth straight. "Now go help Allan and

298

Timothy. They're going through the books in the library one more time."

Kate watched her friend push the man she loved through the door and out of the room. She tried not to laugh but failed. "Is it as bad as all that?"

Hattie dropped her reticule on the table and stripped off her gloves. "You have no idea. And I'm in between ladies so I've no patience for love." Hattie dropped a wink at Kate and sat down at the table.

"No one's good enough for you, that's your problem."

"Only you dear. And you're not lover material."

"I'm afraid I like men. Or one man." She pushed a pile of papers over to Hattie. "I'm still sorting." She pointed to piles on the table. "These three piles are all military. Specifics about regiments, including numbers of soldiers and commanders, here, and supply stuff there and then this pile is for fortification information. There seems to be a lot of information about Washington's defensive positions. Over there is a pile of political stuff, and that far pile is related to the buying and selling of people." Kate paused and added, "I thought perhaps you and Miss Barton? Or Celeste?"

Hattie jerked her head. "Oh, heavens no, not Miss Barton. She's so serious and unbending. An affair with her would be excruciating. There'd be lists and rules and schemes for self-improvement. I prefer my ladies more light-hearted." She pointed at the far pile of papers. "These are all proof that the illegal slavery ring can be laid at Mrs. Greenhow's door?"

Kate heaved out a sigh. "I don't know whether to be relieved that we've caught her or enraged at how cavalier she was about it. You haven't answered my question. What about

Celeste? You two spent a lot of time together on our trip home from New Orleans."

Hattie paged through the pile. "This is depressing." She put the pile down and frowned. "Celeste is wonderful, but she's making a life for herself in Philadelphia. In Mama's dress shop. I can't ask her to come here, not with a war on and the Confederate army within a day's march."

Kate watched Hattie sort papers. Last spring, during their investigation into Juba's disappearance they'd burned down a whore house, one run by a woman with a predilection for mixing sex and violence. They'd rescued several women before the place went up in flames and before Kate killed the Madame who objected to the destruction. Hattie had spent weeks with her mother and the rescued women and eventually developed an intimate relationship with Celeste. "Did her time with the Countess leave Celeste unable to, you know?" Kate's voice trailed off. She had no idea how to talk to Hattie about her sex life.

Hattie leveled a look at Kate. "She seemed enthusiastic at the time. But I don't know if she's always preferred women, or if it was a temporary result of her time with the Countess."

Kate took a breath to speak, but Hattie looked down and kept speaking, words coming out of her in a tumbled rush. "So maybe I'm just a regrettable interlude for her. Something she's come to feel ashamed of? And even if it's not that, how can I ask her to come here to be my, my, well, my paramour. I'd be asking her to prostitute herself again and that would be unforgivable."

Kate watched as Hattie's enormous brown eyes filled with tears, making her beauty even more luminous than usual. "Oh, Hattie." She reached across the table and grasped her

friend's hand. "Has it occurred to you that there's an easy so-
lution to your problem?"

Hattie pulled a snow-white handkerchief from her sleeve
and dabbed at her eyes, shaking her head as she did. "It's never easy when you're like me. It's not like you and Hazzard."

"I won't argue that you've got obstacles, but love is never
easy. You're in love with Celeste and you're making yourself
miserable with questions you can't answer by yourself. Go talk
to her. Philadelphia's a day's train ride away. Whatever she
says, it will be better than this. Once we get this Greenhow
mess sorted, I want to expand the women's bureau to include
more women of color. Maybe she'd like this work." Kate
waved her hand at all the papers on the table.

"When did you get so smart about love?"

Kate snorted. "Other people's problems are easy to solve.
And I'm not so smart. In fact, I need your help with something."

Hattie opened her mouth, but the kitchen door flew open
with such vigor it smacked into the wall and bounced back on
the young woman standing in the doorway.

She caught the door with her hand and announced, "I am
here! How can I help?"

Hattie stared from Kate to the young woman in the door,
as startled as Hazzard had been at her resemblance to Kate.

A startled Kate stood and smiled. "Hattie, I'd like you to
meet Miss Kate Chase. Miss Chase, Hattie Lawton. You two
should get along well. You're both more ladylike than me."

Miss Chase laughed. "I don't have much choice. Father
demands perfection in all things, including his daughters' de-
portment."

Kate watched Hattie and Miss Chase greet and inspect each other. After a few moments, she gestured at the table. "Miss Chase, I've asked you here because, if you are willing, you'd be a great help in sorting and interpreting this mess of papers."

"Oh, I'd love to help. Show me what to do." She pulled a chair up to the table and sat, looking from Kate to Hattie. "And you must quit calling me Miss Chase. Please call me Kate."

Hattie laughed. "Of course your name is Kate. That won't be confusing at all."

Miss Chase looked at Hattie and then Kate in mock astonishment. "Then I will have a special Pinkerton name. You shall call me Kitty. A dear Aunty used to call me that, long ago when I was small. And like a kitten, I appear harmless, though I can draw blood if necessary."

Kate smiled and pushed a pile of papers over to their new helper. "Then Kitty, let me explain what I need you to do."

Odetta and Louisa showed up about midday with two baskets bursting with food. They shooed Kate, Kitty and Hattie out of the kitchen, forcing them to move their piles of papers to the large table in the library, after which they all sat down for a lunch of cold beef, rice salad, sliced tomatoes and oatmeal cookies. Once they'd eaten their fill, Odetta kicked them all out of the kitchen again and sent them back to work.

After the excitement of the previous day, the afternoon stretched into an exhausting slog. Searching for and analyzing the wealth of information stashed around the house just wasn't as fun as arresting people. Allan, Timothy and Hazzard,

302

who'd been working their way through all of Rose's books, added to their piles of papers as they found things.

When the men finished with the books Allan sent Hazzard and Hattie upstairs to search Rose's bedroom again. Rose and Miss Mackall both put a good deal of effort into complaining about being locked into Little Rose's room. At one point Rose shrieked dire threats loud enough to be heard in Baltimore, but she shut up when Allan told her she'd get no lunch or dinner if the noise continued.

Kate stayed with the paper pile for the next few hours because she and Kitty were making headway. If nothing else, she was getting an idea of how the Greenhow network operated. Kitty eventually went home to check in with her father, promising to come back after dinner. Bleary-eyed from sorting papers, Kate went upstairs to Rose's room. From the doorway, she watched Hattie, Hazzard and Allan. From the looks of it, Hattie had worked her way through most of Rose's clothing, while Allan had removed all the lady's books from their shelves. Hazzard had the bed pushed aside and was testing floorboards.

"We need a council of war," Kate said. "Miss Chase uncovered a startling set of letters and I've got a list of people we should arrest before they disappear. Are you almost done up here?"

Just then Hazzard exclaimed, "I thought so!" He held a loose floorboard in his hand. He groped around the hole in the floor and pulled out a bundle of letters tied with a red silk ribbon. He untied the ribbon and fanned out the bundle. Everyone in the room watched him, waiting for his next words. He opened one envelope and pulled out a letter, perused it and said, "It's a love letter."

303

Kate stepped over to Hazzard leaned over to look at the letter. "Who's it from?"

He held the letter out to her. She scanned it. Racy stuff indeed. The bottom of the page read, 'Your Beloved, H.' "Are all the letters signed this way?" She glanced at Hazzard.

He shook his head.

Kate's mind scrambled.

"Ahem," Allan interrupted. "Let us take what we've found, including those letters, downstairs for a brief evening meeting. And we've all earned a drink and some dinner. Odetta left plenty of food and I think we can help ourselves to Mrs. Greenhow's booze."

Kate waved Allan and Hazzard past her and shot Hattie a meaningful look. "Gentlemen, we'll join you downstairs." She watched the men leave, then shut the door behind them.

From her post at the closet doorway, Hattie asked, "What are you up to?"

"I need your advice," Kate said in a low voice. She opened Rose's dresser drawer and removed a small cardboard box. "Is this what I think it is?" Inside the box was an amber colored, translucent rubber cap-like item, not unlike a small, hollow ball cut in half. It had a lip of rolled rubber around the outer edge, which appeared to contain a tiny, coiled wire.

Hattie smiled. "If you think it's a pessary, then yes it is. My mother had one. She called it a womb veil."

Kate looked at the thing, careful to keep her hands off it. "So your mother use it . . . For what? And how?"

Again Hattie smiled. "So she wouldn't have more babies. She explained it to me when she thought I'd end up like her. Before she helped me run away."

Kate held the boxed item under the lamp. "So they work?"

304

Hattie shrugged. "I think so. I suspect the trick is getting it to the right place. Mama was explicit and I nearly died of embarrassment."

"She showed you?" Kate paled at the notion.

"Oh, no, not that." Hattie chortled. "She had this little booklet with instructions. And drawings."

The two women stared at the pessary, careful not to meet each other's eyes for a moment. Kate tried to imagine that booklet. She couldn't do it.

Hattie put the pessary back in Rose's bedside table drawer. "I've seen them advertised in the back of Godey's, but I think you can get one at that pharmacy just down from Willard's. You've seen the sign, even if you didn't know it. They call them Female Preventatives. I've never bought or used one, but I know ladies who have and they all survived the experience."

Kate bit her lip and raised her eyebrows. Hattie saw the look and laughed. "It's about time, that's all I can say. How about you and I stop by that pharmacy on the way home tonight? It'll be less awful if we do it together."

"We'll have to get rid of Hazzard," Kate said. "He'll want to ride home with me."

Hattie laughed again. "You leave that to me."

Her belly full and a glass of Mrs. Greenhow's excellent whiskey in her hand, Kate looked around the table. The gentlemen had a brandy, while Hattie and Kitty drank tiny, ladylike glasses of sherry. Kitty refused a drink at first, on the principle that her father didn't approve, but then declared that in the spirit of adventure she would partake. She took minuscule sips and not very many of them. "Father would give me his most forbidding look, accompanied by a stern lecture on the benefits of water if he could see me." She took another tiny sip and smiled, clearly delighted with her secret defiance.

Kate sipped a smoky Kentucky whiskey she'd discovered

when she was Lord Tracy. She thought Miss Chase's father sounded like a stuffy old fart that loomed too large in his daughter's consciousness. Still, Kitty seemed unaffected by her lofty position as one of the highest ranked ladies in Washington society. "Kate, I mean Kitty," Kate corrected herself with a smile, "would you begin by explaining what you found today?"

"What, me? Oh." She paused, rifled through the papers they'd stacked in the center of the table and pulled out a folder. "Mixed in with everything else, there's a set of papers containing information that could only have come from someone highly placed. There are no names, but rather a certain rhythm to the language the writer uses that suggests someone with an elite education. I recognize it because Father went to Brown University and he is both particular about language and formal in his sentence structure." Kitty waved at the piles on the table. "Most of this correspondence is written in a vernacular style, so this other stuff stands out. I pointed this out to Kate, who kept a look out for such documents in her own sifting of papers." Kitty looked over at Kate. "Would you like me to continue?"

Kate nodded. "It's your discovery."

Kitty looked around the table. "Miss Warne is far too modest. This afternoon we inspected the Brown File, as we now call this collection of papers, and she noticed that the file has two authors."

"And you know this how?" Hazzard asked.

"Handwriting," Kate said.

He pushed the pile of love letters at Kitty. "It might be interesting to know if letters in your file match these letters from H."

Kitty extracted a letter from its ribbon-tied bundle and smoothed it open. She pulled two pieces of paper from her so-called Brown file. She looked at them. Everyone stared at her. She held out one sample. "I'm no expert, but these look like the same hand." She handed the sample and a love letter over to Allan, who perused them and handed them around the table.

Hazzard handed the papers to Kate with a look of deadly seriousness. Like Miss Chase, he understood what they meant.

"What?" Allan blurted, mystified by their reaction.

Kitty and Hazzard both looked at Kate. "A few weeks ago I hired a cadre of street children to watch this house."

"And?" Allan took a nervous sip of his drink.

"One of them, a little girl, is quite a talented artist. She sketched several of the men who frequented this house. Hazzard identified one man, then we took the others to Miss Chase to see if she could identify the others ."

"Which reminds me," Hazzard said. "Allan has my report on that, but we never discussed it as a group."

Allan held a hand up. "We should, but first I want Kate to finish."

Kate looked over at Miss Chase, who shifted in her seat but said nothing. As you know, Miss Chase is the eldest daughter of Mr. Lincoln's secretary of Treasure. She has contact with men in this administration in a way we do not."

"You're stalling Kate," Hazzard said. He winked at her after he said it.

"I know," she said. She took a deep breath and continued. "One man seen coming and going from this house with some regularity is Senator Henry Wilson, chair of the Senate's military committee."

Hazzard tapped the bundle of love letters. "We're fairly sure Senator Wilson is the H who wrote these letters."

Allan leaned forward and pulled the Brown file over in front of himself. "Why am I hearing about this now?"

Kate frowned at Allan. "Did you make me the head of the Washington office? Or not?"

"I did." Allan had the sense to look chagrined.

"Then I could tell you it was my decision and not yours. And it was. We didn't know enough to accuse anyone. I also didn't want you mixed up in it until we were sure."

Allan stubbed out his cigar and looked around the table. "Nicely played. It's what I would have done."

Kate let out a breath she hadn't known she was holding. She was still getting used to this boss stuff.

Allan pulled yet another cigar from his jacket pocket and rolled it between his fingers. "So, we have love letters most likely from a highly placed Senator. And documents exposing military secrets that match the love letter's handwriting. This suggests the same person wrote both sets of documents."

Kate nodded. "And Mr. Lincoln will not want Senator Wilson exposed. He needs his allies. But we can't ignore the problem. Miss Chase has aligned the contents of that Brown file with some of the information Juba stole from General Beauregard's files in Manassas. The information that made its way to the Confederate Army has several sources, among them this H."

Hazzard shook his head. "I'm having trouble believing Senator Wilson would divulge military secrets to Mrs. Greenhow. His anti-slavery record is beyond impeccable."

"I admit, I'm struggling with that too," Allan said.

Miss Chase pointed at the letters. "The proof is difficult to refute. I think he did it. The question is, did he do it on purpose?"

Allan waved his hand over the table. "Let's back up. Hazzard, you said you identified another of Mrs. Greenhow's gentleman visitors. What do you know about this other fellow?"

Hazzard glanced at Kate. "I identified one of Mrs. Greenhow's gentleman callers as Colonel Erasmus Keyes. He used to be an instructor at West Point, but he's spent most the last decade out west with the Third Artillery. General Scott made Keyes his military secretary right after Mr. Lincoln's election. So Keyes' has been in Washington since last fall. By his own admission, he fell into Mrs. Greenhow's social orbit and then into her bed. He says she tried, quite unsuccessfully, to bribe him into giving up military secrets."

"He says?" Kate's face made her surprise clear. "And you believe him?"

Hazzard nodded. "I do. In March he too wrote several love letters to our Rose. She then attempted to bribe him with these letters just after the attack on Fort Sumter. He retrieved his letters one afternoon while she was out. Broke into her house to do it. Then he told the lady if she tried it again he'd have her arrested."

"And you believe him," Kate repeated.

"The president believes him. I met with Mr. Lincoln, General Scott and Colonel Keyes not long after I identified the sketch. Scott brought a report Keyes wrote detailing the whole sordid affair. A report dated April 21st. Keyes made a frank confession to his commanding officer as soon as it happened."

Kate frowned. "But we know he's still visiting her, or that he was just a few weeks ago."

Hazzard nodded. "I think Mr. Lincoln's idea to keep Mrs. Greenhow under house arrest originated with Colonel Keys. Keyes has continued his relationship with Mrs. Greenhow to keep tabs on her. He thought to keep her from entrapping other highly placed men."

"But he threatened her," Hattie said. "Why would she continue the relationship?"

Kate raised a finger. "I have the answer to that. Mrs. Greenhow admires no one so much as herself. She imagines that all men find her irresistible. And Keyes' position would have made him irresistible to her."

Hazzard paused and frowned. "I also get the sense the President and General Scott did not take Mrs. Greenhow very seriously. Both men have rather tender ideas about ladies."

"They take me seriously, don't they? And Hattie?" Kate asked.

Hazzard's teeth flashed in a wide grin. "I think they view the two of you not unlike how one might feel about a unicorn or some other rare and exotic creature."

This time Hattie laughed out loud. "Kate the Unicorn!"

"Don't laugh," Kate grumbled. "You're one too. And you too Kitty."

Miss Chase smiled. "Can we be unicorns if there's three of us? Aren't unicorns rather rare?"

310

"Good point," Hazzard said with a chuckle. "You'll be pleased to know Colonel Keyes disabused the president and the general of their tender notions. Keyes believes lady spies should be in prison. He thinks we should separate them from male prisoners and use female guards who will not succumb to lady spies' feminine wiles."

"I am not spending the rest of the war guarding that aging viper," Kate said with considerable vehemence.

Hattie shook her head. "Me either."

Hazzard's mirth disappeared. "I don't blame either one of you. I'm just saying Keyes ideas about female spies may have rubbed off on the president, thus explaining why Mrs. Greenhow is upstairs instead of prison."

Miss Chase spoke up. "I'm sorry to interrupt, but I believe you all are forgetting something." She inclined her head at Hazzard and Allan. She tapped the so-called Brown file. "There's at least one more high ranking source we haven't identified."

"And?" Allan pinned Miss Chase with one of his steely, squinty-eyed looks.

Miss Chase ignored him. "That man may be Mr. Seward."

Allan gasped. "The Seward? Mr. Lincoln's secretary of State and closest confidant?"

Miss Chase tapped the file again. "We don't know with any certainty he's the other man in this file. But we know Seward's a regular visitor to Rose's house. And he would know the details in these documents."

"We also know the lady upstairs seduces men in positions of power as a method of getting information," Kate added. "And Mr. Seward lives apart from his wife. Even Mr. Lincoln mentioned it."

"You discussed this with Mr. Lincoln?" Allan dropped his head and thumped it on the table. "This just gets worse and worse."

Hazzard leaned back in his chair, grinning from ear to ear. "Maybe. Maybe not. We don't know yet. Mr. Seward and Mr. Wilson could have both avoided the widow's trap, much as Colonel Keyes did. It requires more investigating."

Allan lifted his head from the table and looked at Kate. "And I suppose you have a plan?"

"Sort of. I think we put these letters back where we found them. Rose will think she outsmarted us and it might make her careless. And we need her to be careless. We've got a long list of people working for Madame Rose, but our only evidence is Rose's papers." Kate shuffled through the papers on the table, looking for the list.

"Oh, I've got it," Kitty said. She pulled a piece of paper off the top of a pile at her elbow and handed it to Kate.

Kate glanced at the list, before handing it to Allan.

He took it, eyebrows raised. "All these? That's a lot of people, most of whom we don't have imprisoned in this house."

"Who?" Hazzard asked.

Allan raised the list and read out loud. There were over twenty names on it

Hazzard whistled a low, two-note tune. "We had the dentist Van Camp. And some of the women? But the rest? That's a big network to keep secret, but they seem to have managed."

Kate nodded. She'd helped Kitty put the list together and still, hearing it read aloud alarmed her. "As we know, Miss Mackall and Mrs. Hasler are upstairs, though I'm beginning to doubt Mrs. Hasler's importance. The lady is too unstable for Rose to trust with anything important. And we knew about

Miss Duval. Miss Boyd doesn't appear much in these papers, but Juba and I saw her in Beauregard's camp, where she is much admired, so I added her to the list." She didn't add that she fully intended on putting the lovely Miss Boyd in a prison cell next to Rose.

Allan folded the list and tucked it into his jacket pocket. "I'll put some men on this. I can recall Scully and Lewis from Richmond. And I better go see General McClellan. Kate, you put the letters back and return Mrs. Greenhow to her room."

Kate started to remind Allan he wasn't in charge, but stopped herself. Let Allan bring in Mr. Price, Mr. Scully and the others. The Washington branch of the Pinkertons could use the help.

Hattie stood and gathered a handful of empty glasses. She turned to go into the kitchen and then stopped and stared at Kate. "I wonder if we should get Mrs. Greenhow a maid. You know, to help take care of her needs."

Kate nearly scoffed, but the look in Hattie's eye stopped her. "Ahhh. Yes. I see what you mean." And thus the bare bones of a plan sprang into existence.

Chapter 26

August 25-September 6, 1861
Washington City

*R*ose sat in the corner, seemingly engrossed in her knitting. Over the last few days, she'd found that if she were unobtrusive her captors forgot themselves, or more appropriately, forgot her and accidentally revealed helpful information to her.

The bearded detective, the same repulsive man who'd first arrested her, sat at her dining room table, his elbows on her best tablecloth like he was at a barbeque. The tall Irishman was with him and he was no better. Like all brutes, he was slow-witted and ill-tempered. Why the first night of her arrest he grabbed her arm so roughly that he left marks. And that was after she suffered the awful indignity of that unnatural woman's search of her room and her person.

The bearded man liked to talk and often talked to her. Only days ago he'd revealed to her he was Scotch and Catholic. When she told him her own ancestors were Catholic, he gushed his admiration for her in a manner that was both gratifying and disgusting.

"That a lady of your distinction should be treated as a common criminal astounds me," the man, who called himself

Edward Allen, told her. The fool grew teary-eyed at every discussion of her brave fortitude and once even asked for her
signature, telling her that should anything happen to her "he'd
like to look upon her name and know she'd forgiven him."

At first Rose played along with the man's heavy-handed
flattery. He no doubt thought by currying favor she would
forget the role he played in her arrest and share her secrets
with him. Once he even offered to sneak letters out of the
house for her. She allowed the game for several days, but each
day he became clumsier in his advances. It was exhausting,
this pretending to be stupid. Yesterday she finally gave herself
permission to be rude to the stupid man.

Next, he set about wooing Lily, bringing her candies and
other treats. Lily thought it good fun to lead him on. Their
captors continued their charade as unwilling jailers, their
hearts overflowing with charity towards their female prisoners,
their hands ever ready to accept a bribe, unaware that their
prisoners knew what they were doing.

Life under arrest gradually improved over the last week.
On the third day of what she now thought of as the Yankee
Reign of Terror, they moved her back to her bedroom and
locked her in again. Once she heard the key turn in the lock,
she'd checked all her hiding places. Somehow the wretches
found most of her papers, though they missed the letters under
her floorboards. The fools hadn't thought to move the bed, let
alone check the floor for hiding places.

On the fourth day, the bearded man arrested Eugenia
Phillips and her daughters Fanny and Lena and imprisoned
the women in Rose's attic. Poor Mrs. Hasler came by the
house to deliver a basket of smoked sausages and
they'd arrested her like a common thief. The joke was on them

316

when Betty Hasler cried so long and so loud that her noise drove all their guards downstairs. And for nothing. Mrs. Hasler was only a courier and knew nothing important.

At the end of the first week of her confinement, the bearded man brought her a newspaper.

He'd smiled at her as he held the paper out to her. "Thought you'd like a little reading material."

Rose wanted to refuse, but curiosity got the better of her. The headline read, "The Proclamation of Gen. Fremont." The article outlined the most disgusting news. General Fremont, who everyone knew was an abolitionist lunatic of the most dangerous sort, declared martial law in Missouri. Fremont then proclaimed every man in Missouri who took up arms against the Union would have his property, including slaves, confiscated by the federal government. Worse, the government would confiscate and free the slaves of "all armed rebels."

Freed! Rose could not believe it. While the newspaper made much of the fact that Fremont declared the rebellion treasonous, Rose cared not one whit. They could call it whatever they wanted and it wouldn't change the fact that the so-called rebels were winning the war. And rightly so. She could only imagine the mayhem in Missouri, what with the slaves pretending to be as good as white men. No white Missouri woman would be safe and did these Godless abolitionists care? No, they did not.

Lost in her thoughts, Rose almost missed the two men's conversation. *Had they mentioned the Provost Marshall?*

"That old rascal Mansfield has been interfering with the new Provost Marshal, a man named Porter. Porter didn't know what to do about it. It's like he wants Mansfield back in charge," said the one who called himself Edward Allen.

The other one, who she knew as Tim, seemed excited. "I hope so. Porter's too worked up about duty if you ask me. Old Mansfield knew how to have fun."

Rose's heart sped along with her knitting needles. Dear General Mansfield had been one of her loyal friends. Her arrest no doubt stemmed from this new Provost Marshal. That these police detectives used soldiers to guard the house suggested as much. She should write a letter to Mansfield. She'd already gotten two letters out, one to President Davis and another to Mr. Seward. That black maid they loaned her had been glad to help.

She sighed in happiness, thinking about her letter to President Davis. She told him how much the federals discovered and how much they still didn't know. There was no way her captors could not decipher the code in which she wrote so much of her correspondence. Almost daily they begged her for the cipher code. Naturally, she refused. These regular exchanges were among the most satisfying of her captivity.

"Time for dinner," a female voice called. Rose looked up to see her most hated captor, Miss Barley, in the doorway.

She'd engineered the woman's downfall two days after her arrest. She requested an audience with the bearded Mr. Allen. In the most strenuous language she could muster she objected to her treatment at the hands of Miss. Barley. As uncouth as Mr. Allen was, even he recognized the impropriety. He called Miss Barley into the dining room and excoriated her for her behavior and language. "This woman is our captive," he'd nearly yelled, "and she deserves our respect." Barley had sputtered and protested her innocence, as women of her type always did, but Mr. Allen demoted her anyway.

The man they called Tim stood with a huff and tromped upstairs to fetch the other lady prisoners for dinner. Several days ago Rose established that she would not act as a maid in her own home. On her first day downstairs they'd asked her to go upstairs and tell the other women it was dinner time. She had refused. Rose felt a thrill of triumph each time one of her captors had to fetch the ladies.

She took her seat at the head of the table and watched while the Barley creature set the table with plates and spoons. "I'd like water, as would the other ladies."

"Yes, Ma'am." The now chastened Barley woman scuttled off to comply with Rose's demand. Once the ladies were all seated and the food passed around, Rose considered their dinner conversation. Poor Mrs. Hasler was no help. She spent most of each meal staring at her food and eating little. Their guards paid no attention to her protestations of innocence, proving once more their ignorance of Rose's network. Dear Eugenia, on the other hand, had a true southern woman's heart, for all she was an over-reaching Jewess. She refused to speak to their jailers, except to inquire about the charges against her.

An armed guard or two always joined them at meals, ostensibly to keep an eye on them. Every day Rose and Eugenia endeavored to frustrate and embarrass their captors with some titillating story of her network's success. Rose had a juicy tidbit she'd been saving. Perhaps today was the day? Yes. She quite thought so.

"You men should tell your superior officers we knew all about their clumsy attempts to assassinate President Buchanan. We knew the whole diabolical scheme."

Mr. Allen reared his head back in shock. "What? How can that be?"

"Poor President Buchanan told me himself, you fool. Toward the end of his term, he appeared perpetually nervous. At his weekly socials, he drank four, sometimes five large glasses of brandy. He confessed to his friends he could no longer trust water and drank brandy to keep himself alive. You abolitionists poisoned the water, first at the White House and later at the National Hotel. The poor man. You know where you went wrong? You said the poison was for rats, and yet upon examination, there were no rats in any of either cistern. It was a thin story, concocted by people too arrogant to expect discovery."

She smiled around the table, ignoring poor Mrs. Hasler's head and shoulders slumped in a pose of the most abject submission. Eugenia's little girls had the good manners to never speak at the table, but Eugenia and Lily beamed their approval at Rose.

Mr. Allen spooned up the stew and, with his mouth full, asked, "Why didn't ole Buchanan order an investigation? And arrest us?"

Rose seized on the man's error with silent glee.

His face turned red when he realized his faux pas, "I mean arrest the people who done it."

"Oh, he explained that," Rose said, her victory complete. "He said the constitution bound us to turn over the government to abolitionists and that our duty was to help the nation through the difficult transition to abolitionist rule. Mr. Buchanan, unlike Ape Lincoln, sought to avoid war, not provoke it."

Lilly sniggered at Rose's little joke with the president's name.

With that Rose put down her spoon, rose and swept from the room. Though none of them had finished their dinner, five ladies followed her out.

After the guards locked them in for the night Rose went to her dressing table, which stood just in front of a window and lit her gas table lamp. She smiled to herself. Thank goodness she put a plan in place in the event of her arrest, a plan set in motion when Little Rose alerted Mrs. Mills. The detectives hadn't counted on her daughter's loyalty and training and had mistaken her frantic yelling for the contretemps of a frightened child. *Fools.*

Once alerted, the plan called for Mrs. Mills to alert Rose's most trusted lieutenants, Dr. Van Camp and lawyer Edward Pringle. Both men had instructions that allowed her underground resistance network to continue to function in spite of Rose's arrest. One of their many contingencies was a Morse code message system using her bedroom blinds. She peered out the window. There, across the street under the tree, stood a man shaped shadow. She opened and closed her blinds in quick snaps to indicate dots, longer closures for dashes. Her watcher needn't know Morse code, only record the dots and dashes.

An hour later a knock came at the door, then the sound of it unlocking. Her new maid Lizzie stepped into the room carrying a pitcher of water. She smiled at Rose without meeting her eyes and she lay out her mistress's nightclothes.

Rose appraised the girl. She rarely approved of free black servants, but this girl knew her place and was only too happy to do her new mistress's bidding. Rose had meant for Little Rose to function as her letter courier, but that plan had proven unworkable. The dastardly Yankees wouldn't let Little Rose out of the house. Her back up plan had been to force her house slave to act as a courier, but the woman had disappeared.

Rose had considered bribing a soldier, though the thought of physical congress with one of these crass northern men made her quiver in revulsion. Still, she'd have done it, she was that loyal to the cause. God's approval showed itself to Rose when Lizzie appeared. The mutton-headed men no doubt thought a colored girl would be loyal to the federal cause, but the girl understood something the abolitionists could not— that Africans were a natural servant race, born to serve their betters.

Lizzie helped Rose into her nightgown, poured water into the basin on the dressing table and turned to go. "Anything else, mistress," the girl asked, her tone as submissive as any good maid.

"In fact, yes." Rose held out a folded piece of paper. "Take this to the same man as before."

"Oh, yes ma'am," the girls said, her face shining with gratitude. "He's ever such a gentleman and he gave me two Indian head pennies last time. I bought taffy. It were ever so wonderful. I shared some with Little Rose, remember?"

Rose sighed. The girl really was a simpleton. Still, she got the job done. "You're a good girl Lizzie. Now off you go."

Rose walked the girl to the door and knocked on it. The soldier that guarded her room unlocked the door and let Lizzie out.

Rose leaned against the door and smiled. Life in captivity was proving as busy as life before her arrest. She'd accomplished so much today and she had so much more to do tomorrow.

Chapter 27

September 7, 1861
Washington City

Kate leaned against the closed kitchen door, the same one that somehow inspired so much kissing. She didn't feel romantic now. "One bullet. Just one. Or two, maybe." She glared at Allan, who sat at the kitchen table eating toast like it was just another day. "I've never wanted to kill anyone so much in my whole life. And we could call it self-defense because every time that self-satisfied, arrogant woman talks I want to kill myself."

Allan choked on his toast.

Hattie, who'd been helping Odetta unload a crate of food, sat a glass of water in front of Allan. "Kate has a point. Even I have murderous thoughts about the lady and I'm a model of patience when compared to Kate.

"I hate everything she does. Everything she says." Kate balled up her fists and held them at her side. "She treats Louisa like her personal slave."

"Which is precisely the idea." Hattie slid a tub of butter into the icebox and turned to face Kate. "If she knew the girl was with us she'd kill her."

Peg A. Lamphier

"None of that excuses the woman's behavior," Kate insisted.

Odetta handed Kate a cookie. "She nothin' but wind Miz Kate, you best remember that. You got her under house arrest after all."

Allan drank his water and kept quiet.

Kate pulled out a chair and sat with a thump, staring at her cookie. "I hate her. I hate her for outwitting us for so long. I hate her because she sees things as she does. I hate her snotty attitude and how nasty she is to Louisa"

Hattie laughed a laugh that sounded like tinkling silver bells. "My darling Kate, thank the powers above she is exactly who she is. She's playing right into our hands."

Allan swallowed hard and spoke up. "We're getting good intelligence on her network Kate. You know we are. And, we've created some elbow room to figure out the Senator Wilson and Mr. Seward problem. I know it's galling, having that woman lord it over you every day, but none of it's real."

Odetta chimed in. "Girl, at least you ain't in here cooking her food like she thinks. You outside watching her watchers most of the day. You and Mr. Juba. She got no idea a runaway like me is in her kitchen, doing my part to put a wrench in her wagon wheel." Odetta picked up her empty crate and gave Kate a stern look. "You got no right to be feeling sorry for yourself when you on the winning side." She left by the back door, like a breath of fresh air blowing out instead of in.

Hattie poured a mug of tea from the kettle sitting on the counter and held it to Kate. "It's hot in here. Take this outside and talk to your horse. Maybe go for a ride. You'll feel better. And consider this. Maybe you're just cranky because Hazzard got sent back to Fort Washington. You miss him." Before
326

Kate could argue Hattie dug in a cotton bag and brought out two small apples. "Here. One for each of you."

Kate gave Allan a token glare, just to remind him she was still mad, and took her apples to the backyard. She missed Hazzard, but that wasn't the problem. Rose was the problem. Excelsior head-butted her, interrupting her cranky thoughts. She gave him his apple, which he ate while she saddled him. He gobbled it, then lipped at her, checking to see if she had a further supply of his favorite treat. She relented and gave him the second apple.

Rose didn't keep her own horses and didn't have a stable, but she did have an enclosed backyard. Each morning Kate rode Excelsior to Fortress Greenhow, as the press had dubbed the house, and put him in the yard. Sometimes Monty came with them though lately he spent as many days with Juba as he did Kate. She wasn't sure where her uncle and dog disappeared to, but this morning they'd been up and gone before dawn.

She could have walked the distance, but she liked having Excelsior with her. And they rode out each afternoon between lunch and dinner. Excelsior would trot across the White House grounds to the Smithsonian, where they'd visit Mr. Banks, a friendly stable man Kate met months ago. He generally had a pot of tea ready and a newspaper. They'd pick through the news and talk about the war for an hour or so and then she'd head back to Fort Greenhow.

Mr. Banks, who came from a long line of fishermen, found the war's naval engagements fascinating. Last week he rejoiced in the U. S. Navy's victory at Fort Hatteras in North Carolina and took great pains to explain the importance and difficulty of blockading southern ports. This week they were

327

following the fighting in Kentucky. Confederate forces took the state only days before, though Mr. Banks seemed to think General Grant would get Kentucky back for the Union.

Kate grabbed Excelsior's bridle and looked her horse straight in the eye. "You're a big old goof, you know?" He was too tall for her and old enough to retire, but he was hers and she was his.

Excelsior knew his way to the Smithsonian so Kate let the reins fall slack as her mind wandered. The plan they'd come up with was a variation on Allan's "I'll pretend to be incompetent so no one suspects us" plan. Allan and Timothy often spoke in front of Rose about matters that seemed important but were either inconsequential or fictional. The idea was to trace information as it left the house and see where it led.

They planned for Hattie to act as Rotten Rose's new maid, but four seconds of clear thinking reminded them that Rose had met Hattie, masquerading as a bubble-headed debutante with southern leanings. Instead, they put Louisa into place. Louisa seemed immune to Rose's condescension and she delighted in outwitting the lady. So far Rose had given Louisa half a dozen letters, four of which went to Mr. Pringle, Rose's lawyer and co-conspirator. The other two went to a quack doctor named Van Camp, who they thought might be Rose's second in command. All the letters were chock full of names and instructions the Pinkertons were using to dismantle the network.

They let a letter to President Davis go through, curious to see if Rose's network could get it to Richmond and return a reply to Rose. In the letter, Rose assured Davis that her captors remained ignorant of both the cipher code and the identities of her two highest placed sources of information.

328

Though she named no one, the letter confirmed Miss Chase's analysis of the 'Brown File' documents.

Last night the wretched woman gave Louisa a letter for the ex-Provost Marshal. That letter urged General Mansfield to join her work for the glorious cause by assisting in a plan to free the women imprisoned in Fort Greenhow. They had not bothered to forward that letter because, though Allan and Timothy wanted Rose to believe Mansfield was meddling in the Provost's office and wanted his job back. In fact, the General had retired to Indiana months ago.

Some nights Pringle stood across the street recording Rose's window messages, while other evenings he sent his scrawny clerk. Neither man knew that while he stood on the street recording the lady's flashing blinds, Kate's band of Pinkerton Irregulars perched in the tree just above the men making the same recordings.

When Kate first proposed using the Irregulars for the job Allan strenuously objected.

"What kind of people use children to do their dirty work," he'd half-hollered at Kate.

"Smart ones," she'd replied, using the same voice she used to calm Excelsior when he got himself all worked up about an in-season mare. "Allan, they won't be in danger. Even if they're discovered, and they haven't been so far, they're children."

"Exactly my point," Allan interrupted.

Kate shook her head. "No, I mean they're nimble. All they would have to do is climb higher in the tree and elude capture."

"And what if they're shot at?"

"Mrs. Greenhow's silent watchers will not shoot anyone outside the house, thereby announcing their presence. And they're not likely to think the children anything more than street urchins."

Allan agreed they'd try the children at evening surveillance after Kate promised to pull them off the job at the first hint of danger. The children considered the job a grand adventure and an opportunity to continue the lunch program.

Kate wrinkled her nose at the stench coming from the canal as Excelsior crossed over it to the Smithsonian grounds. Unidentifiable lumps of floating muck rode the sluggish brown water, making the canal almost as revolting to look at as it was to smell. The poisonous stink reminded Kate of the toxic story Rose told about abolitionists efforts to assassinate President Buchanan. Not only had no such attempt been made, but Rose's own people had conspired to kidnap Buchanan as part of a larger plan to subvert Mr. Lincoln's election.

Many things about Rose and people like her frustrated Kate, but their absolute refusal to acknowledge facts drove her mad. They lied easily and casually and then pretended the lies were the truth. Mr. Lincoln was right. They had their own truth. Damned Rose Greenhow.

Kate's hands tightened on Excelsior's reins, causing him to throw his head and snort. "Sorry old boy," she said, remembering where she was. Kate shook her head and loosened her hands. Part of her anger was a simple response to Rose's high handed treatment of herself and Louisa the last two weeks. But it went deeper than that. She'd seen little of Juba lately. He wouldn't come by Rose's house, not even to sort or decode papers. Kate suspected he wanted no reminders of his enslavement, but she still missed him. If truth be told Juba's enslavement was Kate's reason number one for wanting Rose Greenhow in the darkest, dankest prison in Washington. Seeing her hanged for treason and general bitchery would not even begin to pay for what she'd done to Juba, but Kate would take it as a strong start.

Excelsior slowed as they approached the stables at the back of the Smithsonian Castle. Mr. Banks rose from his chair, which he'd leaned against the stable wall, and waved the *Washington Evening Star* at her. "Our boys on the U. S. S. Vincennes burned a Confederate ship to the water line down in Florida," he hollered at her. He rocked back on his heels and grinned.

She smiled back at him as she slid off Excelsior. She'd like to do the same to Mrs. Rose Greenhow. Burn her right down to the water line.

Chapter 28

*ow dare he? The despicable worm of a man. No wonder his
wife Varina could hardly stand to be in the same room with
him. And to think she'd anticipated this letter. This terrible,
wretched, hateful letter.* Her maid Lizzie brought it to her earlier
this evening, secreted in the hem of her skirt, a smile of triumph upon her dusky face. Rose took the letter and laid it on
her dressing table. *Let the little nigger gal think her mistress
received letters from the president so often they provoked no
excitement.* Once the maid left her for the evening Rose
rushed to her dressing table and ripped the letter open. She
turned up the light and decoded it. It began well enough.

*The Confederacy thanks you for your invaluable service. The
intelligence your network gathered exceeded both Captain Jordan's expec-
tations and my own. General Beauregard sings your praises and assures
me his recent, decisive victory can be, at least in part, be laid at your door.*

Rose looked with pleasure at her reflection in her dressing
table mirror. The evening light flattered her looks, but her
looks were less important to her than her life's work. After this
most excellent beginning, this application of praise she had
earned a hundred times over, the letter took a most repugnant
turn.

In light of the discovery of your activities and your incarceration, I urge you to retire from your efforts. You have done all you can, woman that you are, and the Confederacy shall ask no more. You have earned a return to femininity, with all the soft submission that makes women so essential to men's work. No intelligence you gather will address the failure of General Lee's Cheat Mountain campaign, nor General Johnston's refusal to attack Washington. The efficacy of your services has come to its inevitable end.

Rose fought the urge to burn the horrid letter. She'd held the president in such high esteem and he rewarded her with this? Did he not understand she accomplished so much precisely because she was a woman? *Soft submission. Bah.* Submission was for other women, unexceptional women. That while incarcerated in her own house she could get a letter to him in Richmond proved not only of her great skill in organizing a resistance network but the ongoing efficacy of that network. The man was a dullard and an ungrateful dullard at that. He was like a spoiled child, too stupid to recognize the quality of his toys.

I urge you to give yourself over to federal authorities. I would not have you face harsh punishment. Reveal the cipher to them if it will yield any favor to yourself. Jordan has developed new ciphers and a new network to replace yours. Rest easy knowing that the Confederate States of America respects your past contributions and forgives the situation in which you find yourself.

Yours,

JeffersonD avis

Rose stared at the signature. She very much wanted the letter to be a forgery, a false trail laid by her captors designed to break her spirit. But it was not. She knew his handwriting. Besides, Davis had this peculiar habit of writing the first letter of his last name as an addendum to his first name. She supposed that could be faked, but the letter had been written in her cipher—the same cipher her jailers kept asking her to reveal. No. The letter was authentic.

She reread the letter, her rage building with every word. Even Jordan, her onetime lover and confidante, had betrayed her. These men who led the cause to which she sacrificed everything wanted to throw her away as if she were garbage. She grabbed the coded letter, balled it up and hurled it across the room. Her whole being rebelled at the notion of submission, to either her captors or her president. They would pay. All of them. She rose, retrieved the balled up letter and returned to her dressing table. Removing the glass shade from her lamp, she held first the original and then the deciphered letter to the flame before dropping them into her wastebasket. The fire burned itself out in seconds, leaving only ash behind.

That is my old life. It is in ashes.

She stared at her reflection for several long minutes before rewarding herself with a grim smile. *And like the Phoenix, I shall rise again.*

Kate leaned against the brick wall, enjoying the way the day's heat radiated off the house as the day turned to night. Monty pressed against her leg, his furry body a warm spot in the cooling air. Washington natives assured Kate that the summer had been mild, being neither as hot nor as humid as most, but it had seemed plenty warm and sticky to her. Now, in mid-September, the humidity had relented its grip on the city and cooler nights made for cooler mornings and shorter periods of mid-day heat.

She and Monty had taken to spending her evening's out-doors, hiding behind a shrubbery across from Rose's house. The owners of the brick house had no idea that a woman and a small black and white dog lurked in their flower beds most evening. From her hiding place, she had a view of both Rose's bedroom window and the watcher who stood beneath the tree two houses down. The Irregulars had determined that Rose's window messages came after dinner, between 8:30 and 10 in the evening, so that's when Kate and Monty sat vigil.

Ten days ago she made a deal with her gang of misfits. She promised to pay them the same rate she always had, but they were to only watch the house in the afternoons and evening. In the mornings they had to attend school. A minister and his wife, who ran a free school, were only too happy to accept Kate's donations in return for weekly attendance reports, a fact she'd made known to her Irregulars, much to their dismay. So far the deal seemed to be holding. The children attended school in the mornings and took turns watched the house in the afternoons and evenings, leaving when Kate and Monty relieved them.

Kate stole a glance at her pocket watch. The crickets stilled their song at her movement before resuming their nightly serenade. It was coming on 10 o'clock. She stroked the watch with her thumb and thought of Hazzard. Kate couldn't blame General Scott for wanting more soldiers trained in the usage of the big artillery guns, men who could man the series of new fortifications that now ringed the city, but she still missed Hazzard. Plus, she studied the little instruction sheet that came with her "ladies preventative" and practiced inserting the thing. The process had been exquisitely embarrassing.

Rose's window remained dark, though she had sent messages nine of the last ten days. Most of the information Rose transmitted was about the goings-on inside the house and thus not important. Still, it was alarming to know that the Washington underground had a good idea of Fortress Greenhow's daily operations. She'd urged Allan to remove the blinds from the lady's bedroom but he'd argued for keeping them. Kate hated to admit it, but he was right. If they alerted Rose to the fact that they knew about her message system it might suggest that they had deceived her in other matters. The longer the lady thought she was running roughshod over her captors the longer they had to root out the entire network.

After yet another long meeting they also agreed to not move against either Senator Wilson or Secretary Seward as long as both men stayed away from Fort Greenhow. Neither man had been near the house since Rose's house arrest began. The thought of having to charge either man with treason made her sick with anxiety. Hattie, Timothy and Allen felt the same way. No one wanted to expose Mr. Lincoln's administration to corruption and scandal.

At her feet, Kate felt Monty shift his weight. She looked down. His ears pricked forward. A soft, scraping sound caught Kate's ear, so soft it did not disturb the crickets. She sat up, pushing herself away from the house's foundation wall.

Rose's window sash rose. A length of white rope emerged from the window. Monty growled. Kate laid a hand on his back, his tiny body like a coiled spring beneath her fingers. He quieted.

Where was the soldier who was supposed to guard the door? Kate looked at her watch again. Just after eleven o'clock. Every hour the guard left his post at the front door and made a circuit of the house and yard. His eleven o'clock circuit always took longer. Kate assumed he had a smoke in the back alley or used the privy. She had paid little attention to the man's absence, figuring a guard outside the house was redundant when they locked the prisoners in their rooms each night. She'd been wrong.

Kate watched the rope growing longer out the window and wished she had her field glasses. No, not a rope. It was sheets, torn and tied together. *Oh, for goodness sake.* Had the woman been reading sensational novels of the type where brave heroines escaped castle towers on ropes of torn bedding? Really? People didn't do that sort of thing in real life, did they? A milk-white leg appeared over the window sill. A body clad in dark clothing followed the leg. Apparently, people did do that sort of thing in real life.

Kate peered through the gloom. There was a street light just down the block from Rose's house, but its limp yellow light didn't make it this far. Still, the figure inching down the rope looked like a man. *Why would a man escape from Rose's bedroom via the window?* Kate snickered at her own questions. She could think of a hundred reasons a man might make a sheet assisted exit from Rose's room.

Then Kate remembered seeing a suit of men's clothing hanging in Rose's closet, a gray wool so dark it looked black, pushed toward the back as if forgotten. At the time Kate assumed it belonged to Rose's long-dead husband, who surely died from the shame of being married to such an awful woman. Maybe the suit had belonged to Mr. Greenhow, but he wasn't wearing it now.

The black-clad figure reached the ground, rubbed its hands on its trousers and set off walking south, towards Lafayette Park.

Should she raise the alarm? What if Rose injured someone inside the house to affect her escape? She spent a precious second imagining Louisa lying on Rose's bedroom floor, unconscious or worse. Kate shook off the image and set out after the escapee. Louisa visited Rose's room just after dinner. Tonight she'd delivered the letter from Jefferson Davis and appeared back in the kitchen only minutes later. Rose would have wanted privacy to read her letter, a letter Hattie and Kate concocted just that afternoon. They'd had great fun fabricating phrases calculated to insult and enrage Rotten Rose. Apparently letter had succeeded all too well in its intent.

Louisa was fine. Was Rose escaping? Or someone else? Kate had a hard time a woman of Rose's dignity and age climbing down rope of sheets wearing a men's suit. And there was Little Rose to consider. Would Rose leave her behind? But who else could it be?

Kate and Monty followed the dark figure down Sixteenth Street to Lafayette Square, the park just to the north of the president's house. Their quarry made straight for the large, white stone monolith, atop which reared an equestrienne statue of President Jackson. The shadow turned there and struck southeast across the park toward Thirteenth Street. She spared a glance at the statue as she passed it. The sculptor made Jackson look like a pompous ass, but the rearing bronze horse had marvelous style. Her eye caught the words on the statue's base as she passed.

OUR FEDERAL UNION
IT MUST BE PRESERVED.

I'm doing my best. She resisted the impulse to break into a run. No need to get too close.

Kate and Monty followed the Shadow south, towards the river. After several blocks, the shadow turned onto Ohio Street, one of the city's many-angled streets that cut across the grid of north-south and east-west streets. Kate knew exactly where she was. Her target was taking a route to the Smithsonian identical to the one she and Excelsior traveled each afternoon. *What would Rose want with the Smithsonian? Probably nothing. Most likely she'd cross the Smithsonian grounds on her way to her destination.* A profusion of military installations lay near the Potomac River. Or was she going to a friend's house? Kate searched her memory for a Greenhow contact that fit the bill. She found no one and returned to her original idea. Rose was most probably heading to a military destination, one containing a friend of the Confederacy. It would be an officer. A woman as enamored with herself as Rose Greenhow would not seek out an enlisted man for help. No, Rotten Rose would have a friend with epaulets on his shoulders and a weakness for mature ladies of easy virtue.

The further her target walked the angrier Kate became with herself. She should have had multiple watchers on the house. She should have ordered the upstairs windows nailed closed. Most frustratingly, the bitch should have been in jail, where escape would have been impossible. Instead, they let her play lady of the manor in her own house while most of her spy network went around free as birds. That Boyd girl, for example, was still out there somewhere.

Kate gritted her teeth and picked up her pace. Allan, Mr. Lincoln, General Scott, all of them, fundamentally didn't believe a woman, any woman, could be a threat to the nation's

340

security. This near universal lapse in male judgment made opportunities for women spies, including herself. And hadn't her own work proved the effectiveness of female agents? Either they didn't believe in her effectiveness. Or Hazzard was right—they mistook her for a unicorn. How else did one explain this lax treatment of Mrs. Rose Greenhow?

Rose crossed a narrow square, one made by the confluence of Ohio and Louisiana streets, abutting the Smithsonian grounds. Kate and Monty closed the gap between them. As Kate approached the bridge that crossed the canal her patience broke. She could see Rose clearly in the light of the gas lamp that stood at this end of the bridge so she scooped up a small rock and flung the rock at Rose. Kate put all her anger, all her frustration, and all her hate into her arm. The rock chunked solidly into the black-clad figure's back, bounced off and clattered to the ground.

Rose yelped in pain, stumbled and regained her footing. She turned. "You!" Rose Greenhow's face contorted in rage. Swimming in a black suit two sizes too big for her, Rose stepped toward Kate, the bridge at her back.

Monty's hackles bristled. He growled a sound too big for his small body.

Kate reached for her gun, cranky with herself for losing her temper and forgetting it until now.

Rose beat her to it. She pulled a gun out of her jacket pocket and pointed it at Kate. "Get away from me," she said in a voice so low it was almost a growl. "Turn and go or I will shoot you."

Kate stared at Rose's gun. It was a common Philadelphia Derringer. *Where had the bitch gotten a derringer?* It didn't matter. Once again Kate rejoiced in the fact that the man she loved

341

was an artillery officer willing to share his knowledge of guns. One-shot derringers were notoriously difficult to load correctly and wildly inaccurate at any distance over six feet. She and Rose were about ten feet apart and the street lamp created only a dim pool of light. And she'd had already taken one gun off the rebel woman.

Kate flung herself at Rose.

Rose's gun cracked.

Kate hit Rose hard, wrapping her arms around the woman and taking her to the ground in a rush of cold cobblestones and black rage. *Had she been hit?* A needle-sharp pain rushed through Kate's leg. She couldn't believe it. Rose's shot had not missed.

They rolled together, scratching, kicking, spitting. Monty circled them, barking like a canine possessed. Kate struggled to get a grip on Rose with one hand while groping for her revolver with the other. Rose flailed her arms, screeching and spitting like she had rabies. When Kate finally yanked the Colt from her inside jacket pocket she lost her grip on Rose.

Rose rolled over, grabbed a handful of Kate's hair and yanked. Kate used the forward momentum to slam her forehead into Rose's face. Pain exploded between Kate's eyes. It was like slamming her head against a wall. She felt a warm trickle run down the side of her face.

Blood ran down Rose's face as she screeched and batted wildly at Kate. Her hand connected with Kate's gun hand, knocking the revolver loose. Kate heard it clatter across the cobblestones. A blur of black and white appeared in Kate's field of vision a second before Monty sunk his teeth into Rose's arm. Rose screeched again and shook Monty off. The little dog charged back in, teeth bared in canine fury.

342

Kate swept Monty back with a free arm and staggered to her feet, feeling stupid and slow. A few feet away, Rose struggled to her feet, swaying as she did. Monty stood between them, head down, hackles up. Pain sliced through Kate's forehead. Her leg chimed in to keep her forehead company. *I will kill this bitch and be done with her.* She glanced around for the one of guns but in the weak gaslight she saw neither.

Rose swayed on her feet, a handful of Kate's hair still grasped in her hand, her face smeared wetly with blood. She pulled something dark and slim from her pocket and advanced on Kate.

"A button hook," Kate gasped, trying not to laugh at the stupidity of the weapon. Monty growled, evidently finding no humor in button hooks. Kate dared not look down at her dog.

"It won't be so funny when it's sticking out of your eye," Rose hissed. She took another step forward. And then another.

The button hook started to seem less stupid. It was metal and had a nasty little pointed crook at its end. Kate took another step back, her nose telling her the canal was right behind her. She risked a glance over her shoulder. She had less than three feet. All Rose had to do was force her back, back into the terrible muck of the city canal. While Kate floundered Rose could make her escape.

Kate had an idea. It had worked in Libby Prison's waiting room. No reason she couldn't do it again. No reason but the bullet hole in her leg. *The leg will hold. It has to.*

Kate stepped back half a step. "You can't beat me. You're old and used up."

"You know nothing," Rose screeched. "Men desire me and I use them!"

343

Monty bounced on his front feet and growled.

Kate shook her head, and regretted it when pain flashed behind her eyes. "I felt your sagging tits, remember? They disgusted me. They disgust men too."

Kate watched Rose's eyes tighten. She unleashed her worst sentence. "You're no better than a worn out whore."

A howl of inchoate rage escaped Rose's lips. She threw herself at Kate, the fingers of her free hand spread like the claws of a predatory beast. She jabbed the hook at Kate's face.

Kate half turned. She reached up with her left arm, grabbed Rose's arm and pulled it toward her. With her other hand, she grabbed the back of Rose's head. She heaved herself forward, using both arms to pull Rose over. Her leg protested with a flare of white-hot agony. Kate ignored it. She put everything she had into the throw. For a moment Rose hung heavy on her shoulders. And then the burden was gone. Rose flew over her shoulder and splashed into the canal.

Monty ran to the water's edge and barked at the flailing woman. Kate gasped out a laugh. The last time she'd been in a fight near the canal she'd been the one who ended up floating among the swollen animal carcasses and soggy turds. This was much better.

Rose slipped under the dark water.

Kate watched, her leg throbbing in time with her heart. It served the bitch right. If she drowned it would save the trouble keeping her under arrest for God only knew how long.

Great bubbles broke the water's surface as Rose boiled to the surface. She sputtered and spit filthy water. "I can't swim," she cried, waving a hand at Kate. She went under again.

Kate watched Monty, watch the water. She'd killed two people in her life. Both times she had little choice. And still,

344

they weighed on her and troubled her sleep. *Could she stand by and watch this woman drown? Surely she deserved death. For enslaving Juba and dozens more free people of color, for the death and destruction, she caused at Bull Run, for the countless acts of violence her network had nourished with its well of hate. Rose Greenhow was a long distance killer. Was she? Could she stand by and condemn this woman to drown?*

A choking gurgle broke the canal's surface, followed by Rose Greenhow's head, slick and black with filthy water. Her hands waved in the night air like pale starfishes.

Maybe Mr. Lincoln was right. When it came right down to it, was there any difference between the two of them? And if there was, was it enough to justify murder?

Kate kicked off her shoes, shrugged out of her coat. "Stay," she yelled at Monty. She dove into the canal.

Chapter 29

September 16, 1861
Washington City

The front door thumped against the wall Feet pounded up the stairs. Doors slammed. Kate sat in the kitchen, a damp kitchen towel tied around her head, ice chips from the icebox rolled inside. She reached for her teacup, then looked over at Charlotte, eyebrows raised. From his bed, in the corner of the room, Monty raised his head, then returned to licking his white paws. He'd jumped into the canal with her, and been no help at all after he did. Much to his dismay Charlotte had given him a bath. He'd made his preference for canal stench to laundry soap abundantly clear. Kate found him a bone after they toweled him off. The treat made up for the indignity of the bath, but only barely.

From the sink where she was rinsing out the mess left by Monty, Charlotte shrugged and dried her hands. "Before I sewed you up, I sent Louisa to telegram your captain. It seemed only fair."

Kate listened as Hazzard's boots thumped up the stairs and then down again. The kitchen door flew open. Hazzard stood gasping for air in the doorway, collar open at his throat, black chest hair just curling into sight, the hair on his head tussled. His eyes glinted in a manner that made Kate feel shivery all over.

"Shot again?" he yelled at her. "You must be kidding me, woman." He raked his hands through his hair.

"I'm fine." She looked pointedly at her bandaged leg, which lay across a pulled up chair. Turning to Charlotte, she asked, "What exactly did your telegram say?"

"It said," Hazzard roared, "you'd been shot. Again."

"To be fair," Charlotte said in a reasonable tone, "the telegram also said it was a small wound."

"It said she was shot," Hazzard repeated, though much quieter this time. He sunk into a kitchen chair, propped his chin on his hands. "You'll be the death of me, my dear."

Kate tried not to laugh. Instead, as sweetly as she could, she said, "I'm sorry Hazzard. I was going catch up on my knitting last night, but Rotten Rose escaped house arrest and I had to re-capture her."

Hazzard stared at Kate.

She stared back.

Charlotte folded the kitchen towel in her hands and laid it next to the sink. "I've been up all night. I'm off to bed."

The second she left the room Kate pushed away the chair and rose, careful to keep weight off her bad leg. Hazzard stood as well, but she gestured him back into his chair. Instead, she hopped over and took a seat on his lap. His arms circled around her and hers around him. "I really am fine," she whispered into his ear.

He crushed her against him. "I'm the soldier. I'm supposed to get shot. Not you."

"No one is supposed to get shot." She lowered her lips to his.

348

He pulled her in closer, his arms crushing her against his uniform.

Kate explored his mouth, her tongue tangling with his. She nibbled his lower lip, pulling a groan from deep inside him.

After a time Kate asked, "Do you have to leave soon?"

He shook his head. "I've got a 24-hour pass. I have time to hear your story. You know, the 'how I got shot again,' story." His hand moved to the towel tied around her head. "What's this?"

Kate snuggled into Hazzard's arms and regaled him with the story of her and Monty's evening adventure.

Just as she was getting to the part where Rose was cutting across Lafayette Park he interrupted her. "Did the fake President Davis letter set her off?"

"Probably. Maybe. But she didn't say a word after I pulled her out of the canal, I don't know what she was thinking. Not sure I care either."

Hazzard cocked his head at her. "The canal?"

"Well, you interrupted me." Kate continued with her tale, placing particular emphasis on Monty's heroism. At the mention of his name Monty interrupted his paw cleaning to stare at Kate and Hazzard. When it became clear they were not discussing food he returned to his toes.

Hazzard laughed. "So you tossed her into the canal, just like Captain Jordan did to you last spring?"

"It's where I got the idea," she said. "That and my fight at Libby Prison."

"Your fight at Libby Prison?" Hazzard's eyebrow rose.

Kate felt his chest rumble.

A chuckle burst out of him. "That's a sentence no other lady will ever say to me."

349

"Well, you taught me to throw people. What did you think would happen? And you never told me how much head butt's hurt. It's how I got this." She pointed at her head and then continued. "So I provoked Rose and she ran right at me."

He squeezed her again. "I have to admit, I never thought you'd need a fighting technique like that."

"I know. You just wanted to get your hands on my body."

He threw back his head and laughed, exposing his neck to her. She leaned in and kissed him under the ear. It was a minute or two before they spoke again.

When she was ready Kate looked Hazzard in the eye and said, "I almost let her drown."

He regarded her steadily and waited.

"She can't swim. And she was wearing her husband's suit, which was way too big for her. It must have weighed thirty pounds soaking wet." Kate swallowed hard. "I've wanted her dead for so long. I'm so angry at her. For everything she's done. For all the people she's hurt. So I stood there and watched her struggle."

"Mmmhhmm." Hazzard kissed the tip of her nose. "But you didn't let her drown did you?"

Kate shook her head.

"Where's she now?"

"Back at Fortress Greenhow."

"Is that good enough?"

"I don't know."

"I notice you've pretty much forgotten about Miss Boyd and the others on that list."

Kate realized she had. She felt a little ashamed about that.

"It's because you're furious at Rose for what she did to Juba and Columbus, not for the spying and all those dead men at Bull Run. Because that stuff isn't personal. Not to you."

Kate heaved out a big breath of air. "Yes." Her hands tightened around Hazzard's neck. "I know I should care more about the Union soldiers who died or all the other people her spy ring enslaved, but I don't. Not like Juba. I don't know what's wrong with me."

"He's your family. Even before he told you he's your real uncle, he was your family. That means something." He paused. "Let me tell you something I learned long ago. I was just out of West Point. The Army sent me out west to the war with Mexico. I killed men and none of it meant much. And that bothered me. But I had this friend, we were in the same class at West Point and we both ended up in the Mexican War. He wasn't a soldier. His father made him join the Army because he wanted to toughen him up. He wasn't a military sort of fellow, you see? Thomas was . . . . I don't know . . . . Poetical. Soft. I did my best to protect him. I know what it's like to have a father who disapproves of you and wants you to be someone you aren't." Hazzard's voice trailed off.

Kate did the waiting this time. Outside birds began to chirp, greeting the same dawn that slowly brightened the kitchen.

"There was a battle. A messy, chaotic thing. They always are. This big, mustachioed Mexican charged our position. I saw him coming right at Thomas, but I was too far away. The man stabbed Thomas with his bayonet. Thomas fell. The man was stabbing and stabbing him. That was the first time I felt outraged in battle. I killed that man. I've killed a lot of men in battle, but he's the one I remember. And the look on poor

351

Thomas's face as he lay dying. I remember that too." Hazzard's voice trailed off to a whisper.

Kate listened to the birds, unsure what to say.

Hazzard helped her. "Death is theoretical until it happens to someone we care about. You hate Rose Greenhow for what she did to Juba, and by extension, what she did to you. All her other deeds happened off stage. It's not real. Not to you."

"Shouldn't it be?" Kate felt her eyes fill with unshed tears as the big ball of guilt inside her shifted.

"I don't know." Hazzard shrugged and squeezed her a little. "I think we're designed to love and hate. Wouldn't you rather we loved and hated people we knew? Shouldn't it be personal?" He paused. "That's what makes war so god awful. It's impersonal killing. We pretend war makes killing fine, even honorable. Like killing in the name of abstract ideas is somehow better than killing for personal reasons."

"So I should have killed her?" Somehow this idea made Kate's heart sink.

'Hell no." He tightened his arms around her. "You've killed two people. Both in self-defense, right?"

She shook her head. "No. The Countess meant to kill me, but that man on the road, he was going to kill Juba, not me."

"It's the same thing. Killing to defend someone you love is like killing to defend yourself. But if you'd let Rose drown, it would have been murder. It would have sullied you."

She gnawed at her lower lip. "When I was dragging her out of the canal, it occurred to me that punishing her or anyone else isn't the point."

Hazzard cocked his head at her. "What is the point?"

"It's not revenge. The dead are beyond saving. It's stopping the information drain. Saving the next soldiers' life.

352

Because Mr. Lincoln was right about Mr. Seward and Mr. Wilson. There's no point in exposing either man for mistakes they aren't making any more. The scandal would distract from our larger purpose."

Hazzard watched her for a moment and then changed the subject. "So what happened after you pulled her out of the canal?"

She told him how she'd rolled Rose out of her soaking wet coat and pounded on her back until she gushed buckets of reeking water onto the cobblestones. While Rose was coughing and gagging on the ground, Kate removed Rose's wet stockings, wrung them out and used them to tie her hands together. While she did Monty stood at Rose's head, teeth bared like he meant to chew her face off if she moved. Kate guessed that as small as he was his teeth looked pretty big when they were six inches from your face.

Then she put on her shoes back on, which gave her an idea. She tossed Rose's shoes into the canal, along with her husband's jacket. The loss of those two items should keep Rose from making a run for it. She collected her Colt, which she found not six inches from the edge of the canal, but couldn't find the derringer. She gave up the search after less than a minute on the assumption that it was at the bottom of the canal. All the while she searched Rose alternated between coughing and cursing at her. Kate ignored her and hailed a passing hansom cab, which turned out to be easier said than done. She and Rose were both dressed in men's clothing and neither of them smelled very nice. She had to pay him twice his usual fair before he'd let two soaking wet, unpleasant smelling people into his conveyance, though he hadn't minded that the money he took was as wet as his passengers. It was

353

Peg A. Lamphier

after midnight when they pulled up in front of Kate's F Street house. Kate knocked on the door until Charlotte came down while Monty stood guard over their captive.

Charlotte woke up the household and after a brief discussion Timothy took Rose back to Fort Greenhow. Odetta went with them, insisting Mr. Webster needed the help. The grim look on her face suggested Odetta wanted to do more than 'help.' Hattie, Louisa, and Charlotte helped Kate into the house and back to the kitchen. Charlotte undressed Kate and wrapped her in a clean towel while Hattie cleaned the bullet wound and put two stitches in Kate's calf.

As she worked Hattie chastised Kate for making her work on her day off from the hospital. Kate suggested they call Miss Chase so Hattie could go back to bed since she was so delicate. Hattie rapped Kate upside the head. Louisa looked alarmed until the two women grinned at each other and she figured out they were teasing. Charlotte helped Louisa make a poultice of moldy bread, which the girl insisted her granny always used to keep infection at bay. Hattie slathered the gooey mess on Kate's leg and wrapped it up in strips of clean toweling. Afterwards all three women wiped Kate down and wrapped her in her favorite dressing gown.

Kate couldn't articulate how that felt, all those women taking care of her. She'd lost her mother when she was fifteen years old, but tonight it seemed as if she gained three new mothers. Or sisters. It was a startling idea.

"So where's everyone now?" Hazzard asked. "I know Charlotte went up to bed, but the rest of them?"

"Louisa thought someone ought to go look for Rose's coat and shoes. Hattie agreed. The jacket might have clues to where she was going." Kate wrinkled up her nose. "They took

354

the manure shovel and a garden hoe with them." Kate had tried not to laugh at the two of them, armed with yard tools, when they left the house. She'd seen women do wonders with less.

"All's well that ends well." He kissed the tip of her nose again.

Kate thought about it. They'd catch up with Belle Boyd and the others eventually and without a spymaster that whole crew might just fall apart. Still, the Boyd problem was unfinished business.

Kate shifted herself out of Hazzard's lap and perched on the kitchen table. "It hasn't ended well at all." She put her slippered feet up on the edge of his chair, between his legs. "For months now all I could think about was how much I hated Rose Greenhow and how I wanted her hung for treason. But when she was drowning it occurred to me, she's not that different from me. Though to be fair, Mr. Lincoln suggested it first."

"Hmmm." Hazzard learned toward her. "Explain."

"Well, me and Rose are both professional liars. And we both believe we're doing the right thing, though we believe in different things. That's why I saved her. Or one reason. I think I was wrong to hate a woman for doing the same job I do."

"Maybe," he said with a shrug. "But the difference is, you're right and she's wrong."

Kate shifted on the table, reaching back for her mug. "That's what I told Mr. Lincoln. He said she thinks she's right too."

"Yes. But you're right and she's wrong."

She took a sip of her tea, watching Hazzard over her mug.

355

He leaned forward and put his hands on her knees. "It's just wrong to own human beings. It's not debatable. To buy and sell men, women, and children is morally wrong. It's a crime against humanity and a perversion of democracy. It's wrong to believe the group you belong to is superior to some other group, more entitled to basic rights like liberty, safety and self-determination. It's just wrong."

"Says who? You? Me? How convenient for us."

He let go of her knees and leaned back. "Now you're being obtuse. You tell me. Who or what says slavery is wrong? And the ideas that go with it?"

Kate considered the questions. "History. History tells us that tyranny is wrong. The more people who have equality and liberty, the better. Hate isn't just mean or selfish, it's immoral."

Hazzard nodded. "So that's how you're different from Rose and why you're right and she's wrong. You believe until every man owns only himself and is equal to every other man, no man is really free."

"And no woman." She smiled and slid back to his lap, this time straddling his legs.

He pulled her snug against him. "I couldn't agree more," he murmured into her ear. "I like a free woman."

"Rascal," she breathed into his ear before taking his earlobe in her teeth. She nibbled, then slipped her tongue into his ear. Hazzard groaned and his interest became clear. She was, after all, sitting on his lap.

She clasped her hands behind his neck and leaned back. Butterflies did somersaults, frogs stuck in her throat, bees buzzed in her brain. But he'd made it clear time and again, he'd wait for her to be ready. It was her move. "I've come into

356

the possession of an item that prevents married ladies from becoming pregnant."

"Just married ladies?" He leaned back and ran his hands through her hair. "What about unmarried ladies with quicksilver hair?"

Hazzard's predatory grin made Kate go shivery all over. "All kinds of ladies I'd presume."

"And that's what you want?" He held her waist, his thumbs settled just over her belly button. "You still don't want to marry? Because if you've changed your mind I'll ask you. Right now."

She sighed. "No. I meant what I said. I was married and found it not to my liking."

He kissed her once more, this time as tenderly as if she were a child. "You were not married to me."

She nodded. "True. But still. No wedding and no babies. Not right now. Is that all right?"

He kissed again, this time with less tenderness and more passion.

Kate took the kiss as a yes.

When he broke away he said, "But if you change your mind, we can talk about that too. War be damned. But for now, no wedding and no babies."

She opened her eyes wide and batted her eyelashes at him. She'd made no secret of her fondness for the technique when she wanted something from a man she was investigating. "The thing is, I have an injury." She kissed him where his jaw and ear met. "I was shot. In the leg." Kissed him again, just by his ear. "It's quite bad. I don't think I can walk." She nipped at his earlobe. It felt like velvet between her teeth. "I'd feel much better if I were in bed."

He threw back his head and laughed. It was a glorious, full-throated, rolling sound. Kate thought she could listen to it for the rest of her life. He swept her up in his arms and carried her up the stairs.

The End.

It Takes a Village

Thanks for reading *Rebel Belles*. If you enjoyed the book you could help me by leaving a review at Amazon or Goodreads (or both if you're feeling it). I know it's a hassle, but it helps get the books out there. You can sign up for my email list at www.peglamphier.com. I'm not going to spam you or give your information to rebel spies, so there's no downside. If you have a private comment or found an error you can email me at: pegalamphier@gmail.com. And again, thanks so much for reading. Spread the love!

Real (and Not So Real) Things

As in the other novels of this series, the events portrayed are based in reality. I've fictionalized history whenever and wherever it suited the story, but otherwise tried to get it right. Kate Warne, Juba Lane, Hattie Lawton, George Hazzard, Timothy and Charlotte Webster and Allan Pinkerton were all real people, though I have taken considerable liberties with some aspects of their lives. Allan Pinkerton did employ Kate and Hattie, but they both barely appear in the historical record.

Some of the language in this book belongs to my characters, not me. I do not condone usage of the "N" word or any hate-based speech. The racist language in this novel is meant to create historical verisimilitude—people in the past spoke this way (and sadly, some people still do). Racism and sexism are ugly things and to write about the people who believed these ugly things an author must use ugly language.

History criticizes Allan Pinkerton for being a poor spymaster who encouraged George McClellan's tendency to caution. I think a man smart enough found the Pinkerton Detective Agency would be smart enough to be a good spy. Thus I invented the ruse by which Allan pretends to be incompetent to hide his spy operation. The Pinkerton Detective Agency was headquartered in Cincinnati in 1861.

George Washington Hazzard was an officer in the Fourth Regiment, U. S. Artillery, having command of battery A in the summer of 1861. That regiment was out west, but when the war began the regiment was recalled to Fort McHenry near Baltimore, and then moved to Fort Washington. Captain Hazzard was not with his regiment in the months before the war, having been detached to investigate a variety of threats against then president-elect Lincoln. Once the war began the 4th had charge of the defense of Washington. Thus Hazzard and the 4th Artillery were not at Bull Run with the other Artillery regiments, which was handy for me.

Mountain Feists are a breed of dog original to the Appalachian and Ozark Mountains. Abraham Lincoln's poem "The Bear Hunt" features a Feist. Their owners say they are excellent squirrel hunters. I named the dog in this novel after a delightful hound we adopted years ago. The original Monty has since passed to doggy heaven where (I hope) he chases airplane contrails and flashlight beams every day.

The Columbia and Warrenton Turnpikes did once take travelers to Centreville and Manassas. A wagon overturned at Cub Run late in the afternoon of the first battle. There was a field hospital down the road at Stone Bridge. I tried to get the Bull Run details correct, but battlefield buffs should keep in mind that novels are works of fiction and that I cavalierly disregarded any fact that didn't serve the story. Such are the delights of fiction.

Spectators gathered at Centreville Heights to watch the battle, including the congressmen and senators named in Chapter 2. Though it is easy to discount these observers as frivolous tourists, it would be wise to remember that a major battle, close to the nation's capital, would have created a lot of anxiety. In the modern age, when too many people entertain themselves with television shows, movies, and video games that portray the violence of war, we should not be too glib in our condemnation of Civil War Americans who wanted to see Bull Run.

Northerners referred to the battle on July 21 as Bull Run, after the creek that ran through the area. Confederates named the battle after the nearby town Manassas. This follows a pattern where Union officials named battles after natural landscape artifacts while Confederates named battles after towns and cities. I use Bull Run to avoid confusion.

The quotes from the lady with the opera glasses and the gentleman rider come from William Howard Russell's account of Bull Run, which he first published *The Times of London*. It's a gas. You should go read it right now. Kate Chase was in Washington during Bull Run, though she most likely did not go out to Centreville. Clara Barton volunteered at the Washington Infirmary, which saw the first casualties of the First Battle of Bull run.

The note Jordan sent Greenhow thanking her for her contributions to the Confederate victory at Bull Run/Manassas was real. It was not written in code. I accurately described her cipher code (you can find it on the internet if you're interested). As far as historians know, Belle Boyd and Rose Greenhow did not work together. Like Greenhow, Belle Boyd wrote a memoir from which I borrowed words and thoughts. Historians continue to argue about the efficacy of Boyd's espionage efforts.

Rose Greenhow wrote a memoir of her life as a spy and prisoner titled, *My Imprisonment and the First Year of Abolition Rule in Washington*. I borrowed many of her words and sentiments for the chapters written from her point of view. It would be easy to think I have exaggerated Rose's arrogance, hatred of northerners or narcissism. I have not. Read her book and see for yourself. It would be difficult to find a more self-aggrandizing, self-righteous liar in all the annals of history. She was also a more than competent spy who got valuable intelligence out of Washington and to the Confederacy. I've used some of her accomplishments and invented others. Rose invented a good many things for her book so I didn't think she'd mind if I emulated her.

There is considerable disagreement about the importance and quality of Rose Greenhow's intelligence. Many, but not all, academics dismiss her spycraft. I think historians discount her, at least in part, because she was female. I'm not saying she was the most dangerous spy ever, but I think she might have been more dangerous than most modern historians will admit. The same can be said of Belle Boyd and all the women spies of the Civil War.

Christopher Peplin's blog about safe cracking formed the basis for Kate's safe-cracking adventure. The safe types, dialing sequences, and number stuff in that scene are accurate. Also, the internet is full of people, mostly older white dudes, who know a lot about Civil War era guns, including cannons. I thank these gentlemen for providing information that helped me with the guns and artillery in this book.

The Georgetown Market was razed and a new one built in 1865. The Market I describe is a mishmash of the original and the "new" market.

Readers of Arthur Conan Doyle's stories will recognize my homage to Sherlock Holmes' army of street urchins, the Baker Street Irregulars. Child homelessness was a massive problem in the mid-1800s, fed by poverty, immigration, poor health care and general cultural ambivalence about poor children.

Any reader who believes governments should not provide social services or regulate businesses should examine the
plethora of images for homeless children and child factory
workers workers in the decades before and after the Civil War.

The *National Era* was an African American newspaper published in Washington DC. It ceased publication in 1860. I
revived it for this story.

Kate Chase, the daughter of Lincoln's Secretary of Treasury Salmon P. Chase, lived at 6th and E Street with her father
and sister Nettie Chase. They had servants named Cassie and
Marshall. Kate nursed wounded Bull Run soldiers at the
house. Bishop McIlvaine visited and he once chastised a patient for his language. I wrote a biography of Kate Chase long
ago, and co-edited a volume of Chase family letters as well,
and maintain a certain fondness for Miss Chase, as I do for all
strong, misunderstood women.

The nineteenth century contains a good number of exam-
ples of "passing women." Antebellum gender ideologies did
not allow for the possibility of women in men's clothing. Simp-
ly put, nineteenth-century Americans saw skirts and thought
'woman' and thought 'man' when they saw pants. This is how
upwards of 600 women, dressed as men, served in both Civil
War armies. In fact, the numbers might be higher because we
only know about the ones who were caught or later admitted
the deception. Most of these women were not lesbians or
transgender persons (though a few were) but rather were
women who wanted to help their country and make a living
wage (Army pay being a great deal more than most women
could earn at traditional female trades). Some may have just
wanted an adventure.

I described the Cincinnati depot as accurately as possible, along with the steamboat *Cricket* and the Kanawha Turnpike. I borrowed the details for the first part of Kate and Juba's trip into the Confederacy from an adventure Pinkerton operative Lewis Pryce had before the First Bull Run. The *Cricket* took Lewis to Guyandotte, which was a town divided over slavery and occupied by the Union Army in the summer of 1861. Colonel George Patton commanded a Virginia regiment at Charlottesville. He was killed in battle in 1864, leaving an infant son named after himself. He is also the grandfather of the World War II general of the same name.

Former governors Henry Wise and John Floyd were both Brigadier Generals in the Kanawha Valley in the summer of 1861 and they didn't like each other very much. I invented Floyd's camp to put him within a day's ride of Charleston.

Kanawha House was a real place as was the spa at White Sulfur Springs. In fact, the hotel and spa still exist today, though under a different name. The prices and dinner menu for the Hotel Spotswood, which was only months old in August 1861, are taken from handbills I found on the internet. How fun is that?

Congressman Alfred Ely and U. S. Army officers were taken prisoner early in the war and first imprisoned at Lignon's Warehouse. Elizabeth Van Lew first visited Ely at Lignon's. Crowding at that converted warehouse and others prompted the Confederacy to open several new warehouse/prisons, including Libby Prison and Castle Thunder. Ely and others would be transferred to Libby, but records are unclear whether that was before or after August 1861. Because most sources on Ely mention Libby (and not Ligon's) I used that prison to avoid confusion.

Elizabeth Van Lew and her mother were important Richmond Unionists. Commonly referred to as "Crazy Bet" by post-war Richmonders, Elizabeth Van Lew managed multiple feats of bravery including helping slaves escape north, assisting prisoners with jailbreaks, hiding spies and communicating valuable military information to Union Army officials. Most historians considered Van Lew the leader of Richmond's underground resistance movement. General U. S. Grant regarded her as his best spy. Mary Ann Richards, or Mary Bowser, was a free woman of color who may or may not have been born a slave. Information about her is scarce and not entirely reliable but she was a real person and worked with the Van Lews on the Richmond Underground.

Jefferson Davis suffered from chronic ocular inflammation. It may have resulted from a herpes simplex virus, which causes corneal blindness. Davis's disease was so painful that historians believe it interfered with his ability to manage the war. Jefferson and Varina Davis had a difficult marriage. She did not immediately join him when the Confederacy moved its capital to Richmond.

I may have made Colonel 'Shanks' Evans more dastardly than he was. The story about how he had a soldier follow him around the battlefield with a cask of whiskey is true and makes me laugh every time I visualize it. Generals Beauregard and Johnston were key generals in the Confederate Army and were stationed at Manassas and Centreville respectively.

The story about the turtles or terrapins is, in the main, true. I know because the ambassador gave Salmon P. Chase some turtles as well. Both Chase and Lincoln let their turtles escape though I made up the part about Lincoln's sons and the terrapin underground railroad. Alice Johnston was a cook

367

at the Lincoln Whitehouse. Apparently, she made excellent gravy.

Eugenia Phillips has a fabulous, real-life story. The wife of Alabama congressman Phillip Phillips, Eugenia was imprisoned at Fort Greenhow, with two daughters. Her husband used his contacts in the Lincoln administration to order his wife's release three weeks after her arrest. Later Eugenia was arrested in New Orleans under General Benjamin Butler's so-called Women's Order for laughing at a union soldier's funeral cortege. She was imprisoned on Ship Island until September 1862.

The U. S. S. Vincennes burned the Confederate Alvarado on August 5, but I needed a September ship burning for the story so I moved the date. Rose Greenhow's house was called Fort Greenhow while the U. S. government used it as a temporary prison for female spies.

Pessaries came in two types, one to prevent uterine prolapse and another to prevent pregnancy. In the twenty-first century the word is most often used for devices that support the uterus, bladder or rectum, but in the mid-1800s women used pessaries as contraceptive devices. Many modern Americans quite incorrectly believe women in the past had no access to and or interest in contraception. Quite the opposite is true.

Drum Roll Please

First, I gotta thank all the fabulous women from history that have inspired me for decades. When I was a kid I'd walk to the library and hunt for books with strong women in them. They were hard to find.

I owe a great debt of gratitude to my beta readers Paul Lamphier, Jackie Lamphier, Sheila McClintock, Emma Burke and Anna Sorum.

How about that cover? Daniel Aley does all my Kate Warne covers. You can contact him at www.flutterspace.com if you're interested in his work. And thanks to Marvelle Thompson for my author photo.

Last, kisses to my husband Leo Burke. Thank goodness he's self-sufficient and can entertain himself when I ignore him for long swaths of time. Thanks Dude.

More From Peg A. Lamphier

Iron Widow
Kate Warne, Civil War Spy Series, Book 4
(Coming Fall, 2018)

As if Pinkerton Detective Kate Warne doesn't have enough on her plate, what with Confederate spies everywhere in war-time Washington, an old case comes back to haunt her. Five years ago she investigated a Black Widow killer who disappeared before Kate could catch her. Now it looks like the nefarious Lily Winslow is back, and ready to kill again.

The tricky part of the investigation lies in the Black Widow's identity. A client comes to Allan Pinkerton, who's in Cincinnati with General McClellan, hoping the agency will deal with a disreputable spiritualist who has romantically ensnared his boss. Pinkerton has a long standing policy of not taking marital cases, but when the spiritualist's description rings a bell in Allan's memory he sends for Kate.

Kate retraces her investigative trail, hoping to uncover information she can use to link the woman who killed her father and two husbands to the Rochester spiritualist. The new investigation pushes Kate to confront the mistakes she made six years ago. What she learns forces her to think about the Black Widow case differently. Alone in wintery upstate New York, separated from her Washington family and missing dashing Army captain George Hazzard, Kate must confront the social norms that push some women to violence. Kate must ask and answer this question: Do some people have good reason to kill? And do some people need killing?

Peg A. Lamphier

Violent Delights & Vampires
A Perils of Petronella Crabtree Journal

Petronella Crabtree's 1893 journal reveal a perilous world of monsters, some (but not all) more dangerous than a freshly sharpened parasol tip. Only the agents of the International Monster Hunter Organization & Thwarters of Evil Predators (IMHOTEP) stand between humanity and the rapacious fiends who delight in murder and mayhem. Petronella and her IMHOTEP agents disguise themselves as itinerant actors and travel to Elkhorn Montana to destroy a mysterious Giant Bat Monster. Shape shifter Petronella has help from a sword wielding vampire named Emma, Therese, a darkly mysterious Romani medium, Sierra, a six foot tall Fae woman whose second form is a unicorn and the Demon Botis, who masquerades as a mild mannered professor.

Can the Monster Hunters kill this ancient terror before it's too late? Or will the children of Elkhorn continue to die? In the shadow of the northern Rocky Mountains, the troupe must strap on their swords and parasols, don their night vision goggles and brave the lair of an ancient evil in order to end its plan to regain its lost power.

"Soldier, Diplomat, Archeologist: The Bold Life of Louis Palma di Cesnola"

Cavalry Colonel Louis di Cesnola wants acceptance from the Union Army and his adopted country. After fighting for Italian Independence and in the Crimean this son of a Italian count has more military experience than most of the officers in the Civil War. When he objects to a general's orders he finds himself stripped of his saber and under arrest. Major William Parnell tells Cesnola that his regiment will not go into battle without their colonel. As one of the few men to survive the infamous Charge of the Light Brigade, Parnell knows what it means to follow the right man into a unwinnable battle. Cesnola defies his arrest, leads his men into battle without saber or carbine, before he's captured by the Confederate Army. After ten months in the notorious Libby Prison, Cesnola has to decide. Does he go back to war or not? And what of his wife Mary and their daughter? Louis becomes the American consul to Cyprus, an archaeological excavator, the first director of the New York Metropolitan Museum of Art, and a Medal of Honor winner, but every step of the way he must battle prejudice, proving himself again and again.

Peg A. Lamphier has a doctorate in American History she uses to write non-fiction monographs, encyclopedias and a small pile of novels. A native Montanan (Go Bobcats!), she lives in the mountains of Southern California with five dogs, five tortoises, a huge cat, three canaries, one beta fish, one daughter (who's away at college), one husband (who is around *all* the time) and a collection of vintage ukuleles that she plays with more enthusiasm than talent. Oh, and she has a hedgehog now. When she's not writing fiction Peg teaches delightfully diverse young adults at California State Polytechnic, Pomona and Mount San Antonio Community College. For more, see www.peglamphier.com.

www.ingramcontent.com/pod-product-compliance
Lightning Source LLC
Chambersburg PA
CBHW051939240626
47153CB00005B/1549